ACT YOUR AGE, EVE BROWN

Also by Talia Hibbert

Get a Life, Chloe Brown
Take a Hint, Dani Brown

ACT YOUR AGE, EVE BROWN

A Novel

TALIA HIBBERT

AVON

An Imprint of HarperCollinsPublishers

ACT YOUR AGE, EVE BROWN. Copyright © 2021 by Talia Hibbert. All rights reserved. Printed in the United States of America. No part of this book may be used or reproduced in any manner whatsoever without written permission except in the case of brief quotations embodied in critical articles and reviews. For information, address HarperCollins Publishers, 195 Broadway, New York, NY 10007.

HarperCollins books may be purchased for educational, business, or sales promotional use. For information, please email the Special Markets Department at SPsales@harpercollins.com.

FIRST EDITION

Designed by Diahann Sturge

Library of Congress Cataloging-in-Publication Data has been applied for.

ISBN 978-0-06-294127-5

23 24 25 26 27 LBC 14 13 12 11 10

For Corey, who left their mark upon the world—
and what a stunning mark it is

ACKNOWLEDGMENTS

What a journey the Brown sisters have taken me on. I'm so glad I dared to write them.

Thank you to my readers, old and new, for making me giddy with every email you send or Instagram caption you tag me in or book you buy. Thank you to my agent, Courtney Miller-Callihan, and to my editor, Nicole Fischer, for making all this happen. Thanks to Imani Gary and Jes Lyons for presenting this series to the world in such a fun and thoughtful way, and to Laurie McGee for polishing this story until it shone.

Thank you to my beloved friends, who gas me up when I desperately need it, who offer advice or critique when I ask, who inspire me with their own work and thoughts and wonderfulness. Divya, Laila, Maz, I don't know what I'd do without you. Dylan, Kennedy, Therese, KJ, and the countless others who have been so kind and supportive—you guys make this job extra magic.

Finally, thank you to Mum, Sam, and Tru. Writing this book

during lockdown meant you got a terrifyingly up-close-and-personal view of my, ahem, "artistic process." It wasn't pretty. So. Thanks for not burning me at the stake, I suppose? Also, for keeping me alive and making me smile.

This book was powered by family.

AUTHOR'S NOTE

This book mentions childhood neglect and anti-autistic ableism. If these topics are sensitive for you, please read with care. (And feel safe in the knowledge that joy triumphs in the end.) You should also know that, while writing this book, I elected to ignore the existence of COVID-19. I hope this book provides some form of escape.

EVE'S *ACT YOUR AGE* PLAYLIST

- "Don't Rain on My Parade," Barbra Streisand
- "Big for Your Boots," Stormzy
- "hometown," cleopatrick
- "Remember," KATIE
- "Bad Blood," NAO
- "Papaoutai," Stromae
- "Honor to Us All," Lea Salonga
- "Sticky," Ravyn Lenae
- "Hometown Glory," Adele
- "Curious," Hayley Kiyoko
- "Special Affair," The Internet
- "From Ritz to Rubble," Arctic Monkeys
- "Through the Rain," Mariah Carey
- "Make Me Feel," Janelle Monáe
- "Breathless," Corinne Bailey Rae

CHAPTER ONE

Eve Brown didn't keep a diary. She kept a journal. There was a difference.

Diaries were horribly organized and awfully prescriptive. They involved dates and plans and regular entries and the suffocating weight of commitment. *Journals*, on the other hand, were deliciously wild and lawless things. One could abandon a journal for weeks, then crack it open one Saturday evening under the influence of wine and marshmallows without an ounce of guilt. A woman might journal about last night's dream, or her growing anxieties around the lack of direction in her life, or her resentment toward the author of thrilling AO3 fanfic *Tasting Captain America*, who hadn't uploaded a new chapter since the great tittyfucking cliffhanger of December 2017. For example.

In short, journaling was, by its very nature, impossible to fail at. Eve had many journals. She rather liked them.

So, what better way to spend a lovely, lazy Sunday morning in August than journaling about the stunning rise and decisive fall of her latest career?

She sat up with a stretch, clambered off her queen-sized bed, and drew back the velvet curtains covering her floor-to-ceiling windows. As bright summer light flooded the room, Eve tossed aside her silk headscarf, kicked off the shea butter foot mask socks she'd slept in, and grabbed her journal from her bedside table, leafing through gold-edged pages. Settling back into bed, she began.

Good morning, darling,

—The journal, of course, was darling.

It's been eight days since Cecelia's wedding. I'm sorry I didn't write sooner, but you are an inanimate object, so it doesn't really matter.

I regret to report that things didn't go 100 percent to plan. There was a bit of a fuss about Cecelia's corset being eggshell instead of ivory, but I resolved that issue by encouraging her to take a Xanax from Gigi. Then there was a slight palaver with the doves—they were supposed to be released over Cecelia and Gareth for the photographs, but I discovered just before the ceremony that their handler (that is to say, the doves' handler, not Cece and Gareth's (I was their handler, to be frank)) hadn't fed them for two days (!!!) so they wouldn't shit all over the guests. But really, when one wishes to work with the wonders of the animal king-

dom, one must respect their ways and resign oneself to the odd sprinkle of shit. One certainly must not starve the poor creatures to *avoid* said sprinkle of shit. Any sensible person knows this.

So I *may* have lost my temper and released them all. The doves, I mean. Clearly, they were born to be free—hence the wings, et cetera. Unfortunately, the handler demanded I pay for them, which I suppose was fair enough. It turns out doves are very expensive, so I have had to request an advance on my monthly payment from the trust fund. Hopefully Mother won't notice.

Anyway, darling, here is my point: Cecelia and I have sadly fallen out. It seems she was very attached to the idea of the aforementioned doves, and perhaps her tongue had been loosened by the Xanax, but she called me a selfish jealous cow, so I called her an ungrateful waste of space and ripped the train off her Vera Wang. By accident, obviously. I did fix it—after a fashion—in time for the actual ceremony, so I don't entirely see the issue.

But knowing the lovely Cecelia as I do, I'm sure she'll spend her Fiji honeymoon bad-mouthing my services on various bridezilla forums in order to destroy my dream career. Obviously, the joke is on her, because I have no dream career and I have already erased Eve Antonia Weddings from the face of the earth. And Chloe says I lack efficiency!

Hah.

Eve finished her entry and closed the journal with a satisfied smile—or else, a smile that *should* be satisfied, but instead felt a little bit sad and slightly nauseous.

She'd known Cecelia since their schooldays. Had always felt somewhat nervous around her, the way Eve often did around— well, humanity in general. As if she were walking a cliff's edge between being the easy, entertaining friend people kept around, and the irritating mess people kicked off the ledge.

Now she'd leapt off that ledge with Cecelia, and it turned her stomach to a gently writhing pit.

Clearly, Eve was in a mood. Perhaps she should go back to sleep, or binge-read a romance novel, or—

No. No moping. Mood or not, she had responsibilities to fulfil. *Someone* needed to feed Gigi's exotic fish, even if Gigi rarely forgot to do so these days and the fish were getting quite fat now. *Someone* needed to . . .

Hmm. Eve was sure she did other useful things, too, but none were coming to mind.

Shrugging off her funk, she chose her song for the day—"Don't Rain on My Parade," to cheer her up—hit Repeat, and popped in one of her AirPods. Soundtrack established, she got up, got dressed, and headed down to the family home's vast marble-and-chrome kitchen, where she found both her parents in grim residence.

"Oh dear," Eve murmured, and stopped short in the doorway.

Mum was pacing broodily by the toaster. Her pale blue suit made her amber skin glow and really highlighted the fiery rage in her hazel eyes. Dad stood stoic and grave by the Swiss coffee machine, sunlight beaming through the French windows to bathe his bald, brown head.

"Good morning, Evie-Bean," he said. Then his solemn expression wavered, a hint of his usual smile coming through. "That's a nice T-shirt."

Eve looked down at her T-shirt, which was a lovely orange color, with the words SORRY, BORED NOW written across her chest in turquoise. "Thanks, Dad."

"I swear, I've no idea where you find—"

Mum rolled her eyes, threw up her hands, and snapped, "For God's sake, Martin!"

"Oh, ah, yes." Dad cleared his throat and tried again. "Eve," he said sternly, "your mother and I would like a word."

Wonderful; they were in a mood, too. Since Eve was trying her best to be cheerful, this was not particularly ideal. She sighed and entered the kitchen, her steps falling in time with the beat of Barbra's bold staccato. Gigi and Shivani were at the marble breakfast bar across the room. Shivani was eating what appeared to be a spinach omelet, while Gigi stole the occasional bite in between dainty sips of her usual Bloody Mary smoothie.

Unwilling to be contaminated by her parents' grumpiness, Eve trilled, "Hello, Grandmother, Grand-Shivani," and snagged a bottle of Perrier from the fridge. Then, finally, she turned to face Mum and Dad. "I thought you'd be at your couples' spin class this morning."

"Oh, *no*, my lovely little lemon," Gigi cut in. "How could they possibly *spin* when they have adult children to *ambush* in the kitchen?"

"I know that's how I approach disagreements with my twenty-six-year-old offspring," Shivani murmured. When Mum glared in her direction, Shivani offered a serene smile and flicked her long, graying ponytail.

Gigi smirked her approval.

So, it was official; Eve was indeed being ambushed. Biting her lip, she asked, "Have I done something wrong? Oh dear—did I forget the taps again?" It *had* been eight years since she'd accidentally flooded her en suite bathroom badly enough to cause a minor floor/ceiling collapse, but she remained slightly nervous about a potential repeat.

Mum released a bitter laugh. "The *taps*!" she repeated—with frankly excessive drama. "Oh, Eve, I wish this issue were as simple as *taps*."

"Do calm down, Joy," Gigi huffed. "Your vibrations are giving me a migraine."

"Mother," Dad said warningly.

"Yes, darling?" Gigi said innocently.

"For God's sake," Mum said . . . rage-ing-ly, "Eve, we'll continue this in the study."

♫

The study was Mum's office, a neat and tidy room on the ground floor of the family home. It had an atmosphere of focus and success, both of which Eve found singularly oppressive. She fidgeted awkwardly under her parents' stares.

"Where," Mum asked, straight to the point as always, "is your website?"

Eve blinked. She had, in her time, owned many websites. Her oldest sister, Chloe, was a web designer, and Eve had always been a loyal client. "Erm . . ." Before she could formulate a response—a nice, precise one that covered all relevant information in exactly the way she wanted—Mum spoke again. That was the trouble with Mum. With most of Eve's relatives, in fact. They were all so *quick*, and so uniformly relentless, their intellect blowing Eve about like dandelion fluff in a hurricane.

"I directed my good friend Harriet Hains," Mum said, "to your business, because her daughter is recently engaged, and because I was so proud of the success you made of Cecelia's wedding last week."

For a moment, Eve basked in the glow of that single word: *proud*. Mum had been proud. Eve had, for a day, achieved something her brilliant and accomplished mother valued enough to deem it a *success*. Giddy warmth spread out from her chest in cautious tendrils—until Eve remembered that her success was now over. Because, behind the scenes, she'd fucked things up. Again.

Why did she even bother? Why did she even try?

You don't, really. Not anymore.

"Harriet told me," Mum forged on, "that your website URL led her to nothing but an error message. I investigated for myself and can find no trace of your wedding planning business online." Mum paused for a moment, her frown turning puzzled. "Except a largely incoherent forum post claiming you stole an entire bevy of white doves, but that is an obviously unhinged accusation."

"Obviously," Eve agreed. "I paid for those doves, that lying cow."

Mum gave a glacial stare. "I beg your pardon, Eve Antonia Brown."

"Let's focus on the issue at hand, shall we, love?" Dad interjected. "Eve. What's happened to your business?"

Ah. Yes. Well. There was the rub. "The thing is, Dad, Mum . . . I have decided that wedding planning isn't for me after all. So, I dissolved the business, deleted the website and disconnected the URL, and closed down all associated social media accounts." It was best, Eve had found, to simply rip off the bandage.

There was a pause. Then Mum said tightly, "So you gave up. Again."

Eve swallowed, suddenly uncomfortable. "Well, no, not exactly. It was just an experience I stumbled into—Cecelia's original wedding planner was rubbish, so—"

"She was an ordinary woman who couldn't deal with a spoiled brat like Cecelia Bradley-Coutts," Dad cut in, his brow creased. "But you could. You did. And you seemed to enjoy yourself, Eve. We thought you'd—found your calling."

A cold bead of sweat began to drip, slow and steady, down Eve's spine. Her calling? Eve wasn't the sort of woman who had callings. "It's for my own good, really," she said, her voice aiming for *light* and hitting *scratchy* instead. "Everything went suspiciously well—you know I couldn't re-create such success again. Wouldn't want to disappoint myself."

Dad stared, crestfallen. "But Eve. You're disappointing *us*."

Ouch. No pulling the parental punches today, then.

"You can't avoid trying at anything in case you fail," he told her gently. "Failure is a necessary part of growth."

She wanted to say, *That's what you think.* Eve's parents had never failed at a bloody thing. Eve's parents knew who they were and what they were capable of, as did her sisters. But Eve? All Eve really knew was how to be fun, and experience had taught her she ought to stick to her strong suit and avoid reaching too high.

She used to reach, once upon a time. But it hurt so terribly to fall.

"Enough is enough, Eve," Mum said into the silence. "You're twenty-six years old, perfectly intelligent and absolutely capable, yet you waste time and opportunities like—like a spoiled brat. Just like Cecelia."

Eve sucked in an outraged breath. "I am *not* spoiled!" She thought for a moment. "Well, perhaps I am mildly spoiled. But I think I'm rather charming with it, don't you?"

No one laughed. Not even Dad. In fact, he looked quite angry as he demanded, "How many careers do you plan to flit through while living at home and surviving on nothing but the money *we* give you? Your sisters have moved out, and they work—damned hard—even though they don't need to. But you—you dropped out of performing arts college. You dropped out of law school. You gave up on teaching. You went from graphic design, to cupcakes, to those tiny violins you used to make—"

"I don't want to talk about the violins," Eve scowled. She'd quite liked them, but she knew far better than to make a career out of anything she *liked*. Those were always the failures that hurt most.

"You don't want to talk about *anything*!" Dad exploded. "You dip in and out of professions, then you cut and run before things get real. Your mother and I didn't set up the trust so you girls could become wastes of space," he said. "We set it up because when I was a boy, Gigi and I had nothing. And because there are so many situations in life that you've no hope of escaping from without a safety net. But what you're doing, Eve, is abusing your privilege. And I'm disappointed."

Those words burned. Her heart began to pound, her pulse rushing loud enough in her ears to drown out Barbra's comforting beat. She tried to process, to find the right words to explain herself—but the conversation was already racing off without her, a runaway train she'd never been fast enough to catch.

"We have decided," Mum said, "to cancel your trust fund payments. Whatever savings you have will have to do until you can find a job."

Savings? Who the bloody hell had *savings*?

Dad took over. "You can stay here for three months. That should be more than enough time to find a place of your own."

"Wait—what? You're throwing me out?"

Mum went on as if Eve hadn't spoken. "We've discussed things, and your father and I would like you to hold down a job for at least a year before we restart your trust fund payments. We know finding decent work might be difficult with such a . . . unique CV, so we've lined up positions for you in our own companies."

Eve jerked back in her seat, her head whirling as she tried to keep up. "But—I already quit law." It had only taken a few seminars with hyperfocused geniuses for Eve to realize that she wasn't nearly clever enough to get her head around the unwritten constitution.

Mum's mouth tightened. "Well, there's always your father's accountancy firm."

Now Eve was truly appalled. "Accountancy? I can barely count!"

Mum narrowed her eyes. "Don't be flip, Eve."

"You're right. I don't *want* to count. And I don't want my parents to hand me a job because I'm too useless to get one on my own. I'm *not*." Even if she felt that way, sometimes.

"No," Mum agreed, "just too feckless to stick with one. To do the hard work, after the excitement and glamour has faded. Too immature to be an *adult*. When are you going to act your age, Eve? I swear, it's embarrassing—"

And there it was. Eve sucked in a breath and blinked back the hot tears prickling at the corners of her eyes. They were more shock than pain, like the tears that came with a banged elbow— but she shouldn't be shocked at all, now, should she? Of course her parents saw her this way. Of course they thought she was an immature little brat. She'd never given anyone a reason to think she was anything else.

"I—I need to go," she said, standing up quickly, her voice thick with tears. Embarrassing. She was so bloody embarrassing, crying like a child because her mother had told her the truth, running away from everything because she wasn't strong enough to cope with the pressure.

"Eve, darling," Mum began, already sounding softer, full of

regret. Next, she'd say, *I'm sorry, I didn't mean that*, and everyone would decide that was enough for today, and the poor, delicate baby of the family would be let off the hook for a while because everyone knew Eve couldn't handle difficult conversations.

She wanted to be more than this. She really, really did.

She just didn't know how.

"Don't worry," she said sharply. "I've listened to everything you've said, and I'm taking it very seriously. I don't need you to baby me anymore. I will deal with this on my own, and I will try not to disappoint or—or *embarrass* you in the process." *But now I need to go before I completely undermine myself by bursting into tears.* She turned her back on her stricken parents and bolted.

CHAPTER TWO

It had taken Eve seven attempts to pass her driving test. Apparently, she had serious spatial awareness problems that took four years of weekly lessons to overcome. But driving was one of the few things Eve had refused to give up on, because earning a license meant earning freedom.

For example: the freedom to drive fast and aimless down abandoned country roads while blasting a playlist that started with Stormzy's "Big for Your Boots" at full volume. Her mood had taken a sharp dip, and Barbra would no longer do.

As she sped past turn after turn that would take her back to the main road—to the city, to her sisters—Eve debated the pros and cons of running to Chloe or Dani for help. What, exactly, would she say? *Help, Mum and Dad have cruelly demanded I hold down a job and take on some adult responsibilities?* Ha. Chloe was hideously blunt, and Dani was addicted to hard work. They were both intimidatingly no-nonsense and had a shocking tendency to tell Eve the absolute truth, without even the accompaniment of a soothing cup of tea or a nice bit of chocolate. They'd eye-roll her into oblivion, and she would absolutely deserve it.

Eve had told her parents she'd handle things herself, and she would keep that promise. As soon as she finished undoing the instinctive panic caused by this morning's conversation, that is.

She turned up the endless music and drove. The sun faded behind gray clouds, and pre-rain mist soaked into her skin through the open windows, and well over two hours passed without her even noticing. Just when she was beginning to feel the first pangs of hunger, she caught sight of a sign that read SKYBRIAR: FIFTEEN MILES.

"Skybriar," she murmured over the thrum of cleopatrick's "hometown." It sounded like a fairy tale. Fairy tales meant happily ever after.

She took the turn.

Skybriar *looked* like a fairy tale, too. Its main road unraveled down a gigantic hill, the kind usually found in books or Welsh travel brochures. Mysterious woodland stood tall on either side of the pavement, likely containing pixies and unicorns and other fabulous things. The air through Eve's open window tasted fresh and earthy and clean as she drove deeper into the town, past adorable, old-fashioned, stone-built houses and people in wellies walking well-behaved little dogs. She spotted a sign among the green, a gleaming blue board with white lace effect around the edges that read PEMBERTON GINGERBREAD FESTIVAL: SATURDAY, 31ST AUGUST. How absolutely *darling*, and how potentially delicious. Oh—but it wasn't the thirty-first yet. Never mind.

Another turn, taken at random, and she struck gold. Up ahead, guarded by a grand oak tree and fenced in by a low, moss-covered wall, sat an impressive redbrick Victorian with a burgundy sign outside that read CASTELL COTTAGE. EXCELLENT ACCOMMODATION, DELICIOUS CUISINE.

She was feeling better already.

(Actually, that was a categorical lie. But she *would* feel better, once she ate, and took a moment to think, and generally stopped her drama queen behavior. Eve was quite certain of that.)

She threw her car into the nearest sort-of parking space—well, it was an empty spot by the pavement, so it would do—and cut off the radio. Then she slipped in an AirPod, chose a new song— "Shut Up and Groove," Masego—to match her determinedly positive mood, and pressed Play. Flipping down the car's mirror, she dabbed at her red eyes and stared disapprovingly at her bare mouth. Boring, boring, boring. Even her waist-length braids, lavender and brown, were still tied back in a bedtime knot. She set them free to spill over her shoulders, then rifled through her glove box and found a glittery, orange Chanel lip gloss.

"There," she smiled at her reflection. "Much better." When in doubt, throw some color at it. Satisfied, she got out of the car and approached the cute little countryside restaurant thingy through softly falling drizzle. Only when she reached the grand front door, above which sat yet another burgundy sign, did she notice what she'd missed the first time.

CASTELL COTTAGE

BED-AND-BREAKFAST

Eve checked her watch and discovered that it was now far from breakfast time.

"Gabriel's burning bollocks, you have *got* to be kidding me." She glared at her warped reflection in the front door's stained-glass window. "Has the trauma of the morning's events killed off your last remaining brain cells, Eve? Is that it?"

Her reflection did not reply.

She let out a hangry little growl and started to turn—when a laminated notice pinned up beside the door caught her eye.

CHEF INTERVIEWS: FIRST DOOR ON THE RIGHT

Well, now. *That* was rather interesting. So interesting, in fact, that Eve's witchy sister, Dani, would likely call this literal sign . . . a *sign*.

Of course, Eve wasn't Dani, so she simply called it a coincidence.

"Or an opportunity," she murmured slowly.

Eve, after all, could cook. She was forced to do so every day in order to live, and she was also quite good at it, having entertained brief fantasies of opening a Michelin-starred restaurant before watching an episode of *Hell's Kitchen* and developing a Gordon Ramsay phobia. Of course, despite her private efforts, she had never actually cooked professionally before—unless one considered her ill-advised foray into 3D genital cakes *cooking*. It was certainly baking, which amounted to much the same thing. Kind of.

The more she thought about it, the more perfect this seemed. Wedding planning had been too exhilarating—the kind of career she could easily fall in love with. The kind where true failure could break her. But cooking at some small-town bed-and-breakfast? She certainly couldn't fall in love with that.

Your father and I would like you to hold down a job for at least a year before we restart your trust fund payments.

Her parents didn't think she could get a job on her own and clearly doubted her ability to keep one. They thought she needed supervision for every little thing, and if she was honest with herself, Eve understood why. But that didn't stop their doubt from biting like too-small leather boots. So, securing her own job the day she left home? And also, quite conveniently, *not* having to return with her tail between her legs after this morning's tantrum-like disappearance? That all sounded ideal, actually.

One year to prove herself. Surely, she could manage that?

She opened the door.

♫

Contrary to popular belief, Jacob Wayne did not create awkward situations on purpose. Take right now, for example: he didn't *mean* to subject his latest interviewee to a long, glacial pause that left the other man pale and jittery. But Simon Fairweather was a certified prick and his answers to Jacob's carefully considered interview questions were nothing less than a shit show. With each meaningless response, Jacob felt himself growing even colder and more distant than usual. Perfect conditions for the birth of an accidental awkward pause.

Simon stared at Jacob. Jacob, more pissed off by the second, stared at Simon. Simon began to fidget. Jacob reflected on how bloody irritating he found this man and did nothing to control the derisive curl of his lip. Simon started, disturbingly, to sweat. Jacob was horrified, both by the rogue DNA rolling down Simon's temples and by his obvious lack of guts.

Then Jacob's best friend (all right, *only* friend) Montrose heaved out a sigh and leapt into the breach. "Cheers, Simon," he said. "That'll be all, mate. We'll get back to you."

"That's true," Jacob allowed calmly, because it was. He watched in silence as Simon scrambled up from his chair and exited the room, nodding and stuttering all the while.

"Pitiful," Jacob muttered. As the dining room door swung shut, he wrote two careful words on his notepad: FUCK. EVERY-THING.

Not his most adult choice, granted, but it seemed more mature than flipping the goddamn table.

Beside him, Montrose cleared his throat. "All right. Don't know why I'm bothering to ask, but . . . Thoughts on Simon?"

Jacob sighed. "Are you sure you want to know?"

"Probably not." Montrose rolled his eyes and tapped his pen against his own notepad. He, Jacob noticed, had written a load of intelligent, sensible shit about today's applicants, complete with bullet points. Once upon a time, Jacob had been capable of intelligence and bullet points, too. Just last week, in fact. But then he'd been forced to sit through the seven-day-straight parade of incompetence these interviews had become, and his brain had melted out of his fucking ears.

"Well," Mont went on, "here's what I put: Simon's got a lot of experience, but he doesn't seem the sharpest tool. Bit cocky, but that means he'll eventually be confident enough to handle that thing you do."

Jacob narrowed his eyes and turned, very slowly, to glare at his friend. "And what *thing* is that, Montrose?"

"That thing, Bitchy McBitcherson," Mont said cheerfully. "You're a nightmare when you're panicking."

"I'm a nightmare all the time. This is my ordinary nightmare behavior. *Panic*," Jacob scowled, "is for the underprepared, the out-of-control, and the fatally inconsistent."

"Yeah, so I've heard. From you. Every time you're panicking."

Jacob wondered if today would be the day he murdered his best friend and decided, after a moment, that it was entirely possible. The hospitality industry had been known to drive men to far worse. Like plastic shower curtains and brown carpets.

To lessen the risk of imminent homicide, Jacob pushed the fine frames of his glasses up his nose, rose to his feet, and began to pace the B&B's spacious dining room, circling the antique table that took up its center. "Whatever. And you're wrong about Simon—he isn't right for Castell Cottage."

"You don't think anyone's right for Castell Cottage," Mont said dryly. "That's kind of why I'm here. Voice of reason, and all that."

"Actually, you're here because you're a respected local business owner, and proper interviews need more than one perspective, and—"

"What's wrong with Simon?" Montrose interrupted.

"He's a creep."

Mont, who had a habit of leaning everywhere—probably something to do with his ridiculous height and the natural effects of gravity—sat up straight for once. "Who told you that? The twins?"

A reasonable assumption, since Mont's sisters were some of the only women in town who actually spoke to Jacob—aside from Aunt Lucy, of course. "No one told me. Just watch the man sometime. Women bend over backward to avoid being alone with him."

"Christ," Mont muttered and ripped a page out of his notepad. "All right. I know you hated the first two, and you've written off all the *previous* candidates." He paused significantly. If he was waiting for Jacob to feel bad, or something, he'd be waiting a long fucking time. "So that leaves us with Claire Penny."

"Nope," Jacob said flatly. "Don't want her." He stopped mid-pace, noticing that one of the paintings on the aubergine wall—a landscape commissioned from a local artist—was slightly crooked. Scowling, he stalked over and adjusted it. Bloody doors banging all day, knocking things out of whack, that was the reason. "Can't have a chef who slams my doors," he muttered darkly. "Doesn't create a restful atmosphere. Bastards."

"Is that the issue with Claire?"

"What? Oh." Jacob shook his head and went back to his pacing. "Claire knows how to shut a door properly, so far as I can tell. But she smiles too much. No one smiles that much. Pretty sure she's on drugs."

Mont gave Jacob the dirty look to end all dirty looks, which was a natural skill of his. "You can't be serious."

"I'm always serious."

"She's sixty-four years old."

Jacob rolled his eyes. "You think people stop making bad decisions when they hit sixty? Nope. Anyway, you remember before I moved to the city, she used to work at Betty's? I ordered a slice of her apple pie once, and there was a hair in it."

"*That's* why you don't want to invite her back?"

Jacob frowned at his friend. "Why are you using your *Jacob's being unreasonable* voice? I don't want hairy pie, Montrose. Do you want hairy pie? Because if you're that hot for hairy pie, I will make you a hairy pie."

"You couldn't pay me to eat your cooking, which is kind of why we're here." Mont scrubbed a hand over his face and screwed his eyes shut for a second. "Come on, man. You moved years ago. You think she hasn't learned how to wear a hairnet in five years? Call her back, let her cook for us, give her a chance."

"No." Jacob knew he sounded like a dick. He knew even Mont, who got him better than everyone, probably thought he was being a dick. But sometimes it was easier to keep his thought processes to himself because other people had trouble following them or thought they were unnecessarily blunt.

Bluntness was never unnecessary.

In the case of one Claire Penny: she was cheerful, she was gentle, and then there was that fucking pie. Jacob didn't like poor cooking hygiene, he didn't like working with nice people—too easy to accidentally hurt their feelings—and he didn't like compromising at a time when he needed the absolute best. He had plans. Carefully laid, highly detailed, suddenly derailed because sod's-bloody-law, *plans*. Plans that involved the upcoming Pemberton Gingerbread Festival, high-quality cooking, and a shit-ton of professional success. Entertaining a candidate who didn't meet the criteria to fit those plans would be a waste of time, and he did not have time to waste.

"So what the hell are we going to do?" Mont demanded. "Because the festival is in four weeks, and—shit, isn't there a meeting next week? If you don't show up with a chef, you're going to lose the opportunity."

"I know," Jacob gritted out. It was all he could think about. How typical that the *one* time he managed to wrangle something useful out of someone, his chef ruined it all by pissing off to Scotland.

"Aside from which," Mont said, "you're fully booked for the next five days, and I can't keep—"

"I know you can't keep cooking for me. I *know*." Jacob collapsed back into his chair, dragged off his glasses, and pinched the bridge of his nose.

"If you don't loosen up and hire someone, you're screwed."

"I don't need to hear that kind of negativity." Jacob Wayne was never screwed. Well, not like *that*—obviously he was sometimes screwed in other, better ways. Although not as often as he'd like, but—you know—ah, fuck it, never mind. "Look, failure is—it's not an option." Not when he'd spent years working at the best hotels to learn everything he'd need to make this work. Not when he'd sunk all his savings into this fledgling business. It couldn't be.

A sharp knock at the door interrupted their depressing conversation. Jacob frowned, sat up straighter in his chair, and called, "Who is it?"

The door opened a crack, which was fucking annoying, since he'd said *Who is it?* not *Sure, help yourself, come in.* But they weren't expecting any more interview candidates today—Skybriar, while it had grown in recent years, was still a small town, and unemployed chefs weren't exactly rolling through the hills like stray acorns. Which meant this could be a guest, come looking for him. So Jacob arranged his expression into something neutral (Mont had suggested he try *friendly,* but Jacob didn't see the point of that with people who weren't his friends) and waited.

After a moment's hesitation, an unfamiliar face popped itself through the gap in the door. Jacob assumed the face was attached to a body, but all he could see right now was a head, a little bit of neck, and a whole lot of purple braids.

"Hello," the floating head said. "I'm here for the interview."

Assertive and straight to the point: good. Complete stranger, unscheduled: bad. The kind of crisp accent Jacob usually heard from the guests themselves: potential issue. Hovering in the door like a supernatural creature: undecided.

Since she wanted a job, Jacob started cataloging visible details. Big, dark, Disney princess eyes, purple braids, chubby cheeks, and smooth brown skin. She was young, which suggested unreliability. Orange lip gloss, which clashed with the purple hair, but since chefs weren't front of house, he'd let it slide. She was smiling at him, which Jacob found infinitely suspicious, but then Mont kicked him under the table, and he remembered he was supposed to relax. Maybe her inane expression was a good thing: someone in this place needed to look approachable for guests, and clearly it wouldn't be Jacob.

"Hi," Mont said. "You want to come in?"

"Yes, thank you." The head and neck became a complete person.

She stepped into the room, shut the door behind her, and assaulted Jacob with her T-shirt. Bright orange like the lip gloss, with words written across her chest in turquoise block capitals: SORRY, BORED NOW.

Ironic clothing. *Rude* ironic clothing. *Apathetic*, rude ironic clothing. Bad, bad, bad. He couldn't take his eyes off it. It was like a car crash. Even worse, it must be raining outside, because the T-shirt was wet. All of her was wet, her soft, bare arms gleaming obnoxiously. What, she'd gone out in the rain without a bloody coat? Ridiculous. Even more ridiculous, he could see the outline of her bra under the T-shirt. No one should let themselves get wet like that. She could catch her death. Then Mont kicked him again, and Jacob realized it probably looked like he was staring at an interviewee's tits right now. Jesus Christ. He looked down at his notepad, cleared his throat, and scrawled down three Os and an X. Three positives, one negative. He'd given her an extra positive to make up for the chest-staring.

"My name is Eve Brown," she said, coming to sit down. More confidence. Good. He circled one of the Os again.

"I'm Eric Montrose," Mont said. "I run the Rose and Crown over on Friar's Hill. And my silent friend here is the owner of Castell Cottage, Jacob Wayne."

Silent? Oh, yeah. That was Jacob right now. He was just taking things in. He had things in his head. Eve Brown, she said her name was, but it seemed so unassuming compared to the lip gloss and the T-shirt and the way all those long, fine braids spilled over her shoulders. Very dramatic, was the spilling. And the wetness of her skin made it look less like skin and more like some kind of precious metal or silk or whatever. Her neck reminded him of a wood pigeon's breast, that soft sort of curve. But no feathers here, he assumed. Just kind of velvety, the way they looked. He was still circling the O on his notepad. Crap.

Jacob put down his pen and cleared his throat. "Sorry. Autism. I occasionally hyperfocus."

She nodded and kept her mouth shut. No thrilling stories about her sister's husband's cousin's neighbor's five-year-old autistic son. Wonderful. Another O.

Jacob made the mark, then got down to business. "Obviously, we weren't expecting you."

"No," she smiled. Again. For what possible reason, Jacob couldn't say. Perhaps she was trying to be charming? Definitely suspicious. "I was actually just passing through," she went on, "when I saw the notice on your door."

Jacob stiffened. Disorganized, unintentional, *just passing through.* Bad, bad, bad, X, X, X. "Do you often roam the Lakes, passing through random small towns, looking for work?"

"The Lakes?" She blinked, then smiled again. "Is that where we are? Good Lord, I drove quite far."

Jacob had changed his mind. Her neck did not look like a wood pigeon's breast. It looked like the rest of her: untrustworthy and highly annoying and possibly on drugs. He was allergic to cokeheads. He had been overexposed during his childhood, and now they made him leery. "You don't even know where you *are*?"

Beneath the table, Montrose kicked him *again.* He followed it up with a glare, which Jacob knew from experience was code for, *Tone, man.* Eve, meanwhile, narrowed her eyes until they went from wide, innocent, puppy-dog things to flashing slits of night. Then they returned to normal, so fast he wondered if he'd imagined that moment. "I'm afraid not," she said sweetly. "Or at least, I didn't know before. Thank goodness you were so chevalier as to tell me."

Jacob stared, perplexed. Then Mont said, "Er . . . did you mean chivalrous?"

"No," she replied calmly. "I'm quite certain I meant chevalier. Would you like to hear about my experience now?"

The answer should be no. She was disorganized and unreliable; therefore, Jacob did not want her anywhere near his masterpiece of hospitality. On the other hand, she was clearly cool under pressure and very self-assured, and he appreciated the firm conviction with which she spoke utter nonsense. Conviction was a very important quality. He jotted down another O. Her pros and cons were practically even, although the fact that she had any cons at all should make her an automatic failure.

Jacob opened his mouth to tell her as much, but Mont, the bastard, interjected.

"Sure. Tell us all about it."

"Do you have a CV?" Jacob demanded, because *he* wasn't about to let this process go to the dogs, thanks very much.

"No," she told him with another one of those sweet little smiles. She really was like a Disney princess, except her clothes were awful and everything that came out of her mouth was wrong. He felt a bit dizzy, which in turn made him more than a bit irritated.

Who in the bloody hell was this woman, anyway, turning up at his B&B with her posh, southern accent, making him draw far too many Xs and Os? He didn't like her, Jacob decided, his mind snapping into a new direction like a whip. He didn't like her at all.

"I studied at a pastry school in Paris for, er, a period of time," she went on, which was the vaguest bullshit he'd ever heard, "and I'm an excellent baker. Really, since this is a practical position, I was hoping I could simply take you to the kitchen and prove my abilities."

Jacob was frankly appalled. "No. Nope. No. For one thing, practical skill doesn't cover things like health and safety experience."

"Oh, but I have all of that," she said brightly. "I had to, so I could join my friend Alaris's Mindful Juicing Experience back in 2017. Juice recipe development," she told them in a conspiratorial tone, "is an underrated form of meditation."

"Really?" Mont asked.

"Mont," Jacob said, "why are you responding to this rubbish?"

Eve ignored him, or perhaps she didn't hear. He'd noticed she was wearing one of those earbud things, peeking through the braids, as if her T-shirt wasn't offensive enough.

"Oh, yes," she was saying, her eyes on Mont as she nodded pleasantly. "It does work. My grandmother is a great fan."

"Hmmm. You know, I've been looking for ways to turn the pub into a kind of events hub for the town. Maybe something like that would work. Holding classes, or . . ."

"I'd be happy to discuss it with you," Eve said. "I could even give you Alaris's number. She's a true pioneer."

Jacob wondered if perhaps, when he had gotten up to pace twenty minutes ago, he had actually tripped and fallen and hit his head and was now in a coma. "Look," he said sharply, attempting to drag the conversation back into the land of good sense and logic. "I can't interview you without a CV. You have no references, no solid evidence of education or employment—"

"I studied at St. Albert's," she told him, her tone a little colder, "from two thousand—"

"That won't be necessary," he interrupted. "What I'm trying to say is, applications are still open, and if you're serious about this, I'm sure you'll email me your CV as soon as you can get to a computer." *If you're serious about this.* Ha. Clearly, this woman had never been serious about anything in her life.

Which made her exactly the type of person Jacob despised.

She pursed her lips as if he'd demanded something wildly unreasonable, like the deliverance of a magical scroll from the Andes by tomorrow afternoon. "But," she said, "I don't have a CV. Or a computer, right now. Actually, I was rather hoping I'd come in here and wow you with my incredible cooking skills, good looks, and general charm, you'd employ me, and I'd have a salary, and a house, and all those lovely things."

Jacob stared.

Montrose laughed.

Jacob realized that must have been a joke. "Ha. Ha. Hilarious." Then he remembered that sometimes jokes were kind of true and wondered if she didn't have a computer because she didn't have a home, and if she was wandering around looking for jobs because she really needed one.

But she sounded like the queen, and her shoes, he'd noticed, were white Doc Martens with red hearts, probably limited edition and very expensive. If he were homeless, he would sell his expensive shoes. Except, no, he wouldn't, not if they were warm and waterproof and sturdy and possibly the only pair he had, because that wouldn't make long-term sense.

"Are you homeless?" he asked.

She blinked rapidly.

"Jacob," Mont scowled, then looked at Eve. "You don't need to answer that. Listen, Eve, let me level with you."

"Oh, God," Jacob sighed, because Mont *leveling with people* usually involved a vile amount of needless honesty. People complained Jacob was blunt, but at least he'd figured out when it was polite to lie. (Mostly.)

"Jacob here is knee-deep in the shit," Mont said cheerfully.

Great. Absolutely *brilliant*. Jacob's second-in-command had gone rogue.

CHAPTER THREE

Eve had never had the pleasure of staying at a B&B. In fact, she rarely ever stayed at any sort of hotel—why bother, when Grandpa's home in Saint Catherine was always open? Her vision of a B&B owner, therefore, had been cobbled together from vague ideas and possibly a few books she'd read as a child. Jacob Wayne should, by rights, be an old married couple with a twinkle in their eye who looked upon the world at large with kindness and goodwill and would be happy to hire Eve so that she could start her journey to self-actualization in a job she'd never get too attached to.

Instead, Jacob Wayne was a single man, not much older than her, and the twinkle in his eye was more of a steely, judgmental glint. Or maybe that was just the light flashing off his silver-rimmed glasses. Those glasses were balanced on a strong, Roman nose that someone should probably break, because all his features were strong and Roman and that likely had something to do with how he'd become so arrogant. The man was disgustingly, inescapably, thoroughly handsome, and as Gigi often said, *A handsome man is a fearsome liability to everyone but himself.*

Jacob had high cheekbones and a hard, sharp jaw, a terminally unsmiling mouth, pale skin, and rainy-sky eyes that had speared Eve through the chest from the moment she'd entered the room. Everything about him, from his severely side-parted blond hair, to his blue button-down shirt with its crisply rolled-up sleeves, suggested brisk efficiency. Even the way he talked, staccato bursts that zipped from point to point, said he was irritated by the irrelevant chatter the rest of the world wasted its time on.

Most of all, he seemed irritated by Eve.

Which was, frankly, his loss. Eve was an absolute *delight*, everyone knew that—yet it was abundantly clear that Jacob believed himself to be better than her. And perhaps, in certain respects, he might be right . . . but she wasn't overly fond of people who made judgments like that without the proper evidence. She wasn't fond of them at all.

Honestly, she *barely* wanted to work here anyway. In fact, what she wanted to do with Jacob sneering Wayne, after just ten minutes of acquaintance, was conk him on the head with a saucepan.

But watching a scarlet flush creep up his chiseled cheeks was also enjoyable, and since that's what happened when Mont said, *Jacob here is knee-deep in the shit*, Eve decided to listen instead of storming off.

"Jacob's last chef won the lotto down at the corner shop last week," Mont went on. "Fifty grand, so she's jacked work in and moved back to Scotland to marry her fella—long distance, they were—and start her own business."

Eve arched a dubious eyebrow. "Well, that's nice for her. But I doubt she'll get far with fifty thousand."

"That's what *I* said," Jacob burst out. "What's a house deposit without a guaranteed income to pay the mortgage?" He frowned and snapped his mouth shut as soon as the words escaped, looking thoroughly displeased at having agreed with Eve on any level.

Of course, Eve hadn't realized fifty thousand pounds was a house deposit. What she'd meant was that fifty thousand pounds hadn't been even half of the budget of the wedding she'd planned for Cecelia. But she decided to keep that minor detail to herself.

You waste time and opportunities like—like a spoiled brat.

She pursed her lips and turned away from Jacob's sharp, clear energy, focusing on Mont, who was considerably less unsettling in every way. Oh, he was as handsome as Jacob, with his smiling mouth, dark skin, and warm eyes—but he didn't vibrate with iron control and never-ending judgment, which made him far easier to look at. "Please," she said politely, "do continue."

Mont smiled a little wider. Jacob, meanwhile, narrowed those frosty eyes of his. Not that Eve was looking.

"Point is," Montrose went on, "the chef's gone, and Jacob doesn't know how to boil an egg."

"Yes," Jacob growled, "I do."

"Correction: Jacob was cursed by a witch at birth, so no matter how carefully he follows a recipe, it always comes out like shit."

Jacob opened his mouth as if he wanted to argue, then closed it again as if, on second thought, he really couldn't. Eve was suddenly glad she'd stayed; though she had no intention of taking this job, hearing all about Jacob's problems was rather entertaining.

"Plus," Mont said, "it's the Gingerbread Festival over in Pemberton at the end of the month." He must have seen Eve's expression, because he explained: "Old-school gingerbread bakery with a bit of a cult following. You should try some, it's bloody good. Anyway, they have this annual foodie event and Castell Cottage is running a breakfast for dinner stall."

Eve hadn't realized that breakfast for dinner was a legitimate thing, as opposed to evidence of her own chaotic lifestyle, but she decided to take this new knowledge in stride. "So they chose your B&B—"

"*My* B&B," Jacob interrupted. God, what a prat.

"*This* B&B," Eve went on smoothly—she was rather proud of herself—"to lead such an important event, despite your not even having a chef?"

Jacob's jaw tensed and his cold eyes flashed with irritation, which was rather fun to see. It was rare that Eve's natural skill at annoyance gave her such satisfaction. "We *did* have a chef when I secured the opportunity," he corrected her. "An excellent one."

"Also," Mont cut in, "there are multiple food stalls, all with different themes and providers. Pemberton Gingerbread is a bit of a patron for local business, like in the olden days with kings and . . . harp players. Or whatever." He shrugged his massive shoulders. "Point is, tourists come from all over the place, so it's an unmissable chance to reach new customers. Plus, there's always press. Jacob wants it to go well. Badly. But, as you pointed out, it kind of requires a chef."

Eve assumed that last part was the understatement to end all understatements.

"Suffice to say, we really can't afford to be picky at the moment. So here's what I think: let's go to the kitchen right now—"

Jacob's head whipped around as he glared at his friend. "*What* are you doing?"

Somehow, Montrose ignored the rigid command of that tone. In fact, he ignored it with a smile. "You show us what you can do, Eve, and if you're good—"

"Mont, no."

"If you're good," Mont continued firmly, "maybe Jacob will get his head out of his arse and take you seriously."

"I bloody won't," snapped the man in question.

Her patience snapping, too, Eve produced her sweetest smile. "You *won't* get your head out of your arse? Aren't you concerned about potential suffocation?"

A muscle began to tick at his jaw. "I—you—that is *not*—" Jacob cut off his own spluttering with a sharp inhalation. In an instant, he went from flustered irritation to rigid disdain, his gaze drilling into her.

For some reason, Eve's breath hitched a little. As if that harsh focus was something other than rude and alienating. Which it was not.

Jacob said, steel braided through every word, "I'm sorry, Ms. Brown, but my friend is mistaken. It's clear to me, based on this interview, that the two of us would not suit."

"I couldn't agree more," Eve said calmly, and she had the great satisfaction of making Jacob Wayne look like he'd swallowed a wasp. She rose to her feet and said to Mont, "It was absolutely wonderful to meet you. Perhaps I'll loiter around a certain pub this evening. Where did you say it was?"

Mont had been shooting Jacob some serious side-eye, which

was rather enjoyable, but now he turned his attention to Eve and gave her the sort of charming and indulgent smile she should always be treated to. "Friar's Hill, sweetheart. You come and see me. Don't worry," he added darkly with another glare at his friend, "Jacob won't be there."

Eve beamed. "I can't wait to talk . . . juice."

Jacob threw up his hands, clearly disgusted. "Are you flirting with her?" he demanded of Mont.

"Of course he is," Eve said pleasantly. "I'm delicious." She turned on her heel and sailed out of the room, tossing a look at Mont over her shoulder in the doorway. *Call me,* she mouthed with an ostentatious wink.

"We don't even have your bloody contact details!" Jacob yelled after her.

"Darling," she replied, "if you wanted them so badly, you should've asked."

Eve was fairly sure she heard a volcanic *boom* from the dining room as she left. Which kept a smile on her face for . . . precisely as long as it took to reach her car and realize she'd found the perfect opportunity to prove herself to her parents and had immediately, childishly, *recklessly* fucked it up.

At which point, every drop of her satisfaction went right down the drain.

♫

The minute Eve shut the door behind her, Mont turned to Jacob and demanded, "What the bloody hell was that?"

"You're asking *me*? That whole interview was betrayal, Mont.

Rank and utter betrayal. Guillotine-worthy. What were *you* doing, you sack of shit? Bending over backward for that—that *chaos demon*."

"You mean the woman who could have saved your arse," Mont corrected. "She was perfect!"

"She was unprepared, unprofessional—"

"Because you were such a shining star, there," Mont said. "I bet you know her fucking bra size."

"*I was reading the bloody T-shirt,*" Jacob roared.

"You were acting bonkers, is what you were doing. I've never seen you . . ." Mont trailed off and narrowed his eyes.

"What?" Jacob demanded. He hated trailing off. Hated unfinished sentences. Hated ominous ellipses that other people could mentally finish, but that left him utterly in the dark.

Mont continued to look weirdly suspicious. "I have never seen you speak so much to a complete stranger."

Heat crept over the back of Jacob's neck, prickled at the bends of his elbows. "I lost my temper. You know better than anyone how talkative that makes me." But the truth was, Mont made a valid point. Jacob didn't typically waste so much of his breath on interacting with untried strangers, because 90 percent of humanity was eventually proved useless and/or infuriating without any exertion on his part. He suspected Eve Brown was both, but he'd exerted himself for her, anyway, and behaved quite badly, too.

He must be at the end of his tether.

Mont shrugged and shook his head. "Whatever. Look, I know you didn't like her, but just think for a second. She was charming as fuck, which is something the B&B needs that *you* don't provide—I'm sorry, man, no judgment, but you don't."

"I know," Jacob replied sharply. It had never been a problem at the luxury hotel chains he'd used to gain experience in the city. Precision, perfectionism, clear communication—those had all been points in his favor. But it turned out B&Bs had different requirements. People wanted to feel *cozy* and *at home*. Well, Jacob had gotten that down with the decor, the amenities, the marketing—but his manner didn't exactly fit in with the crackling log fire and hot tea.

"Not only that," Mont went on, "she didn't bend for you one bit—"

"That's a bad thing, Montrose."

"No, it's not, you absolute tyrant. And *finally*," he said with a flourish, "I know she can cook."

"How?" Jacob demanded.

Mont got a familiar and annoying expression on his face: the Stubborn and Superior one. "I can just tell."

"*How?*"

"It doesn't matter how, because we're going to go after her and apologize, and then she'll cook for us and prove it."

Jacob shot him a disgusted look. "I hate it when you do this."

"When I'm right, you mean?"

"When you're full of shit." Jacob took off his glasses and cleaned them on the edge of his shirt, thoughts flying. The fact was, Montrose's points weren't entirely inaccurate or illogical. Eve *was* undeniably warm, excessively so in his opinion, but Jacob was aware he had unusual parameters. She was probably funny, too, if you liked that kind of bollocks. Much as Jacob hated to admit it, he could see her making customers laugh, could see the Trip Advisor reviews with little throwaway comments about *that adorable cook*—and her attitude, while infuriating, suggested she wouldn't be prone to breaking down in tears when under pressure. Jacob couldn't abide tears in the kitchen. He didn't need rogue DNA in his guest's eggs.

He would never have hired Eve back when he was working hotels, but the dynamic in B&Bs was different, and those who didn't adapt . . . well, they died out. He refused to die out. Although, if he spent too much time with such an infuriating woman, he might die anyway—of frustration. Or frustrated rage. Or—something.

So what was more important—his survival, or the B&B's?

Absolutely no question.

Jacob sighed, put his glasses back on, and stood. "If she can't cook, I'm going to skin you alive."

They broke out of the cottage's front door and into a steady drizzle that was rather typical of the Lake District, even in August. Less typical was the angry yellow tinge of the clouds, the roar of thunder in the distance, and the near-instant flash of lightning that followed.

"Fuck's sake," Jacob muttered as tiny raindrops beaded on the lenses of his glasses in record time. "Electrical storm," he shouted over the thunder. "Better get inside, Mont."

"Really? Height jokes? Now?"

"Always."

Mont rolled his eyes. "You go left, I'll go right."

They split up just as the sky above them cracked open. Rain

spilled to the earth as if each drop weighed a ton, and in the few seconds it took Jacob to scan the cottage's small gravel driveway, he was already soaked to the skin. His shirt clung to him, his jeans grew stiff and heavy, and his glasses slid down his rain-wet nose. He cursed, pushed them back up, and squinted at the cars lining the gravel. Every space was taken by a familiar vehicle—guests—so he jogged out onto the street and turned left.

"This *bloody* woman," he shouted to no one in particular over the rain. An irritating voice at the back of his brain reminded him that he wouldn't be looking for her if he hadn't chased her off in the first place, but Jacob swept the voice aside with only a whisper of guilt. Who the fuck wore ironic T-shirts to a job interview, showed up without a CV, and rambled on about her posh mate's juicing experiences? *Who?* Feckless, irresponsible ne'er-do-wells, that's who. He knew the kind. He'd been plagued with the consequences of their actions since birth, the same consequences *they* always seemed to outrun.

But he was desperate, and he did try to listen to Mont every six months or so, which meant Jacob had no choice but to continue searching. He passed parked but deserted cars on the street—and pulled up short when he found a moon-blue vintage Beetle he'd never seen before, parked at an outrageous angle a good two feet from the curb. There was a pink sticker on the back window that read SEYCHELLES SLUTS OF '16—*dear God*—and he could see a familiar silhouette in the driver's seat.

Great. He'd found her. Now he'd have to actually *say* something to her, something that would convince her to come back and try again.

Clearly Mont hadn't thought this through, or he never would've sent Jacob to do this on his own.

"Get on with it, Wayne," he muttered under his breath, and ran both hands through his dripping wet hair, pushing it off his face. Then he stepped out onto the street, ready to walk around the car and knock on her window.

But in the end, he never made it there. Because the moment Jacob left the safety of the pavement, the car's lights flicked on, and the car itself jerked backward. Directly into him.

Hard.

Trust Eve fucking Brown.

CHAPTER FOUR

Jacob wasn't an expert in physics, but he didn't think the force of one little Beetle should hurt this bad. Then again, the whole event took him completely by surprise, so he didn't do much to save himself.

First, the car's bumper slammed him bodily into the Porsche Cayenne behind him. His head jerked back and hit the windscreen so hard, it was a miracle he didn't crack the glass—or maybe he did. He wasn't sure, since a moment later, he was busy sliding to the ground like a stunned sack of potatoes. Landing was awkward as fuck, his right wrist taking almost all his weight and bending hideously. So he gave up on the whole "staying upright" thing and let his body flop back onto the road like a fish.

After all that, Jacob decided the most sensible thing he could do was lie very still and make sure he wasn't dead.

"Oh, shit in a sweet pea."

His thoughts exactly, but the voice that floated to him over pounding rain definitely wasn't his own. It was too posh and too pretty. Could voices be pretty? Jacob wasn't sure. He'd take a look at the voice and check.

He opened his eyes, felt a stab of pain shoot through his head like a sharpened ice pick to the skull, and closed them again. His glasses were missing, anyway. No point doing eye stuff. Bugger eyes. Who needed them?

"Oh no, oh no, oh no, oh no." There was that voice again, strange and yet familiar. His mind was hot and sticky like fudge. Yum, fudge. Was this a guest, maybe? A yummy, fudgy guest? Fuck. No lying around in the street in front of guests. It was inappropriate and irresponsible and very bad business.

Jacob tried to sit up, but several points of agony screamed at him simultaneously to stop that shit and lie down again. So he stopped that shit and lay down again.

Then the voice said, "Are you a dog? Please don't be a dog," and memory came to him like a bolt of lightning.

He croaked accusingly, "*Eve.*"

She was supposed to wilt with guilt under the mighty power of his voice, but all she did was sigh, "Oh, thank goodness you're not a dog."

Rage was an excellent method of clearing the head. Jacob forced his eyes open, even though he couldn't see for shit and felt kind of dizzy. The sky above him was a sickly yellow, staticky with the motion of still-falling rain. He didn't spot any Eve-shaped blobs in his line of sight, but he hoped she could see him—or more specifically, that she could see the burning hate in his eyes. "You'd rather hit me than hit a dog?" he demanded. "Interview was . . . so bad?"

His words were wonky. Goddamn it. He didn't want his words to be wonky.

"Don't flatter yourself," she said primly. "It has nothing to do with you in particular. I meant that I'd rather hit a *person* than a dog."

His lurching mind grappled with that drivel for a moment before he announced, "You are joking. This is a joke."

"Of course I'm not joking! Dogs are so small and sweet and vulnerable. Humans are much sturdier. See how well you're handling this?"

Jacob might be having an out-of-body rage experience right now, because his pain was growing oddly distant, and he barely even noticed that the storm was slowing as suddenly as it had begun, and really, all he could feel was this overwhelming urge to bury Eve Brown in a hole somewhere, or possibly dump her at the bottom of a well. "How well I'm *handling* this?" he echoed, his shout making his battered lungs ache. "Woman, I am one wrong move from vomiting blood."

There was a slight pause before Eve said reasonably, "Ah, but if you were a dog, you might be dead right now."

Jacob was searching for the strength to drag himself up and strangle her, even if it killed him, when a new smudge of blurry color appeared before his eyes: an oval of rich brown, surrounded by ribbons of pastel purple. She came closer, closer, and he made out the details he'd rather forget. The rounded cheeks and the big, dark eyes behind rain-wet, spiky eyelashes. The stubbornly pointed chin and glittery, glossy lips. She was biting those lips, if he wasn't mistaken, and quite violently, too. Not to mention, there was a deep furrow on her formerly smooth forehead. Maybe she *was* racked with guilt.

Or maybe she was just worried about a potential manslaughter charge if he died.

Probably the latter.

"Would it take your mind off things if I showed you my tits?" she asked out of the blue.

God, concussions were strange.

"Jacob?"

"What?" he bit out.

"Did you hear me?"

"Did I—?" He stopped. Oh. Had the tits comment *not* been some kind of auditory hallucination? "Dunno," he slurred. "Maybe it would help. Wait, no it—what the hell is wrong with you?"

"Several things." She'd disappeared from his line of sight, which was honestly a blessing, and her voice came as if from a distance. "I only asked because when I came to the interview you seemed very distracted by my chest, so—"

"*I was reading the T-shirt,*" he insisted for what felt like the thousandth time.

"If you say so," she murmured, clearly amused and absolutely infuriating. Then she cried, "Ah! Found them," and reappeared again. Slowly, carefully, she slid his glasses back onto his face.

His glasses. She'd found his glasses. He hadn't even asked. And now here she was, putting them on for him.

Of course, that task was not as easy as certain films and TV shows liked to make it look. As a general rule, Jacob made sure no one ever did it to him. Similarly, when women tried to *remove* his glasses in fits of passion, or whatever the fuck they thought they were doing, it usually pissed him off enough to take him out of the mood, and then he had to think about messy blow jobs for a solid five minutes to get going again. So when he realized that a complete stranger was attempting one of his least favorite things in the world, he tensed.

Which hurt like a motherfucker and turned out to be a waste of energy when she pulled off the move without a hitch.

Well, mostly. She avoided all the big no-no's, like stabbing him in the cheek or the eye or the ear. She didn't get the glasses quite straight—but he suspected they were no longer straight at all. Plus, one of the lenses had cracked, which was utterly her fault, so he refused to give her 10/10 for cautious glasses-sliding. But still. Pretty impressive.

And now her face was in focus, he could see something unexpected: those huge eyes of hers were shimmering with something that might actually be tears.

But she didn't let the maybe-tears fall. She offered a smile that was a shadow of the cheerful, dimpled thing she'd flashed in his dining room and said, "There. Now you can glare at me properly."

Jacob really must be concussed, because instead of telling her to fuck off, he said softly, "Thanks."

Thanking her. He was thanking her for putting his shattered glasses back on his face after she'd knocked them off *with her car*.

But her smile was wider and realer now, and if she gave him just a little more, that dimple would appear, and . . .

"Jake?" The shout was Mont's, clearly nearby. "Where are you, man?"

Eve looked up. Jacob blinked and wondered why he felt so off-balance, now her gaze wasn't on him anymore.

Concussed. He was definitely concussed.

"Montrose," she called, and rose to her feet.

Jacob, for some reason, tried to sit up, as if there was a string attached between them. He made it roughly halfway before pain wrapped a fist around him and squeezed. Shit, shit, shit. He clamped his jaw shut because he refused to throw up in front of Eve—or rather, in public—or rather, at all. Then he sat up the rest of the way, realized he'd done something terrible to his arse, and tried to roll up on his knees instead.

"Christ, mate," came Montrose's voice from above. "You're a mess. What the bloody hell happened?"

Eve wailed, "I hit him with my car," just as Jacob snapped, "She *hit* me with her *car!*" Then he registered how teary Eve sounded and felt like a bit of a bastard.

Hang on—*she* was the bastard. Her! Good God, what the hell was wrong with him?

"I'm going to call an ambulance," Eve said.

"You bloody well aren't," Jacob snorted, then instantly regretted the snort. Could lungs be broken? His lungs were broken. "*Ambulance,*" he wheezed contemptuously. "What a fuss."

"Jacob," Mont said sternly, "don't be a prick. You need medical attention."

"I realize that," Jacob said, "but there's no need for an ambulance." Waste of public resources. He was perfectly fit. There were people dying, for Christ's sake. "I'll drive myself." He started to rise to his feet, but the world swung sideways and a gang of vicious pixies set fire to his skull. He was all charred and crumbling inside and he felt violently dizzy again. "Montrose's going to drive me," he corrected, and looked up at the man in question, studiously avoiding Eve. Everything would be a thousand times better if she wasn't here, so he had decided to pretend she wasn't. "Give us a hand, Mont."

Mont gave a long-suffering sigh and knelt down, sliding an arm around Jacob's back—which hurt like a motherfucker, but there was nothing to be done about that—and muttering "Hold on to me. Properly. I mean it, you bastard."

"Yes, sir." Jacob attempted to sound grudging or maybe indulgent, as opposed to pathetically grateful. In the end, he missed all of the above and simply sounded drunk.

As they staggered to their feet together, Eve fluttered around like an especially annoying, orange butterfly. "What shall I do?" she asked. "He's driving you—what shall I do?"

"Disappear," Jacob suggested wearily. "Down a well, maybe. Or up a mountain. Or to the moon."

"Watch the cottage," Mont said.

"*What?*" Jacob wasn't sure who said it first—him or Eve.

"Well, I'm taking you to the hospital," Mont scowled, "my sisters are working, and so's your aunt Lucy. Looks like Eve's all we've got." He turned to the demoness in question. "We were looking for you, anyway, hoping to give you a trial, so here it is. Trial by fire. Tell all the guests what's happened and wing it."

Jacob wanted to tell Mont he'd lost his mind, but he was growing incredibly exhausted with every second they spent standing up, and the connection between his mouth and his brain seemed to have become dislodged at some point in the last few minutes. So all he could do was croak out, "But—serial killer—very sophisticated con woman—industry spy—she's going to *steal my complimentary organic shampoo provider.*"

There was a startled pause before Mont said sadly, "Look what you've *done* to him."

Eve winced and focused on Jacob, speaking as if to an infant. "I'm not a serial killer," she told him slowly, "or . . . any of the other things you just said, whatever they were. But I am really, really, awfully, terribly sorry about hitting you with my car. And I promise I will look after your B&B as if it's my very own." Or at least, that's what he thought he heard. It was hard to tell over the ringing in his ears.

Jacob tried to say, *Take your promise and stick it up your arse, Madame Spy,* but what came out was a raspy "Jesus, fuck, my *head.*"

And then the fuzziness got even fuzzier and Mont dragged him away, and Jacob . . . just sort of . . . went.

♬

Warm and dry in the B&B, Eve could almost convince herself that the past twenty minutes had been a dream. Of course she hadn't run over the most infuriating man alive! Of course he hadn't been dragged off to the hospital by his best friend, leaving Eve behind to watch a goddamn bed-and-breakfast. Really, why not take things even further? *Of course* Eve hadn't driven miles in a teary fit of pique before interviewing for the first job she came across as if that would solve all her problems! Because only a spoiled brat, or, alternatively, an adorable dog with a very tiny brain, would ever do such things, and Eve was surely neither.

Which didn't explain why her jeans were still damp from kneeling beside Jacob's crumpled form, why her hands were shaking something awful, or why she was currently standing nervous and alone in Castell Cottage's welcoming foyer.

Well, shit sticks and fudgesicles.

Eve found a handily placed chaise longue by the stairs and summarily collapsed. She'd been aiming for an elegant lounge of the type Gigi might do, but her jeans were stiff and her frigid, fear-stricken bones were stiffer, so she ended up falling like a pile of bricks. The chaise was upholstered in burgundy silk that matched the Edwardian—or was it Victorian? Oh, who gave a shit—wallpaper and rugs. There were a lot of rugs in this high-ceilinged room, she noticed, as well as mahogany floors polished to a gleaming shine, and glowing wall sconces and various other things that said *coziness* and *comfort* and *gravitas*.

Was this really Jacob's B&B, or did he just manage things? Only, she'd have taken him for a fan of cold, impersonal, modernist decor. Traditional vibes that she actually *liked* were not what Eve expected from the man.

He'd probably hired a decorator.

And she should probably stop thinking uncharitable thoughts about someone she'd just put in the hospital.

When Eve's phone buzzed from her back pocket, she jolted in a manner that screamed guilty conscience. The vibration popped her bubble of shock, making her suddenly, uncomfortably aware that she was now responsible for the house in which she lounged. Better make a good show of it. Arsehole or not, Jacob *did* deserve to have his obvious B&B standards upheld. And she had said . . . She'd said . . .

I promise I will look after your B&B as if it's my very own.

Which, in hindsight, had been a reckless promise to make. Already regretting her words, Eve huffed out a shaky breath and sat upright (in order to seem more commanding and less, er, collapsing). Unfortunately, regardless of her physical position, she was clearly incapable of looking after a damned flea. This morning alone, she'd failed at running away, failed at her first job interview, and failed at basic car safety. By the time Jacob returned she'd probably have set his roof on fire.

Rolling her lips between her teeth, she wiggled her still-vibrating phone from her pocket. It was set to Do Not Disturb, so someone must have called multiple times. The name FLORENCE LENNOX flashed up on the screen. Eve sighed, hesitated, then pressed Accept. In her experience, the best way to deal with Bad Feelings was to avoid facing them by any means necessary. Whatever Florence wanted would do wonderfully as a distraction.

"Hello?"

"Darling! *There* you are, I texted *twice*."

"Twice?" Eve murmured. "Goodness. Please thank your fingers for their service."

Florence released a waterfall of tinkling laughter, which was strange, since she never usually laughed at Eve's jokes. In Florence's circle, Eve was the Baker Friend—which meant they called her up when they needed event cakes, then invited her to whatever said event happened to be, as a form of payment. Following which, they gently ignored her until the next party.

Eve had a designated status in every friendship group she belonged to. That was how she managed to cling to the periphery of them all.

"Oh, darling, you're *hilarious*. But, do listen—I have a proposition for you."

Eve frowned at the phone. *A proposition* was not how Florence usually spun, *A request for you to bring a three-tiered topsy-turvy cake to my mother's fiftieth birthday.*

"Yeees?"

"Don't sound so nervous!" Flo had a charming habit of noticing and immediately articulating weakness. A bit like a wolf that could talk. "It's about your little events company. Now, I know you love to take over the cakes and things for all my parties."

Love might be an overstatement, but Eve didn't *hate* it. Fucking up a favor was nearly impossible—and people were always so pleased when they tasted her double-fudge.

Causing happiness was about the only thing that still made her sparkle.

"I *thought* cakes were your only real skill," Florence was droning on, "but it seems you've been hiding other talents, you naughty thing. Because I've heard amazing things about the wedding you planned." She paused. "Well, except for that odd rumor about your biting off a dove's head and spitting feathers into the bride's face, but never mind that. My point is—it's little Freddy's birthday in February, and he's just given our original party planner the clap, so we need a new one. One he probably *won't* give the clap."

Little Freddy Lennox was Florence's twenty-year-old brother. Eve considered several responses—for example, *I actually just closed my company down*, or, *All I did was free the doves, that lying cow*. But in the end, she settled on stammering, "Er—Florence, does that—well, what I mean to ask is . . . Erm, *the clap* is some sort of euphemism, isn't it?"

Florence laughed. "Silly goose. Of course it is!"

Eve relaxed.

"It's a euphemism for Freddy shagging the party planner and giving her chlamydia, darling. And what a frightful fit she's thrown about it, too."

"I . . . see," Eve croaked. *I see* was a lovely, neutral phrase. Much more socially acceptable than *Bloody hell, Florence, what the fuck is your family on?*

But really. If you were going to sleep with staff, practicing safe sex seemed the very *least* you could do. Or perhaps she was being judgmental?

"Now, darling, we will of course be paying you—you're an entrepreneur now!" Florence trilled. As Eve wasn't particularly close to, well, *any* of her friends, none of them had a complete picture of just how many times she'd been an entrepreneur. Her failures were her own private wounds to lick, thank you very much. "And since the party's not until February," Florence went on, "we won't need to start consultations until . . . September."

Eve blinked. "That's six months before the actual party, Flo."

"Well," came the frosty reply, "this is Freddy's twenty-first, Eve. If you can't take that fact seriously—"

"No," Eve blurted, that disapproving tone making her stomach roil. It reminded her of being at school, when life had revolved around avoiding too much soul-shriveling attention from students or teachers. "No, that's not what I meant. But, Flo . . . I'm not sure if I'm up to this at the moment." *Understatement of the year.* Eve had rather a lot on her plate, what with today's mild familial disowning and mild vehicular maiming. Plus, September was only a month away, and she should probably spend that month job-hunting.

She braced herself for a Hurricane Florence tantrum, and possibly for temporary ostracism from one of her many friendship groups. Instead, after a slight pause, she heard . . .

A sniffle?

"Evie," Flo said, sounding rather damp. "Please. I know it's a sudden ask, and Freddy can be a bit difficult, but he's really fluffed things up with this party planner woman and our parents are going absolutely bonkers and—well, I need your help, Eve. You wouldn't let me down, would you? Not when I need your *help*? It would be so terribly cruel."

Eve bit her lip, a worried frown creasing her brow. Florence sounded quite upset, which made the stress and annoyance sloshing around Eve's stomach swirl predictably into concern. The fact was, Flo had a problem, and Eve—her currently messy life aside—could fix it.

So after a moment's internal wobbling, she inevitably gave in. "Oh, all right. If you need me, Flo, you know I'll do my best. So . . . six months of party planning it is." What were friends for, after all?

"*Really?*" Florence squealed. "Oh, that's wonderful, Eve, absolutely wonderful. Knew you'd see reason." Her tone zipped from squeaky pleasure to smooth business in the blink of an eye. "Since I've got you on the phone, we might as well talk details. Venues are the priority at this point, of course—when are you available for viewings? Never mind, I'll email you an invite to the Google Calendar."

Eve blinked. Gosh. Florence was very focused when it came to this birthday party.

And the more Eve thought about it, the more she realized this might be a blessing in disguise. Party planning was different from planning a wedding—significantly less time, less pressure—but still a *job*. The beauty of it dawned on her slowly, like an early-morning sun. Six months spent planning Freddy's twenty-first, then another six months planning some other party, and she'd have done it. She'd have held down a job for a year, proved her parents wrong . . .

And maybe done them proud?

Let's not get out of hand, here. Scraping together a couple of parties was hardly running a business like Chloe or being a professional genius like Danika. But Eve had officially secured gainful employment—even if it wasn't precisely what Mum and Dad had had in mind—and she really, really intended to keep it this time.

Absolutely nothing would go wrong.

CHAPTER FIVE

By the time Jacob returned, Eve was beginning to worry she'd actually killed the man.

Hours had passed. The sun hung low in the sky, and several guests had already returned from their days out. She knew that the National Health Service, being currently underfunded, came with heftier waiting times, but good Lord—how long did it take to check a man's skull and whack a bandage on him?

In the time since he and Mont had left, she'd found the (rather impressive, if terrifyingly clean) kitchen, helped herself to a sandwich (plus a teeny, tiny baked potato with beans and cheese, for dinner), and relocated to the dining room to avoid any further guests. She found undefined interactions with strangers to be incredibly awkward and had decided not to expose her delicate nerves any further. And anyway, this was a bed-and-breakfast—not a *bed and make uncomfortable eye contact with the strange woman hovering in the foyer*. She was here to prevent grand disasters and answer urgent requests, not to ask various hikers if they needed fresh towels.

Even if a little voice in her head suggested she was absolutely supposed to ask about the towel thing.

Oh, well.

Eve was considering calling the local hospital and demanding to know if she was an accidental murderer when she heard the distinctive heave of the front door opening. As had become her habit, she leapt to the window and craned her neck to see who was there.

It wasn't a guest. Nor was it a rogue burglar she'd have to fight off to protect Jacob's livelihood. No; it was Jacob himself. She only caught the barest glimpse: a head of ice-blond hair resting on Mont's broad shoulder, and then they were gone.

Suddenly, all those hours of wishing they'd hurry back turned into a desperate wish for them to *not be here*. Because it finally occurred to Eve that Jacob coming back probably meant Jacob ripping her a new arsehole for, you know, running him over. Which she would richly deserve.

Wincing, Eve tiptoed over to the dining room door—which she'd left open a crack, in case any of the guests rang the bell at the front desk or screeched "Argh! A murder most foul!" or something like that. Nudging it slightly wider, she peered out into the foyer just as Mont used his free hand to shut the door. His other hand, you understand, was engaged in Jacob-hoisting.

And Jacob clearly needed a lot of hoisting. The viciously upright posture she'd noticed earlier that day had vanished; his long, lean body now wobbled like a kite in the wind, except for his right arm, which was held at a rigid angle by . . . oh, bloody hell, was that a cast? She had literally broken him. Fabulous.

It occurred to Eve that Mum might not be pleased about this new party-planning contract if it came alongside a lawsuit for dangerous driving.

Sigh. Ever the disappointment, Eve.

Was that Mum's voice, or Eve's own?

"Nope, nope, nope." Mont's words dragged Eve back to the scene playing out before her. She choked on a yelp of laughter when she saw Jacob trying to get behind the ornately carved reception desk. By climbing over it.

Mont yanked him back with both hands. Jacob grunted, "Gerroff. Gotta check the—the check-in—ow!"

"Sorry, mate. Bit difficult, at the minute, to grab you without grabbing a bruise."

Eve bit her lip and attempted not to die of guilt. She estimated she could survive another three to four minutes without perishing, but then Jacob turned, and she finally saw his face, and her survival time dropped to approximately five seconds.

He looked absolutely nothing like himself. She barely knew the man, but his transformation was dramatic enough to be obvious. Behind his glasses—which he'd knocked askew during his attempt to vault the desk—those blue-gray ice-chip eyes had melted into hazy springs, his pupils big enough that she could see them from here. His high cheekbones were flushed like strawberry ice cream.

Strawberry was Eve's favorite flavor. (Which wasn't remotely relevant.)

And his perfectly coiffed hair, with its severe side part, had turned into baby duck fluff. That was really the only way to put it.

He looked like a toddler who'd been tossing and turning in bed. A *drunk* toddler. Wearing a cast.

At this rate, Eve was going to bite her own lip bloodless.

"Now, come here," Mont was saying, "and be good, or I'll go into your sock drawer and unpair all your—"

"No!" Jacob gasped, as if this threat was too dire to bear.

Eve slapped a hand over her mouth to stifle a giggle. Good Lord. If you'd asked her this morning whether Jacob Arsehole Wayne was capable of being adorable, she'd have bet her left tit the answer was no. And Eve's left tit had always been her favorite.

"Jus' lemme do the . . . thing," Jacob scowled as Mont tugged him toward the stairs. "The work things . . . and thing . . . We going to my office? Yeah? Yeah, Mont?"

"Christ," Mont muttered, "when did you get so heavy?"

"I have heavy bones," Jacob said proudly.

Mont snorted. "If I'd known concussions could be this funny, I'd have borrowed my sister's GoPro. And don't worry about work stuff, Jake. Eve's watching the place, remember?"

The sound of her own name made Eve jump. And then Mont's dark gaze swung directly to hers through the gap she'd made in the door, and she jumped again. So much for her cunning spy skills.

Mont arched an eyebrow as if to say, *Now would be a great time to come out.*

Eve shook her head as if to say, *No, thank you, I am a monumental coward.*

"*Eve*," Jacob muttered darkly. So darkly that, for a moment, she worried he'd seen her, too. But no—he was staring into space, glaring with impressive focus at a spot on the wall. "*Eve*," he repeated. "She! Broke my *arm*."

"Yeah, Jacob. She did."

Well! So much for Mont's comparatively sweet and kind nature, the bastard. And he had the audacity to grin as he spoke!

"She can't watch Castell Cottage," Jacob growled as Mont dragged him up the stairs. "She is a disaster!"

"Bit harsh, mate."

"She has no idea of the proper—the proper—*protocols!*"

"Well, we were in a pinch, so—"

"She's obnoxious and disorganized and *posh*." This last was said as if it might be the most grievous crime of all. "And," Jacob went on, as Mont towed him away, "she is *hideously* pretty."

Eve blinked. Had she . . . had she misheard that last part?

"Interesting phrasing," Mont said mildly. "Would you mind explaining . . ." His voice faded as they disappeared, and Eve barely restrained herself from kicking the wall. She wanted that explanation, too, goddamn it. *Hideously pretty?* What on earth did that mean? Jacob must be confused. He must have said it wrong. He probably meant *hideously petty* or something along those lines.

She shook her head and backed away from the door, considering her options. Since Jacob was now back—and clearly under proper supervision—Eve was technically free to go. She'd promised to watch the B&B, but it no longer needed watching. She could run from the scene of the crime right this second, return home in time for a late yoga class with Gigi and Shivs, and tell Mum and Dad all about her day's successes while completely leaving out the part where she bombed an interview and drove over the interviewer.

Except . . .

Well. Except that seemed a little bit terrible. Jacob might be an arsehole, but in this situation, she was even arseholier, which was really saying something. She should stick around to make sure he was okay, attempt to apologize to his annoying, strawberry ice cream face, et cetera.

Plus, whispered a voice inside her head, *no job in the world will regain Mum and Dad's respect if you keep running away from the trouble* you *make.*

Hm. Eve usually kept that annoyingly sensible voice—a voice that sounded irritatingly like her eldest sister, Chloe—under strict lockdown. The stress of the day must have released it from its chains.

After a few moments of deep breathing and loin-girding, Eve swallowed her anxiety and forced herself out of the dining room, across the foyer, and up the stairs. She hadn't ventured onto the upper floors of Castell Cottage at all today, but now she found them much the same as the lower ones—if a little lighter and brighter, the corridors narrow but well-lit, the walls covered in ditsy, yellow flower prints and the floors covered in plush, emerald carpet. She kept an eye out for Jacob or Mont as she climbed to the first floor, then the second.

Only at the top of the third set of stairs did she see the door that might lead to her doom. It was a slab of imposing mahogany with a pearlized handle and a gold sign marked PRIVATE.

Yep. Jacob was probably in there.

She smoothed out her braids and straightened her T-shirt as she approached. Then she hovered, awkward and uncertain, for a few seconds before raising a hand to—knock? Shove the bastard open like a TV detective?

In the end, it didn't matter, because the door swung open before she could touch it. There stood Mont, who looked surprised for a moment, then pleased. "Oh," he said. "You came up."

"Well." Eve fidgeted on the spot. "It seemed as if there were things to discuss."

Mont arched an eyebrow. "Interesting. And here I had you for a runner."

"A *runner*?" she repeated with all the righteous outrage of a woman who had totally been moments away from running. "Never."

"Never?"

"Never."

"Right." He grinned. "Then what I'm about to say won't bother you at all."

Eve experienced a deep and powerful sense of foreboding. "Have at it." Her voice squeaked on the last word. Oops.

"Come in," Mont ordered—and it clearly was an order. Eve stepped through the doorway, jumping a little when he closed the door behind her. She looked around to find herself in what could only be described as Jacob's *quarters*. This section of hallway had five doors: one that showed a glimpse of bathroom counter and neatly folded towels, one open cupboard with a washer-dryer thrumming away, two doors that remained neatly closed, and one at the end of the corridor that was slightly ajar—but not enough to see through it.

Eve's nosiness was therefore thwarted.

Mont led her to one of the closed doors, which turned out to be locked. He produced a key and she found herself ushered into the most anal-retentive office she'd ever seen in her life. It was a box room with a desk set in front of tall, wide windows, a trio of filing cabinets lining the magnolia walls, and absolutely nothing else. No books, no photographs, not even any of the old, jazzy rugs thrown about elsewhere in Castell Cottage. A blank slate.

"Is this—Jacob's *office*?" she managed.

Mont, who was already standing behind the desk rifling through drawers, shot her a look. "It helps him focus."

Well, Eve bloody bet it did. The only possible distraction in this room was the window, and Jacob apparently sat with his back to it.

Mont straightened up, a stack of notebooks in his hands. "All right, listen up. I don't know if Jake got a chance to mention it before you ran him over—"

Wow. Okay, they were being blunt, then. She could respect that.

"—but we were chasing after you to give you the job." When Eve stared blankly in response, Mont added, "The chef job. Here. Jacob figured out a couple seconds after you'd gone that you're pretty much our only hope, so yeah."

Was Eve imagining things, or was the guilt being piled rather high in this conversation?

"Then things went left," Mont continued, "and now I'm a little worried you don't intend to take the job you apparently wanted so badly. I'm especially worried because of this Gingerbread Festival thing, which he's worked incredibly fucking hard for—and because, if you waltz off and leave us in the lurch, you're also leaving Jacob in an even worse position than he was in before. What with the fractured wrist, and all. So. That'd be fucked up. Right?"

Eve wasn't mistaken at all; the guilt pile was indeed high, and it was working.

Cooking at Castell Cottage was, logically speaking, a horrible idea: Eve had no clue what she was doing, the owner had hated her on sight, and that was *before* she'd run him over. Plus, she was employed by Florence now—or she would be, come September. But the weight of her need to atone pressed heavier and heavier, squeezing an unauthorized reply from her throat.

"Of course I'm taking the job," she croaked.

And immediately wanted to kick herself.

Mont brightened. "You are?"

I'm not. "I am."

"Oh, *perfect.* Thank you. That's—really, thanks, because we're in a bit of a bind here. Now, I hate to throw you in at the deep end, but Jacob's got a concussion and a fractured wrist and a seriously bruised arse—"

Eve wrestled with an involuntary wince.

"—so he's not exactly going to be better in the morning. Do you think you could . . . take over for a little while, just while he's recovering?"

Eve blinked. "*Take over?* But I—I only interviewed for the chef position."

"Yeah, but then you hit Jacob with your car."

"Well—doesn't he have any other staff?!"

"No."

"No?!"

"No," Mont repeated calmly, striding across the room toward her with his mysterious pile of papers. "Here. These should help."

Eve opened the first notebook to find a handwritten title page in impressive calligraphy.

HOW NOT TO FUCK UP MY HEALTH RATING
By Jacob Wayne

She stared. "Are these . . . employee handbooks?"

"Basically."

"That he . . . that he made *himself*?"

"Yep," Mont said. "Now, I need to see to the pub, and you need to be prepared for breakfast tomorrow morning, so—"

A thought struck Eve on a wave of horror. "What *time* is breakfast tomorrow morning?"

Mont ignored her. "So I'm going to rush you through the ropes. Okay?"

Okay? *Okay?* A very large part of Eve wanted to scream that no, this was *not* okay—mostly because holy shit, there were seven notebooks piled in her arms, and this bed-and-breakfast seemed properly run and generally good and therefore intimidating, and she already knew she couldn't possibly take over in a manner that would please the Prince of Perfection Jacob Wayne.

Didn't they realize she wasn't up to much? Didn't they know she never quite got things right? Putting her in charge of anything would be a mistake, but putting her in charge of *this*—

And yet . . . who else was going to do it?

Eve bit her lip as realizations racked up in her head. The basic facts were these: Jacob was out of commission. It was her fault. And even before all this happened, he'd been woefully down on staff.

Someone needed to step up here, and it looked like she was the only otherwise unoccupied person around.

"Fine," she said. Her voice was slightly shaky, but it was clear. "Fine. I'll do it. So show me the ropes."

♫

God, sleep was good.

As he snuggled deeper into his nest of pillows and blankets, Jacob wondered fuzzily why he insisted on getting up at 5 A.M. every morning. Something something, work, something something, routine. He had a vague recollection of doing push-ups before breakfast, or some such bullshit. But right now, he couldn't comprehend why any sensible human would ever do any of that when they could just . . .

Stay in bed . . .

Forever.

Even better: when they could *sleep* forever. He'd been in the middle of a bloody brilliant dream about devouring an orange, segment by sweet, juicy segment, when something had woken him up. Hmm. Should probably investigate that.

Scowling, he opened his eyes.

The barest hint of moonlight trickled through his curtains, but the darkness didn't matter; without his glasses, Jacob couldn't see for shit, anyway. It was sound that made him realize someone was in his room: the creak of slow, easy footsteps, the steady huff of gentle breaths. He clenched his right hand into a fist, or tried to. But it turned out his right arm was still broken—had that really happened?—so he ended up shouting in pain. Also known as *completely giving himself away to his possible murderer.*

"Jacob?" the murderer said, her whisper all velvet and smoke.

And now he had the funniest sense of déjà vu.

"*You,*" he croaked, squeezing his eyes shut. This—*woman*—this lilac and orange—*female*—this—destroyer of fucking *worlds*—

"I came to check on you," she whispered. "I read on the internet that you should check on people with concussions or they might, you know, die."

This human bloody *wrecking ball*—

"Did you know you're speaking out loud?" the demoness asked.

This gorgeous fucking *nitwit*—

"Is this negging? Are you negging me right now?"

Jacob's thoughts lurched along like a series of disjointed train carriages, but they were all aimed squarely at one thing: getting rid of Eve Brown. "Piss off," he growled, trying—and failing—to sit up. Turned out his arse was broken, too. That's what it felt like, anyway.

"Your arse is *what*?"

"Stop reading my thoughts." With his left hand, he fumbled for his glasses.

"I'm not reading your thoughts! You're speaking out loud, genius."

"That's right," Jacob muttered soothingly to himself. "I am a genius. Everything is fine. Here are my glasses, I will just put them on and be happy."

"Oh my God, concussions are so weird."

For once, the harbinger of evil made a valid point. Jacob shoved his glasses onto his face, scowled at the crack across his lens, then got on with the very necessary business of glaring at Eve Brown. "Go. Away."

She came closer, because she was the bane of his existence. Her steps brought her into the slice of watery moonlight that had snuck through his curtains. She was still prettier than she had any right to be, with those wide eyes and that glowing skin. Her mouth was free of obnoxious gloss and therefore looked even better than before. He wanted to bite it. He wanted to bite *her*. She had many, many bitable places. He was busy cataloging them all, from her chest to her waist to her hips, when he realized that Eve wasn't wearing her obnoxious T-shirt anymore. She was wearing a loose, oversized shirt, and—

And he never figured out what else, because at that moment, she reached out and touched him. Her cool palm pressed against his forehead, and Jacob's mind went a little haywire.

Well. A little *more* haywire.

"Hmm . . ." she murmured. "You're warm. But that's probably because you're covered in a thousand blankets."

"It's my nest," he said. His nests kept him safe. Even when he didn't know where he was, or where Ma and Dad might drag the family next, his nests had always helped him fall asleep.

But Jacob had never told anyone about his nests. Especially not as an adult, for God's sake. He clenched his jaw to stop his uncontrollable mouth spilling any more embarrassing secrets.

Instead of laughing or asking questions, Eve just nodded absently. "Yes," she said, "nests are useful things. This one could do with a reduction, however." And then she . . . she fucked with his nest!

Well, she removed one of the blankets. And then another, and another, and while Jacob did start to feel a little cooler—funny, since he hadn't realized he was hot—he also felt completely outraged.

"There," she said softly. Soft, soft, soft. "Is that better?"

"Get off," he mumbled. "Off my . . . nest . . ."

"Pardon?"

"Gerroff my . . ." He broke off into a yawn.

"I think you're tired." He felt the weight of another blanket lift. "You should probably go back to sleep. There's fresh water on your bedside table, and I'm right next door if you need anything at all. Okay?"

"Fuck . . . off . . . awful woman."

She laughed. She *laughed*. For God's sake, Jacob was going to push her out of a bloody window.

After he took a little nap.

CHAPTER SIX

Eve's Monday mornings were always wildly unpredictable, but she could never in a thousand years have seen *this* coming. It was 5:56 A.M. and she was standing in someone else's sterile, steel kitchen with the memory of a thousand employee handbooks spinning through her mind, preparing to make breakfast.

Good God.

It wasn't as if Eve had never made breakfast before. She really had taken several cooking courses. It was just, she'd taken those courses for fun—to pass time, to learn a new skill. They were a party trick to impress friends with, a way to devise the perfect hangover breakfast for Gigi or comfort food for Chloe.

She *hadn't* taken those courses to be an actual bloody chef, a professional who was held to specific standards and on whose shoulders the weight of a bed-and-breakfast guest's morning experience rested. And yet, here she fucking was.

Delightful.

Huffing out a breath, she bent to check the fresh pastries she'd chucked into the oven, tapping her thighs in time with the hypnotic beat of KATIE's "Remember" blaring in her ear. Mont had arrived half an hour ago to check on her—but Eve, like a witless fucking oblong, had sent him home because he looked *tired*. Who gave a damn if the man looked tired? *She* was tired. She'd spent last night on Jacob's pullout sofa, courtesy of Mont, sleeping on lumpy pillows he'd dragged out of some cupboard, wearing pajamas he'd apparently borrowed from some mysterious—and outrageously long-limbed—sister. She'd been up for hours reading Jacob's various employee handbooks—

And checking on his adorable sleeping face.

—and googling bad bed-and-breakfast reviews to torture herself with the various ways all this could go wrong. She'd gotten ready that morning under the cover of darkness, trying to put off the moment Jacob discovered her presence for as long as possible because she *knew* he'd be unreasonable about it. Really, under such stressful circumstances, it was only a matter of time until she crumbled into dust and contaminated the croissants. This entire endeavor was doomed to go tits up with her at the helm.

"Excuse me?"

Eve jumped so violently, she was surprised she didn't bump her head on the ceiling. Smoothing down her apron and adjusting her hairnet—HOW NOT TO FUCK UP MY HEALTH RATING: Chapter One, Section A, THE BASICS: *Wear your fucking hairnet*—she turned toward the source of the sound.

There was a windowlike hatch in the kitchen wall, and the employee handbooks had revealed that it was meant to be opened. Eve had done so when she came down that morning and discovered the window let her see into the dining room, sort of like an olden-days shop front. Now that window was occupied by what appeared to be—*shudder*—a guest.

"Hello in there," he said brightly. He was a man of middling age, pink cheeked and gray haired, with far too friendly a smile for this time of day and a waterproof parka covering his torso. "Bit early for breakfast, am I?" he asked cheerfully.

Eve stared at him in disbelief. Who in God's name was early for a 6:30 A.M. breakfast? "Yes," she said faintly, then rallied. HOW NOT TO PISS OFF MY CUSTOMERS: Chapter Three, Section B: *Harmless rule breakers are to be humored, however much it might pain you.* "But I'm sure we can accommodate you, sir. The pastries are still in the oven, but I can take an order for a cooked breakfast?" Eve approached the window, produced her little notepad, and steeled her spine. *Do not fuck up. Do not fuck up. Do not fuck up.*

But already, she was starting to doubt her memory of the employee handbooks. She knew she'd memorized them, but she also knew she had a tendency to mess things up at vital moments, and therefore her memories of memorizing were not to be trusted, and—

Oh Christ, the man was talking. "—sunny-side up, and the stewed tomatoes, ta."

Eve scribbled dutifully and hoped like hell she'd just caught the tail end of a request for a Full English. Because that's what the poor bastard was getting. "Right. If you'd like to take a seat, I'll bring it right out."

"Cheers, my darling," he said, but he did not take a seat. *Why didn't he take a seat?* "This hatch wasn't open yesterday," he went on conversationally.

Eve froze in the act of reaching for some eggs. "It wasn't?" But it was supposed to be open, wasn't it? Or had she misread, misunderstood, mis—

"Nor the day before, when I arrived. Nice to see what's going on behind the scenes, though. Say, where's Jacob this morning?"

Oh dear. This particular question was the one Eve had been dreading. She'd hoped no one would miss the man's icy presence and she therefore wouldn't be asked about him, but apparently, no such luck. "Jacob is, erm, indisposed."

"Indisposed, is it?" The man chuckled. "If it were anyone else, I'd think that was code for a hangover."

Eve laughed nervously. "Right. But not Jacob!"

"Lord, no, not him. So what's up with him?"

"Erm . . ."

"I hope he's not poorly. He's a lovely lad, he is."

Eve blinked. "*Erm . . .*"

"This here's the only place that guarantees us a ground-floor room every time. My Sharon's got dicky joints, bless her. Puts us on a special list, he does."

Eve's sister Chloe required similar accommodations, so Eve knew some people were horribly unreasonable about that sort of thing. But apparently, not Jacob. *Typical.* She'd feel much better about her rather shocking sins toward him if he could be a little bit evil. The bastard.

"Barry?" A voice trilled from the dining room doorway, out of sight. The man in the window turned toward it, his smile growing impossibly wider.

"There y'are, Shaz! Sleepyhead. I've ordered my breakfast, babe, didn't know what you wanted."

A woman appeared in the hatch, as smiley and pink faced as the man. "Hiya, darling," she beamed at Eve. "I'll have what he's having."

Of course she would. "Right," Eve stammered. "Which, er, which is . . . I mean, rather, would you like your eggs—"

"Sunny-side up, thank you!"

"Fabulous." Eve stared at the couple with a rictus grin she hoped they might find encouraging. Any further instructions? No? Fine. "Can I get you anything to drink? Tea? Juice? We have a selection of both this morning."

IT'S NOT JUST BED AND BREAKFAST: Chapter Two, Section F: *There's no such thing as too much.*

"I'll have a coffee," the woman said. "He'll take a green tea."

"Shaz!"

"Don't start." She patted Barry's chest, then linked her arm with his and tugged him off toward the tables. "Now, leave this poor woman to her work."

Yes, thank you, Shaz. Eve waved them off with what she hoped was a sunny smile, then returned to anxiety-cooking as soon as their backs were turned.

Okay, Full English. She presumed.

Eve grabbed Jacob's premium-grade, locally sourced pork sausages from the fridge—LOCALS LIKE MONEY: Chapter Eight, Section N: *Skybriar's butcher is named Peter, he is very old, do not question his maths or he will provide inferior sausage meat*—and got started. She was, under ordinary circumstances, quite an excellent cook. Despite this fact, Eve stared at the sausages for a moment, gripped by the fear that she'd put the wrong oil in the pan. She was humming frantically along to the beat of Teyana Taylor's "How You Want It?," trying to recall the basics of cooking oil usage, when the kitchen door opened behind her.

She froze, dread catching her by the throat. Dear God. Jacob was awake. Jacob was *here*. And she was—

Frazzled. To say the least.

But she was also trying, and that should count for something. So Eve cleared her throat, lifted her chin, and turned around—to find that Jacob wasn't standing in the doorway after all. No; Eve had been joined by a tall, slender woman with sharp blue eyes, her graying blond hair pulled into a no-nonsense ponytail and her jacket open over a uniform apron of some sort.

The woman stared at Eve. Eve stared at the woman.

Then the woman said, "You're not my nephew."

Eve blinked rapidly. "Erm," she replied, "no. No, I'm not." Hadn't Jacob mentioned an aunt, yesterday? Yes, he had. What was her name? Laura, Lisa, Lilian—

Aunt Someone gave Eve a very searching look. Really, it felt rather like an x-ray. "Well," she barked, "where is he, then?"

"Lucy," Eve blurted.

The aunt raised an eyebrow. "Yes?"

"Er, sorry, I meant, erm . . ." Eve didn't think she'd *erm*ed so much in her life. "I believe he's in bed. He was last I saw, anyway."

A beat passed. Lucy's other eyebrow arched to join the first.

"Not," Eve said quickly, "that *I* was—that I saw him because—what I *meant* was that—"

"Go steady, girl, before you swallow your tongue." The ghost of a smile passed the woman's fine mouth. "What's your name?"

"Eve," Eve mumbled. Then a thought hit, and she spun around. "Shit, my sausages."

"I'm Lucy Castell, which you seem to know already. New chef, are you?"

Castell. Hm. So Jacob had named his bed-and-breakfast after his aunt? That had to be dull and uncreative or weird and sinister, somehow. Because if it wasn't either of those things, it might be cute.

"Yes, I'm the new chef," Eve tossed over her shoulder, snagging a tin of tomatoes from the pantry. Christ, now her timings were all off.

"And Jacob's in bed because . . . ?"

Eve wondered if she could politely elect not to answer.

"Is he ill?" Lucy nudged. Lord, the woman was like a diamond drill.

"Not exactly," Eve murmured, pouring tomatoes into a saucepan and opening up the spice rack. "He just—well, he got a little bit run over—"

Lucy's air of calm evaporated. "He *what*?"

Eve spun around to face the other woman, hoping her own guilt wasn't patently obvious. "Oh, it's nothing to worry about. Just a broken wrist and a very mild concussion, so—"

"Run over by *who*?" Lucy demanded. Diamond. Drill.

"Erm," Eve squeaked. "Me?"

Lucy stared in a very violent manner.

Eve began mentally cataloging all the knives in the kitchen and their whereabouts in relation to Lucy's hands.

After a tense moment, the older woman said, "Are you . . . are you trying to tell me that my nephew, your employer, is currently in bed because you hit him with your car?"

A new guest popped up at the window like a video-game toadstool. "What's that? Someone hit Jacob with a car?"

"No," Eve said.

"Apparently," Lucy said.

"Blimey. Any hash browns going?" asked the guest.

Eve bit her lip. "I'm—I'm certain I can whip some up if you give me just a—"

Lucy held up a hand. "Please, don't let me keep you. I will be upstairs, checking my nephew's still alive." She swept out of the room.

Oh dear.

Eve supposed, all things considered, she'd better do a damned good job with this breakfast.

♫

"Why in God's name didn't you call me?!"

Leaning against his dresser, Jacob squeezed his eyes shut and pressed his thumbs to his temples. Didn't help: his headache still flared in time with every outraged lilt in Aunt Lucy's voice. He sighed and opened a drawer, rifling through it for his spare glasses. "Because you were busy."

"*Busy?!* A couple of clients and a weekly book club is not busy, Jacob!"

"I didn't want you to worry." He found his old case and pulled out a pair of glasses identical to his current frames, except for the fact that these were undamaged, and also weaker by 0.75 in the right eye. Sliding them on, he blinked until the slight blurriness became almost unnoticeable. These would do, for now.

"It's my *job* to worry about you, you plonker," Aunt Lucy said. He turned to face her, and this time, he could see her furrowed brow and pale cheeks clearly. His gut squeezed with guilt. And with a little pain from the ache in his skull and his back and his stomach. The stomach was hunger. But he hadn't even managed to shower yet, so hunger would have to wait.

"Sorry," he said, because he knew from experience that she wouldn't leave him in peace until he apologized. "But in my defense, I was concussed when I told Mont not to tell you."

"Ha! I'll be having a word with young Eric soon enough," Lucy said, looking menacing.

Sorry, Mont.

"But first—what on earth is the woman who hit you doing in the kitchen? I mean, I'm all for forgive and forget, babe, really, I am, but I know very well that *you* aren't."

Jacob opened his mouth, then closed it. *The woman who—?* "I'm sorry, what?"

Slowly, Lucy said, "The woman. Who hit you. Is in. Your kitchen."

Oh. Oh shit. "*Eve?* Eve is still here?"

"That is what she called herself, yes. Purple hair, about this tall, wearing a T-shirt that I'm sure belongs to one of the twins."

One of the . . .

Jacob set his jaw and sucked in a breath. No. No way would Montrose actually hire the living terror who *literally* ran Jacob over yesterday—

Except someone needed to take over, and Mont is even more practical than you sometimes. So this is exactly the kind of thing he would do.

"Fuck," he hissed. Then, "Sorry, Aunt Lucy."

"Don't mind me, sweetheart." Lucy was already straightening up his perfectly tidy room, throwing back his bedcovers and opening the window. She gave his curtains a considering look. "Would you mind if I just popped these off and gave them a quick iron? They'd look proper smart with a nice crease in the—"

"Whatever you want," Jacob called over his shoulder. He didn't have time to argue about the relative merits of curtain ironing. He had an Eve to remove.

♫

Righteous outrage propelled Jacob out of his private quarters, but when he hit the staircase, reality kicked in. Specifically, the reality of his body, which fucking *killed*. Gripping the banister with his good hand—his left hand, and what bloody use was that?—Jacob eyed the steps warily before tackling the first one.

Pain sang to life along the length of his spine, from the dull ache near his shoulders to the sharp stab at his tailbone. When his foot made contact with the next stair down, his head throbbed inside his skull like he'd jumped off a building.

"For shit's sake," he muttered. "You have *got* to be kidding me." His injuries definitely hadn't hurt this badly yesterday

Then again, much of what he remembered about yesterday wasn't exactly coherent. Except for the part where Eve Brown stormed his very serious interviews with her utterly unserious self, thoroughly got on his nerves, made him chase after her like an undignified puppy, then ran him over for his troubles. Yes, that part was crystal bleeding clear.

Gritting his teeth, Jacob took the next step.

By the grace of some merciful god, he made it down all three flights without running into a single guest. Clearly, he'd gotten up during the lull between early birds and those who liked to sleep in—and thank Christ for that, because as he finally reached the polished wood floors of the foyer, he felt a bead of sweat trickle down his temple. When Jacob sweated in front of people, he preferred it to be on purpose: because he'd chosen to run, or he'd chosen to lift, or he'd chosen to go out in some god-awful sun. Not because he'd unexpectedly lost the ability to walk down his own bloody stairs without gasping for breath.

He was swiping the sweat away with an irritable grunt when he heard footsteps approaching from a nearby corridor—the *kitchen* corridor. And then, wouldn't you know it, Eve fucking Brown appeared.

She was walking with brisk efficiency, a plate of steaming breakfast balanced in each hand—just one plate per hand, which told him she'd never waitressed before. Inefficient method. Lack of confidence. And yet, her hold was steady and her spine was straight and her focus was undeniable, her trajectory taking her toward the dining room.

Until she noticed him and froze.

Wide-eyed, she gasped, "Jacob?" As if he'd died yesterday and she might be communing with a ghost right now.

"Eve," he replied. The word was meant to sound dignified, possibly cold—cold was always safe, after all. But instead, her name fell from his lips like a fistful of sand, his voice a strained rasp.

She looked different this morning. It wasn't her lack of obnoxious T-shirt, or the Castell Cottage apron she wore, but something . . . else. The steadiness of her stride, maybe. The lift of her chin. Yesterday, her braids had spilled around her shoulders and even the soft, baby curls at her hairline had been . . . styled, somehow, but today her braids were pulled back in accordance with health and safety, and her little curls frizzed around her face. Her skin was glowing and he suspected that if he touched her cheek—not that he ever, *ever* would, dear God, *unless* he suspected she had some kind of deadly fever, in which case he would of course have to, as an act of human decency, but never mind that, what had he been saying? Oh, yes. If he touched her cheek, he had a feeling she'd be warm like the air in a busy kitchen.

Even though he knew very well that Eve did not belong here, for a second, standing in his hallway with her hands full, she looked as if she might.

Jacob shook his head sharply. Must be the concussion.

"Are you okay?" she asked, frowning as she stepped closer. Her expression screamed such obvious—and unexpected—concern that Jacob looked down at himself reflexively, just to check his arm hadn't dropped off while he wasn't paying attention.

What he found was even worse. He was still wearing his fucking pajamas.

He realized with a jolt that he'd jumped out of bed and rushed down here to throw her out without even making himself presentable first. He was roaming the halls of Castell Cottage in gray jersey and flannel, which meant he'd come to work inappropriately dressed, which made him undeniably unprofessional. Even worse, Eve Brown was looking at him like he was an adorable but endangered baby animal, which was especially annoying, for some reason.

Shit. Shoving a self-conscious hand through his hair, Jacob set his jaw and steeled his spine. He was already down here, and he wouldn't be climbing those fucking stairs without a ten-minute breather and a cup of tea, so he might as well act natural.

But this disaster, just like everything else wrong with the world, was completely Eve's fault.

Coating himself in ice like armor, he said stiffly, "I'm fine." The *no thanks to you* part was unspoken, but he hoped she sensed it. "You and I need a word."

Literally just one word: *Go.*

"Well, that sounded appropriately omniscient," Eve muttered. Then she paused, shaking her head. "Or is it—?"

"I know what you meant," Jacob snapped.

"*Really.*" She gave him a skeptical look, then rolled her eyes and lifted the plates. "Look, if you don't need anything—I'll be right with you, but I need to serve these before they get cold. No one likes cold tomatoes, Jacob. Be reasonable. All right?" Before he could begin to formulate a response to that, she'd swept off into the dining room.

Leaving him and his annoyance with the uncomfortable feeling that they'd just been dismissed.

And with the—admittedly obvious—realization that he was late for breakfast. He'd slept in by his own standards, and now, according to his watch, it was 6:44. Breakfast had already begun without his supervision.

Jacob rushed into the kitchen, expecting chaos, chaos, more chaos, and a flagrant disregard for the health and hygiene posters he'd stuck to the walls. You know: filth, disorganization, rats scurrying toward the open pantry, maybe. At least a small microwave fire. Instead, he stared in shock at a kitchen that appeared to be . . . absolutely fine. Exactly as it should be. Clearly in use, but safe and orderly all the same.

Well. That was a bit fucking anticlimactic.

Eve had even opened the dining hatch, a feature that provided an authentic behind-the-scenes glimpse for guests and one that Mont had steadfastly refused to use. *I'm not a fucking fry cook anymore*, he'd bitched, *and I look like a twat in this apron*. Blah, blah, blah. Well, apparently Eve had no such concerns, because the window was rolled up and Jacob had a direct view into the dining room.

A direct view of *her*, actually. She sailed into his line of sight, approaching one end of the mammoth dining table with that infuriating smile. Although, now Jacob saw the smile directed at guests, he had to admit its obnoxious beauty and objective cuteness had some benefits. Feeling himself bamboozled by the thing was unsettling, but watching it have the same effect on Mrs. and Mrs. Beatson wasn't all bad.

He stared, semimesmerized, as she fetched salt and pepper for the couple from two feet down the table—as if they couldn't reach it themselves. He frowned, genuinely perplexed, as she poured tea for another party like the three of them didn't have six clearly functional hands. He glowered with increasing annoyance as Eve whipped around the room being infuriatingly, impressively, undeniably helpful.

It was like she saw people's needs before they'd even noticed themselves. Which was, obviously, an excellent skill for a hospitality employee to possess.

But goddamn it, he wasn't supposed to think this kind of thing. He wasn't supposed to think *anything* complimentary about Eve. She'd fractured his bloody wrist, for fuck's sake. Had anyone else broken Jacob's arm, and therefore messed with his ability to carry out key aspects of his daily routine—push-ups, sudoku, et cetera—he'd be fuming for at least a week.

And he was angry with Eve. He *was*. Even if he also, suddenly, remembered the tremor in her voice when she'd knelt over him on the road, offering an entirely insufficient apology. Bugger that tremor, and bugger her.

By the time she returned to the kitchen, Jacob was determined to despise her the same way he did everything: thoroughly.

"What is going on here?" he demanded as she entered. He kept his voice low so the guests couldn't hear, stalking over to her as she approached the sink.

"What's going on where?" she asked lightly, rinsing the clean plates she'd brought back and . . . *stacking them in the dishwasher correctly.*

For some reason, this only pissed Jacob off further. "Here, damn it. Here! What is with all this—this—" *Order, perfection, prowess.* Any of those words would apply, but he didn't want to say them. In the end, he whisper-hissed, "How the hell do you know what you're doing?"

Eve blinked those long lashes, then smiled, so quick and sharp it flashed behind his eyelids like lightning. "Oh, I see. So the bug that's crawled up your arse this morning is down to the fact I'm not crashing and burning yet?"

Yet, she said. Something about that word snapped against his skin like a rubber band. But Jacob was quickly distracted by his own embarrassment, because her accusation was technically correct and it made him sound ridiculous. "Well," he ground out, "obviously I'm pleased that you're doing—actually, you know what, fuck that." He stopped, then said sharply, "How well you may or may not be doing is irrelevant, because you shouldn't be here at all. I didn't hire you."

She set down the last plate and turned to face him, eyes narrowed and hands on her hips. "You were going to."

"You don't know what I was going to do."

"Mont told me," she shot back.

Making a mental note to smack Montrose later—twice—Jacob

powered through. "Any decisions I may have come to before you hit me with your car were invalidated the moment you *hit me with your car.*"

Eve had the grace to look awkward. "Er, yes, sorry about that." She turned and hurried over to the stove, grabbing a box of eggs. "The thing is, I thought helping out while you were under the weather might go some way toward atoning for that grieving mistake."

Jacob scowled at the back of her head. There was nothing worse than someone making a valid point during an argument he intended to win. "Look," he began. But then Eve moved toward the pantry, grabbed a fresh loaf of bread, and shut the pantry door . . . with her hip.

And good God, what a hip.

Jacob's jaw clenched as several muscles in his body tightened without permission. His eyes glued to Eve's back of their own accord, focusing on the place where her knotted apron strings grazed the strip of bare skin between her borrowed T-shirt and her jeans. "Don't do that," he growled. Really, it was a growl. Like a dog. Jacob immediately wanted to shoot himself.

She turned around, a line appearing between her eyebrows. "Do what?"

And now his choices were: either to say out loud *Don't move things with your body that belongs to you*, or to pretend he'd made an involuntary noise as part of a concussion-related seizure. "Nothing," he muttered, biting the inside of his cheek. "Look, I'm . . . glad things are going well down here. And that you started breakfast, and so on."

Eve smiled, a real smile—the bright, sunshine one that lit up entire rooms, possibly entire worlds. He felt a bit dazed. As a concussed man who'd only just woken up, it probably wasn't safe for him to be exposed to such things. "I'm sorry," she said teasingly, "was that a compliment?"

His reply was automatic. "No."

"A positive comment of some sort directed at me, then? Ah, ah." She held up a finger to cut off his response. "Don't bother to answer. I'm quite certain it was." And then she was off, back to the stove again, leaving Jacob feeling . . . odd. Flushed. Perhaps he should go back to the hospital. His reactions were all wrong this morning, and he was becoming concerned.

"This conversation isn't over," he said, which made no sense, because it clearly should be. He was sliding backward down a very steep hill, and Eve was pushing him with one finger and laughing all the way. "The fact remains that I didn't hire you, and—" He paused beside her, squinting at the flash of white hiding beneath the braids she'd pinned over her ears. "Bloody hell, are you still wearing that fucking earbud?"

She flicked him a cool look. "Language, Mr. Wayne. I'm sure the guests don't want your foul mouth served with their tea."

"I—you—" Jacob was pretty sure steam had just shot out of his ears.

"Trust me," she went on, "you want me to wear the earbud. Music helps me concentrate on the order of things."

That made not a lick of sense.

But then, Jacob supposed, his own methods of focusing had never made much sense to other people, either.

"And the alternative," she went on, "is to let me sing to myself, which would probably disrupt the guests' eggs something awful."

"I can't decide if you're serious or if you're just being a—"

"Returning to the subject at hand, I think I have a solution to your latest stick up the arse," she said, briskly cutting him off. "Yesterday, before—well, *before*—you were blathering on about a trial, correct?"

"Incorrect," he shot back. "I do not blather."

She stared at him for a moment before murmuring, "Dear God, you are so much fun."

He hadn't picked up any of the usual indicators—excessive emphasis on unexpected words, for example—but that absolutely had to be sarcasm. Even if Eve was currently watching him with a gleam of amusement in her eye.

"Anyway," she continued, "the point is, you wanted to trial me. So trial me."

He frowned. "I beg your pardon?" A trial? Surely she didn't mean—

"Let me make you breakfast." Apparently she *did* mean. Interesting. "Here, sit down." She wrapped a hand around his elbow, and Jacob jolted like he'd been shocked. Shit. She snatched her hand away. "Sorry," she said quickly. "Er, sorry. Do you not like to be—I shouldn't have—"

"Bruises," he lied through gritted teeth. Because he couldn't exactly say, *It appears physical contact with you has an atypical effect on my nervous system.* And yet, it did. An effect that made him hyperaware of the flimsy jersey pajama pants he currently wore, pants that did nothing to hide an erection.

Not that he *had* an erection. That would be ridiculous. That would be obscene.

He was just a little bit worried that he might eventually get one, perhaps, for some reason. Who knew? You could never be too careful about these things.

"I'm going back upstairs," he blurted, striding toward the door. "Going upstairs to . . . change. And things. Later. I'll come down later. To . . . test you. Erm . . . keep up the barely acceptable work."

"Barely acceptable?!"

"That's what I said," Jacob sniffed, and then he made good his escape.

CHAPTER SEVEN

It took Jacob so long to come back, Eve was almost convinced he'd forgotten about her.

Almost.

But a man with that level of dogged focus probably didn't forget much. Except, apparently, for the little chat they'd had last night, while he'd been curled up in bed like the world's most adorable wolf. Because she had a feeling that if he'd remembered that, he would've ramped up the arsehole behavior by at least 50 percent this morning.

As it was, he'd been practically cordial.

Eve was waving off the last of the guests with a smile when the kitchen door swung open behind her. Her tentative glow of success faded like sunlight behind a cloud, because the snick of that door handle brought her earlier challenge flying back like Thor's hammer.

You wanted to trial me. So trial me. Let me make you breakfast.

A test. She had *volunteered* herself for a test—also known as her number one weakness and natural enemy.

For fuck's sake, she didn't even *want* this job. What in God's name had she been thinking?!

That everyone assuming you're useless and incapable is starting to get old.

Hm. Well. There was that.

Still, she was already feeling the familiar high-pressure jitters that accompanied formal judgment of any kind. Her palms were clammy. Her pulse vibrated in her veins. Had she always produced this much spit? Slowly, she turned around to face the man she knew was waiting.

And almost dropped down dead when she laid eyes on him. "Good *Lord*," she murmured.

Jacob—or rather, Super Jacob, because that's how he looked—arched a pale eyebrow. "Pardon me?"

If he was any other man, this would be the point where she made a comment about his outrageous hotness.

After his earlier disheveled appearance, which had honestly been—gag—*cute*, Jacob had clearly decided to remind the world exactly how put together he could be. The razor precision of his close shave displayed those unholy cheekbones to unfair advantage. The bladelike part of his blond hair somehow emphasized the sharp line of his jaw, the unfair symmetry of his face, the angular shape of those pale, wolflike eyes. He'd managed to put on a crisp, gray shirt despite his cast, the right sleeve folded up around his biceps. And the jeans he wore hugged his lower half in a way she could only call *subtly obscene*. One probably wouldn't notice the slight outline of his massive fucking package, unless you were looking (and Eve had *no* idea why she'd been looking), in which case, you really couldn't *un*-notice it.

Gosh.

He cocked his head. "Eve?"

She swallowed, clearing her throat. Time to say something un-affected and totally professional. "How'd you get the shirt on?"

His eyes narrowed.

Yes, brilliant, Eve. Question him about his clothing habits. Evoke mental images of him naked. Well done.

After a frigid moment, he muttered, "I cut the sleeve."

Despite herself, she squinted at the sleeve in question. "Did you?"

"I shortened it, then cut along the hem so it would fold higher, then stitched the edges so it would look neater."

When she moved closer—all the better to stare at his impossible handiwork—Jacob shifted to the side as if to hide it from her. "Christ, woman, don't inspect it. I'm shit with my left hand."

She paused. "You mean, when you said *you* did all that—"

"Yes." He sighed, rolling his eyes. "I did mean the literal interpretation of the word *I*. Most people do."

"But your wrist is broken!"

"Believe me," he said dryly, "I'd noticed."

Eve flushed. No wonder he'd been gone for hours—from the sound of things, it must have taken him that long to get dressed. "You do realize that broken limbs are usually a valid excuse to dress . . . a little differently than usual?"

"You do realize," he drawled, "that excuses are not something I've ever been interested in?"

Well, yes, she was starting to get that vibe.

"Now," he continued, "if we could return to the point—you're supposed to be making me breakfast."

Oh. Yes. Eve gulped and turned away from him, heading to the shiny, double-doored fridge. "You know, I would've cooked for you regardless," she quipped, except her voice wasn't as light as she'd like. "You don't need to dress it up like an exam."

"If I remember rightly, you were the one who came up with the idea."

Yes, she was, and she sincerely desired to travel back in time and kick herself. When she faced him again, Jacob had made himself comfortable leaning against the wall. The pose seemed so casual, with his long legs and his lean hips and the easy angles of his body, that it took her a moment to notice the slight wince on his face. He hid it well. But it was still there, shadowing those icy eyes and twisting his fine mouth at the corners.

Throwing sausages into a hot pan, she said, "You should probably sit down." There were a couple of stools at the central island—uncomfortable, steel-looking stools, but stools all the same.

Jacob grunted and shifted against the wall, a sinuous predator trying to get comfortable. "Can't."

Oh. Ah. Yes. Eve remembered Mont's comment about arse-bruising and tried not to drown in this brand-new influx of guilt.

"Didn't I tell you to take that out?" he went on, nodding at her.

It took Eve a moment to realize what he meant. Her hand rose automatically to her ear, as if to protect the source of NAO's "Bad Blood" from his evil eyes. "And didn't I tell you," she shot back, "that I work better with it in?" She sounded a hell of a lot more confident than she felt—because that, she'd discovered, was the knack with Jacob: confidence.

He might be tough, might be harsh, but he didn't do it in the hopes of crushing those around him. He did it with the assumption that if they were stronger, better, *right*, they'd push back.

So he reacted just as she'd expected, tilting his head like a wolf examining strange prey instead of biting its head off. After a moment's consideration, he said, "You mentioned before that you could sing instead."

She pressed her lips together as she soaked bread in egg and cinnamon. "*Could* being the operatic word."

His lips tilted at the corner into something that was almost—a smile. A smile like slow-dripping honey beneath the summer sun. She faltered, a little bit stunned. Jacob made ice look good, but apparently, he made warmth look even better.

Oh dear.

"Since it's an option . . . I would rather you sing," he said, "even if it's terrible, than appear ignorant toward guests."

"Ignorant?! I'm only wearing one."

He straightened, strolling over to the dining room window and pulling down the hatch with his good hand. Eve tried not to be salty about the fact that rolling the thing up had taken two hands and a few hops on her part. "I see that, Eve. I also see a Trip Advisor review titled RUDE CHEF, WEEKEND GETAWAY RUINED. People find unusual habits more charming when *they* are included. So, if singing is a viable alternative for you—consider it."

People find unusual habits more charming when they are included. Eve had always known that, in the back of her mind, but it was something she'd resented, and so she tended to ignore it. Now, though—now, here was Jacob, laying it out like a military tactic rather than some sort of moral directive. Like a strategy they were smart enough to deploy upon people who just didn't understand, rather than a behavioral correction.

Slowly, cautiously, she found herself saying, "I'll . . . give it a try."

He met her eyes for a moment. "Well. I appreciate that." Then he faltered, as if he hadn't meant to say something so reasonable. Within seconds, his familiar glare was back, scalping her with its mighty force. Eve didn't mind.

Actually, she found this much easier to deal with than Jacob Masquerading as a Nice Man. That whole *us against them* routine had threatened to do something terrible and ominous to her nether regions.

"As for right now," he went on, his tone frostier, "you might as well play your music out loud. Unless you find it more helpful when it's directly in your ear."

And there he went again—even cold, he illustrated an understanding of how her needs worked. Or maybe it was simply an *attempt* at understanding, which, for some reason, Eve found just as satisfying. Either way, he needed to stop before she got all confused and started to accidentally enjoy his presence a bit. This was meant to be a test, damn it. She was supposed to be sick with nerves right now, and also with hating him. He was ruining everything, and it would serve him right if she threw her fried bread mixture over his head.

But Eve was a reasonable, responsible, semiprofessional woman these days, so instead, she set the mixture aside, put her soaked bread in the pan, then pulled out her phone and uncoupled her AirPod. Lilting piano notes filled the room, accompanied by a pounding beat and rhythmic French rap. Watching Jacob as he returned to his spot leaning against the wall, she explained, "It's—"

"Stromae," he finished. "What's this one called?"

She stared. *Stromae*, he said, all casual, as if it made perfect sense that he'd know such a thing.

He clicked his fingers, then nodded. "'Papaoutai.' Right?"

She stared some more. "You listen to Belgian rap from 2013?"

"No," he said.

Well, at least that made sense.

"I *listened* to Belgian rap *in* 2013."

And, she was back to the staring. "Est-ce que tu parles français?"

"Oui. Toi aussi?"

"Passablement. Mon vocabulaire est faible."

"Un enfant m'a appris, il y a des années, donc ma grammaire est pauvre."

"Your grammar doesn't sound poor to me," she said pertly.

"And I see no holes in your vocabulary. I suppose we'd have to talk a little longer to discover all that, but this isn't a tea party."

Eve huffed out a breath. "Oh, yes. How could I forget? I'm being tested, and you're impossible."

"Usually, people who want a job from me are a bit more polite."

"I've come to the conclusion," she gritted out as she flipped his eggs, "that you are incredibly difficult to be polite to." *And I don't want your bloody job.* Even if she had sort of accidentally enjoyed herself this morning, once she'd gotten the hang of things.

She was jolted out of that unexpected thought when Jacob released a bark of laughter. It was so sudden, and so completely surprising, that she spun to look at him—as if further inspection might reveal that the noise had come from someone else.

But no: judging by the ghost of a smile still on his lips, and the lines fanning from the corners of those piercing eyes, it had definitely been him. Even if he cleared his throat and iced up under her gaze faster than a puddle in December.

Still, she had to ask. "Did you just laugh? Did I just make you laugh?"

"Woman," he sighed, "you couldn't *make* me do anything, even with a gun in your hand."

Funnily enough, she believed him. But he *had* laughed. She'd heard him. The sound, wry and rusty, had been a little bit like music.

"Hurry up with the breakfast, would you?" he said, and though his tone was lazy, she had the distinct impression that Jacob was changing the subject. "If you're not up to scratch, I'll need to find another replacement, and the clock is ticking."

Turning her back on him, Eve rolled her eyes. "*Up to scratch.* It's only eggs and bloody sausages."

"Actually," he said sharply, "it's much more than that. This is hospitality. Hospitality matters. Creating a home away from home matters. And I prefer staff who take this business—this *responsibility*—seriously."

She faltered as his words sank in. Responsibility. Taking things seriously. Those were the things Eve had failed at most of all, and she was supposed to be fixing that.

She swallowed.

"Furthermore," Jacob went on, "while my standards are high at all times, they are even higher when people from all over the country will soon be tasting Castell Cottage's food."

She blinked rapidly, shoving her discomfort aside as she stirred the scrambled eggs. "The whole country?"

"Yes. You do remember the reason I hired—*considered* hiring you, correct? The festival in Pemberton?"

Oh, shoot. "Yes," Eve said brightly. "Of course." Telling the truth—*No, actually, I had entirely forgotten*—seemed like it might cause an argument. But shit, now she felt even worse, because this Gingerbread Festival (whatever *that* entailed) was important to Ja—to the business, and it had dropped clean out of her head. She'd planned to stick around until the man she'd injured was somewhat back on his feet. But she couldn't do that only to disappear when he really needed her, could she? For heaven's sake, she'd messed him up so badly it took him hours to get dressed, never mind to hunt down another willing human-sacrifice-slash-chef.

Aaand there was her guilt again, like clockwork.

"What would—*do* I have to do?" she asked casually, her back still to him. "For the festival, I mean. What does it involve?"

Jacob gave a long-suffering sigh, as if she'd asked him to recite the periodic table. (Although, knowing him, he could probably do so with little difficulty.) "Don't worry," he drawled. "It'll be quite simple, since my previous chef already planned everything. A few menu options—similar to those we offer during this breakfast service—will be written up on a board. Some can be prepared in advance; others are simple enough to make using the equipment I've already purchased."

Already purchased? Eve wasn't the greatest with money, but she did know a new business couldn't buy equipment without earning something back to make the purchase worth its while. Yet another reason why Jacob was so determined to go forward with this festival, she supposed.

"You will be responsible for cooking to order at the stall, and I'll serve customers," he continued.

"Ah—putting your winning personality to good use."

"You have a very poor sense of humor," Jacob said steadily. "If I were you, I'd keep that to myself."

Eve rolled her eyes, but she was too busy wrestling with her own thoughts to really take offense. Because the more Jacob spoke, the more she became dreadfully convinced that staying in Skybriar longer than planned was her only moral course of action. The man needed her help—even if he'd likely rather die than phrase it that way. And Eve owed him said help, probably more than she'd ever owed anyone anything.

Which made her choice crystal clear. For the next month, whether he liked it or not, Eve Brown would work as a chef for Jacob Wayne. She would serve breakfast for dinner at a ginger-bread parade or whatever, and only *then* would she disappear in a puff of smoke to begin her party-planning profession. All things considered, it seemed the least she could do.

Jacob cleared his throat, rudely interrupting her Very Serious Thought Process. "Am I getting this breakfast, or are you going to stand there looking grim all day?"

"Grim?" Eve yelped. "I never look grim. My resting expression is general delight."

"Your resting expression is *princess*," he muttered.

Princess. Her hands curled into fists.

"What?" Jacob barked at her silence. "Are you actually nervous about this? Because if you've been merrily feeding my guests substandard food all morning without saying a bloody word—"

For some reason, Jacob questioning the deliciousness of her breakfast was starting to piss Eve off. "Hard to speak to a man who's asleep," she pointed out sharply.

He flushed, strawberry ice cream again. Just a hint. But he also stood tall and narrowed those flinty eyes behind his glasses. "I have a concussion." The *Because you hit me with your car* part did not need to be said.

"Yes, you have a concussion," she replied, "but you were a prick to me even before that event, so I don't see how it's relevant."

Jacob's jaw dropped. Pettily, she enjoyed the sight.

"Now, shut up about it," she finished, slapping his breakfast onto a plate. Funny, how she'd made all this food without really noticing. Arguing with him had worked wonders for her nerves. "Here's the plan. Since your wrist is broken and your arse is also broken—"

"I'll give you this," he muttered, "at least you're thorough when you run a man over."

Eve valiantly ignored him. Or was it Valium-ly? "—you can't sit at a table and you can't hold your own plate."

"I can hold my own plate, genius," he said, waving his left hand.

"And can you also feed yourself, *genius*?"

He glared. "It's very irritating when you say logical, intelligent things. Stop it. Now."

Ridiculous, to take such sideways words as a compliment. It was just—well. Eve's *sisters* were smart. They passed exams and built careers and did incredible things with computers or peer-reviewed research. *Eve* failed exams, attended drama school, failed that, too, and mixed up all her words because focusing on conversations was beyond her. Family never called her stupid, and her friends only ever implied it—but *intelligent* wasn't a word she often heard directed at herself.

Jacob cocked his head, watching her steadily. "You keep zoning out of this conversation. Have you suffered a blow to the head too, or do you find me that boring?"

"You are the exact opposite of boring," she blurted out before she could stop herself.

Jacob blinked, and she had the pleasure of seeing him look genuinely at a loss for the first time since they'd met. "Oh. Erm . . ." He cleared his throat. She watched his Adam's apple bob as he swallowed. "Right. Well. That's true."

Eve shoved the plate of breakfast at him, pleased when he took it reflexively with his good hand. "This'll probably be cold after all the babbling we've done."

"Excuse me," he said severely, "I don't babble."

"I am ignoring you and your smartarse interruptions," she replied, "because they do not deserve acknowledgment. As I was saying—"

"You do realize that claiming you won't acknowledge something is an acknowledgment in itself."

You already injured him yesterday, Eve. At least let him recover before you beat him over the head. "As I was saying, here is the plan. You hold the plate, and I," she murmured, fighting a smile as she picked up his fork, "will feed you."

He reacted just as wonderfully as Eve had expected. Which is to say, his eyes widened with comical horror, that vicious mouth fell into a rather satisfying O, and more strawberry ice cream crept up his pale cheeks—the outraged kind, this time, which had a sort of raspberry tinge.

"Feed me?" he sputtered.

Eve couldn't hold back her smile anymore. It spread evilly across her face. A snicker might have escaped, too. "That is what I said."

"Are you taking the piss? I'm not having you feed me. That is unnecessary—"

"Do you have another solution, then?"

"—and completely inappropriate."

"Inappropriate?" Eve blinked, taken aback for a moment. "Oh—you don't mean to say you're sensitive about the idea of me shoving a sausage down your throat?"

To her surprise, instead of scoffing at her admittedly risqué joke, Jacob simply blushed harder. "Do you ever shut up?" he muttered.

"Do you?"

"Of course. When I'm *alone*," he said, "which I seriously wish I was right now."

"But then how would you eat my delicious test breakfast?"

"Oh, fuck off. I told you about the logic and the intelligence and the making points. It unsettles me. Stop."

Eve didn't mean to grin. It just . . . happened.

"How about this," Jacob said after a moment. "You hold my plate, and *I* feed myself."

"I had considered that," she said.

"And disregarded it *because*?"

"Because feeding is a dominant action. A helpful action. An action that inf—infant . . ." Oh dear. There was nothing worse than confusing her words when she was trying to be badass.

She waited for Jacob to pounce on her stutter, but all he did was sigh and drawl acidly, "I'm assuming you are searching for the word *infantilize*."

"Oh. Yes. Thank you." Eve brightened. Let the badassery continue. "Feeding is an action that infantilizes *you*. Whereas holding something, like a table, is servile, and I am not servile."

Jacob stared. "First of all, you think like a wolf under all that pastel hair."

Said the wolf himself.

"And second of all, you literally work for me. You *should* be servile."

"I thought I didn't work for you yet?"

"Well, you're trying to," he snapped. "Embrace servility in your soul, and maybe I'll hire you."

"Do you often encourage servility in the souls of the black women around you?"

"Do I—the—" He shut his mouth with a *click* and glared. "Again. You think like a wolf."

"Thank you. Now open up for the choo-choo train."

"Murder," Jacob murmured. "I am going to commit a murder."

But to Eve's surprise, when she stabbed some egg and a chunk of sausage onto the fork, Jacob opened his mouth and took it.

He really . . . really . . . took it.

She found herself dazed by the sight of Jacob Wayne, usually all frost and superior self-control, parting those fine lips for her. His teeth were so white and his tongue was so pink. Those were quite ordinary colors for tongues and teeth to be, and yet Eve found herself unfairly fascinated by the contrast. And then . . . and then he bent his head forward and *closed* his mouth around the fork. The fork she was holding. She felt the action, the slight pressure, even as she saw it.

His gaze was lowered, focused on the fork, presumably to make sure she didn't accidentally stab him with it. Which, in fairness, she might, because her limbs were feeling oddly distant and her brain was starting to hum. Behind his glasses, his eyelashes were long and thick. She hadn't noticed before, since they were the sort of golden color that didn't exactly catch attention in a face like his. But here, now, all she could *do* was notice them.

Jacob released the fork, and chewed, and swallowed. His eyes fluttered shut for the barest second, and a slight grunt of pleasure escaped him before he could stop it. Eve knew she should be punching the air with pure, professional satisfaction—or better yet, *told-you-so* satisfaction.

Instead, all she could do was suck in a breath and press a cool hand to her suddenly feverish throat. Because *shit*. Jacob made pleasure look and sound rather good.

Wait—no. No, no, no. Eve had an unfortunate habit of forming attractions to unsuitable men. Her sexual choices, like her other choices, had always been utterly terrible. But since she was currently on a voyage of growth and self-discovery, gaining maturity points like the intrepid heroine of a bildungs-whatever-the-fuck, she would *not* develop the horn for this incredible arsehole of a man. She absolutely refused. She didn't even *like* him.

Of course, Eve had certainly lost her head over men she didn't like before.

But this was different. This was absolutely different. *So*, she said to her stirring libido, *don't let me catch you mooning again.*

Jacob opened his eyes just as she finished scolding her vagina. "Okay," he said grimly, as if she'd presented him with something awful rather than the very best British breakfast had to offer. "*Maybe* that was *possibly* quite decent."

Thankfully, as soon as he spoke, every ounce of Eve's physical appreciation drained away like hot water down a plughole. How convenient.

"Is that French toast?" he went on, eyeing the plate. "Let me try some of that."

"Why? At best it'll only be maybe possibly quite decent."

He rolled his eyes, then winced as if the action had hurt. "Fine," he said, "it was good. You're hired. Now give me the bloody toast."

And just like that, she was walking on air. "Really? You mean it?" Her smile practically stretched from ear to ear, so intense her cheeks started to hurt.

"Yes. Toast. Now."

Still beaming, Eve dropped the fork and picked up a slice of French toast, holding it to his lips. But her mind was elsewhere. Specifically, itching to grab her phone so she could change the music filling the kitchen from Stromae to some miraculous hymn. How odd, to feel this helium balloon of excitement in her chest over a job she barely wanted, one she was only taking for various moral reasons, et cetera. Hm. Satisfaction was such an unpredictable thing.

Maybe she was pleased to have secured a proper job on her own—something her parents assumed she couldn't do. Yes, that must be it. And, of course, it didn't hurt that she'd enjoyed cooking this morning. Once she'd gotten over her nerves, chatting to guests and playing with ingredients in the kitchen had been rather fun. Not reading-Vanessa-Riley-in bed fun, but completing-a-puzzle fun. Which—

Eve sucked in a breath, pulling back her fingers when they touched something soft and warm and . . . human. Before her, Jacob blushed like a traffic light, his chin snapping up so he was staring straight ahead. Or, more specifically, over *her* head.

"Did you just *bite* me?" she asked. Except it hadn't been a bite, because there were no teeth involved. Just the velvet brush of . . .

Jacob's mouth?

"No!" he barked. "I was—the toast was very good. I, erm, got a bit carried away, and I wasn't paying attention, so. Sorry."

Oh. He'd been so busy eating the toast, he'd almost eaten her. Usually, Eve would laugh about that. Tease him mercilessly, at the very least.

Instead she found herself staring at her still-tingling fingertips.

"Well," Jacob said into the silence. "I think that's enough breakfast for today." It wasn't until he turned and walked away that Eve realized how close they'd been standing. He put his plate down on the counter with a clatter that seemed distinctly un-Jacoblike, then continued speaking with his back to her. It was a very broad back. It seemed to rise and fall with his breaths quite frequently. Or maybe she was just looking very hard.

"Mont must have set you up for this morning," he said. "Are you aware of afternoon tea?"

Eve bit her lip. RHYTHM AND ROUTINE: Chapter Three, Section A, THE FULL EXPERIENCE: *Afternoon tea and cake is to be served in the yellow parlor daily at four o'clock.*

"Yes," she murmured. "I'm aware of afternoon tea."

"And you can bake?"

"Of course," she snorted, momentarily affronted.

"Good. Other than that, I'll need to meet with you at some point to go over basic paperwork, and there's a meeting this week amongst the Gingerbread Festival organizers that we should both attend. Oh—and, since I'm currently down an arm, I'll need your help with housekeeping after breakfast." He paused, cleared his throat, and added quickly, "But not for the next few days. No. Er . . ."

Eve tried to shake the feeling he was making this part up as he went along.

"My aunt," he said finally, "has rearranged a few appointments so she can help me. Which means your only remaining duties today are afternoon tea. If you need anything, I'm usually in my office. But I'll probably be very busy so you might not find me there or, you know, I might not answer when you knock." With that, he turned away from the counter and stalked toward the door.

"Okay," Eve said. "Erm . . . Jacob, are you—?"

He left.

Eve had intended to keep the details of yesterday's disastrous in-terview private, which is to say, completely off her family's radar. But later that day, she made the fatal mistake of calling her sisters for a post-shopping phone call that quickly veered from the price of a decent bra (astronomical) to Eve's latest goings-on. After a valiant three minutes of prevarication, she unfortunately sang like a canary.

"Oh, Eve," Danika said. "You can always be relied upon for an interesting story. Really, with you to live through vicariously, Chloe and I barely need to leave the house."

"And a good thing, too," Chloe murmured absently, "because I'm far too busy to bother."

For some reason, the word *busy* made Eve think of Jacob. Too many things were making her think of Jacob, at present—probably because his sudden disappearance earlier had jabbed at an old and much-disturbed scar.

Eve hefted the shopping bags weighing down her arms—she really needed to start working out, if her current exhaustion was any indication—and continued the uphill trek back to Castell Cottage. "I should stop telling you two my stories, then," she said, "because you both need to get a bloody life."

Twin gasps hit her, one through each AirPod. Left for Chloe, right for Dani.

"How dare you, darling." That was the left. "I *have* a life. I built it myself."

Eve rolled her eyes.

"I'm simply incredibly bogged down with work at the moment," Chloe went on, and in fairness, Eve could hear the telltale rapid taps of Chloe working at her laptop in the background.

"And I *also* have a life," Dani said.

Somewhere in the background, her boyfriend, Zaf, called, "Nope."

"Shut up, you."

"Nope."

"*Zafir.*" There was the sound of a scuffle, followed by a few grunts. Then Dani laughed, "Let go of me, you awful man."

"Are you going to stop throwing cushions?" he asked reasonably.

"Do you two mind?" Chloe demanded. "Eve is in the midst of a crisis."

At the sound of her name, Eve blinked. She'd been drifting off a little bit, there. Thinking about . . .

Well, not about Jacob. Not specifically. More about people in general—about how her friends never liked her quite as much as she liked them. How they dropped her as soon as someone better came along, or pushed her to the edge of the circle when space was tight, or generally treated her as optional rather than vital. She had a little scar on her heart from all those tiny, vicious prods, and Jacob walking out abruptly this morning had left that scar sore and aching.

Not that she'd wanted Jacob to stick around. She might be

slightly hard up for friends—real friends, the kind you read about in books—but that didn't mean *Jacob* made the cut.

Which was just as well, since he clearly didn't want to.

"*Is* it a crisis?" Dani was saying. "Because it sounds as if she's landed on her feet completely by accident, what with this insta-job. Are you enjoying yourself, Evie-Bean?"

Enjoyment was something Eve rarely considered, when it came to the world of work. Work was something you did to try and feel useful—until you fucked it up. Work was something you did to help the people around you until you weren't needed anymore. Work was not something you enjoyed in and of itself, because that would only make the situation worse when everything collapsed.

Yet Eve knew she had enjoyed herself that morning. The creative chemistry of cooking, the social aspect of starting her day with so many people—even working in relative solitude, being in control of her own environment, had given her a little thrill.

It was incredibly odd. She assumed the sensation would wear off soon.

"I'm not having a *terrible* time," she hedged to her sisters, and ignored their laughter.

"What glowing praise," Dani snorted. "Have you told Mum and Dad?"

"Yes," Eve said, which wasn't technically a lie. She had sent Mum a text that said,

Parents,
I've found a month's interim employment and secured an event-planning contract beginning in September. My

current job has provided temporary lodgings, and I'll deal
with the rest later, so don't worry about me coming home.

Then she'd muted their texts and firmly ignored all their calls.
Nothing personal. She was just afraid that if she heard her parents' voices again before she'd gotten over their last conversation,
she might do something mortifying, like cry.

"So where's the crisis part?" Dani nudged.

"That would be the bit where she ran over her employer, darling," Chloe said helpfully.

Eve had finally crested the hill and reached her car. She unlocked it, trying not to look at the bumper where there may or
may not be a Jacob-sized dent (she didn't know, having refused to
check), and shoved most of her shopping bags inside. Her current
housing situation was . . . well, more like a squatting situation,
and until that was resolved, she probably shouldn't traipse into
Castell Cottage with all the new clothing and toiletries she'd just
bought.

Since Jacob had no idea she was living in his spare room,
and all.

She was going to tell him, of course! At some point.

"I don't see how that's crisis-y," Dani was saying, "unless he's
dead. Or suing. But it doesn't sound like he's doing either of those
things, is he?"

"No," Eve muttered, "just killing me slowly via frostbite in re-
venge."

"Pardon?"

"He's a bit of an arsehole, is all." In fact, she felt a rant on the subject building in her chest, like a bubble that needed popping.

"Due to the car-hitting thing?"

"Yes, and also due to his personality."

"How unfortunate," Chloe murmured absently.

"He's—completely unreasonable," Eve said, warming to the topic. "Intimidatingly focused and alarmingly straightforward and apparently determined not to like anyone."

"Sounds like Chlo," Dani said. Which brought Eve up short for a moment, because actually . . . well. That *did* sound like Chloe. Very like her, on a superficial level at least.

"Charming," said the woman herself. "And accurate. Just feed him, Evie, that'll soften him up. Everyone likes food."

And now Eve's mind was thrust backward to that morning, to the curious zip in her belly when she'd felt Jacob's mouth on her skin. His mouth. On her skin. Goodness gracious. She sucked in a breath and started walking again, stomping over the B&B's gravel drive. "Maybe. I don't know. This morning, he did seem like he might . . ." She trailed off, suddenly hot all over and ever so slightly confused.

"What?" Dani prompted. "Like he might what?"

"Never mind. I've got to go now."

"*Do* you? How sudden and suspicious," Dani drawled.

"Are you perchance *hiding* something, little sister?" That was Chloe.

"No," Eve lied. "It's just that, if he catches me on the phone, he'll probably flush it down the toilet."

"I beg your *pardon*?"

"So I'll text you later, love you, bye." Eve hung up with a twinge of guilt toward her sisters and absolutely no guilt toward Jacob, who totally deserved to be mischaracterized as a phone-flushing prison warden so Eve could avoid awkward conversations.

Totally.

CHAPTER EIGHT

One upside of having his brain slammed against his skull? It made Jacob sleep like the dead. Or rather, he had slept like the dead last night, and had fallen asleep easily this evening. But now he was awake again, so maybe his sleeping superpower had already gone.

He rolled over and eyed the blinking blue light of his alarm clock in the dark. 1:11 A.M. For fuck's sake. He was in the process of burrowing deeper into the blankets when a particular awareness zipped down his spine.

He'd woken because something was wrong.

With a grimace, Jacob threw off the covers and dragged his aching bones out of bed. Striding to the window, he snatched open the curtains and was hit in the face by a waft of warm, summer-scented night air. He stared out at the grounds for a moment, letting his eyes adjust to the moonlight. When adjustment failed to happen, he realized he'd forgotten to grab his glasses.

Bloody concussion. Since when did a man who'd been short-sighted since childhood *forget* his glasses?

He was just turning back to get them when he heard it. Loud. Harsh. Unmistakable. The sound that'd roused him from his sleep, a siren of danger and destruction.

Quack. Quack. Quack.

Ducks.

Gripping the windowsill with his good hand, Jacob stuck his head out of the window, then remembered that bellowing at ducks at 1 A.M. with a houseful of sleeping guests was not conducive to five-star reviews. Crap. He turned and stomped out of the bedroom, snagging his glasses on the way. Maneuvering quickly and quietly through the B&B was a familiar act, if a little more difficult now his body had become a giant bruise. Still, the knowledge that ducks were defiling his precious, perfectly arranged garden—*shitting* in his pond, no doubt, the bastards—pushed him harder and faster.

He broke out of the back door minutes later, only realizing he was shirtless when a breeze bathed his bare torso. For fuck's sake. He always wore his pajama set—always—but on the *one* night he couldn't face wrestling his cast through the armhole . . .

Whatever. Didn't matter. He had ducks to shoo.

Although, as Jacob strode across the grass, he realized he couldn't hear the ducks anymore. Instead, he caught snatches of a voice, low and pure and kind of pearlescent, singing like a fairy-tale siren. Notes rose and fell on the wind, and he stopped walking, vaguely hypnotized. What the bloody hell was that? He rather liked it. Unless it belonged to an inhuman creature luring him to his death, in which case, he hated it, but damn, it was bloody effective. He stared into the darkness of the garden for a moment, trying to locate the source, until—QUACK. The voice cut out and the ducks returned. Fuck. He shook himself and started toward the pond again.

Past the cherry tree, around the folly, left at his carefully arranged wildflower planter—because meadows were pretty but order was prettier—and . . . there. The pond. It was a lovely sight, with the moonlight slanting off its narrow surface, and all that crap. There were just two things wrong with the whole scene.

One: the ducks. The fucking *ducks*. Two of them. The first was gliding over his pond as if it had the right, and the second was waddling about the banks, foraging for food.

Which brought Jacob to problem number two: Eve goddamn Brown, sitting there with a bag of bread, *feeding* the bastards. Encouraging their presence. Ruining everything, which he suspected was a particular talent of hers.

Although that thought came with a niggling sense of unfairness, because . . . she hadn't ruined breakfast. Quite the opposite. She'd been thrown in at the deep end and it turned out he admired the way she swam. He'd been dangerously close to not-hating her presence—until the Accidental Finger Lick had brought him back down to earth via the power of embarrassment.

But he'd decided to wipe that unfortunate incident from his mind. So. *Focus on the issue at hand, Jacob.*

"What are you doing?" he demanded.

She jumped half a foot in the air, slapped a hand to her chest, and released a little scream. Christ. Hadn't she heard him coming?

Did the woman have any situational awareness at all? Now he was worried about her being murdered or kidnapped when left unattended.

Worrying because such an event would leave him chefless. Obviously.

"Oh," she said, slightly breathless. "Jacob." She twisted to look at him, the side of her face softly illuminated by the moon. This sort of light turned her dark skin silvery and made her wide eyes into mirrors. Her braids were loose, spilling over her shoulders, practically forcing his gaze downward, at which point he discovered she wasn't wearing a bra.

It was difficult to miss, really. Her top was thin and kind of loose, and the armholes hung low, and the sides of her breasts swelled—

Jacob put a fast and violent stop to that train of thought. It wasn't hard. All he had to do was look at the ducks and fury welcomed him back into its cold embrace.

"Yes," he agreed, "Jacob. Me. Here." Hm. Maybe he hadn't fully woken up yet. "Which means," he continued, trying to snatch his thoughts back from their duck-Eve-boob precipice, "*you* are *caught*."

She blinked slowly. "Caught . . ."

"Feeding ducks!"

She blinked some more. "Should I . . . *not* be feeding ducks?"

"No!" he burst out, then realized he was almost loud enough to wake the dead, never mind Castell Cottage's guests. "No," he repeated again, more quietly.

"But they seemed so hungry," she said, and the worst part was that Eve appeared genuinely concerned. For *ducks*. For the vermin of the waterfowl world. Good God.

"They're not hungry," Jacob scowled, "they're wild animals who know how to feed themselves, so stop it. You'll encourage the bastards. They'll make a habit of returning. They'll treat my pond like a common watering hole and bring their friends. Next thing you know, the whole garden will be duck shit and duck sex—which is an extremely disturbing event, let me tell you—and aggressive duck demands for food. Aside from which, you're not even supposed to give them bread."

A pause. Eve cocked her head. Then, instead of addressing the substance of his speech, she asked in tones of great surprise, "You aren't? Oh dear. Why on earth not?"

"It's bad for the digestion! Christ, woman, read a waterfowl blog."

"Which *you* do because . . ."

"Because," Jacob sniffed, suddenly aware that this conversation had spiraled out of his control. "Know thine enemy."

"Ah," she murmured. "Yes. Of course." The moon had shifted, so Jacob could no longer see her face. But he had the strangest suspicion that she was smiling.

He wasn't entirely sure how he felt about that.

"What are you doing here, anyway?" he demanded. "Aside from sabotaging my garden."

"Nothing." Which was a nonsense answer if he'd ever heard one, but she rose to her feet and went on. "If you're so antiduck, I'll get rid of them. Not that I brought them here in the first place."

Bloody ducks. They should know by now that Jacob's property was off-limits to their foul ways.

"Well," he muttered. "Good." Except it wasn't good, because Eve was still here, and he really didn't want her to be. He was starting to find her . . . charming. Jacob usually saw charm as useless and insubstantial, but somehow, she made the damn thing stick. Made it solid and welcoming, like a well-built brick house rather than smoke and mirrors.

That was technically a good thing, but he hadn't expected it, and so he decided to resent it. He'd always hated surprises. "What possessed you to come over here at this time of night and waste perfectly good bread? *My* perfectly good bread?"

"I'll buy some more tomorrow," she said, throwing what remained of the bag—yes, *throwing* it!—casually on the ground.

"You'll fuck up my supp—"

"Supply is my responsibility now, anyway," she cut in, and Jacob was left to wonder how the bloody hell she'd known that. He hadn't mentioned it, because frankly, he hadn't wanted her to do it just yet. Supply monitoring was a delicate business, and Eve seemed a bit bloody ditsy, to say the least. Plus, he'd only known her for a few days. Putting her in charge of securing sausages and whatnot seemed premature. They hadn't even had their first post-employment meeting yet.

Because you've been avoiding her.

Blah, blah, blah. The point was, she knew too much. "Who told you that?" he demanded. "It was Mont, wasn't it? I heard him come and visit you today, you know. While you were baking."

Eve, who was windmilling her arms at the first duck with almost no effect, snorted a laugh. "Visit *me*? I thought he was on his way to visit you."

"Well, yes. Wanted to check I hadn't died while he wasn't looking. But I don't see how that mission took him to the kitchen."

Earlier, it had occurred to Jacob that he'd left a bit abruptly after the Finger Licking Moment, and he'd started to feel almost . . . bad. After all, Eve was so unrelentingly earnest, she might as well be a puppy, and if you kicked a puppy, even by accident, you had to pick it up and rub its belly and say sorry. Not that he'd intended to do something so awful as apologize. Or rub Eve's belly. He'd just planned to pop into the kitchen and say something vaguely friendly, to negate his earlier awkwardness.

So down he'd gone, only to find her laughing. With *Mont*.

"You should be aware," Jacob said now, "that I think he likes you." It would make sense, after all. Eve was technically attractive, and technically interesting, and really quite capable in a way that made Jacob's stomach tighten, but also quite silly in a way that made his chest fizz, so, yes. He could see it. Why Mont might like her, that is.

"Everyone likes me on first acquaintance," Eve said, then flicked a look at Jacob. "Well. Except you."

"I—" He snapped his mouth shut before it could betray him.

"Aha! Success!" The first duck had finally taken the hint and fucked off, waddle-flying away with an affronted squawk. Eve clapped her hands and did a little jump, and Jacob thanked every god he knew that the moon was currently covered by cloud, because if he'd seen that movement in any kind of light he probably would've noticed something awful. Like her tits.

Or her thighs, in those tiny shorts he absolutely hadn't been looking at.

"And by the way," Eve went on, "Mont didn't tell me anything. I read about it in the handbook."

Jacob froze.

"SUPPLYING ONESELF: THE ART OF REMAINING READY," she went on.

Jacob froze some more.

She walked toward him in the dark, her shadowy outline drifting closer. "Are you all right?" she asked. "Is this some sort of concussion thing? Do I need to reboot you?" And then she reached out a finger and tapped him on the nose.

He caught her wrist automatically, trapping her hand in front of his face. Her skin was soft—almost unnaturally soft. She must bathe in butter or milk or something because if he didn't know better, he'd think her whole body was wrapped in satin. He could feel her pulse beneath his fingers and it was fast. Probably because she'd just been grabbed by a strange and silent man in the dark.

He let her go.

"Well," she said cheerfully, "I wasn't expecting that to work." But she moved away with a speed that didn't quite match her casual tone.

Damn. Every time they did something other than argue, he managed to fuck it up. Surprising, how tense and unhappy that made him. Jacob wasn't in the habit of giving a shit about people who weren't on his pre-approved list. It was complicated and it always ended badly.

Badly, as in: with him dumped on someone else's doorstep like a bag of rubbish.

Now, why was he thinking about that?

With effort, he wrenched himself back to the conversation they'd been having before everything had somehow gone off the rails. "You've been reading my handbooks."

"Oh, yes. Mont gave them to me."

"And you—actually read one."

She sounded confused when she corrected him. As if she didn't understand his disbelief. "I read all of them."

"You—read—all of them."

"I can read, you know."

"You've been here for two days!"

"Technically three, since it's past midnight."

"Days don't count until they end," Jacob snapped. "And—and you should know, I really wrote those manuals for myself more than anyone else. To get my systems clear in my head."

"Ah—that explains the rampant swearing and generally un-professional tone."

He was so beside himself with astonishment, he didn't even scowl at the *unprofessional* comment. Even though it was bullshit. Jacob was the soul of professionalism. Although he had a feeling that if he said that out loud, she might laugh in his face.

Didn't matter. He couldn't get over the fact that she'd apparently taken his weird manuals—yes, he knew they were weird—and read them as if they were very *serious* materials and applied them with impressive commitment.

Serious. Application. Commitment. All these things added up to one impossible conclusion.

"Eve," he said slowly. "Are you . . . do you . . . by any chance . . . *respect* my B&B?"

"What on earth kind of question is that?" she demanded. "Of course I do, you widgeon."

Well. *Well.* He'd expected someone like Eve—someone carefree, someone flexible, someone who could bend without breaking—to look down on his rigidity. To laugh at it, maybe. But this . . .

"In that case," he said stiffly, his mind still sifting through evidence, "it is entirely possible that I have been operating on some incorrect assumptions about you, based solely on your horrific taste in T-shirts and your annoyingly whimsical manner."

"Is that your way of saying you've been a judgmental prick?" she asked. "Gosh, I hope so. Say sorry next. Go on. You can do it."

"Piss off."

"*There* he is."

Jacob was disturbed to find himself grinning ear to ear. God, why did she have to be *funny*? He felt himself being dragged against his will toward the certain doom of not-hating her. Dangled over the explosive volcano of enjoying her as a person.

"And what exactly is horrific about my T-shirts?" she asked, as if she'd just remembered the comment.

"Everything." Except for how tight they were. He was a fan of the tightness.

Wait, what?

Jacob was busy checking his own pulse (because his thoughts indicated a lack of oxygen to the brain, possibly caused by some kind of cardiac event) when the clouds covering the moon danced away again. Eve came properly into view, but this time, she wasn't standing—or duck-chasing—safely on the banks. This time, she was at the very edge of the pond, waving her arms like a wind turbine and muttering, "Shoo! Shoo!" at a certain beady-eyed minion of poop and destruction. Which was wonderful, except for the part where she was leaning perilously far.

"Eve," Jacob said.

"Go on, Mr. Duck. Bugger off."

Make me, said the duck's tranquil glide and vicious gaze.

"*Eve.* Be careful. The banks are uneven and you're too—"

"Shit sticks," said Eve, and fell right in.

♫

The night was warm, but the pond, as it turned out, was not.

Eve sucked in a breath as she plunged into cold water, then choked and coughed when she got a mouthful of pond for her troubles. Oh, fudge knickers. Now she probably had tuberculosis, or something. Lung mold, or something. She was diseased, and all because Jacob was ridiculously anal about ducks. She would kill him. She would murder him. She would—

Another splash sounded beside her, and then a steely arm wrapped around her waist, and Eve found herself turned around and smushed chest-first against some sort of wall.

She blinked water droplets from her eyes and squinted up. The wall had a marble-carved jawline and a wintry gaze and slightly lopsided glasses. The wall was Jacob.

Her mind momentarily glitched.

He shook her about like a terrier shaking a rat. The fact that he did this with only one arm made the whole ordeal even more undignified. His other arm, or rather, his cast, was held in the air, clear of the pond, because even when leaping into bodies of water to physically assault his staff, he remained coordinated and sensible. The bastard.

"Eve," he said, shaking her some more. "Say words. Proper words. Together."

She slapped his arm—his strong, strong arm, which was lean and corded with muscle, and currently getting up close and personal with her not remotely lean or muscular waist. It was an . . . interesting contrast, one she absolutely did not enjoy because that would be weird. "Get off me, you prat!"

"Oh good," he said, "you're all right."

She paused, then glowed for a moment. He'd been checking she was all right? He *cared* that she was all right? Maybe he wasn't the worst human being on earth after all.

Then he added, "It's far too late to find someone else to do this morning's breakfast," and Eve decided she'd been mistaken; he was definitely still the worst.

"Fuck off," she muttered and shoved him away. Her brand-new pajamas were ruined. Her braids were swirling around in algae. Her mouth still tasted of tuberculosis or fungus or something equally terrible, and when she tried to step back, her shoe sort of . . . *squidged* in something, and the something gave way, and suddenly she was sinking.

"Oh no you don't," Jacob said and grabbed her again. Now she was back against the wall of his chest.

"Why," she gritted out, "is the water up to my neck, but only up to your . . . boob area?"

He stared down at her. "Because we are different heights, Eve."

"I *know* that!" She scowled, then blinked. "Er, Jacob, are you shirtless?"

"Let's not discuss it."

"Bloody hell." She hadn't noticed before, in the shadows, but it was difficult not to notice now, with his bare skin pressed against hers. She prodded experimentally at his abs. "Bloody *hell*."

"Stop that," he snapped. "Do you think we could get out of here now? There's . . . algae on me." Apparently he found that even more abhorrent than she did, because he shuddered. It was a full body movement, one that seemed involuntary—and pressed the aforementioned abs against her tits. Which might have been enjoyable if he hadn't muttered darkly, "Slime. Can't stand slime."

Actually, even with the mutterings, it was still enjoyable. How dare *Jacob* of all people have this . . . television body?! He must have made a deal with the devil. She'd seen evidence in the kitchen of him eating microwaved spaghetti Bolognese for dinner. Men who ate nice food like spaghetti Bolognese were not supposed to also have abs. There was a balance to the universe that had to be observed and he was shamelessly flouting it.

"Well, not to be ungrateful," she shot back, unreasonably irritated, "but why on earth did you jump in? You're injured, you clod."

He gave her a severe look and said stiffly, "Obviously, I came in to rescue you."

"*Rescue* me? It's a pond, Jacob." Still, the word *rescue* fizzed through her mind with all sorts of soft and pleasant meanings.

"And you're a disaster. I'm surprised you didn't slip under and crack your head open on a rock and drown on my property and send my insurance through the roof. Or something like that."

"Oh, insurance." She laughed. "That's why you jumped in to rescue me?"

"Obviously," he bit out.

Funny how she didn't believe him. Jacob's attitude was rather like a barbed-wire fence: designed to rip you to shreds if you got too close, but only to protect something special.

No matter what he said, injured men who were obsessed with cleanliness didn't jump bodily into ponds over *insurance*. No, people did things like that because they were secretly halfway nice, even if they didn't want anyone to notice.

But if she pointed that out, he might sputter his way into an embolism. So instead, Eve kept her smile hidden, rolled her eyes, and pulled away from his chest. His hard, naked, shockingly well-muscled . . . ahem. His chest. "Whatever. Come on, then. Let's get out."

"Gladly," he said. Then he waded through the water with sickening ease, plopped his left forearm on the banks, and heaved himself up one-handed. Eve watched the entire maneuver very, very closely, for research. In the conveniently broad shaft of moonlight glowing down on them, she observed—for science!—the following:

- Jacob's biceps and shoulder muscles, tightening and shifting beneath his skin as they worked.

- The long, lean line of Jacob's torso emerging from the water, his abs dripping wet, beads of moisture trailing down the sharp V leading into his pajama pants.
- The curve of his arse and bulge of his thighs through the aforementioned, soaking-wet pajama pants as he scrambled fully onto the ground.

For science. Obviously.

He stood, then turned around and blinked, as if surprised to find her still in the pond. "Oh. Er. Didn't we decide to get out of there?"

"Yes," she agreed, "but as you've previously mentioned, you and I are different heights. And possess different levels of upper-body strength. And so on."

Snorting, Jacob sat down on the banks with a wince. She tried not to think about his various Eve-inflicted bruises. He propped his elbows up on his knees and leaned forward, arching an eyebrow. "Does this mean you need my help?"

"No," she said automatically.

He arched another eyebrow. And, if she wasn't mistaken, the corner of his mouth tilted into what *might* be a smile. "No?"

"No," she repeated. "But. Well. I just thought, since you're so concerned about your insurance, and whatnot, that you might like to oversee my exit from the pond—"

"*Oversee*," he echoed, and this time his smile was unmistakable. There were teeth involved. Strong, white teeth, with slightly turned-in incisors. She couldn't speak for a moment, at the unexpected sight of his grin—wolfish and unrestrained and mildly sarcastic.

Then she swallowed and pulled herself together. For heaven's sake, she was in a pond. Now was not the time to mentally wax lyrical over the smile of a man she barely even liked.

"Yes," she said, "oversee. Without your uptight—um, I mean, *masterful* intervention, I could easily make some sort of mistake and fall and hit my head and die."

Jacob snorted and shook his head, but he was still smiling as he reached out a hand. "All that to avoid asking for help? No wonder you went to a performing arts school. You're even more of a drama queen than I am."

Eve pressed her lips together as she bobbed toward that outstretched hand. "Clearly I'm not that much of a drama queen," she muttered, her attention focused on not slipping again. "Or I wouldn't have failed."

She barely realized she'd said those words out loud before Jacob reacted. Cocking his head in that sudden, predatory way of his, he asked, "Failed?"

Oh dear. Ohhh dear. Why in God's name had she said something like that? The fall must have shaken her brain loose. Or perhaps it was the pond-based bacterial infection currently multiplying in her lungs. Eve shrugged, though he probably couldn't see the action, since she was underwater in the dark and everything. Then she reached out and grabbed his hand.

Their fingers actually *squelched* as they interlocked. Disgusting. Definitely disgusting. Except for the breadth of his palm, and the long delicacy of his fingers, and the firmness with which he held her, as if nothing on earth could make him let go because he simply wasn't a letting go sort of man. Those things were . . . not disgusting. Not quite.

He was silent, for a moment, staring at their joined hands, probably thinking about that hideous squelch. Then he shook himself slightly and looked at her again. "How do you *fail* at drama? Well, I know how I failed at drama. I hated it. Also, my acting was more wooden than a plank. I should've been chucked out after my first class, except Aunt Lucy made me take it as an elective to improve my confidence." All this came out in an absent-minded stream before he snapped his mouth shut and looked askance, as if he had no idea why he'd said such a thing. Maybe they'd both been infected with some kind of loose-tongue disease, or maybe oversharing was a natural side effect of interacting with another human being in the dead of night.

Eve fought a smirk. "Improve your confidence, hm? Did it work?" She could just imagine a younger Jacob, doubtless twice as irritable and ferocious, refusing to talk to the other children because he found them all incredibly dull. And his aunt, deciding this was an issue of confidence, nudging him toward a class he hated with the best of intentions.

Or maybe that wasn't right at all. Because now she was imagining a different younger Jacob, eyes huge behind his glasses, hair like duckling fluff, standing rigid at the back of a class while everyone else paired up and pretended with an ease he couldn't quite access. And her heart sort of . . . squeezed.

Jacob scowled and shook his head. "No, it didn't help, because drama is soul-destroying. For me, anyway. I would've assumed it came quite easily to you." He untangled their hands, the same hands Eve had almost forgotten were joined. The connection had started to feel natural at some point, much like their bickering.

"Need more leverage," he explained when she jumped a little, and then his hand slid down her forearm and wrapped around her elbow. "So," he continued, planting his feet. "How did you fail at drama?"

"The same way I fail at everything," she said breezily, wrapping her own hand around his forearm. "With pastiche." She had the vague idea she'd misspoken, but Jacob didn't correct her, and then her thoughts were sweeping off, anyway, too fast for specifics to matter. Eve had been searching for a foothold in the edge of the pond, but she froze as the connotations of her *other* words sank in.

I fail at everything.

It was technically true: she'd bombed school, every one of her professional dreams had died, none of her friends cared enough to hold her braids back while she threw up, and her last boyfriend had believed vaccines were a front for a government tracking system based around injectable microchips. She quite literally failed at *everything*, from meaningful employment to sound relationship choices. But she certainly wasn't in the habit of admitting that out loud, and especially not to her employer.

"Erm," she added after the mother of all awkward pauses. "Not that I'm going to fail *you*. I mean, this job. Or anything."

Jacob looked down at her seriously. "That hadn't even entered my mind."

"Oh." Tentatively, she smiled.

"Until you brought it up."

"Oh." Her smile was replaced by a scowl—until she caught sight of *his* smile in the moonlight, another subtle tilt of the lips, a wicked gleam in his eyes. "Oh! You bastard."

"You're not supposed to call your boss a bastard. Pull." As if following his own instructions, he began to heave Eve upward. She squawked and grabbed a fistful of grass with her free hand, until he barked, "Do *not* fuck up my lawn."

Scoffing, she let go and grabbed his calf instead. "Fine. And I will call my boss a bastard when he teases me with such a ruthless lack of concern for my sensitive soul."

"I don't tease," Jacob said, his voice low and strained as he dragged her bodily from the pond. For a moment, Eve thought of those same words in a different context. They flashed through her, hot and glittering and entirely inappropriate. "And," he went on, "I don't give a damn about your sensitive soul."

"Clearly," she shot back. She was almost out of the pond now, her upper body completely clear. Jacob's muscles were straining and his jaw tight, yet somehow he managed to balance lifting a woman who clearly weighed more than him—one-handed!—with trying not to tumble back into the pond himself. It was slow, but it was steady, and Eve had the sneaking suspicion that despite her own best efforts to clamber out, she wasn't doing much to help.

"Look," he said, the word a rasp. "There are many ways to fail—"

"Trust me, I'm aware."

"And very few of them are actually controllable. Life has too many moving parts." He managed to sound resentful of the very nature of human existence, which Eve found impressive despite herself. "So when it comes to this job, and failing, or succeeding, there's really only one thing you can promise me. And," he added sharply, "you *will* promise."

"What?"

His response couldn't be more surprising if he'd delivered it while butt naked and standing on his head. "Try for me, Eve. That's all. Just try."

She stared. Had she misheard him? King of High Standards and Anal-Retentive Rules? "That's . . . all? That's all you think it'll take, for me not to fail."

"Why not? You're a relatively smart woman—"

"Relatively!"

"Relatively. No common sense, but other than that: smart." Eve wanted to be offended, except he was wearing that tiny smile again. So she found herself trying not to laugh instead of ripping him a new arsehole.

Only Jacob could make *relatively smart* sound like a genuine and unreserved compliment.

"You're also a good cook," he went on, "and I get the sense that you try to be a nice person, when you're not running people over. Plus, you're . . . determined. I can work with determined. I can respect determined. I can trust determined. So, yes, I think trying will do it. That's all I need from you."

Trying. Just trying. She should probably still be hung up on that part, but instead she found herself echoing with obvious surprise, "Respect?"

"Yes, Eve. I respect you just fine." He met her gaze as he gave one last, good pull.

Eve was just thinking that perhaps she didn't hate Jacob after all—and perhaps, even more shocking, he maybe possibly didn't entirely hate *her*—when she found herself free from the pond and flying through the air. That flight ended when she bumped into Jacob, knocking him backward and probably breaking several of his already bruised ribs.

"*Fuck*," he barked.

"I'm so sorry!" As quickly as she could, Eve shifted her weight onto her hands and knees, hovering over him. She bent her head to . . . inspect him for damage, or something, God, she didn't know. But at the same time, Jacob pushed himself up on one elbow, and she thought for a moment they were going to bump heads, but somehow they both managed to stop moving—

Which left their faces less than an inch apart.

She assumed that was his face, anyway. She couldn't quite see, with the fall of her hair surrounding them and blocking all the moonlight. But she could feel his breath ghosting against her cheek. He smelled like toothpaste and fresh lemons. And pond, yes, but it was the lemons that had her attention. Something about it, or the heat of him, or his *closeness*, made her feel slow and stuck, like she'd just waded into honey.

"Sorry," she repeated softly. The word was a barely there breath.

Then he pulled back a bit, or tilted his head, or *something*, and she could see him now. He had warm, summer-sky eyes, although he wasn't smiling. Not at all. His mouth was a soft, slack pout, lips slightly parted as if he'd just been kissed. Such a sweet mouth, now that she looked at it, for all the sharp things it said.

"Are you sure you didn't come here to kill me?" he asked.

"Quite sure."

"But you'd be so good at it. You half murder me on a regular basis completely by accident."

"Shut up," she said. "I'm trying to admire your mouth and you are ruining it."

"Admire my—?" He choked a little bit. Choked, and blinked rapidly, and then, if she wasn't mistaken in the moonlight—he blushed.

For such a hard-hearted arse, he certainly blushed a lot.

And for such a smart woman—because Eve *was* smart, she had decided—she sure made a lot of bad decisions around him.

I'm trying to admire your mouth? Why on *earth* had she said that? Was she high? Were there shrooms growing in that pond and had she managed to . . . to huff them, or whatever one did with such things?

Flushing with mortification, she scrambled backward and hopped to her feet, brushing the dirt off her knees. "Ha. You should see your face."

A muscle in Jacob's jaw ticked as he stood. "Has anyone ever told you your sense of humor is shit?"

"*You* have told me."

"I was right." He turned on his heel and stalked back toward the house.

"Where are you going?" she called, shifting awkwardly—and wetly—on the grass.

He shot a look over his shoulder. "To clean up."

She waited.

He sighed and stopped walking. "You should probably come and drink some Coke at the very least. If you die of pond disease, my insurance will be even higher."

"Coke?"

"To kill whatever was in that water you swallowed. It's a thing," he said stiffly, and started walking again.

Fighting a smile, she rushed after him. "You know, if you're so worried about insurance, you should probably put a fence around that pond."

"It doesn't need a fence, Eve. Only you would fall in."

CHAPTER NINE

They took turns in the shower.

Eve went first, of course. He wasn't going to send her home soaking wet and filthy—and anyway, Jacob needed to think, and he couldn't do that if she was roaming around unattended. Better to shove her into the bathroom, to hear the lock click, to lean against the door and quietly lose his mind while safe in the knowledge that Eve was contained to one room only. So that's exactly what he did.

Of course, what he'd *meant* to lose his mind about was his current situation: shirtless, covered in algae, forced to share a bathroom with an employee he couldn't stop staring at. So many layers of inappropriate and uncomfortable and just not right. He should've been turning this awful night over in his head for hours.

Instead, Jacob leaned against the bathroom door and heard the rush of water over what must be Eve's naked body, and lost his mind in an entirely different way.

Admiring your mouth. Fuck. *Fuck.* He wanted to ask himself what that meant, but even to a serial overthinker there was only one possible answer. It was very straightforward, really. She liked his mouth. She'd claimed to be messing about, but Jacob didn't believe her. He didn't know why. He was hardly an expert in reading people—quite the fucking opposite.

But still, he didn't believe her. He just didn't.

So this, then, was the state of things: Eve liked his mouth, disliked the things that came out of it, and was currently naked in his shower.

That last part wasn't meant to be relevant, but he couldn't stop thinking about it.

Jacob was staring at the wall, tapping the fingers of his left hand against his thigh in a rapid rhythm, when the lock behind him clicked again. He had just enough time to straighten up and turn around before the door swung open to reveal Eve. There she stood in nothing but a towel—one of *his* towels—her shoulders bare and glistening with water, her braids piled on top of her head and dripping wet. The scent of lemon hung about her like a cloud, and something low in his gut clenched like a fist. She'd used his soap. There were three different kinds of body wash in the shower, just in case Jacob ever felt like changing things up, but he rarely did, so the lemon one was way emptier than the mint or the raspberry. She must have seen that, she must have noticed that, but she'd used the lemon anyway.

She'd used his soap.

Jacob knew there was nothing strange about that fact, under the circumstances. Nevertheless, it joined the list of things in his head that he couldn't get rid of.

"Don't worry," she said. "I didn't break anything." Which is when Jacob realized looming in the bathroom doorway wasn't a normal thing to do.

"Sorry," he muttered, and stepped aside. "Listen—my room is down there. I put some clothes on the bed for you. Get . . ." His cheeks heated, his voice catching on the words, though fuck only knew why. "Get dressed. And, you know, go home. I'll see you tomorrow."

"Um," she said, "about that—" But she'd made the mistake of leaving the bathroom, which meant Jacob could *enter* the bathroom. He did so, quickly, and shut the door fast and firm behind him. Then he leaned against that door—again—and blamed the steam in the room for the fever rushing through his body. When he closed his eyes all he could see was Eve's bare shoulders, water droplets winking like diamonds in the light.

And her smile. He could see that, too.

It took a long, burning-hot shower to scald away whatever weirdness was messing with Jacob's head. But by the time he was clean—properly clean, his skin fizzing with it—he felt like himself again. Normal. Balanced. In control. Not in danger of fixating on any part of his employee's anatomy. Excellent.

Then he left the bathroom, entered the bedroom, and found her sitting at the end of his bed. In his clothes. His soft, white T-shirt pulled tight over her chest, his basketball shorts practically cut into her thighs, and Jesus Christ he hadn't thought any of this through.

He could see her nipples beneath the thin fabric of the T-shirt. Shit. That wasn't supposed to happen.

She looked down, presumably following his line of sight, then back up at him. Without hesitation, she threw a pillow at his head.

Jacob cleared his throat, averted his gaze, and said with complete sincerity, "Thank you."

"Yes, you're welcome, I am a goddess of mercy. Were you staring at my tits?"

"No," he said honestly. She really ought to ask more specific questions. "What are you doing here? I told you to go home."

"Hm, yes, about that—"

"Could you just . . . get out, for a minute?" he cut in. "I'm tired and I really want to put some clothes on." *And you're making me dizzy. You and your eyes and your body and everything I know about you now, it's all making me dizzy.* That disorientation sharpened his words and his expression. Eve, most likely offended by his shortness, pressed her lips together and left.

Which was the desired result. So why the fuck did he feel deflated as soon as she'd gone? It was the puppy effect, again. Jacob didn't want to kick her, and so when he did, he felt the urge to apologize. With a sigh of resignation, he threw on some pajamas and rushed out of his room, hoping to catch her before she disappeared to wherever the hell it was she lived. But when he opened the bedroom door she was standing right there in his hallway, staring at the picture on the wall.

So he hadn't kicked too hard; he hadn't hurt her too badly or scared her off entirely. Perhaps she was starting to understand that most of the time, his sharpness had more to do with himself than anyone else. He released a pent-up breath and moved to stand beside her, staring at the picture just like she was.

What did she see?

Well; he knew what she saw. Aunt Lucy, and Jacob, and his cousin Liam, clustered together at the pointless "graduation" ceremony their sixth form held, like some American school in a glossy film. Except this was Skybriar, so there hadn't been gowns or caps and the blocky comprehensive building sat in the background of the photograph like a crumbling spaceship. Jacob looked stiff and uncomfortable, because he had felt stiff and uncomfortable. Lucy looked proud, and also short, standing between two teenage boys like that. Liam was grinning at the camera like some kind of supermodel because he was a prat.

So that was what Eve saw. But what did she *see*? Must be something beyond a family photo, judging by the expression on her face. It was soft, her eyes like melting chocolate, her mouth a gentle curve. Her hair was still up, and for once, she wasn't wearing her AirPods. She had small ears that stuck out slightly. He had the strangest urge to flick them, which made no sense at all.

Then she said, "You grew up with Lucy, didn't you?"

Jacob ran his tongue over the inside of his teeth. "I met Lucy when I was ten."

Eve nodded before pointing at Liam. "Is that your brother?"

"Cousin. Liam. He's away right now. For work."

"Oh." She paused. "So Lucy really is your aunt. I mean—a relative kind of aunt, not a mum's friend kind of aunt. Because you and your cousin look so alike."

Jacob stared. "We don't look alike." Liam was handsome and charming and probably could've played the badboy love interest on a daytime soap opera if he hadn't been born to play with engines instead. Jacob saw the family resemblance, but he knew he was sharper and harsher and altogether more awkward in a way that drained the handsomeness right out of him.

But Eve frowned as if he wasn't making sense and said, "What? You're practically identical. You see that, right?"

Jacob tried to compute the many implications of that statement and developed a small headache that encouraged him to stop. "You thought Lucy wasn't my aunt?"

"She's protective over you like a mother. You have different surnames but you love her enough to name Castell Cottage after her. And you never talk about your parents. I thought maybe she'd adopted you or fostered you or something, and you didn't want to call her Mum."

"She did adopt me. I'm her son." He cleared his throat. "Legally, I mean."

"Not just legally, from where I'm standing."

Jacob supposed that was a comment on love or emotional connection or what have you. He shifted uncomfortably and searched for a new topic.

But Eve apparently wasn't done. "I'm sorry about your parents."

He blinked. *So am I.* "Sorry for what?"

"That they . . . um . . ." For once, she looked awkward, lacing her fingers together and shrugging her shoulders. "Sorry . . . for your . . . loss?"

Jacob realized what she was getting at and snorted. "*Are* you? You don't sound certain."

"Oh my God, Jacob." She squeezed her eyes shut and winced.

He decided to put her out of her misery. "My parents aren't dead."

Her eyes flew open. "Aren't they?"

"Well, I suppose they might be. I'd hardly know, at this point. But last I heard, they were alive and well, terrorizing a small village in southern Italy. Mind you, that was a few Christmases back. This time of year, they're probably in . . ." He thought for a moment. "Thailand? Cambodia? Maybe Laos."

Eve stared as if he'd started speaking a foreign language.

With a sigh, Jacob did what he'd always done, right from his first day at school, back when he'd arrived in Skybriar. He ripped off the bandage and splayed his guts out there like they didn't matter one bit. All the better to speed up everyone else's eventual boredom with his life story.

"My parents are international adventurers, also known as spongers, grifters, or childish twats. They had me by accident and weren't pleased with the result. After about a decade, they gave up and came back to England long enough to dump me on Lucy's doorstep." He made his voice as flat and robotic as possible during this recitation, because if his words were impenetrable iron bars, no one bothered to look beneath. To see the anxiety he'd grown up with, waking up somewhere different every morning in the bed of his parents' truck.

To hear the things they'd told him, as they arrived in Skybriar on that final day: *You'll be happier here, Jacob. Lucy has more time to deal with your . . . quirks.*

To understand how humiliating it had been, that first day at school, when he'd realized all the other children could read, and he'd had to put his hand up and whisper to the teacher that he . . . couldn't. Because his parents hadn't cared enough to teach him. Because they'd assumed, thanks to his slow speech and his atypical processing, that he was unable to learn.

No, no one was supposed to notice all those parts. And yet, when Eve turned those huge, dark eyes on him, her brow furrowed and her soft mouth pressed into a hard line, he had the oddest sensation that she'd noticed it all.

Which was obviously impossible. But still.

"So you met Lucy when you were ten," she said finally, "because your parents showed up and . . . gave you to her?"

Jacob decided not to mention that the *giving* had been more . . . dropping him off on the doorstep and telling him to ring the bell as they drove away. "Yes."

"And before that, you—what, traveled the world with them?"

"Yes." Most people thought of that as an idyllic childhood. He was aware that millennial hippies in particular would call it parenting goals.

But Eve looked horrified, probably because she'd read all his guidebooks and seen his meticulously cleaned bathroom and realized that spending the first ten years of his life on the road had grated against his fucking soul and turned him into the most nervous and unsettled child on earth. "Shit."

"Yes."

"I mean, *shit*, Jacob. I bet you hated that. Did you hate that?"

He opened his mouth to say *Mind your business*, but three completely different words emerged on a sigh. "God, so much." He heard a hint of something vulnerable in his own voice and tried not to die of embarrassment. Attempting to lighten the mood after that little spillage of angst, he cleared his throat and said, "Thank God they eventually came to their senses and dumped me somewhere nice and quiet." On second thought, maybe the word *dumped* wasn't a mood lightener after all.

It certainly didn't have that effect on Eve. In fact, when he flicked a quick look at her, she was clearly the opposite of amused.

Her expression was smooth, blank, almost serene. But her eyes burned. Badly.

"Your parents," she said, "sound like pricks."

Jacob instinctively wanted to argue, even after all these years. Instead, he took a breath, remembered how many times he'd woken up alone in the dark, and nodded. "Mm."

"There's a story, in my family, you know." She looked up at him suddenly. "It happened before I was born, but my grandmother loves to tell it. Back when my oldest sister was crawling, our family lived in some big old mansion. But the more my sister explored, and the better she got at communicating, the more she made it clear she didn't like all those empty rooms. She liked the smaller spaces where she felt safe. She wanted a little bedroom and hallways that didn't echo." Eve was watching him steadily as she talked. "So my parents sold the house."

Jacob wished he could look away from her, wished he didn't understand what she was getting at. But he did understand, and his stomach twisted with envy. Still, he managed to quip, "Is that a *my family's rich* story? Interesting timing."

Eve rolled her eyes. "You know it isn't. That is a story about my mother, who always wants the best and biggest of everything, not understanding her child's needs but taking them seriously anyway. Because that's what parents do. They take you seriously and they put you first. When I was at St. Albert's, I knew a girl whose mum and dad both worked two jobs to pay her fees. Four jobs, Jacob, to support something as unlikely as a career in performing arts. But she needed it, and they could make it work, so they did. Because parents put you first. And I can hear in your voice—I don't even need to ask—that yours didn't. They didn't put you first. They didn't even try."

No. No, they hadn't. They'd treated him like an inconvenience at best, and they hadn't been apologetic about it. He remembered, sometimes, the agony that used to cause him.

But it didn't hurt too badly anymore. "You're right," he said stiffly. "They didn't give a shit. But Aunt Lucy did."

Some of the murderous fire left Eve's dark gaze. She nodded with an air of satisfaction. "Good. Then clearly she deserves you far more than they ever did."

Deserves you. He couldn't touch that phrase, with all that it implied. It might make him feel too much. *She* was making him feel too much.

Maybe she could see that, because she softened and smiled and asked different questions, lighter ones. "You said a child taught you how to speak French. When you were—?"

"I made friends with a boy in the Congo. We stayed there longer than usual. I think something was wrong with the truck." Jacob shrugged, the movement smoother than it should be. The way Eve was looking at him made this topic easier. She didn't gawk at him like he was a lab rat, or act like he'd been raised by rock stars and failed to appreciate it. She looked like she understood a little bit and wanted to understand even more.

His left hand flexed at his side.

"Anyway," he said firmly. "It's late." And it was. His eyelids felt weighted, his mind a little hazy, even as his blood fizzed with electricity in her presence. "You really need to go home."

"Ah. Hm. Yes." Her steady serenity was replaced by a sheepish expression that did not bode well. "About that—and don't interrupt me this time."

Jacob stared. "Pardon?"

"Just . . . don't interrupt me, because every time I try to explain this you cut me off, and if I don't let it out soon I'm going to lose my nerve."

"What are you—?"

"Shhhh," Eve said. "Just shush." Then she stepped around him and opened the door to his sitting room, the room he never actually sat in. He'd turned it into a kind of gym, cramming his weight bench and his running machine in there—not that either were much use to him now, since he'd fractured his wrist.

And since, apparently, his weight bench was being used as a clothes hanger.

Jacob stared, slack-jawed, through the open door at what *should* be an unoccupied and organized sitting room. There were clothes on his equipment. There was makeup sitting on top of his old television, the one he never watched. And his battered pullout sofa was now a battered bed, strewn with his spare winter duvet and his cushions.

"What. The. Fuck."

Eve flashed a nervous smile and waved her hands. "Surprise! I live here!"

Surprise. I live here.

Jacob turned slowly toward her. "I beg your pardon?"

Her smile faltered. "Oh my God, you look like you're going to murder me. Don't you dare murder me."

"I have to confess," he said faintly. "I'm considering it."

"Well, don't! My mother is a lawyer, you know."

Was she, now? Interesting. He'd assumed, based on the accent, that Eve came from the kind of family where women didn't work. He'd also wondered if she might be secretly pregnant, and therefore disgraced and cast out, which would account for her slumming it over here in his B&B. But now he looked at the room she'd apparently been squatting in, and he decided that whatever had brought this particular princess into his life must be far worse, because . . .

"What sentient human person would voluntarily sleep on that sofa bed? It's practically springless."

She ignored his question. "Mont told me to sleep in here. You know, to keep an eye on you—with the concussion—and also because I had nowhere to stay and the B&B is booked up to the eyeballs, which, well done, by the way. And really, it's more convenient if I live here anyway, what with the early hours, and all, and clearly I'm no trouble since you didn't even notice I was here, so—"

"Hang on," Jacob said sharply, a thought occurring to him. "Have you been using my bathroom?"

"Only a little bit," she said. "Like, the teeniest, tiniest bit. While you were asleep. And I cleaned up after myself so you wouldn't even know I was there. But also because I'm a superconsiderate roommate."

He looked at her. "Tell me the truth. Have you ever had a room-mate before? Ever? Shared a bedroom with a sibling, bunked in college, anything?"

There was a pause. "Well, no," she said. "But I do share a floor with my grandmother and her girlfriend."

I share a floor with my grandmother and her girlfriend. I share a floor. With my grandmother. And her girlfriend. "Where did you *come* from?" Jacob demanded. "Some kind of *palace*? Some kind of elderly lesbian palace?"

"Gigi isn't a lesbian. She's pansexual."

Jacob stared at Eve, then stared at the sitting room. "You know what? I'm too tired for this. I'm going to bed."

She beamed. "So you don't mind? I can stay?"

"Yes, I absolutely do mind, and no, you absolutely can't stay. We'll figure something out." He wasn't entirely sure what, but something. She couldn't sleep next door to him, for Christ's sake. That just . . . wasn't right. Wasn't safe. Or something. Somehow. "Christ, I can't believe you're on the sofa bed. I should've thrown that thing out ages ago. If it weren't for—"

"I know, I know," Eve said. "If it weren't for your many injuries and the space you need for your arm, you'd be a gentleman and switch beds with me."

Jacob snorted. "Would I fuck. No, I was *going* to say—if it weren't for the fact that I poured all my money into this bloody business, I'd have already replaced the damn thing." He shook his head and turned, leaving her to it. His own bed was calling him like a siren song. Even if he *did* feel slightly guilty at the thought of her lying on that monstrosity.

Like she said, it wasn't as if they could swap. He had to sleep with his cast propped up on a pillow.

So why don't you share? It's a big bed.

Jacob froze, then forced himself back into motion. *Get. Out. Before you say or do something incredibly terrible.*

"Whatever," he managed, hoping he sounded exactly as bored and unaffected as he should be. "You want to sleep here, then sleep here. Just don't wake me up."

"*Well.* Charming. Absolutely charming."

"No one," he said over his shoulder, "has ever accused me of that."

CHAPTER TEN

The gingerbread meeting, as Eve had begun to think of it, happened two days later. Eve had fallen into a steady routine: she made breakfast, cleaned up, and spent a while calling her sisters or reading Mia Hopkins or painting tiny ladybirds on her fingernails. Then she went back to the kitchen, made and served afternoon tea, gossiped with the guests a bit while Jacob hovered broodily and disapprovingly in the background, before retiring for the evening.

It wasn't exactly thrilling, but it certainly wasn't terrible. Actually, Eve was rather enjoying herself.

Today, though, her new routine broke down somewhere post-afternoon tea. Instead of disappearing back to his office once cleanup was over, Jacob hung about by the thundering industrial dishwasher and said, "Meeting's tonight."

Eve blinked. "Pardon?"

"The—"

"Oh, the gingerbread meeting! I'd quite forgotten."

"I know you had," he said, sounding incredibly long-suffering.

"That's why I'm reminding you. Again. And stop calling it the gingerbread meeting. It is the meeting of the Pemberton Gingerbread Festival Committee."

"Right," Eve said slowly. Sounded dull, dull, dull. Then a thought occurred, and she brightened. "Will there be free gingerbread to keep us going?"

Jacob sighed. "I'll meet you out front at six."

Since this whole gingerbread situation was clearly Super Important and Very Serious, Eve changed into one of her favorite new T-shirts—READ LIKE YOUR BOOK IS BURNING—and put on a shit ton of pink eye shadow. Then she remembered that Jacob found excess color offensive, and added pink lip gloss as well. It was good for him to be kept on his toes.

They met outside on the gravel drive, the evening hot and sticky and golden. He was in Ultimate Jacob mode again, everything about him even more pristine and precise than usual. Eve took in his perfectly sewn-up shirtsleeve, the razor-sharp part in his hair, and his gleaming, polished glasses with a single look.

"Are you *nervous*?" she demanded, shocked and yet utterly certain.

He flushed, but his expression remained severe. "No. Are you wearing *glitter*?"

"Absolutely." She waited for a glower of disapproval. Instead, he studied her for a long moment before sucking in his cheeks and looking away. "What?" she prompted.

"What?" he shot back.

"What have you got to say about my glitter, Wayne?"

"Nothing."

"Oh, come on. Be a big boy."

"Fuck off."

"Just *say* it—"

"I think you look nice," he blurted.

Eve's mouth fell open, but her capacity for words had been stolen by the power of her astonishment.

Setting his jaw, Jacob met her eyes again. "What? You asked. Pink suits you. It's my opinion. I think you look nice. Okay?"

She choked. "Um. You're saying a lot of words right now."

"You were right," he said shortly. "I'm nervous. And concussed, don't forget. Your fault, of course. Oh, look, here's the car."

A black Volvo with a taxi company logo on the side pulled up just beyond the gate, and Eve blinked, momentarily distracted. "You ordered a taxi?"

"Of course I ordered a taxi," he said, striding across the gravel.

"I thought you were going to drive."

He gave her a pointed look, one she supposed she deserved. "Eve. My wrist. Is broken."

"Well—well—*I* can drive!"

"I'm not going to dignify that with an answer."

Before she could defend herself, the taximan stuck his head out of the window and asked, "Jacob Wayne?"

"Yeah. Cheers." Jacob opened the door and stood aside.

Eve stared, uncomprehending. Was he—opening the door—for *her*? She rather thought he might be, unexpected as such politeness was.

Before she could overcome her surprise enough to actually move, however, Jacob rolled his eyes, slid into the car, and slammed the door shut.

Bastard.

♬

Pemberton was a bustling town with a booming food industry, multiple nature walks, and a history of producing mildly famous writers and engineers. It was also responsible for 100 percent of Skybriar's fledgling tourism trade: they were the overflow town, offering Pemberton's sightseers a quaint home base that possessed regular transport links to the county's main attraction.

Jacob had always planned to take advantage of that fact, but he'd never expected an opportunity like this: the chance to take part in the widely known Gingerbread Festival, to have Castell Cottage's brand stamped into the minds of Pemberton regulars. It was an incredible marketing opportunity that would take what he'd done with the business so far and boost it into the next stratosphere. Or rather, it *could* boost the business—if the food they served at the festival was actually mind-blowingly good.

This time last week, he'd been quietly disintegrating with worry that he wouldn't have any food, never mind the good stuff. And now—well. Now, he had a chef who'd recently run him over, who was squatting in his sitting room, and who sang made-up nursery rhymes about his grumpiness every morning at breakfast. He really shouldn't feel as confident as he did.

But he entered Pemberton's town hall feeling rather good about the entire situation.

Pessimism was Jacob's natural state, but today, his dark thoughts were vague and abstract, rather than real and specific. And he knew that fact was down to Eve. Over the past few days she'd proved herself shockingly competent, culinarily talented, and, most importantly, bloody hardworking. He was starting to actually admire her. It was sickening, and slightly worrying—because Jacob knew himself, and admiration would only worsen his inappropriate physical attraction to this woman. Which was something he really couldn't afford.

He snuck a sideways look at her as they approached the table. Her expression was alight with something that might be interest, her glossy lips curved into a gentle smile and her dark eyes gleaming. He tried to be irritated by the obnoxious pink scrawl on her white T-shirt, but when he read the words READ LIKE YOUR BOOK IS BURNING, all he wanted to do was smile. Eve, he'd noticed, read using an app on her phone. Dirty books, if her laughably easy-to-read expressions were anything to go by. She always got shifty and furtive whenever anyone passed too close, as if they might catch a glimpse of the words she devoured so eagerly.

He shouldn't have noticed that. Just like he shouldn't notice the shape of her beneath that T-shirt, or the little glances she flicked up at him now, as if she was noticing things about him, too.

Fuck, fuck, fuck, fuck, fuck.

"Jacob!" The leader of the festival's committee was Marissa Meyers, Pemberton Gingerbread's marketing director. For a small, still family-owned business, the popular bakery had a very well-developed staff. That was what Jacob wanted, one day: an establishment run firmly in the black, *known* for what it did, and staffed by the best. Marissa, for example, was incredibly good at her job.

"Please, sit. And help yourselves," she smiled, indicating the jugs of water and plates of gingerbread at the center of the big, circular table.

Eve made a stifled little squeaking sound as she sat, and Jacob knew without looking that she was shooting heart eyes at the gingerbread.

"Thanks, Marissa," he murmured. Then he snagged a plate of gingerbread and held it out to Eve, because, well—her arms were shorter than his, so she'd have to lean over to reach.

She stared at him wide-eyed, like his basic courtesy was some kind of miracle, and Jacob felt himself grow irritable and overheated. For fuck's sake. Just because he wasn't a sunny cartoon character didn't mean he couldn't be nice, too.

"Stop looking at me like that," he muttered, "and take the gingerbread."

After a moment, her surprise dissolved into a smile. "Yes, boss," she whispered impishly, and took two.

He ruthlessly squashed his grin.

Then a voice to his right popped the little bubble that had formed around he and Eve. "All right, Wayne. What's up with the arm?"

Ah. Yes. There were . . . other people here. It looked as if almost everyone had arrived, in fact: the ice cream people, the artisanal cheese people, the teacher in charge of the floats by local children, the Thai street-food people, and so on. The man speaking was Craig Jackson, a florist from another nearby village. He was a loud and nosy type with beady, judgmental blue eyes and a love of speaking over people. Including Marissa. Jacob privately suspected that the man would not be contracted again for next year's festival.

Jacob, by contrast, had been on his absolute best behavior during all meetings. After all, Marissa was the one giving him this opportunity based on nothing but the essay he'd emailed her months ago outlining point by point why he would be an excellent bet for one of the stalls on offer. He certainly owed her the bare respect of paying attention to whatever she said.

Turning to look at Craig, Jacob said stiffly, "I have fractured my wrist." He'd have thought that much was obvious, what with the cast and all.

Craig released a snicker that signaled incoming bullshit. "How'd you manage that, Spock? Sudoku-ing too hard?"

Jacob set his jaw. He didn't appreciate Spock comments. He'd received a lot of them over his lifetime, and he knew exactly what they were supposed to imply, and they made him want to throttle people before sitting them down for a long and detailed chat on why the world would be a much better place if they stopped congratulating themselves on being normal and started to accept that there were countless different normals, and Jacob's kind was just as fine as everyone else's.

In his head, that detailed chat usually involved a lot of curse words and multiple threats of violence.

Unfortunately, he wasn't in much of a position to carry out

threats of violence, since a woman whose professional respect and continued grace he very much relied on was watching this entire interaction with an unreadable expression. He resigned himself to squashing down his anger for the greater good—well, for his own greater good—when Eve leaned forward to glare flintily at Craig.

Jacob blinked, momentarily taken aback. He hadn't realized she could glare like that. But it turned out that big, expressive eyes, while very good at sparkling adorably, were just as good at delivering death stares.

"Spock," Eve repeated after swallowing her mouthful of gingerbread. "What does that mean?"

Craig faltered for a moment. "He's, er, a character from one of them—"

"No, I know who Spock is," she said dismissively, as if Craig were being excessively stupid. "I meant, what did you *mean* by it?"

Craig paused. "Well," he said after a moment. "Would've thought that was obvious."

Eve produced a lovely, vacant smile. "No," she said. "Explain it to me."

Once, as a child, Jacob had seen a mongoose eat a snake. He was now experiencing a similar fascinated, secondhand alarm.

"Welll," Craig repeated, drawing out the word uncomfortably this time. "Obviously, Spock is . . ."

Eve waited, blinking slowly.

"Spock is . . ."

"What?" she nudged.

"Well, you know that Jacob is . . ."

Eve waited. Then she repeated, "*What*? Jacob is what?"

"Yes, Mr. Jackson," Marissa interjected. "Jacob is what?" Much like Eve, she waited for his answer with a deceptively patient smile.

"Erm," Craig mumbled. "Er. Ah. Never mind."

"Are you sure?" Eve asked.

"Doesn't matter."

"But—"

"I said it doesn't bloody matter!" Craig barked, his face flushing red.

Jacob's amusement drained away at that, replaced by a cold fury. "Do not," he said quietly, "raise your voice at my employees."

Craig shifted uncomfortably, looking away. "Christ," he muttered. "Let's bloody get on with it."

"I couldn't agree more," Marissa said severely. "If you're done disrupting proceedings, Mr. Jackson, we are all busy people and have no time to waste."

Craig's redness ratcheted up to fire engine, but, with a wary glare in Eve and Jacob's direction, he kept his mouth shut.

Marissa opened the notebook in front of her and flicked through a few pages before starting a speech about schedules and orders of events. But, honestly, Jacob barely heard a word. He was too busy staring at Eve, who had produced a notebook of her own from somewhere and was already scribbling bullet points as Marissa spoke.

He looked at the downward sweep of her dark lashes, the sugar-sweet pink gloss on that lovely, clever mouth, the quick glide of her hand over the page. And then he saw the title she'd written on the clean, white paper.

Notes for Jacob.

All the breath swept out of him in a long, quiet wave. Eve, he had noticed, helped everyone. So it shouldn't hit him like a fist to the chest when she helped him, too—yet his heart stuttered a bit beneath the blow of his surprise.

This woman—he kept waiting for her to hate him more, but she appeared to be hating him less. They were moving backward, firmly away from safe, spiky interactions and closer to something dangerously like friendship.

Jacob really wasn't sure what to do with that.

CHAPTER ELEVEN

Eve's family saw her as "the social one"—but only because her eldest sister was a hermit, and her middle sister was a book-worm with a vague disdain for human contact. If Chloe or Dani cared enough to collect friendships, they'd probably be far more successful than Eve—because Eve's method of socializing had been born out of desperation and careful observation, a shield of giggling charm and always-up-for-it flair designed to hide the ways she didn't quite fit in.

It was odd, really; the more she thought about it, the more she occasionally reminded herself of . . . Jacob.

Well, only a little bit. Just the awkward parts.

So when the man himself announced on Friday morning that they'd finally be doing the housekeeping together, *alone*, Eve waited patiently for self-conscious anxiety to consume her. She should be a nervous wreck, frantic about maintaining a persona that worked best in group situations, worried he might see right through her and find her irritating or unnerving or just not right.

Instead, she surprised herself by feeling utterly serene. Because, honestly? Jacob wasn't like other people. He'd found her irritating from the start, and he hadn't bothered to hide it, so she'd long since bothered to care. It turned out there was a difference between the heavy weight of wondering what people might think, and the easy acceptance of *knowing* what Jacob thought because he bloody well said it out loud.

Plus, she was pleased to finally offer some help.

So when he dragged Eve off to get cleaning supplies, she found herself skipping merrily after him, singing, "We're off to see the storeroom, the wonderful storeroom of Oz."

"Good God, woman," Jacob muttered. "Your energy is indecent. Weren't you moaning this morning about how early we have to wake up?"

"I think I'm getting *so* little sleep it's making me hyperactive," Eve said.

"Like a toddler," he replied. "Delightful."

"Anyway, you said I could sing. You said, something something, blah blah blah, no AirPod, Eve can sing."

She expected him to express regret over that fact. Instead, all he did was murmur gravely, "Ah. So I did." Then he shut up about the singing thing completely.

For an outrageous grump, he could be incredibly reasonable sometimes.

They entered a green-and-white wallpapered hallway where Jacob caught her wrist and tugged her to a stop. You'd think, after all the touching and rescuing there'd been the other night, Eve would be accustomed to physical contact with this man by now. But when his long fingers pressed firmly into her skin, she felt as if he'd shocked her—tiny, delicious bursts of electricity sparkling over her flesh.

He touched her casually, as if he had a right to do it, as if they were like that now. She supposed they *might* be like that now, because she knew him, at least a little bit. And somehow, despite his many infuriating qualities, she liked what she knew.

"You have to be quiet in the storeroom," he murmured. "We both do. There's a very thin connecting door to the bedroom beside it, and a shared air vent."

"Oh," she murmured back. "So . . . we whisper?"

"We whisper," he agreed. Then he grabbed the big old ring of keys from his pocket and unlocked the storeroom door. The room inside was small and cramped, filled with well-stocked shelves, lit only by a high, round window on the far side. "You'll have to grab the sheets," he said, nodding at a fresh stack on those shelves, "since a dangerous driver recently incapacitated my right hand."

A dangerous—?! Well, perhaps that wasn't entirely inaccurate.

Pushing down a now-familiar wave of guilt, Eve shot him a glare—purely on principle, obviously—and took the sheets. She managed a basket of cleaning supplies, too, just to show off. Then a distracting hum of voices drifted in from the next room, and Eve willed herself not to drop a bottle of bleach or knock over a shelf or anything like that, because Jacob would probably murder her. He would bludgeon her to death with the box of little biscuits and tiny milks he was currently balancing in his left arm.

"Grab a blanket, too," he said, nodding toward a separate pile of bedding.

Eve followed instructions—which was a rather novel experience for her—and asked, "What's this for?"

"It's weighted." When she raised her eyebrows in question, he sighed. "Some people prefer weighted blankets, Eve. Such as the gentleman currently occupying the Peony Room. Let's move on."

"Fine," she muttered, and made a mental note to research what the bloody hell weighted blankets were for. "You know, you should really have a trolley for all this stuff."

"I do have a trolley. I just can't push it at the minute, because, arm."

"I could push it for you."

He whisper-shouted a laugh. "You think I'm going to let you run around my B&B with a bloody trolley? You think I'm going to facilitate your reign of terror like that?"

"Oh my goodness. You run a man over once—"

"You will have to carn the trolley, Ms. Brown," he said dryly, shoving his box of biscuits at her. Then he turned and reached up to the highest shelf for what looked like the world's hugest spray bottle of glass cleaner. Good God, she hadn't even thought about glass. He would be beyond anal about glass.

Haha. Anal.

"What are you smirking at?" he demanded, shooting a suspicious sideways look at her. He was still reaching, his left hand fumbling about on a shelf too high for him to actually see. But Eve, standing feet away, could see it fine, and he was nowhere near the bottle. She decided not to tell him just yet.

"I was thinking about you being anal," she whispered instead. "It's funny, because, you know. You're anal, er, anal-re . . ."

"Retentive," he supplied. "Wait—no I'm *not*. I'm thorough, thank you very much. I am thorough and committed and—"

"Jacob."

He scowled. "Fine. I'm anal-retentive. Please, continue to thrill me with your bonkers train of thought."

"Gladly," she beamed, leaning back against a shelf. At the same time, a door slammed somewhere, and she jumped.

Jacob smirked.

The prick.

"You're anal-retentive," she continued, "and you're an arsehole. So. It's like a pun. Or a double ingenue. Or something."

"Do me a favor," he snorted, "and shut up before I am overwhelmed by the urge to sack you."

"But it's so much fun watching you restrain yourself."

He opened his mouth, but whatever he might have said was cut off when a voice floated through the grate, faint but clear. "You were a dick at breakfast."

A pause. Then a low, baffled response. "Huh?"

"You. Were a dick. At. Breakfast."

Eve widened her eyes at Jacob. "OMG. Drama."

"Shush!" he hissed. Then he fumbled about for the window cleaner with renewed vigor, grabbed it, and was clearly readying to leave when the voices grew louder.

"What the fuck, Soph? What's your problem lately?"

"What's *my* problem? Do you know why I booked this holiday, Brian? I thought it was the pressure of work making you such a fucking bastard all the time—"

"Oh, don't go there, Sophie."

"But it's just *you*—"

"You think this is a holiday? Coming to the fucking Lake District and staying at some shitty B&B?"

Jacob, who had been in the process of quietly shooing Eve toward the door, froze. Then he turned his head slowly, slowly, slowly, and glared daggers at the vent.

It turned out, every evil look he'd ever shot at Eve had been nothing. Practically heart eyes. She'd had no idea one man could produce this much tangible malevolence with nothing but his eyeballs. If Brian collapsed at this very second, she might have to report Jacob as the cause of death. "*Shitty?*" he repeated quietly, with the air of a volcano about to erupt and burn everyone in the vicinity horribly alive. "*Shitty?*"

"See, that's your problem!" Sophie was saying. "You think you're above everything. You can't enjoy anything. This place is adorable."

Jacob closed his Eyes of Violence. "Yes," he muttered to himself. "Adorable. Fuck you, Brian."

Eve knew this was not an appropriate moment to giggle, but she might have to do it anyway.

As if he'd read her thoughts, Jacob cracked open one eye and ordered, "Keep. Quiet."

She stuck out her tongue.

"Maybe my problem is that *you're* boring," Brian was saying, although he sounded as blustery as a hurricane and nowhere near as impressive.

Eve rolled her eyes and mouthed, *Men.*

Jacob, to her surprise, gave her a look of approval. "Quite."

"You don't like men?" she whispered.

"It depends. I don't like imbalanced relationships, and men are frequently the perpetrators."

"*I'm* boring?" Sophie sounded like a woman on the edge. "Brian, you haven't made me come in six weeks and five days. You think Fish and Chips Wednesday at Wetherspoons is a decent date night and you missed my best friend's thirtieth because fucking *Holby City* was on. You're boring as shit and I'm sick of you acting like it's me!"

"Not a fan of the romance thing, then?" Eve asked.

"Not exactly," Jacob said. Honestly, she was surprised he'd admitted that much. But then he added, the words low and quick, "I'm not principally opposed. I'm not opposed at all. There's nothing wrong with—with love. I just think truly happy relationships are hard to find. Often, someone's disappointed, which makes their partner the disappointment. You're either Brian or Sophie, and I'd rather be neither."

Those words were so similar to Eve's own (occasional, totally depressing) thoughts, she almost fell over in shock. "Good to know I'm not the only one with terrible taste in men," she muttered. "Or whoever it is you . . ."

"Women," he supplied crisply. "And I don't have terrible taste. That's simply the way things turn out, sometimes. Happy endings aren't as common as car crashes."

Eve blinked. She shouldn't want to cling to the romantic opinion of *Jacob Wayne*, of all people, but—gosh. "That's an attractive idea," she said ruefully. "That bad relationships are just probability."

He arched an eyebrow. "Yours aren't?"

So he assumed she had bad relationships. She couldn't feign outrage, since she'd once dated a white guy who'd said *Wha gwan, rastaman?* to her father. "I make bad choices," she explained with a teasing smile, because teasing smiles softened everything. They were her safety net. Was she joking? Was she deadly serious? Who could tell? "In case you hadn't noticed, I'm a part-time hot mess."

Jacob's lips quirked. "Part-time?"

"Yep. My other hours are spent as a sparklingly responsible Castell Cottage employee."

"You're damn right they are."

"Sophie—I—you . . ." A tragic pause floated through the vent, dragging Eve's thoughts back to the drama next door. "Six weeks and five days?"

"Oh, *I'm* sorry—did you think ten to fifteen minutes of pumping away in silence was doing it for me? Did you imagine I was coming really quietly and in absolute stillness? I've been seriously considering having it off with my electric toothbrush, Brian."

Jacob made a strangled sort of noise and dropped the glass cleaner. He almost caught it—except he reached out to do so with his *right* hand, so the bottle slipped from his grasp yet again.

On a reflex, Eve fell to her knees and caught it a foot away from hitting the ground. Kind of like a superhero catching a baby or something equally impressive. It was quite satisfying, avoiding disaster instead of causing it. Beaming, she looked up—

And found her face directly in front of Jacob's dick.

Although she probably shouldn't think of this area as *Jacob's dick.* That was sexy romance novel talk, and this was not a sexy romance novel situation. She should think of it as, like, his groin, or the fly of his jeans, or something equally unsexy and non-dick-related. She stared for a moment at the outline of that heavy shape just below his belt, and narrowly resisted the urge to lick her lips. Not because of his di—groin. Just because her mouth was suddenly, unexplainably dry. Must be all the excitement.

"Get up," he whispered, an urgency in his voice that she'd never heard before. Not even when she'd tumbled into that duck pond. "Get *up*," he repeated, and Eve realized her brain was doing the thing where it stuck, like a scratched CD, on one particular element of the world around her. (Jacob's di—*fly*, in this case.) She was about to start moving when he wrapped a hand around her upper arm and hauled her to her feet with a strength that was as impressive as it was unexpected.

She popped up beside him feeling slightly breathless, waving the glass cleaner like a trophy. "Got it." Probably a redundant comment, by now, but her brain was still feeling sluggish.

That bulge had been very big. Very . . . thick.

And Jacob seemed, in the low light, to be blushing. Why was he blushing?

Probably the electric toothbrush comment.

"Yes," he was saying, his voice oddly stilted. "Good . . . good catch. Very good catch. Cheers."

"No problem. I didn't want to interrupt next door and put an end to the juiciest conversation I've ever overheard."

Jacob blinked as if he might have misheard her. She waited for his confusion to be replaced by a dry look of disapproval. Instead, after one shocked second, he . . . smiled. "You're so fucking shameless," he said, but he made it sound like a compliment. And he'd cursed. She had noticed, over the last few days, that Jacob only swore when he was pushed to the absolute limit or when he was pissing around with Mont. So, in short, when he was being himself.

Fucking had never sounded quite so lovely.

"I could never admit that I wanted to listen to this shit," he said.

"But you do. You do want to listen."

"It's like a car crash. The first car crash in recent memory that I haven't been a victim of."

She scowled through the tug of guilt in her stomach. "Holy ginger biscuit, Jacob Wayne, are you *trying* to make me crumble into a pile of sad and sandy regret?"

"Yes," he said. "It makes you awkward and babble-y, and then you say things like *holy ginger biscuit.*"

Well. Eve certainly hadn't expected that response. She hesitated, trying to unravel all the threads in his voice—the warmth and the familiarity and the amusement. Because surely uptight and impatient Jacob Wayne wasn't trying to say that he *enjoyed* her rambling?

Before she could decide, he spoke again, all business now. "We should sneak off before one of them storms out into the hallway and we're trapped." He turned away, as if he didn't want her to examine his face in the fine light through that one window any longer.

And she had the oddest feeling that he did enjoy her rambling, after all.

♫

Fifty minutes and two bedrooms later, all such wonderings about Jacob's inner mind had ceased. Instead, Eve had started to fantasize about hitting him with her car again.

"Tighter," he said, sounding bored out of his mind. "Eve. Seriously. *Tighter.*"

It turned out, making beds to Jacob's ludicrously exacting standards was really fucking hard. Changing sheets? Even harder. Changing duvet covers? The single attempt she'd made would haunt her nightmares forever. Really, didn't most sensible people accept that the duvet would always be a little bit bunched within its cover?

Apparently, not Jacob Wayne.

Then again, she had never believed him to be sensible.

"Tighter," he repeated for the fifty thousandth time.

Tighter, she mouthed, scrunching her face into a scowl.

"I saw that."

"No you *didn't*!" she gasped, outraged. "You're behind me!"

"There's a mirror in front of you."

"Oh." Eve looked up, and so there was. Over the dresser, right there. She could see herself, bending awkwardly as she attempted the pristine hospital corners Jacob was still somehow capable of without his dominant hand—the corners *she* couldn't seem to manage. They'd barely been at this tidying nonsense an hour, but Eve's brand-new T-shirt—CERTIFIED HEROINE—was already clinging to her slight sheen of sweat, and her braids were spilling out of their ponytail. She looked a mess.

Jacob, meanwhile, was sitting comfortably in the wingback

chair behind her, arching a sardonic eyebrow and looking generally villainous. Even the white cast on his arm could be mistaken
for a white cat. Any moment now, he'd start stroking himself ne-
fariously.

Heh. Stroking himself. Amusement struck her for a moment
before the image of Jacob in that same chair, bare-chested and
maybe a little wet, with one hand on his hard cock, wiped her
smile away.

Gosh. Where on earth had that come from? She really needed
to read less AO3 smut before bed.

Or possibly more.

Jacob's reflection frowned at her. "Why are you looking at me
like that?"

Good question. *No dirty thoughts about your boss, Eve.*

"I was thinking," she said, pushing all illicit fantasies firmly
away, "that your arse must be better. Because all you've done today
is sit on it."

She'd intended to annoy him with that comment, but instead,
he grinned. His sharp, wolfish smile—with its turned-in incisors
and the lines of pleasure fanning out from his pale eyes—made
her think of sunlight beaming off fresh snow. "If you have enough
energy to give me lip," he said, "you have enough energy to pull
that sheet tight."

"Give you lip? You're enjoying this far too much."

"Of course I am." He shifted back in the chair, sprawling like
some indolent prince. "I am beginning to think I was born to boss
people around."

"You're only *beginning* to think that?" she muttered.

"You're right. I've always known." He watched her struggle for a moment longer, then sighed and stood up. "But I think that's enough torture for one day."

"No," Eve said, looking away. "It's just a bed. I can do it."

"You—"

"I can do it! Just give me a minute." Except he'd already explained they were on a strict schedule due to check-in times, and Eve knew she'd made him slower today. "I'm supposed to be *helping* you, not making more work."

"Eve." He was standing beside her, looking down with an expression she couldn't quite decipher. One part frown, two parts something that might be tenderness. Or possibly the urge to tenderly strangle her.

"This is your first day on housekeeping," he said slowly. "I'm teaching you things. You're practicing. I do not need or expect you to get everything instantly right, and contrary to your mother hen instincts, *help* doesn't mean *doing everything for me.*"

She huffed out a breath and straightened, inadequacy tangling around her limbs like vines. "I'm not a mother hen," she mumbled, but she wasn't really thinking about Jacob's words. She was thinking about the vines.

Usually, when Eve experienced this feeling of not-good-enoughness, she did the sensible thing and got out. Gave in. Gave *up.* Anything to stop the inadequacy from dragging her down again. But this time, she refused to—because, for God's sake, it was only a bloody bed. And because giving up on Jacob's job would mean giving up on Jacob. It would mean letting him down. Which she didn't want to do, since she, erm, owed him, or something.

Anyway, she kind of liked this job. She liked *Castell Cottage*. So. No giving up today.

"You *are* a mother hen," Jacob was saying, "but luckily for both of us, I don't care. Now, come here. Press down there for me, to keep the tension." He pointed at a spot farther up the bed, then bent over to fold the sheet she'd just been wrestling with. Within seconds, he was making a perfect hospital corner. Left-handed. Eve hurriedly pressed down as instructed, slightly dazed by the sight of his long, dexterous fingers tugging and folding. And by the thought that he was bent over, and what a view she'd have if she were standing behind him. Tragically, though, she was standing in front.

Damn you, situational physics.

"Erm, sorry," she said awkwardly, "for slowing you down today—"

"Actually," he cut in, "I accounted for the possibility that things would take a bit longer. We're not behind schedule."

"I'll be better tomorrow," she offered. "I'm always better at new things once I've had a while to wrap my head around it. Or daydream it. Or break it down or—you know."

He gave her a strange look and said, "Funnily enough, yes. I do know. But—listen . . . Eve . . . you did . . . *acceptably* . . . today."

She stared. "Pardon?"

"At breakfast." He paused, pulling the sheet even tighter—probably tighter than necessary. Possibly so tight he was in danger of ripping the thick, high-quality cotton. At some point during

the conversation, his face had become a rigid mask of awkwardness. She had no idea why. "You . . . Good food."

Dear God, he'd stopped using verbs.

"And you multitask," he continued. "You . . . you talk to guests
very well, you know. As you work. I couldn't do that. You . . .
impress me, when you do that." He almost choked on the word
impress.

But, to be fair, Eve almost choked, too.

You impress me when you do that. Well, all this explained why
he sounded so bloody uncomfortable. She tried to remember Jacob praising anyone, ever, including the local milkman who delivered his product in clearly labeled glass bottles and of whom
Jacob seemed very fond, and came up a complete blank.

"And the meeting we attended," he continued. Good fluff, he
was still going. He'd straightened now, rubbing his palms against
his trousers. He was all raspberry ice cream and diamond-hard
jaw and uncertain flicks of those frosty eyes, as if worried Eve
might throw his tentative compliments back in his face. But he
was still going.

"You were . . . good," he said. "You—just—you're not a hot mess,
that's all. Not as far as I can see."

She looked up at him, dazed and confused by this sudden
barrage of what could only be called reassurance. Compliments
would be one thing—one strange and unexpected thing—but
what really got to her, what hooked her with compelling claws, was
the suspicion that he'd started reeling off positives to make her
feel better.

He was worried she felt bad. He was trying to comfort her. He'd listened to what she said about bad choices, about being a failure, and he was trying to . . . to *disagree*.

"Thank you," she said softly, a smile spreading across her face.

He shot her a look of mild alarm. "Well. You don't need to sound so pleased. I am simply updating you on your professional performance."

A laugh crept up on her. "I can't believe this."

He snorted, looking down his nose. "Believe *what*?"

"I can't believe that beneath all the indelible rudeness, you apparently possess great buckets of emotional intelligence. Far more than I do, anyway. Where in God's name have you been hiding that?"

He rolled his eyes. "Fuck off, Evie." But the words couldn't erase his blush. "This corner is done. Now, lean here so I can do this side."

She obeyed in silence, still watching him with a hint of disbelief. Waiting for someone else to rip off the Jacob-costume and jump out at her. But that didn't happen; of course it didn't. Because he'd been this way all along.

He just saved it. Like a secret. For those who made him want to share.

The idea that she made Jacob want to share had Eve uncomfortably close to a swoon.

"Thank you," she said finally. "You're sweet, you know. Thank you."

"If you ever call me *sweet* again, I'll report you to HR."

"Who's HR?"

"I'm HR."

She grinned, and, judging by the glimpse she caught of his profile as he turned away, so did Jacob.

Then he ruined a perfectly platonic moment by bending over the second corner, this time with Eve standing behind him. Now, she didn't just *assume* the action displayed his arse beautifully; she saw. It was a high, tight peach filling the dove-gray trousers he wore today, stretching their seams with its curve as he leaned forward. Eve felt vaguely hypnotized. Her mouth may have hung open. Drool threatened like the promise of rain in May. This did not bode well.

Eve Brown was a generally horny woman; she knew this about herself. She appreciated all kinds of maleness, such as overlong eyelashes or fingers peeling off a beer label or legs stretched out and crossed at the ankle. If she tried, she could get going over just about anything. So noticing Jacob in certain ways shouldn't technically be a cause for concern.

Except she wasn't simply *noticing* him. Sometimes his smile drew her eyeballs like fucking gravity, and that was a serious problem. She liked it here at Castell Cottage, liked working hard and feeling semicapable for once, liked acting like a bloody grown-up. She wasn't going to fuck it up by developing a completely juvenile crush on her boss. Especially not when said boss might also be— kind of—sort of—her friend.

"Are we friends?" she blurted out, just to make sure.

Jacob looked up at her, appearing genuinely startled. Which made sense, since this was kind of a subject change. "Er . . ."

"Sorry, I was just thinking—you know. We get along much better now."

"Compared to last week, when I was trying to chase you off with rudeness and you were—"

"If you say *hitting me with your car* one more time, I will eat you."

"Battering me with a motorized vehicle?"

She rolled her eyes heavenward. "Yes, Jacob. Since then."

There was a pause before he answered. "Well. I don't know. We're certainly more *friendly*—but then, that wouldn't be hard."

"You know, when I started this conversation, I really thought it was a yes/no question."

"It is," he said immediately. "I mean, it would be. It should be. I just . . ." He trailed off, and she noticed that familiar blush creeping up his cheeks.

The sight took the sting out of his hesitation and pumped her full of glitter. Eve found herself grinning, leaning closer to him, teasing with a song in her voice. "You just . . . what?"

He cleared his throat. "I just don't know. How one technically. Officially, that is. Decides, erm. Well, the thing is, when I made friends with Mont, we were children, and he kind of took charge, so. And since then, I haven't really bothered, so. Hm."

Eve stared, fighting a grin. "Oh my God, you're just like Chloe."

"I beg your pardon?"

"My oldest sister, Chloe. She spends all her time scowling at the postman and avoiding human contact, so when she actually wants to be friends she doesn't know how to get started."

Jacob released a breath that seemed almost relieved. "Ah. Yeah. Chloe does sound quite . . . familiar."

"Oh, good." Eve smiled. "Because I know how to deal with her particular brand of social awkwardness. And I know how to deal with yours, too." In fact, she had the perfect idea already. A silly idea, probably, but she might do it anyway.

Jacob blinked. "That sounds ominous."

"Does it?"

"Yes."

"Okay, but *does* it?"

"Eve. Yes."

She grinned. "Just you wait."

CHAPTER TWELVE

JACOB: What the hell are you doing in there?

While he waited for an answer, Jacob lay back in bed and stared at the sun-washed ceiling. The mysterious groans and thumps from next door continued. He'd had to text Eve about it, not because he thought she was doing something terrible in there, but because the nonstop noise was making it hard to ignore her.

It was always hard to ignore her.

They'd now been semiroommates for a week. He heard her in the mornings, stumbling around at dawn, yawning like some sort of adorable cartoon character. At breakfast, he went down to help, and tried not to marvel at the person she became in the kitchen—the way she whipped around like controlled chaos, like the eye of a storm, cooking and charming and cleaning and still managing to tease him all the while.

Then, later, he'd take her upstairs and watch her wrestle with bedsheets and polish mirrors with impressive determination and place the complimentary biscuits just right, and it turned out that seeing Eve try and try and ultimately succeed—succeed, when she obviously expected to fail—*well*. It turned out that Jacob struggled not to think about things like that.

Struggled not to roll the memories over his tongue later, like a fine chocolate truffle.

Struggled not to drift off into recollections while he soaped himself in the shower, or while he lay in the dark each night, or even—fuck—even during quiet, less busy moments in his office. Sometimes he thought of Eve's easy jokes and Eve's determination and Eve's bubbly chatter, and his blood almost burned its way out of his body.

He'd decided not to examine why.

His phone buzzed, and he grabbed it with a speed that had nothing to do with expecting a text from Eve. Which was just as well, because it wasn't a text from Eve; it was a message from a couple arriving in the morning, confirming their check-in schedule for the third time—as if he hadn't sent them a highly detailed itinerary email complete with FAQ.

Despite priding himself on his swift responses and at-all-hours customer service, Jacob sighed and tossed the phone away.

Another bang sounded through the wall, followed by a yelp. He tensed, ready to jump up and investigate Eve's welfare, then wondered what the fuck he thought he was doing. She was a grown woman. She didn't need him running around after her like a nervous parent. He shouldn't have even sent that text, because he didn't care what she was up to. He didn't—

The phone buzzed again. He grabbed it. And smiled.

EVE: Is harassing me in my own home a proper use of employee information, Mr. Wayne?

Because she hadn't technically given him her phone number; she'd filled it out on her employment forms, and he'd put it in his phone. Which was a perfectly ordinary thing to do—in fact, it was Castell Cottage procedure, enshrined in his personal handbook. He'd had his previous chef's number too, in case he needed to call her to investigate lateness, or some such.

Of course, with Eve, he could always just go and knock on her temporary bedroom door.

Not that he had, in the days since discovering her presence there. Because what if she was—what if she was changing? Or lounging around naked, painting her toenails pink, which seemed like something she would do. Or . . .

He pressed the heel of his hand against his cock, not for any particular reason. Just because.

JACOB: YOUR own home, is it?
EVE: Squatter's rights.

He laughed—actually laughed out loud, and felt the accompanying spark of warmth that had become so familiar around her. He didn't think he'd ever been this easy with someone so quickly, didn't think he'd ever learned another person's rhythms enough to joke around like this without months of observational research first. But she was so open, and so reliably kind, that he couldn't help himself.

And since she'd called it friendship, he didn't even have to worry that all this warmth might mean something else.

EVE: Am I being too loud? I didn't mean to disturb you.

JACOB: You're fine. Just making me curious. You're not using my weights, are you?

EVE: Is that not allowed?

JACOB: It's allowed. I just don't want you to break your own foot.

EVE: Because it would increase your precious insurance. But it would also be payback for the wrist, so . . .

Truthfully, he'd been thinking less about insurance and more about keeping Eve safe and uninjured. If she hurt herself, she might cry, and if she cried, he might die.

Or something.

At the hospital, they'd told Jacob his concussion was mild. But after a week of thinking increasingly strange thoughts about his chef, he was beginning to suspect they'd misdiagnosed him.

JACOB: Making you change a thousand beds this week was payback for my wrist. So no foot-breaking please. What are you doing?

EVE: It's a surprise.

A surprise? Jacob turned those words this way and that, examining them from every angle, before deciding that—yep. They kind of suggested she was doing something for him. Or something that would impact him. Maybe she was painting his original antique end table a hideous shade of orange.

Or maybe . . .

EVE: It's a friendship thing. Are you free this evening? For a
    friendship thing?

Or maybe that. Maybe that.

♫

Eve was, not to put too fine a point on things, bricking it.

She stood, arms outstretched, in the center of the sitting room (as if her body could hide the "surprise" directly behind her) and waited for Jacob to come. He hadn't texted her back, but she could hear him shifting around next door, could hear the springs of his bed creaking as he got up.

Her phone buzzed in her hand, and she looked quickly at the screen. She had five unread messages from Flo—Pinterest links and theme ideas and various other party-related things that, for some reason, made Eve's stomach drop. She didn't want to think about why, so she ignored Flo completely and checked the sisterly group chat instead.

You can't ignore Florence forever. You can't ignore your future forever.

No, not forever. Just . . . for now. While she was here, waiting for Jacob. Just for now.

DANI: Who's up for a phone call tonight? I just finished a horrifically limited essay about the future of feminism and require a palate cleanser.

CHLOE: This is Red. Chloe says she can't talk right now because she's playing comp. But I reckon she'll be done in fifteen.

Eve tapped out her own answer in a rush as she heard Jacob's bedroom door open.

EVE: Can't, about to have a meeting w my boss.

DANI: At eight o'clock in the evening?!

EVE: Could last all night, he's a sticker for details.

And she was looking forward to hearing him nitpick.

A gentle knock sounded at the door. Eve threw her phone onto the nearby weight bench and called, "Come in."

The door swung open to reveal Jacob in the jeans and shirt he considered casual, his expression uncertain. But there was a relaxation about his mouth, a smile about his eyes, that had developed over the last few days of cooking and bickering and scrubbing bathrooms together. She liked that relaxation. She liked that smile.

Because they were friends, obviously. As she was about to prove.

"Ta-dah," she said, giving him jazz hands as he looked around the room she'd rearranged. "Friend stuff."

Jacob didn't reply. He just . . . stared, in that very sharp and precise way he had, his gaze flicking about the space to catalog it all. She wondered what he saw.

Well—she knew what he saw: his various exercise apparatus pushed to the edge of the space, and the cursed sofa bed she'd been sleeping on—or rather, tortured by—dragged until it sat in front of the window. The curtains spread wide open, revealing the hot, drunken retreat of the sun, which lit up the mountains of pillows she'd stolen from the storeroom. Because Jacob, she remembered from their first strange night—the night he didn't remember at all—liked nests.

So she'd made him a nest. Not to sleep in, obviously. No, they were just going to sit here and watch the sun set and listen to music because she'd noticed that every song she sang, he seemed to know, and she wanted to test him and show him things he might like and maybe learn new songs *she* might like. And there were snacks, too, because every friendship date needed snacks.

Although, the longer he stood in silence, and the more Eve thought about the bed she'd moved and the lights she'd lowered, the more this seemed less like a friendship date and more like a clumsy, low-budget, actual date.

Which it absolutely was not meant to be.

And which he certainly would not want.

Oh, good great shit.

"It's a bonding experience with clear perambulators," she blurted out, because an explanation suddenly seemed quite urgent. "I mean—per—um—"

"I know what you meant," he said.

She swallowed and waited for him to say more. He did not. Righto, then. "Because, you know, you weren't sure how to officially become friends. So I thought . . ." Well, there hadn't been very much thought involved. It was more instinct that had driven her to this. Or some weird, unexplainable desire to sit beside Jacob with no other distractions, and just . . . talk.

Oh dear.

"I thought," she said finally, "that I could make a specific evening for you to say, *Yep, only friends do that, that's the moment we became friends*, and then—"

"Well," he cut in, "it's working. Because I'm pretty sure only friends do something this nice to make their friends feel comfortable with calling them friends. Or—oh, for fuck's sake, I don't know. Only you, Eve. Only you." He shut the door and rubbed a hand over his face, as if trying to hide his smile. Except he couldn't hide it, because gosh, it was big. Big enough that Eve's clammy palms started to calm down and her hammering heart became a much more respectable drumbeat.

She was relieved, obviously, that he hadn't taken this the wrong way. She'd been silly to think he would take it the wrong way. Why would he possibly take it the wrong way?

"So," Jacob said, walking toward her. His eyes slid over everything, everything, again and again, as if he was greedy to see it. And it occurred to her for the first time that Jacob, for all he seemed not to give a shit, might be just as pleased by the thought of being liked as she was.

He *looked* pleased. She'd made him pleased. The idea started a bloom of happiness in her chest that threatened to grow into a garden.

"So," he said again. "We're . . . sitting on your bed?"

"And listening to music and eating crap," she said firmly. "Basically a teenage girl sleepover."

"Ah." He nodded gravely. "Because no one knows how to have fun better than a group of teenage girls."

"Exactly."

He started to sit down on the bed, which made Eve realize she wasn't sitting down at all—just hovering awkwardly around the room like a nervous hostess at her first dinner party.

Arching an eyebrow, Jacob nudged the bed's duvet slightly aside to look at the sheets beneath. "Nice corners."

She flushed. Okay, yes, she'd been practicing her bed making on her own bed. She had to get good somehow. "Thanks."

He grinned that wolfish grin and finally sat. Eve swallowed. The sofa bed had seemed a perfectly reasonable place for them both to sit, until Jacob had actually done so. Now it looked like a den of lascivious temptation. Possibly because *he* looked like a lascivious temptation.

He lounged comfortably among the blankets and pillows like a prince, his long, lean body taking up space unapologetically, spread out as if on display. The breadth of his chest was emphasized by that neatly buttoned shirt, the one she'd ironed for him because she'd caught him trying to do it himself and he'd almost set his bloody cast on fire. The length of his thighs was emphasized by those jeans she *should* find unattractive, because he ironed those, too, but actually found drool-worthy, because they clung to the slight curve of his muscles in a way that told her entirely too much about how he might look naked . . .

And now she was getting all hot between her thighs on their very first friendship date. Perfect. Just perfect. Thoroughly annoyed with herself, Eve sat down.

"What are we listening to?" Jacob asked, all calm and pleasant like a . . . calm . . . pleasant thing. Meanwhile, Eve's eyes were glued to the shift of his jaw as he spoke, because Eve's eyes were very badly behaved and had no consideration for her feelings or for the feelings of her vagina.

"I set up a queue," she said, passing him her phone. "I thought, you know, we could both add to it as we went."

"I get to add to the queue?" he asked, raising his eyebrows in mock astonishment. "Me? Even though you called me a heathen for not liking Kate Bush?"

"You are a heathen for not liking Kate Bush. But I caught you humming along when I was singing 'Honor to Us All' the other day, so you do have some taste."

In the dying light of the setting sun, his blush was deep and glowing. "Liam had a mild obsession with Disney princesses, growing up."

"Oh, sure. Your cousin, definitely."

"He really did. As for myself, that's classified information."

She laughed while he tapped through her music app and added who knew what to their queue. When he passed the phone back, the tip of his middle finger grazed the curve where her palm flowed into her wrist, and Eve had to clamp down on this outrageous full-body shiver. *Friends*, she told her nervous system firmly. *We are friends.*

Her blood continued to pulse hot and stormy through her

veins, regardless. Good Lord. Jacob, poor, unaware soul, was leaning back against the cushions and cracking open a packet of crisps. Meanwhile, here she was feeling her knickers get damp. It was depraved. And also kind of hot. Wait, no—bad Eve.

"Hang on," he said, going momentarily still. "Are those biscuits? Are there biscuits in the snack pile?"

"You like biscuits?" She hadn't been sure.

"I fucking love biscuits. My first hotel job, I—" He broke off with an embarrassed little wince before pushing through with a grin. As if he was mortified, but he knew she'd like this, so he'd say it anyway. "I was sacked for eating the complimentary biscuits."

"What?" Eve's gasp was so mighty it probably drained half the oxygen from the room. "*Jacob*! I can't believe you stole. I can't believe you've been *sacked,* ever in your life."

"It wasn't stealing!" he said. "Well, it was, but I didn't mean it to be stealing. I was fourteen!"

"You were working at fourteen?"

He shot her an arch look. "You're doing that spoiled brat thing again."

"Oh, yes, sorry." She waved the question away. "You were morally bankrupt at fourteen?"

"*Hey.*"

"What? That's what I heard."

"Fuck off, Brown," he grinned, and then he leaned forward to snag a biscuit. She let the rising beat of Ravyn Lenae's "Sticky" bounce the happy bubbles in her tummy higher, while Jacob bit into a gingersnap, chewed with a slow frown, then examined the plate. Finally, he asked, "Where did you get these?" Because he was a man who noticed things, such as the lack of logo stamped into the biscuits and the crisper, more buttery taste that came from being freshly baked.

"I made them," she said.

He looked at her sharply, his head held at the lupine angle that meant he was assessing or investigating. What, she wasn't sure, until he took another bite out of the biscuit and said, "Well, fuck."

"What?"

"It never occurred to me until now. I could've been forcing you to make biscuits all this time."

"Oh, yes, add to my to-do list, you absolute slave driver."

"Maybe we could serve these at the festival."

"Not very breakfast-for-dinner-y," she reminded him mildly, "and Pemberton might get a bit pissed off if we muscle in on their gingery turf." But she was smiling because if Jacob wanted something of hers for the B&B, that meant he liked it. A lot.

"Oh. Yes. Hm. All entirely valid points," he allowed. "I suppose the sugar is going to my head. But adding sweets to the menu—we should think about that. It may be breakfast for dinner, but it *is* still dinner . . ."

"And I make a gorgeous sponge cake, which is the sort of talent one should never waste," Eve finished, nodding slowly. "Thank you for the compliment, darling."

"Er, I don't think I compli—"

"Cracking idea, really. I could bake a few cakes—they're easy enough to finish in advance and they'd make for a pretty display. £2.50 per slice, and we draw in the pudding lovers and the foodies who'd rather snack from each station than commit to an entire meal."

Jacob stared at her, looking mildly astonished. "I . . . well . . . yes. That's a very sound strategy."

She arched an eyebrow. "Try not to be so obvious about your surprise. I *can* be clever sometimes, you know." The words felt slightly foreign in her mouth, more spur-of-the-moment bravado than actual belief—yet once they were out there, Eve found she didn't want to laugh them off. In fact, they were sort of . . . true. She *could* be clever. She'd just proved it, hadn't she?

Maybe. Gosh, what a thought.

Jacob, meanwhile, was rolling his eyes. "I know you can be clever," he said in long-suffering tones. "I hired you, didn't I?"

"Barely," she snorted.

"You persuaded me into it, then. Which is more evidence of your cleverness."

"Because you're sooo difficult to outsmart," she snickered, at which point Jacob picked up a pillow and whacked her with it. So she picked up a pillow and whacked him right back, and in the midst of all that delicious immaturity, she barely had time to glow over their conversation.

It still stuck with her, though.

Clever, clever me.

♫

Hours after that sweet, surprise text, the sun had fully set and the moon had finally risen. The night sky was star-studded, the breeze through the open window smelled like cool grass, and Jacob felt a little drunk. But he'd felt this kind of drunk before—the spontaneous, can't-stop-grinning kind where, for once, he didn't care too much—and he knew what had caused it.

The woman sitting beside him, solemnly waving an empty Pringles tube in the air like it was a lighter at a concert.

"*What* are you doing?" he demanded, mostly because he couldn't fucking wait to hear it. He wanted inside her confetti-strewn head every chance he got. It was the only foreign country he could remember wanting to visit.

Now, when had that happened?

Maybe on Wednesday, when he'd asked what she was muttering to herself as they walked down the hall, and she'd said she was ranking his signature scowls from 1 (Disdainful Glare) to 10 (Torturous Stare of Imminent Death).

Or maybe it had started before then. He wasn't sure, suddenly. So it was a relief when she scattered his thoughts with her response. "I'm getting into the solemn spirit of 'Hometown Glory.' Great pick, by the way. Hey, do you think anyone's ever gotten their dick stuck in a Pringles tube?"

Christ, the shit she came out with. And what a fuckup he must be, because when she said this barely sexual nonsense so matter-of-factly—when she made silly dick jokes or winked after outrageous double entendres—he always found himself shifting in his suddenly tight jeans.

Like now.

He leaned over to grab a glass of water from the side table, which had the added benefit of hiding his groin from her view. Not that he was hard. That would be ridiculous. If he could maintain his control while lying in bed with her—while the moon turned her skin silver-dark again, and her T-shirt (TOO SOUR TO BE YOUR SWEETIE) had ridden up to reveal the swell of her bare belly—then he could maintain his control over a question about Pringles.

He sipped his water, relished the cool slide down his throat, and settled beside Eve again. "I think anyone who's big enough to get stuck in a Pringles tube has better places to put it," he said finally.

"*Jacob.*" She turned sparkling eyes in his direction. "You absolute size queen."

"Er . . . what is—?"

Eve waved an urgent hand. "Shh, shh, I like this part." She grabbed her phone and turned up the music. A dreamy expression took over her face and all the breath trickled out of her. She'd been doing this periodically—shutting him up at the crescendo of this or that song, closing her eyes and humming along like she *felt* it. Like every note ran through her blood and some hit her heart harder than others. Since Jacob could be obedient, when he felt like it, he shut his mouth and watched her in the moonlight— watched her tip her head back, watched those wide, warm eyes slide shut, watched a dreamy little smile curve her lips.

What he didn't expect was for her to sing instead of hum.

He'd heard Eve sing before. Of course he had. She sang all the time, especially when she wasn't wearing her AirPod—repetitive snatches of this chorus or that refrain, tongue-twister lines she repeated over again, instruments she imitated with unnerving accuracy. If anyone asked him, *Hey, does Eve Brown sing?* he'd roll his eyes and say, *Only all the fucking time.*

But he would've been wrong. Because apparently, all those other times, she hadn't been singing at all: she'd been playing. She'd been messing around. She'd been entertaining herself absent-mindedly, kind of like a knife-wielding assassin spinning a blade harmlessly between her fingers instead of filleting you alive in twenty seconds.

She wasn't playing this time.

This time, Eve opened her mouth and moonlight came out. Like the silver-dark of her skin, like pearlized smoke, like the siren he'd heard that night in the garden because for God's sake, Jacob, *she'd* been the voice in the garden, obviously. The voice so sweet and sharp at the edges, so husky and effortlessly *strong*— strong enough to easily seem fragile—that he'd assumed it was just his imagination.

She drew out the last, long note in the chorus like silk between her fingertips, and then she gave a breathless little laugh, opened her eyes, and took a bite out of her Mars Bar like nothing had happened. If Jacob was cool, he'd probably act like nothing had happened, too. Jacob was not cool.

"What the shit was that?"

She chewed chocolate and caramel and wrinkled her nose. "I don't know. Nothing. You're not going to be weird about it, are you?"

"Do you know who you're talking to?"

She snorted, then slapped a hand over her mouth. "Look what you're doing. I almost spat Mars Bar at you, and then you might have died. You might have gone into antigerm shock and died."

He kind of wished the thought of her spit freaked him out. If it did, the idea of swapping various bodily fluids with her might stop lurking at the edge of his consciousness.

And shit, now he'd faced the thought, he couldn't pretend it wasn't there anymore: he wanted to kiss Eve Brown. Very, very badly. In a few different places.

But not while she was eating a Mars Bar. A man had to have his limits.

You will not kiss her at all. Sensible, starched Jacob rose from the ashes of himself and corrected tonight's giddy, contact-high, Eve-addicted Jacob with a stern look and a sharp tone. There would be no kissing. It wasn't proper or practical and there were ten thousand issues of consent, and anyway, what would happen after the kiss? Jacob knew what he'd *want* to happen: when he liked a woman enough to kiss her, he liked that woman enough to keep her, too.

But there were social scripts to be observed beyond fondness > physical contact > emotional commitment, and even if those scripts had never felt natural to Jacob, he'd learned them well enough to copy. So. No kissing and claiming. It wasn't fashionable, and if you did it too quickly, you wound up with a woman who was more interested in what you could do with your tongue than she was in your sudoku skills or your conversation. The kind of woman who left.

None of which mattered in this situation, because a man simply could not *claim* his chef. Aside from anything else, it would take him straight back to the ten thousand issues of consent.

"Oh dear," Eve was saying, "you have. You have gone into shock and died."

Jacob realized he had been silent for far too many seconds. "Stop talking rubbish. When were you going to tell me you could . . ." He trailed off for a moment, uncomfortable with every description of her voice that came to mind. They all seemed too gushing, or too distant, or too inadequate to describe a talent that felt embedded into her soul. He didn't want to treat this as a party trick when, apparently, singing as if she should be on a stage was just *Eve*. In the end, he vaguely motioned to her throat and finished awkwardly, "When were you going to tell me you could do that?"

"When it became something that matters, which—oh, look, it hasn't."

"Eve," he said, "everything about you matters." And then he briefly but seriously considered ripping out his own tongue.

CHAPTER THIRTEEN

Everything about you matters.

Eve might have fainted—might have swooned into a pile of dust, kind of like she did when she reached the romantic declaration part of her favorite horny fanfics—if it weren't for the rest of Jacob's little speech.

"We're friends now," he said. "Friends share, correct?"

Ah. Yes. Friendship. That was how she'd ended up lying in bed beside him under a gorgeous night sky, her skin fizzing with the electricity of his quiet, contained nearness and her mind veering into forbidden territory every five minutes. *Friendship.* Obviously. Hm.

"It didn't seem relevant," she said at last. "So I like to sing. You know that. What else is there?"

"You can't tell me," he said, "that it's not important to you. When you sing like that. It has to be important to you."

She knew what he meant. People had their things, right? You could be shitty at this or that, but everyone had at least one *thing*, and they loved their thing, and they were proud of their thing.

She'd been proud of her thing, too, until she'd tried to make it her life and failed. Now it was just . . . there. Part of her, a pleasure, but a reminder, too, when she was in the worst of her moods.

Whatever Jacob read in her silence, or saw in her face, it made him shake his head and put a hand on her shoulder. That hand seemed so heavy, so hot, she was surprised it didn't slide right through her bones like a knife through butter. "Don't," he said.

"Don't what?"

"Whatever you're thinking. Don't. There isn't much that takes the smile out of you like this, so whatever's on your mind can't be good."

His words were a soft and tender shock, bare of all sarcasm or dry critique, like he'd taken off his clothes just to show her his naked skin. Like maybe he was waiting for her to do the same.

Not that this topic was half so serious as her melodramatic mind always made it out to be. As proof of that fact—for him, for herself—she huffed a sigh and stared at the stars as she spoke. "I used to think I would perform. Always, you know? That it would be my future. Because I was so good—everyone swore I was good—so that had to be my destiny. But good isn't all it takes. Especially when you look like me."

"You look perfect," he said, the words quick and razor-sharp with their certainty. They caught her unawares, like a flash of lightning in the dark. When she turned her head to look at him, he wasn't blushing or figuring out how to take it back. He was watching her steadily, as if he'd known she'd instantly try to poke holes in his statement, and he refused to let her. "You look perfect," he said again, each word falling like a petal onto a tranquil lake.

She smiled, then, because he deserved it. And a little bit because . . . well, because he seemed to mean it, which fluffed her up inside like cotton candy.

Jacob Wayne thought she was perfect.

And, beneath all the barbed-wire keep-your-distance ice-god bullshit, she thought there was no one sweeter in all the world than him.

"Thank you," she said. "But you realize plenty of other people disagree."

"I don't give a fuck about other people."

"Neither do I," she said honestly. When it came to her appearance, Eve had long since learned that giving a shit about others' opinions meant slipping under an ocean of negativity. So she'd decided a while back that she was beautiful, and her body was lovely, and she would accept no other judgment on the subject. "But I used to. Back when I wanted to be the star of the show so badly, I cared a lot. You see, I was always rather shit at school. I was slow on the uptake and I didn't test well and my memory—let's not even talk about it. So I told myself, you know, it didn't matter, because I wasn't meant for that sort of thing. I was meant to be a star. I got so convinced that I just stopped trying. I was never going to be smart like my sisters, and I was never going to need it, so I might as well give up.

"But then I finished secondary, and my parents sent me to a performing arts college, and I wasn't . . . I wasn't the best. I'd convinced myself I just had to wait, and I'd eventually be the best at something. But I'd been wrong. I didn't hit the right emotional marks, and my memory issue was a problem, script-wise, and I was terrible at being told what to do. And then, on top of it all, there was the look." She pressed her lips together and flicked a glance at Jacob because, well, this part was so excruciatingly awkward to speak about. Some people wanted to pretend they didn't understand, as if her prettiness negated all the other things she was, and all the ways those other things didn't fit in with society's expectations.

Then there were the people who acted like it shouldn't hurt, being rejected by the status quo like that. As if, because it came from a twisted place of inequality, it shouldn't have any hold on her. Which was a nice idea in principle, but Eve found it mostly came from those who'd never been personally crushed by the weight of all that disapproval.

Jacob wasn't reacting like one of those people, though. He was simply sitting quietly, watching in silence, letting her speak. Because he was like that, when it mattered. He was like that.

"The look," she said again. "I didn't have it. I was too fat and too dark and not entirely symmetrical, so I had to be the evil background character or the comedic relief or whatever. People told me to pay my dues and change things from the inside, and I saw others doing that. But I didn't want to. And none of us should have to. So I left.

"And I think that was my first taste of failure. I didn't entirely blame myself—I couldn't, all things considered. But it was still so . . . bitter." She could taste it now, on the tip of her tongue, a thousand flavors piled high—from all the classes she'd once escaped by fantasizing about her star-studded future, to the day she'd thrown her gnome costume at that uptight director and walked out. And even though the gnome thing gave her a little aftershock of satisfaction, it just wasn't enough.

"I probably should've kept trying, somehow. It was what I really, really wanted, after all. But I was so exhausted. I loved it, but I was done." And then the rest of her failures had started. "Being done meant going back to the real world. New A levels, university, choosing a career path. My parents were understanding and supportive, my sisters were always on my side, and I had—God, Jacob, I had every fucking option. Sometimes I feel ashamed, I had so much in front of me. And I didn't want any of it. I couldn't *do* any of it. I went back to school and I failed in a thousand different ways. My parents practically cheated my way into university but I failed my first year. And I'd *tried*, Jacob. I actually tried."

She'd never told anyone that. She'd gotten her last coursework grade just before finals and accepted, once and for all, that even a perfect score couldn't save her. All the hours at the library making her eyes bleed, all the desperate emails to professors clarifying this point or that point because she struggled to follow the lectures, it had been for nothing.

She'd tried and she'd failed. So she'd told her parents she was bored, and weathered their disapproval, and chosen a new course and tried again.

And failed, of course.

But she didn't need to get into all that—even if she had a sneaking suspicion that she just had, that Jacob could read between her every line even if she stopped the pity party here. Which she fully intended to do. How had she gotten this far off the rails? He'd asked about her voice. She'd told him . . .

Everything.

"Sorry," she said. "Sorry. It doesn't matter."

"Doesn't it?" he asked. Except it didn't sound like he was really asking; it sounded like he was giving her an opening to keep going, to talk more, to release the rest of the bottled-up poison inside her. To say things like, *I think I'm only capable of fuckups and not-quite-enoughs*, just to get it out there before it burned up her insides.

She was about to take that opening. She could feel the words crowding the tip of her tongue. But then something else came along: a memory of the way she'd felt that morning, serving a fluffy tomato omelet and having old Mr. Cafferty from the Rose Suite dimple up at her and say, *You know how I like it, Eve. Oh, you are a wonder.*

That hadn't felt like failure at all. It had felt like creation and nourishment and openhearted generosity—and syrup-sweet success.

"I told you before," Jacob said into the silence, "that there are different ways to fail. Imperfection is inevitable. That's life. But it doesn't sound to me like you've failed at all, Eve. It sounds like your dream broke, and you've been picking up shattered pieces and blaming yourself when your hands bleed." In the low light, his gaze almost seemed to shine at her, slices of summer sky warming her up. "Performing was your dream, yeah. Is it still?"

She blurted out the truth without thinking twice. "No." Because she really did hate being told what to do—or she *had*, when it came to something that should stem from her soul. To have someone directing her voice, her emotions, her interpretation of words and characters she'd understood in her own way; that had seemed a violation every time, and deep inside she'd hated it.

She loved music, loved performing, but she didn't want to make it her livelihood. It wouldn't suit her. She'd learned that at some point over the years.

"Well," Jacob said reasonably, "do you know what you want instead?"

She couldn't answer. She couldn't answer because she'd never had a chance to ask herself that question. She'd been too busy expecting herself to simply know, and get on with it already, and succeed.

Oh, gosh.

Oh, fudge.

What if the thing she'd failed hardest was . . . herself?

Some thoughts were too big to accept all at once. She shoved this one frantically to the back of her mind before it could crack her wide open, but traces of it still lingered—like the ghost of a sparkler after you'd waved it through the air. Bright and dangerous and not-really-there.

"I like it here," she said out loud. "I like—my job."

Jacob's serious expression dissolved into a beaming smile. "You do?"

Oh, she did. And not just because so much of it revolved around this man, with his insatiable curiosity and his blunt impatience and his intense eyes. Not just because of Jacob.

But he was on the list of things to like.

"I do," she confirmed, and for a moment that pleased her—she had a job, just like her parents wanted, and she was getting along very well, and she was even having fun. But then she remembered that all this was temporary. It was a favor Jacob didn't know he'd asked for. It wasn't real. In three weeks, she'd be gone, back to her old world, planning obnoxious parties for Florence's shitty brother even though she barely liked Florence or Florence's brother or anyone else she knew.

Fuck.

But maybe that was why Castell Cottage came so sweet and so easy; because it wasn't really for her.

She shoved the last bite of her Mars Bar in her mouth and chewed as the music went from introspective piano to the staccato beat of Hayley Kiyoko's "Curious." This conversation was dragging her down, down, down into a mire of confusion when what she wanted was to stay *up*. For goodness' sake, this was a friendship date. She was supposed to be enjoying Jacob's rare and adorably earnest happiness, not sloshing her life's woes all over him.

So she turned to face him with an almost-smile that would become real in a minute, if he'd take the hint and help. "I think that's enough talk about *my* life choices."

He hesitated, but she saw the moment when he decided to let it go.

She also saw that he wouldn't let this go forever.

"How did you know," she asked, "that you wanted to do this? Run a place like this, I mean?"

He shrugged, turning to stare out of the window. "I . . . you know about my childhood. I never did enjoy traveling. But when I was twelve—a couple of years after I arrived in Skybriar—Lucy said we were going on holiday. I was horrified. I suppose, in my mind, you either went on holiday forever or you stayed at home, and one of those things was good and one was bad."

Her heart squeezed for all the things he didn't say. Because the fact was, plenty of people lived their lives on the road—entire communities, entire cultures. And *those* travelers never seemed hollow and restless when they talked about a life on the move.

But those travelers had homes and families that moved with them, and it sounded like Jacob's parents had provided neither.

"I didn't want to go, but Liam was excited, and Lucy was pleased she'd managed to save up, so." He shrugged again. "I kept my mouth shut. And in the end . . ." A slow smile spread over his face, unexpected and twice as lovely for it. "In the end, I had a great time. It was nothing like before. I could shower whenever I wanted, I didn't have to stay with strangers or be alone in strange places. We all stuck together—we enjoyed things together. It was the best week of my life, at that point. We stayed at a bed-and-breakfast, and it almost felt like being at home. I left wanting to be that—wanting to do that for people. Any way I could. To provide everyone with a home, so when they traveled, they could enjoy it instead of wanting to die."

The way he said *everyone*—the burning passion in his voice, it made her heart smile. "And that's why you mention additional needs so prominently on your website," Eve realized out loud.

He turned to look at her. "What?"

"Oh." *Don't blush. Don't blush. Don't*—she felt heat flood her cheeks and wanted to roll her eyes. All she'd done was read the man's bloody website, for Christ's sake. It wasn't as if she'd spied on him naked or . . . or hovered by the partially open doorway of his bedroom to take another look at the cool world of order hiding inside and enjoy the sheer Jacobness of it.

Ahem.

Okay, maybe she had done that last one a few times.

"I ordered a tablet," she said casually. "I've been researching Castell Cottage. Amongst other things."

He gave her a look of squint-eyed disbelief, but she couldn't tell if checking out the website had been that weird, or if he was hung up on her ordering a tablet. She had noticed that her own idea of *No money* and Jacob's idea were vastly different. Trying to be sensitive about that difference was an interesting learning curve.

Her sisters weren't like this. Her sisters already knew how to budget, how to work hard and pay bills and all those other normal, adult things. Eve really was a joke.

Used to be, she corrected herself. But she was changing, now.

"It was on sale," she said quickly, which it had been, "and you mentioned I'd be getting paid, soon, so—"

"You don't have to justify what you buy to me, Eve. But I should've thought to offer you my computer."

"It's fine. Anyway. Back to the point," she said, because something about the tap of Jacob's long fingers against his thighs told her he was avoiding this topic. "On your website, I noticed you have a section encouraging people to contact you directly about any particular needs, including those relating to sensory or other issues."

He flushed beautifully, which she enjoyed more than a friend should. "Erm. Yes. Well. Some people like different sheets, or weighted blankets, or they can't cope with certain scents, or a thousand other things, and I like to be sure that—that everyone who stays here is perfectly comfortable."

Eve bit her lip on a hopeless grin. This man wasn't just softer and kinder and sweeter than anyone suspected, he was practically *made* of *cake. Good* cake. With chocolate-fudge icing. She wanted to eat him so badly. Instead, she waved her hands around and sputtered, "For God's sake, Jacob, you—do you have to be so bloody—"

He shuffled away from her flailing arms, then winced and adjusted some cushions. He'd probably fallen foul of the sofa bed's awful springs. Served him right for shorting out all her circuits with his cuteness.

"Why—this is—"

"Are you all right, Eve?" he asked, raising an eyebrow.

"I'm fine," she managed. "Just trying to come to terms with the fact that you work so hard at this B&B stuff because of your *principles*. And your passion. And all sorts of other . . . *p* words." She paused. "Not penis. I didn't mean penis."

"Why on earth would I think you meant penis?"

Genuinely surprised, she cocked her head. "That isn't the first *p* word that pops into your mind?"

"Jesus Christ, Eve, no."

"Ohhh. Is it pussy?"

"*Stop* saying—" The muscle in his jaw performed a fascinating dance and his left hand dug into a cushion so hard she was worried he might rip it apart. "Stop saying . . . those things."

Oh dear. She cleared her throat and moved swiftly on. "I'm just in a constant state of mild shock-horror over your high levels of decency." Mostly because she herself couldn't fathom such thoughtfulness, and also because he was so good at pretending to live in a mental ice palace.

Jacob shifted uncomfortably under her praise and muttered, "Please. If I was that decent I'd be paying you for all the extra work you do."

She blinked. He'd said something like this before, but she'd assumed he'd been joking. Apparently, it was actually bothering him. "Don't be silly. I know you can't afford overtime."

Because Jacob was Jacob, he didn't snarl at the implication or sink into a manly spiral of despair over his reduced circumstances. He just laughed and said, "Oh, so you've noticed I'm poor as shit. I wasn't sure you understood how money worked."

"Har-har. You've told me before that you put all your savings into Castell Cottage. And since I help with the ironing, I am aware you only have three work shirts." She supposed he spent his clothing budget on those little complimentary soaps, the artisanal ones with local honey in them that he arranged just *so* in every guest bathroom.

"You've been counting my shirts, Evie? That is beyond a man's dignity." But he was still smiling beneath his injured expression.

It was a tiny quirk to the lips, a brightness in his eyes that made everything between them as golden as the honey in those soaps.

They could tease and they could share and they could be comfortable together, and she loved it. She loved it.

So she did some more teasing, since he took it so well. "I think it's charming that you are poor as a noble church mouse."

"I think you must've been raised in a palace on Cloud Unicorn because you are the most ridiculous thing." But he said the words fondly. He said them so fondly, with such tenderness in his eyes, that she felt slightly faint for a moment. She felt like squirming under that gentle smile, like covering her heated face with both hands or collapsing at his feet or . . . or . . .

That was definitely enough teasing for one day. She cleared her throat and got back to business. "Don't forget the extra work is because I broke your wrist. And anyway, I researched, and I know you actually pay higher than average."

"I pay a living wage, Eve. The real one, not the government bullshit."

"Do you pay *yourself* a living wage?"

"Quiet, baggage." He reached over and pushed at her shoulder—just the quickest, lightest touch, one that barely connected, as if he was afraid she might topple off the bed and knock herself out on the side table. Or maybe he touched her so lightly because he felt the same thing she did: the electric shiver down her spine, a silver streak of heat, every time his skin brushed hers.

Maybe.

"And what do you mean you *researched*?" he snorted. "What, you had no point of reference?"

Eve shrugged. "You've read my CV."

"You mean the document you emailed me that included two weeks spent as a fire-eater at a resort hotel? I have to say, Sunshine, I assumed you were taking the piss with that."

Her mind stuttered and restarted over *sunshine*. Had he . . . just said that word? Or rather, had he just said it *at* her? As in . . . *she* . . . was the sunshine?

"Please tell me you were taking the piss," he went on. "I am begging you. Because if you weren't, I now have to come to terms with the fact that you spent a month as an abseiling instructor in Wales."

This was the part where she passionately denied her checkered past as an abseiling instructor, or threw caution to the wind and boldly admitted to it. But her whole mind, possibly her entire nervous system, was still occupied with that little *sunshine* slip.

I have to say, Sunshine . . .

Perhaps she'd misheard him. Perhaps he'd developed a stutter or he was so high on sugar he'd started to slur.

Except, after the beat of her silence, he gave a wry smile. "You seem distracted."

"Mmm," she managed.

"I can hear you overthinking."

"Well," she blurted, "you can't blame me."

"Because of the sunshine thing." He didn't make it a question, but she answered anyway.

"Yes indeed."

"I was hoping you hadn't noticed."

"Silly of you."

"Yes. I have come to realize you notice everything." He looked personally inconvenienced by that fact. "I know you think you aren't clever, Eve. You are."

"Are you trying to distract me from the sunshine comment?" she asked hoarsely. Because it was sort of working. He gave a lovely compliment, did Jacob. The part where it seemed like pulling teeth for him made it extra genuine.

"Yes, I was trying to distract you."

"Ah."

He ran a hand through the soft mess of his hair. Eve's own fingers twitched, just a little, in her lap. "I expect it's thrown you. The sudden nickname thing."

"Oh, it has," she said. *Into a pool of pleasure.*

"But we are official friends, now. You should've known I might get carried away."

Truthfully, she murmured, "I didn't think anything could carry Jacob Wayne away."

He met her gaze. "Apparently, you can."

She tried not to choke on her rocketing heart or her sudden, horny feelings.

"Usually, I try to compliment you," he said, "and it comes out like an insult. So. When I accidentally say something true, something that matches what's in my head . . ." He lifted his chin and looked at her steadily, as if daring her to argue. "I'm not going to take it back."

Slightly breathless, she murmured, "I don't think you should. Take it back, I mean. You should be as . . . *yourself* as you can."

"It takes practice, around people I haven't known very long. But with you it's coming along nicely."

She swallowed hard. "Practice makes perfect. Do it again."

"No."

"I'll wait." A smile spread across her face. "Hey—does this mean I get to give you a nickname?"

He gave her a withering look. "Absolutely not."

"But, Mushroom!"

"Piss off, Eve."

"But—my dear, sweet Raspberry!"

"Just for that," he said, and then he snagged the box of Jaffa Cakes and ate the last one.

She released a gasp of genuine horror. "*Jacob!*"

"That's better."

"You *bastard*."

"You were warned, woman."

"Don't you mean Sunshine?"

He swallowed the last bite and grinned. "Don't let it go to your head." Just as quick, the smile was replaced by a frown as he shifted and looked down at the bed. "For fuck's sake, these springs. What . . ." He trailed off as he rummaged among the sofa cushions. "Oh. I think I'm sitting on something."

And then he rummaged some more and produced a giant purple dildo that may or may not have belonged to Eve.

CHAPTER FOURTEEN

If there was one thing Jacob hadn't seen coming, it was to find himself holding a glittery, silicon dick before the day was out. But he should've known to expect the unexpected around Eve.

Still, the idea that he could've predicted *this* was . . . he wanted to think *impossible* or maybe even *horrifying*, but all his brain threw up was *fascinating*. He gripped the sturdy length—Christ, what was this thing, twelve inches?—and held it up to the moonlight, watching it sparkle. Because of course, Eve's dildo sparkled.

And now that he'd actually thought the phrase *Eve's dildo*, every filthy desire he'd crammed into his mental Don't Think About It cupboard simultaneously kicked down the door and burst free.

"Oh my God," she said, her eyes wide and her hands pressed to her cheeks. He imagined those cheeks were hot and blushing under her palms, and then he imagined a similar heat flushing her entire body as she lay back on this bed—*this fucking bed*—and eased off her underwear and rubbed the head of this toy over her pussy. Would she do it under the covers or on top? Would she slick this big thing up first? With lube, or with her mouth?

"Jacob," she practically shrieked, "say something."

He dragged his gaze away from the toy and back to her. "Does it vibrate?"

"What? I think I've broken you. You're broken. Admit it." She sounded genuinely worried. Looked it, too. She'd sunk her teeth into the plump pillow of her lower lip, and Jacob, still drowning beneath the murky waters of sudden lust, wanted to know if she bit her lip just like that when she came.

"I am so sorry," she was saying. "I have no idea how I—um, I completely forgot to—Jacob, you should probably put that down." But her voice wavered on the last word, her chest rising and falling with each breath.

He met her gaze. Arched an eyebrow. Asked calmly, "Why?" And was gratified when she sucked on that bottom lip rather than answering.

He didn't want to let this thing go. He couldn't, not right now. He was . . . studying it. Every plastic ridge and vein. Did she feel that, when it was inside her? Did she care about the finer details, or was she just chasing the thick stretch, the snug fullness a toy like this must give? And she'd never told him if it vibrated or not. He hadn't heard anything through their shared wall—but God only knew when she'd been using it.

Christ, what if she'd been using it next fucking door while he'd been staring at the ceiling, determinedly thinking of anything but Eve's arse in her jeans and Eve's hands as she sliced tomatoes and Eve's mouth, smiling at him? He'd spent half of last night wide awake, playing fucking sudoku, trying to ignore the fact that it was her presence keeping him on the edge. And this whole time she'd been over here with *this*. He hadn't even stroked himself in the shower, this last week, because he'd known deep down inside he'd think of her.

Maybe that's why the voice of reason that usually controlled his actions was growing softer and softer, violently muffled by all his want. Maybe this was exactly what people meant when they used the phrase *Tipped over the edge*.

"You . . . don't want to touch that," Eve managed. She sounded like she was reassuring herself, reciting the rules of Usual Jacob in the face of a Jacob who wasn't behaving usually at all. "You should've dropped it five minutes ago. You—you—it's a foreign object and you don't know where it's been."

"I know where it's been," he said, and his voice came out . . . different. Like the smoke and desire in his head was ripping through his throat, too, coloring every word. He thought about exactly where this toy had been and felt his cock press stiff and fat against the zipper of his jeans, the slight bite of pain the only thing bringing him back to his senses. Back to a point resembling cool control. He had to retain control, because only then could he push delicately at Eve's embarrassment.

He was fascinated by it—just as surely as he was fascinated by the toy she'd been fucking. Not half an hour ago this woman had been nattering about penises and pussies with laughter in her voice; she made dick jokes every time she cooked sausages; she came out with *That's what she said* more often than a fifteen-year-old boy. Yet now she covered her eyes with her hands, practically vibrating with a discomfort that gleamed like ripe fruit in the sun.

"You're blushing," he said.

She peeked at him through her fingers, those cautious dark eyes sending a thrill over his skin. "You are holding my dildo, Jacob."

"So you admit it's yours."

"No, it's yours. You must have lost it on the sofa months ago." But the joke lacked her usual humor, the words softening until they were just gasps with shape. He wondered if she was thinking of him lying here with something just like this, fucking himself. He hoped she was, even if that seemed anatomically unlikely. What did he know about the sexual capabilities of his arse, anyway? Maybe it was perfectly possible.

Maybe she was imagining all the ways it could be perfectly possible.

Or maybe she was so mortified right now because Jacob was utterly alone in his illicit feelings and making a complete fool of himself.

Now, wasn't that possibility a bucket of ice water?

Abruptly, Jacob put the toy down on a side table.

Eve released a sigh of relief and flopped back on the bed, flinging an arm over her eyes.

"I apologize," he said.

"No," she murmured. "No, it's . . ." and then she trailed off. God only knew what *that* meant.

If he had an ounce of sense or self-respect, this would be a great moment to de-escalate the situation. But he must have lost those somewhere down the line, because instead of changing the subject—or, you know, throwing himself out of the window—Jacob simply looked at her. Looked, and let himself notice the soft plumpness of her arms, the dark and delicate lines etched into her palms. The fat curve of her breasts beneath her T-shirt. The hem had ridden up a little and he could see the strip of skin just above her leggings. He could see her bare hips. He could see the beginnings of a scar on her right side—appendectomy, it looked like. He'd seen that kind of scar before.

But it felt like he'd never seen Eve. Or rather, like he'd been working incredibly hard to keep his eyes closed, and now he was exhausted so his eyes were wide open. Only, she was hiding, which suggested she did not want to be seen.

Jacob was gathering the frayed edges of his control when she peeked out at him and asked, "Are you going to make fun of me for the next thousand centuries?"

"You think I'm going to make fun of you," he said. Thank God his voice was strained enough that the words came out flat and harsh, instead of dripping with inappropriate desire and—and hope. Because Eve was gloriously unselfconscious about sex, and she certainly didn't give a damn for his opinions—not usually, anyway. Only when it mattered. So why would this matter?

Some people talked about their feelings sneaking up on them, but Jacob's feelings tended to smack him over the head with a baseball bat. Right now he was seeing stars and fighting a second concussion, because he'd just learned something about himself: he didn't really want to be Eve's friend.

No; that was wrong. He did. He definitely did. He wanted to be Eve's friend, *plus* . . .

God save him, he should not investigate that plus.

But when she muttered, "I *know* you're going to make fun of me," he felt like a wolf catching sight of soft, sweet prey. Like he couldn't give up the chase if he'd wanted to.

"And why's that, Sunshine?" he asked softly, holding himself very, very still, because if he moved, she might look down and notice his massive erection.

"Because you're too sensible to masturbate," she said, but as soon as the words were out, she seemed to realize they were ridiculous. She bit her lip and shook her head and started again. "You're too sensible to masturbate the way I do."

Dear God, he almost collapsed. His muscles almost gave out, possibly because every last drop of his blood had just reported for duty at his cock. He twisted his fist into the sheets so he couldn't grab himself to ease that heavy pressure.

"And what way is that?" he asked. Impressive, how there was only a hint of gravelly, *I'm so horny I might die* filth in his tone.

"With a glittery dildo and fanfiction about Captain America's tits," she said.

Jacob made a mental note to double up on chest day once his wrist had healed.

"Look! Look!" She pointed at his face. "You're freaking out."

"I'm not."

"You are. You're horrified. You wank quietly and efficiently in the shower so all the evidence is washed away, don't you?"

He swallowed, hard. His hips punched up, just a little, when she said *You wank*. She was talking about him. She was thinking about him. Had she thought about him? "It's easier, doing it in the shower."

"I knew it. And you probably think about, like, disembodied tits or something equally inoffensive and—"

"Have you thought about this a lot? What I think about?" The question was out there before he could stop it.

And her response was just as quick, just as reckless. "Well, yes. But when I think about it, your fantasies aren't inoffensive at all."

♫

Was it possible to stuff words back into your mouth? Eve had asked herself that question several times over the years, but never quite so passionately as she did now.

What the ever-loving fudgesicle had she just said?

Bad enough that she'd forgotten all about the dildo hidden beneath the cushions. Even worse that it had disturbed Jacob deeply enough for his jaw to clench this tightly—so tightly she was genuinely worried he might crack a tooth. But to top it all off, she'd sort of accidentally given him a hint that she desperately fancied him. Him, and his big shoulders, and the way he nudged his glasses up his nose, and that air of calm control he had over everything, and the way that air vanished abruptly whenever he lost his shit.

He was probably going to lose his shit right now. He was probably going to give her the mother of all lectures about appropriate workplace relationships and friendly interactions, and then he might throw several handbooks at her head and lock her in this room and possibly call a priest to cleanse the horniness out of her.

Except he . . . didn't. Instead, he leaned closer—so close she stopped breathing. She actually held her breath, and the tightness in her chest was mirrored by a sudden, delicious squeeze in her lower belly. Even lower, if she was being honest. She'd been hot and glittering inside since the moment he'd examined her sex toy with such laser focus. When he'd wrapped his long, strong fingers around something she'd orgasmed on just last night, she'd felt her clit swell. He'd tilted his head as he stared at it, questioning her in that steel-and-stone voice, and her breasts had felt heavy. Her pulse throbbed between her thighs. Every fold of her pussy grew slick and sensitive, rubbing against the dampened cotton of her underwear.

And now here he was, leaning so, so close, and everything was getting worse. Arousal wound through her body as slow and sinuous as the music playing in the background. Which was "Special Affair" by The Internet, because of course a sexy-as-shit song would start playing right now. Of *course* it would.

She shifted slightly in her seat, hoping the action was subtle, but apparently it wasn't.

"You're wriggling, Eve."

"Well," she huffed, "you could be a gentleman and not point it out." But there was no irritation in her voice; she was too breathless, and too desperate, for that.

"I could," he agreed, before continuing to ask questions that made her bare skin feel electrified. "Are you uncomfortable?"

"I—" She shifted just so and the cushion beneath her became a sweet pressure between her thighs.

"Oh," he said softly. "Not anymore."

She looked up at him sharply and saw, in those cool eyes, a

white-hot understanding. One so certain, it made her wonder what he saw in *her* face. "Jacob—"

"What do I fantasize about, in your head? Tell me. You might be closer to the truth than you expect."

Oh. Oh, gosh.

It had occurred to her occasionally over the past week (mostly when he looked at her chest for a moment too long): *Maybe Jacob is attracted to me.* But she'd dismissed the thought every time, because Jacob was too sensible for inconvenient feelings, and because they'd barely even liked each other for five minutes, and because—because *she* was attracted to *him*, so clearly her perception couldn't be trusted. She'd chalked it all up to wishful thinking and attempted to move on.

But now common sense was slapping her in the face with a list of facts a mile long, starting with him calling her Sunshine and ending with the way his tongue slid out to wet the curve of his lower lip. His eyes were hungry on her, his focus dizzying. *Not just wishful thinking.*

Not at all, apparently.

If she was smart, she would end this conversation now. After all, she *wanted* him, which meant he couldn't possibly be good for her. Eve's wants, Eve's choices, were always mistakes.

But she did have a habit of making those mistakes. So it was no surprise, in the end, when she opened her mouth and gave in.

"I think you fantasize about me." She'd seen it in her mind's eye a thousand times, now. Had heard the shower turn on from down the hall, and imagined his grip harsh and punishing over his flushed cock. Imagined him gritting his teeth as he came in his own hand and breathed her name.

She'd just never expected, in a thousand years, to say as much to him. And she'd never expected to have him reply—"*Yes.*"

He came even closer to her in the semidark, and then the knees of their crossed legs were nudging together, and his good hand created a dip in the mattress as he leaned on it, and his forehead bumped hers. Eve's eyelids fluttered shut as his breath, still biscuit-sweet, ghosted against her mouth. "Yes," he said again, "I think about you. I've been trying to stop. I haven't—I haven't even touched myself because that would make it wrong, Eve, really wrong, but I've been thinking and I haven't been able to stop."

Her breaths were quick and so, so loud over the background hum of the music, but his were quicker and louder and that turned her frenetic, nervous lust into something slower and more sure. He'd pushed out his words as if his throat was thick with this forbidden need, as if he didn't even want to say them—like he was clinging to them desperately with bloodied hands but they escaped on an uncontrollable wave anyway. She was being wanted, if not completely then too passionately to deny, and it settled over her like a blanket of snow and a wall of midsummer heat all at once: bright and fresh enough to suck the air from her lungs, but languorous and sensual, too.

"We should do something about this," she said.

"No." But he didn't sit back, didn't stop touching her. He touched her *more*. He leaned an elbow against the high sofa cushions, because his wrist couldn't support him, and then he used his other hand to—to touch her cheek, a barely there caress.

She shivered.

"It would be a terrible idea," he went on steadily. "I'm too hard, at present, to remember *why* it would be a terrible idea, but I feel certain that it would."

"Probably because we're trying to be friends," she supplied, "and because of the whole employ—"

"Don't say it," he cut in. "At least, not before I kiss you."

"You're going to kiss me?" She swallowed, a heavy swirl of pure want spiraling out from her pussy to skate through her entire body.

"I don't know," he said softly. "I shouldn't. I didn't intend to. But look at your *face*."

She flushed. "What—what about my face?"

"You're so obviously horny," he said. Which was rather mortifying, until he followed up with, "It's very difficult to resist. So, yes, I think I'll definitely be kissing you. As long as you'd like me to. Would you like me to, Evie?"

It was the understatement of the century, but all she could manage was, "Yes."

And apparently that was all it took for Jacob to be done talking. His hand slid from her cheek to her hair, and he gathered her braids in a gentle fist and angled her head with the same aching precision he used to angle display pillows. Then he kissed her with a lack of restraint that blew said precision out of the water.

Her pulse fluttered, desperate and relieved. A pool of liquid light glimmered behind her closed eyelids. For a moment all she could think was, *I must be yours and clearly you are mine.*

Fortunately, her vagina quickly took over proceedings and replaced all those fanciful feelings with good, old-fashioned arousal.

Eve moaned against the firm press of his lips, because her sensitized nerves had been ready for more of his delicacy, yet he'd given her pure passion instead. His tongue flicked out against the inside of her upper lip, a subtle yet insistent whip of warm, wet softness. Her mouth opened on a gasp and his tongue slipped deeper, teasing and taunting as his big body pressed against hers.

She could feel his cast resting on the sofa cushions behind her head, the heat of his broad body directly in front of her, his left hand in her hair completing the cocoon of Jacob she'd been trapped inside. And she liked being trapped by him, being close to him. Liked it even more when he grunted and dragged his hand lower, down her throat and over the swell of her breast. She arched into his touch and he squeezed—sudden, strong, unapologetic. He just—he fucking *groped* her, and it was so un-Jacoblike and yet so completely *him* in its ruthless demand, her pussy seemed to dissolve into a pile of glitter. Wet glitter, if the sudden flood in her underwear was anything to go by.

She shifted a little, searching for the pressure her body demanded, wanting this—wanting him—too much to be slow and measured. Sometimes, when Eve had sex, she felt like she should be stiller, quieter, in case whoever she was with realized that she genuinely lost her mind when she was horny, and they found it weird or overwhelming.

Quite a few people had found it weird or overwhelming.

But she felt oddly certain that Jacob wouldn't be one of those people. And when she whimpered a little and sort of humped a pillow, she was proved right. Because all he did was break the kiss and pull back to look at her writhing body, and all he said was, "God, you're amazing."

Eve bit the fleshy part of her hand, just under her thumb, because if she didn't, she might bite him.

"But we should stop," he said. Only, he sounded a little hypnotized and he was still watching her with burning blue eyes. "We should really, probably stop. For the sake of professionalism, if nothing else."

"No, thank you," Eve said. "Here, let me get rid of my bra."

He released an agonized sound and fell back against the cushions. "I'm going to have to take my glasses off, aren't I?"

"And why's that?" she asked, wriggling frantically out of her T-shirt and fumbling with her bra clasp. Jacob appeared outright inebriated with lust right now, his pupils blown and his cock a solid column beneath his jeans—but God only knew when he'd find his usual sternness and really put a stop to this. She wanted as much pleasure as possible before he came over all sensible again.

"Because," he said, removing his glasses carefully as he spoke, "if I kept them on while I buried my face in your tits, I'd probably bend the frames."

"Oh," she said faintly, collapsing under the weight of her enthusiasm. "Gosh. Okay. Off with the glasses, then."

"Mmm." He put them on a nearby table, then turned and grabbed her hip. His hand was strong as steel, almost as if he was pinning her in place so he could lower his head and stare at her body the same way he stared at everything: with unnerving focus and obvious intent. He exhaled, hard and sharp, as his gaze moved worshipfully over her curves. Then he pressed his face against her belly and grazed his teeth over her flesh.

"*Oh*," she gasped, the sensation shooting straight to her clit.

He licked the spot he'd bitten before moving upward. "Sorry. You look like you taste good."

"And do I?"

His gaze flicked up to meet hers, his voice a low growl. "Eve. You must know that you do." And then his inexorable examination continued. His hand slid up, up, up the length of her body, until he was cupping her bare breast, his thumb sweeping over the peaked nipple.

A whimper fell from Eve's lips as she arched against the pillows, her thighs spreading automatically, the space between her legs feeling hollow and hungry and aching for—something. Pressure. Pleasure. Him.

Jacob drew her nipple into his mouth and sucked hard for one torturous moment before licking softly, softly. The contrast set a series of tiny fires across her body, from the pit of her stomach to the bud of her clit to the place just beneath her breastbone.

"You never told me," he said, "if it vibrates."

For a moment, she was so dizzy with sensation she barely knew what he was talking about. But then she remembered Jacob holding up her sex toy, studying it with those all-seeing eyes and asking careful, clinical questions. She squirmed, breathless, and found herself wrapping a leg around the length of his body, as if she could pull him between her thighs.

"I—it—does vibrate," she said, "but I never turn it on because I don't want you to hear."

His gaze darkened at that, his strong hand kneading her breast. The way he touched her—he was like some marauding bandit claiming the gold he'd plundered, and the decisive, shameless want of it all made heat creep up her throat and desperation slick her thighs.

"That was probably for the best," he informed her, before bending his head to suckle her again. Long, hot, slow pulls that tugged at her clit just as surely as they tugged her nipple.

Eve whined and arched her back. "I need to . . ." Her hand slid down toward the apex of her thighs—but on the way she got distracted by Jacob's delicious body, still fully clothed but so hot and so *his*. She ran a hand down his side, and he looked up.

"Hard," he said. "If you touch me, make it hard."

She blinked before pressing firmer against him. "Like this?"

"More."

For a moment, she wanted to hold back, but—well. He was literally asking for it. "This?" She pressed harder and sank her nails into his skin through his shirt.

He released a hiss of pleasure, his eyes drifting shut. "Yeah. Fuck." His voice was hoarse.

"Everywhere?"

"Everywhere. Always. Can you do that for me?"

"Oh, happily."

His grin was a quicksilver thing made crooked by arousal. "Good."

She dragged up his shirt, raking her nails over his chest as she went, exposing him inch by inch. "Mmm. Keep licking me. Wait—can I take this off? Wait—would you lick me somewhere else?"

He laughed softly against her skin, then laved his tongue over her breast again before murmuring, "Can't decide, Sunshine?"

"I think I just want it all."

"Then you can have it." He paused. "Except taking my shirt off is a bit of a mission, so we'll just have to undo the buttons for now."

Eve giggled, and then he rose up for a moment to let her carry out the task. She splayed the halves of his shirt open and tried not to drool at the raw power of his long, lean body while he reached for the table and produced—oh, God—her dildo. Also known as M'Baku. Not that she'd ever admit to naming it.

"So," he said as he crawled down the bed, "you fuck yourself with this."

Her throat felt thick as she replied, "Yes."

"Fuck yourself, and nothing else?"

"Yes." The word was strained and breathy this time, because he was tugging at the waistband of her leggings. Tugging them down, down, down, and when they didn't come easy, he tugged harder with an impatience that made her moan. She rushed to aid him in the leggings removal, kicking them off and laughing when he literally threw them aside.

"And you like that?" he asked as he settled between her thighs. His face hovered right over her cotton-clad pussy, and fuck, all she wanted to do was grab him by the hair and shove his mouth against her clit, hard—but he was being focused again, which was just as good. Focused on her, focused on words, his hazy blue eyes focused on her mouth. "You like fucking yourself, and nothing else?" he repeated, the question a growl. "That makes you come?"

"If I do it hard enough," she whispered, "and deep enough."

He grunted, squeezing his eyes shut, and she felt the bed rock as he thrust his hips against the mattress. "Yeah?"

"Yeah," she whispered, watching him in fascination. He was . . . losing it. Losing it in a way she'd never seen before, his hand shaking as he toyed with the lacy edge of her knickers. Losing it because of her.

God, that was hot. That was so fucking hot she might die.

"I'm going to do this," he said, almost to himself, "and then I'm going to leave you the hell alone."

She bit her lip. "What if I don't want you to leave me alone?"

His jaw tightened. "There are—rules, Eve. Social rules. I know what they are. I learned them."

"So did I," she shot back. "Maybe I just don't care."

"Because you want me so badly?" he asked sardonically. As if that couldn't possibly be the reason, and he'd hear nothing to the contrary. Before she could begin to formulate the right response to that—before she could even put her finger on just how wrong it was—he continued. "I shouldn't be doing this, but look . . ." His voice cracked as he finally glanced down at her pussy. "God, look at you. I'll just—"

"What?" she demanded breathlessly, her hips lifting without permission, chasing the soft, swollen invitation of his mouth.

"I'll just help you a little bit," he said, as if that was a perfectly reasonable way to describe fucking someone with a giant purple dildo. And she was pretty sure he intended to fuck her with a giant purple dildo. Because he put it carefully down beside him, as if he'd need it later, and then he hooked a finger into the damp fabric of her underwear and pushed it aside, just enough to expose her desperate pussy. "I'll warm you up," he murmured, "and then I'll help you."

"Jacob—"

He bent his head and pressed his tongue against her pussy. Eve almost screamed, the rush of pleasure was so intense. It seemed to fold out and out and out from her middle until it had taken over her entire body. Violently.

"Mmm," he murmured, the sound vibrating through her, and then the breadth of his tongue spread her open. Slowly, thoroughly, he laved the swollen bud of her clit.

"Oh, God," she whined, her hands falling to grasp his hair. "Oh, *God.*" She tugged, almost viciously, and he moaned.

Then he licked her again. She might have screamed a little bit, at that point.

Jacob looked up, his grin wicked and satisfied, his lips glossy with her wetness. "You better tell me what you want."

"*Jacob.*" She raised one hand to her own breast, squeezed it hard and pretended it was him. All she needed was him.

"Tell me exactly what you want. Tell me," he ordered, "and I'll learn this, too."

"God," she choked out, "why the fuck are you so—*sexy*?"

"For you," he said, "obviously."

She kind of wanted to smack him, but, like, in a hot way. More than that, though—"I want you to fuck me."

"Is that so?" he asked softly, bending his head to her cunt again. His mouth, tender but firm, brushed against her folds as he spoke. "Let me guess. You want something nice and long and thick inside you. Here." He pushed the tip of his tongue into her sensitized entrance and Eve's entire body jerked as if shocked with pleasure.

"Now," she gasped, her nerves humming with the urge to just—to just grab him and drag him higher and yank him out of those jeans.

Then he picked up the dildo and said, "Good thing we have this."

It was strange, the way her pulse leapt with anticipation even as her heart drooped a bit. "I want *you*."

"I'm right here," he said, his gaze on hers, something solemn and more serious than she'd ever seen in his eyes. "Just let me do this. Okay, Evie?"

Little fragments of reality crept up on her then. Like the fact that what they were doing would complicate things, and Jacob hated complications. Or the fact that *she* shouldn't have *time* for complications, since she was busy learning to make sensible, adult decisions, not hormone-led messy ones.

They were floating together in a bubble of lust, a fragile sheen of protection against hard questions like *What did that mean?* and *What are we now?* Maybe Eve wasn't the only one who'd learned to dread the inevitable, negative answers to questions like that.

Smoothing a hand through his hair, she asked, "What do you want, Jacob? Really?"

His eyes slid closed for a minute before he answered, his voice aching with honesty. "A lot. But most of all, I just want to know you like this."

Those words were such a sweet surprise, she laughed as her arousal hummed back from the brink of concern. "Why does everything you say have to be so hot?"

He looked surprised at that, then pleased. "The talking is usually my weak point."

"Give me a warning before we hit your strengths, then, or I might be in danger of passing out."

"Okay," he said. "Here's your warning." His thumb parted her folds, pressed firm against her cunt, pushed inside. Then there was nothing but fullness and pressure, a pressure that turned into zinging, overwhelming energy when he found her G-spot and rubbed in a slow circle.

"Oh, fuck," she managed, her voice catching. Pleasure pulsed through her veins as he bent his head and sucked—*sucked*—on her clit, gentle and wet and insistent. Time blurred a bit. At some point he replaced his thumb with two fingers, thrust harder and deeper, then gave her another. Her clit grew more sensitive, so he licked instead of sucking, tapping the hood lightly when she shook beneath him. And with every dizzying second, that rabid desire at her core grew worse, or maybe better, depending on your perspective.

"There you go," he said softly, looking down at the place where he fucked her. Eve couldn't see it herself, and her stomach muscles weren't really working at the minute, so she couldn't sit up and take the sight in fully. But she *could* see his expression, his eyes dark like a storm and his lust obvious in the swollen, satisfied curve of his mouth. He watched his thick fingers sliding in and out of her cunt, and he liked it.

When he withdrew fully, she moaned in protest and he laughed. "Be patient, Sunshine." Before she could find a decent comeback in the melted puddle he'd made of her brain, Jacob did something that made the rest of her motor functions evaporate. He picked up her vibrator and ran his wicked tongue, the same one that had just unraveled her so easily, along the toy's length.

Eve's breath huffed out of her in one long, horny rush. She watched through heavy-lidded eyes as he worked his gorgeous mouth over the purple silicone until it glistened in the half-light.

Then he looked at her and said, his voice low and raw, "Spread your legs wider."

Yes sir. She spread, and blushed a little at the slick sound of her folds parting, at the feel of cool air against wet skin.

"Good," he said. "Now bend your knees."

More blushing, but gosh, she didn't think she was physically capable of disobeying the steel in his voice. Still, as she exposed herself fully, she couldn't help but mumble, "At this rate you'll be able to see what I had for dinner."

He arched an eyebrow. "That's not how anatomy works, Eve."

"I *know*—"

"And actually, what I can see is every inch of your wet little cunt, begging for it." He pressed the dripping head of the dildo against her pussy. "Which is exactly what I wanted." He pushed.

The noise Eve made at that moment was less words and more a garbled tangle of OhmyGodJacobnoyesfuckyou. It was like he'd heard everything she'd told him and then more, the secret parts, the unspoken parts, the parts where she wanted that abrupt stretch, the feeling of fullness forced on her. Because he shoved the toy's merciless girth inside her without hesitating, and when she squirmed away from the pleasure he put his right arm across her belly to pin her down.

"Want me to stop?" he asked in a voice that said he knew very well the answer was *no*.

"Oh my God," was all she could say, every one of her nerve endings a firework. "Oh my God."

"No. Say my name."

"*Jacob.*"

"That's better." The toy bottomed out inside her, and he looked down. "You're so pretty, Eve. God, I want to be in you."

She was near mindless, at this point, rolling her hips desperately as if she could fuck herself, when she knew he wouldn't let her. "You do?"

"Of course I do. Look how perfect you are." His gaze was still on her pussy, his body shifting as he rocked against the mattress, too. "Look how much you want it." Slowly, he pulled the dildo out, then shoved it back inside her without warning. "Look how you take that," he said, and God, she'd never heard a man sound academic and aroused all at once. "It's so hot," he told her, "you're so fucking hot," and then he groaned and licked her clit again, as if he couldn't *not*, and he kept drilling into her with the toy, and, *fuck*.

It surprised absolutely no one when her legs shook and her voice cracked and she came hard as hell, all over his face.

CHAPTER FIFTEEN

Watching Eve come was like watching the northern lights, except better. Because Jacob could explain the northern lights, which took some of the beauty out of it, for him. But he couldn't explain this woman. He couldn't explain why everything about her flung him off the cliff of control and into some reckless abyss. He couldn't explain why he was already dreading the moment when he'd get up and leave her alone in this room—because he would leave, for a thousand valid reasons, and because that was what Jacob always did. Left before he could *be* left.

He just couldn't explain why, this time, the thought of his usual routine felt like dying.

He couldn't explain anything.

So he simply enjoyed the taste of her on his tongue, and the look of sheer ecstasy on her face, and the sound of his name on her lips. *Jacob, Jacob, Jacob,* steady as a heartbeat.

When she was done, he put the toy aside and kissed her thigh and sat up. Found his glasses. Dragged the covers over her limp, naked, beautiful body and tried to think of the right thing to say.

It was incredibly difficult, and not just because his dick was harder than it had ever been and all he wanted was to feel that magnificent pussy tightening around him and— *Stop.* That was not a constructive train of thought.

Eve opened her eyes and rolled over to look at him. There was a hint of resignation in her smile. "You're going to be weird about this, aren't you?"

"Not weird," he said, but even his voice was incredibly weird, all hoarse and thick, so it wasn't the most convincing statement he'd ever made. The problem was, when Jacob had sex, it was always under very specific circumstances. Either he'd taken a woman out on five to ten dates, decided he liked her, and discovered she felt the same, or . . .

Actually, that was the *only* time he had sex, and it always followed the same pattern. They'd fuck, he'd call the next day, and either she'd pick up and they'd go on another date, or she wouldn't pick up but she *would* periodically text him to come over, very late at night.

When Jacob had been younger and more hopeful, both of those arrangements usually ended because he was "too much." Now that he was older and wiser, they ended because he was "emotionally distant"—or, as he liked to call it, sensible. Whatever the case, when it came to women, he always knew exactly what was going on. Exactly how things would end.

But Eve was different.

She was his employee, for one thing, and also kind of his tenant, which meant he'd just landed himself in a potential ethical minefield, but she was also—

She was his friend, and friends were diamonds to him. Sometimes, when they worked together, she felt kind of like his partner. She was *permanent*, that was the issue, or rather, he wanted her to be. But Jacob's romances were never permanent. Whether they were the dating kind or the 1 A.M. fucking kind, they were never, ever permanent.

So if they did this, got too close like this . . . experience dictated it would end sooner or later, and then she would be gone.

Which was simply unacceptable.

Jacob cleared his throat. He knew what to say now. He just hoped he wouldn't fuck it up. "Thank you for tonight. All of it. You're . . . you're a very good friend."

She laughed a little. "Ouch."

Great. He was fucking up already. "What? What's ouch?"

"You know that *you're a very good friend* is code for *I don't want to sleep with you again*, right?"

Ah. "Well, yes, I did know that, but I more meant that we *shouldn't* sleep together, not that I don't want to."

Eve bit her lip, pulling the covers over her chest as she sat up. "Oh. Okay. Well . . . yeah. Honestly, you're probably right. I mean—" She laughed, though the usual sparkle in her eyes was absent. "Why did we even do this? It's not like we could date."

Those words really shouldn't feel like a punch to the gut, but Jacob was apparently ridiculous over this woman, so they did.

"Right," he said awkwardly, when what he wanted to ask was, *Why? Why couldn't we date? Am I so unsuitable? Or are you thinking of the problems I'm thinking of? Or—*

Didn't matter. Couldn't ask. If she said something all sweet and brilliant and overwhelmingly Eve, he might throw caution to the wind and do whatever it took to make her his . . . person. And she couldn't be his person because his people didn't last.

"Well. Then we're in agreement," he managed. "The trouble is, whether we agree on this or not, we will probably continue to be attracted to each other." He was impressed with himself for making such an understatement with a serious face. "And we spend so much time around each other, mistakes might easily be made." Even as he said the words, a solution presented itself, glaringly obvious and wonderfully convenient. "But," he said slowly, his mind still whirring, "there's an easy way to reduce the risk." *An easy way to put you out of my reach, at least some of the time.*

"Is there?" She arched an eyebrow, yet he couldn't shake the impression that all her expressions were less full of life than usual, a little more mechanic.

Of course, that couldn't be the case. Because if something was wrong with Eve, she'd just—well, she'd say. She always said. She was beautifully blunt, even now, during the most awkward conversation they'd ever had. So it was probably wishful thinking on his part, his mind searching for evidence that she was dying inside, just like him.

Which she obviously wasn't, because it was insensible for Jacob to feel this way and no reasonable person should. Not after so little time and so little encouragement. For God's sake, this time last week they'd hated each other.

"Go on, then," she said, her voice strangely sharp. Irritated with him already, no doubt. "Give me this mystical solution."

He cleared his throat. "Well—we agreed, last week, that you couldn't stay here forever." Then she'd charmed him so thoroughly that he'd forgotten to mind the fact she was sleeping in his sitting room. But he certainly minded now. For entirely different reasons. "Perhaps the best thing is for you to move out. I—I have alternative accommodations in mind." Or rather, he did as of ten seconds ago. "We could go and take a look on . . ." He flicked through his mental diary, the pieces of this half-arsed plan flying together because he was that desperate to avoid temptation. "Thursday. No check-ins on Thursday. We could make that our house-hunting day."

There: that meant he'd only have to live beside her, to know she was in here alone at night with nothing but the toy he'd used to make her come, for another four days.

Dear God, it was going to be hell.

"Fine," Eve said after a moment's pause. "Fine. Yes. Thursday. If that's what you want."

"Yes. Thursday. Good." He forced the words out of his throat. She lifted her chin. "Good."

His eyes caught on her mouth, and he remembered the moment he'd kissed her, and he wanted to relive it again and again and again for the rest of his life.

"I should go," he said stiffly.

She didn't stop him.

♫

Eve held her breath and counted to ten. The door clicked shut behind Jacob before she'd hit four, because he wasn't the long, lingering-looks sort, and even if he was, he wouldn't have given them to her.

Sigh.

She tried to tell herself it didn't matter, because it didn't. Or rather, it *shouldn't*. She barely knew the man, and she wasn't permitted to have him. He was a bad choice, of course he was: her employer. Her temporary employer. A high-handed, frosty, impossible man who'd probably end up married to someone severe and put together and dear God, why the bloody hell was Eve thinking about marriage right now? The point was, sleeping with Jacob had been one of her life's many terrible, thoughtless, immature choices, and she should be grateful he'd put such a firm stop to things.

It was both senseless and pathetic to wish that Jacob had said something entirely different. To wish that he'd asked her for something she couldn't give and shouldn't want. Eve repeated this mantra to herself several thousand times over, until it took on a little rhythm inside her mind, one she was too hollow to actually sing. Then she heard the faint sound of the shower turning on down the hall, and instead of smirking because she knew *exactly* what Jacob must be doing in there, her lower lip wobbled dangerously because he wouldn't be doing it with her.

She looked around the room that had been filled with so much hope and happiness at the start of the evening, and then breathless lust, and now disappointment, and she sort of cracked right down the middle.

Which is how she found herself sitting butt naked by the window, crying very quietly, while waiting for her grandmother to pick up the phone.

The moment Gigi answered with a drawled, "*Sugar lump. Is something on fire?*" Eve's senses returned.

"Oh, God," she said, swiping the tears from her cheeks. "It must be so late—"

"Shush, shush. Not to worry. Vani and I were just watching *Cat People.*"

"Sorry," Eve sniffled, her voice a whisper. Because Jacob could get out of the shower at any minute, and then he might hear her.

"Why are you whispering, my darling little Coco Pop? Cough twice if you're in a hostage situation."

Eve laughed, but somewhere along the way her voice got confused and the laugh turned into a sob.

"Shivani," she heard Gigi say, voice slightly muffled. "I require a recess. Yes. No, darling, don't worry."

Oh, God; now her grandmother was interrupting date night to deal with the sobbing granddaughter on the phone. Eve was suddenly mortified by the childish behavior she'd reverted to. Steeling herself, she said quickly, "No, please, don't let me interrupt you."

"*Sweetness*, you quite obviously need to talk. And so, we shall talk."

"No—that's not—I'm terribly sorry, Gigi. I suppose I called you out of habit, but I'm a big girl and I can solve my own problems." She didn't even have a problem, for heaven's sake: she was just a bit upset by a decision that made perfect sense.

And slightly annoyed, perhaps, by the fact that it hadn't been *her* decision. That Jacob had so cleverly and decisively taken it all out of her hands. It didn't take two people to decide they wouldn't sleep together again; it only took one. But it certainly took two people to decide that Eve urgently needed to move out, didn't it? Surely it wouldn't kill him to discuss things rather than bossing her about as if they were—well, as if they were at work?

The sadness in her chest became a sudden, unexpected spark of irritation.

"Darling," Gigi was saying, "are you listening to me?"

Oh, Christ. Not only had she disturbed her poor grandmother in the middle of the night, she'd then completely zoned out of their conversation. "Yes. Absolutely. Sorry, Gigi."

"Don't apologize. I know how you get when you're thinking. But I have to say, my little muffin case, I cannot allow you to behave as if calling me when you're upset is some sort of childish tantrum."

Gigi sounded unusually disapproving, her severe tone unfamiliar enough to capture Eve's attention. "Erm . . . you . . . can't?"

"No. I'm glad you're taking life by the bollocks, and what have you, darling, but that doesn't mean renouncing all human connection to become an invulnerable monk type out in the woods. It's perfectly reasonable to call someone you trust when something's bothering you."

"Oh. Well," Eve said slowly, "when you put it like that, I suppose it is." She certainly wouldn't think her sisters were childish if they reached out to her with a problem or just a dark mood—in fact, she wished they'd do that sort of thing more often. They were very self-sustaining, but they'd also struggled with certain things for far longer than necessary, simply because they refused to ask for help.

Eve rarely did anything *other* than ask for help. That was on the list of things she wanted to change. But it struck her now that there was a balance to be observed.

"Thank you, Gigi," she said softly. "I think you're right."

"Of course I am, my precious little plum. Now, what's gotten you into a tizzy at such a disgraceful hour?"

Eve opened her mouth, then realized that (1) she didn't want to discuss mind-blowing sex with her grandmother, even if said grandmother would thoroughly approve, and (2) she didn't actually need to. Eve knew how she felt, what she wanted, and what options were available to her. Just talking to Gigi had calmed her down and untangled her frantic thoughts.

"I think," she said slowly, "that I don't exactly need to talk about it. I think I just wanted to hear your voice."

"What a sweet little nugget you are, Evie."

Trust Gigi to end a depressing phone call by making Eve laugh.

By the time Jacob's shower ended, Eve had restored her bedroom to some semblance of order, put her dildo in a box and put that box in a drawer so she could never stumble upon it again, and gotten into her pajamas. Order. Routine. All very important things for a woman who *felt* raw inside, yet wanted to appear ordinary, to observe.

She would pretend to be fine until she *was* fine—because regardless of her feelings, the facts were clear: she wanted something impossible. If Jacob had wanted the same, she might be brave enough to reach for it, anyway. But he didn't, so she wouldn't.

She would go back to the way things had been only yesterday, and she would try to be as satisfied as she'd been then.

Which must be the adult choice, because she didn't bloody like it. Not one bit.

♫

Amazing, how quickly Thursday had come despite Jacob's sleepless nights.

This week, breakfast had continued to go smoothly, as had afternoon tea. Housekeeping had gone less smoothly, at least for him—because controlling himself, even controlling his *thoughts*, around Eve Brown was a fucking roller-coaster ride. But he'd successfully performed their new, stiff choreography without cracking, never touching her as they worked, talking about nothing but the necessities because any other conversation might see him pulled under the wave of her loveliness. So perhaps he should call that a win.

Now they were walking through the streets toward Aunt Lucy's to start their tour of local, affordable accommodation, and he should call that a win, too.

He really should.

Less of a win was the fact that he remained utterly fascinated with Eve, and mostly unable to hide it. Like right now; his eyes were staring straight ahead, his feet were obediently walking, step by step, down the street—but his mind was out of control, pouring all its considerable attention onto Eve. He imagined he could feel the warmth of her as she walked beside him, slightly hotter than this mild afternoon. He imagined, every so often, a glittering sensation caused by her gaze on the side of his face. As if she were sneaking looks at him, and he was so in tune with her every move that he could sense it.

But those things were just fantasy, in reality, all Jacob could do was hear her. How lucky for him that she was never silent. After a few awkward moments of quiet at the beginning of their walk, Eve had started up this odd, humming lilt, the same snatch of a tune repeated again and again in slightly different ways. It was a habit of hers, a vocal tic he'd gotten used to. But now, on his way to Aunt Lucy's—on his way to lose Eve, just a little bit—Jacob found himself desperate to *understand* everything she did rather than simply enjoying it.

So he asked on an ill-advised rush of curiosity, "What are you doing?"

At his question, Eve looked up sharply. Almost guiltily. "Sorry," she said. She was so on edge, now. Ever since—well, ever since. It was obviously his fault, and the knowledge squeezed at his lungs.

That tightness, that lack of air, made his next words come out clipped. "I didn't say to apologize. I said, what are you doing?"

Predictably, his sharpness chased the embarrassment from her eyes. Now she looked pissed off with him, which he far preferred. "You said I could sing. You even said it was better to sing than to wear the AirPods. I *told* you it would be annoying."

"I don't find it annoying." Which was the truth. He found it . . . familiar.

"You don't find it annoying?" she echoed skeptically, one eyebrow arched.

"That's what I said." Jacob paused, considering his next words.

He wasn't sure if he should say them; after all, this woman wasn't his business, not in the way he wanted her to be. Restless, he even pulled out his phone, hoping for a distraction that would stop him from speaking. No new notifications. Nothing particularly interesting on his live video feed of the cottage. Fine.

He put his phone away, and next thing he knew, the question he'd been avoiding slipped out. "Have you ever heard of stimming?"

She kicked a twig onto the grassy path beside them, then tipped back her head to squint at the low-hanging sun. "I don't know. Maybe. Remind me what it is?"

Jacob allowed himself a moment to watch the fall of her hair, the way one fine lavender braid caught and coiled in the soft space between her neck and her shoulder, before dragging his gaze away. "It's a kind of . . . repetitive action, to find comfort or focus or self-stimulate. Lots of autistic people do it."

"Oh," she said. There was a pause. "Well, if you want to . . . stim, go for it. I don't mind. I'm never going to mind."

Jacob blinked, then narrowed his eyes. She thought—she was giving *him* permission to—? He didn't know whether to be pleased or pissed.

Not pleased. Pleased is not allowed.

Fine, then: pissed. "I don't need permission to be myself, nor would I ever ask you for it." He'd grown out of that the hard way.

She huffed. Folded her arms. Flicked Jacob an utterly unreadable look. "So—do you think—" She broke off, pressing her lips together. "Then why did you bring it up?"

Good fucking question. His feelings for her must be causing

some kind of brain hemorrhage, because this conversation wasn't his to have. You couldn't just tell a woman that she often behaved in a way you read as autistic. Not if you weren't said woman's behavioral therapist. There were rules—or—ethical boundaries, or—something. Or maybe there weren't; Jacob didn't fucking know. He'd only been twelve when Aunt Lucy had told him they were just going to the doctor's to sort something out, and really, the something didn't matter, except school might be easier if people knew what she already suspected, that was all.

So he didn't really know how this stuff worked for adults. He *did* know that he could very easily be wrong, and that he'd already crossed enough lines with this woman, so he should stop while he was ahead.

"Don't worry about it," he said finally. "Just—don't worry about it."

She seemed to deflate, though he didn't understand why. "Okay. Whatever." A moment later, he watched as her odd mood drifted away like clouds from the sun—because she was Eve, and Eve was never one thing for long. She turned the golden ray of her attention upward as they wandered down an avenue of old oak trees. The sunlight through the verdant leaves sent dappled patterns across her skin and brought out the ocher in her dark eyes. She released a sigh that thrust him right back to last weekend, to her shaky breath when he'd kissed between her thighs.

He wrenched himself back to the present before his dick could start to react. Wandering down the streets of Skybriar with a hard-on wouldn't do his reputation much good, professional or otherwise.

"Oh look," she said, pointing. "A gingerbread sign."

Jacob eyed the banner advertising the Gingerbread Festival, and instead of his usual anxiety to get said festival absolutely right, all he felt was a quiet confidence in Eve. Which wasn't a feeling conducive to caring about her less, so he squashed it down and simply grunted.

"This is such a lovely town," she murmured. "I don't know how you manage to stay so grumpy when you live here."

"Through great force of will," he replied.

"I've never seen this street before. It's pretty."

"Never seen—?" But no, he supposed she wouldn't have. He knew that Eve had gone shopping, and that she made trips to the supermarket, but aside from that, well.

"There's not much time for exploring," she said. The words were light and even, a simple statement of fact, but they hit him like a hammer made of guilt. Christ. The more he thought about it, the more Castell Cottage looked like some kind of labor camp, lately.

"I'm sorry," he blurted. And it was the truth. As a child, he'd caught a butterfly in a jar, and though he'd given it air holes and fed it as advised by the quick facts section of his insect encyclopedia, it had still died.

Aunt Lucy had told him butterflies needed somewhere to flutter about. Just like Eve.

Eve, who was looking at him with a hint of surprise, probably because he never apologized more than three times per annum. "That's okay," she said. "I could explore, if I wanted to, after tea, or—"

"Except you're usually bone-tired because I work you like a dog."

She laughed out loud. "You're so dramatic."

"Tell me I'm wrong."

"Jacob, you're wrong."

"Things will be different when my wrist is healed. In four weeks, your workload will be greatly reduced, I promise."

She turned and flashed him another look he couldn't decipher—one completely devoid of levity or even sarcasm. "Right," she said softly. "Just four weeks." Then she swallowed, and turned away, skipping ahead of him. "I bet you make sweet promises to all the indentured servants."

He snorted, then caught a familiar movement up above. Wrapped an arm around her waist and dragged her back against him without even thinking. The instant her soft, round arse pressed into his thighs, bird shit splattered on the pavement where she'd stood.

Eve, predictably, screamed. It was only a little scream, but *really*. "Jesus, woman," he muttered.

"*Poop!*"

"Yes. Welcome to the countryside. What were you saying about lovely towns?"

"Fuck you," she laughed.

He found his own mouth curling into a smile, an automatic response. Then he ruthlessly corralled it back into a straight line, because he'd read many books over the years, and one of those books had been about how not to break under torture. Your tormentors would start with little things, easy concessions to get you used to cooperating with them. If he allowed himself to smile when Eve was lovely—and she was often lovely—next thing he knew he'd be laughing with her, and talking to her properly—and surely the next step was dragging her up to his room and fucking her into the mattress. He could even imagine the sounds she'd make, the way her hands would glide over his skin as if just the feel of him turned her on. He could imagine, when he allowed himself to do so, *everything*.

Hence why he could give no quarter when it came to smiles.

He rolled his eyes at her instead, and let her go. Well, almost. Two of his fingers snagged the belt loop at the back of her jeans, hooking around the fabric, staying there. But only, he told himself, because someone needed to guide her around. This was unknown terrain. There was bird poop about. It was his responsibility to hold on to her like this.

Clearly she agreed, because she stayed close as they walked.

♫

The first place on Jacob's accommodation list was, as it turned out, his aunt's house.

Lucy's was a lovely little place, a bungalow being eaten alive by wisteria in a way Eve quite adored. And it had a spare room—the one Jacob and his cousin Liam had shared, growing up, which was now an immaculate double bedroom. Apparently, Eve might rent said bedroom for a nominal fee.

"So he's chucking you out," Lucy said from the doorway as Eve looked politely around the space. "Have you pissed him off that badly?"

Eve tried not to be intimidated by the other woman's impassive expression or horrifyingly mature work boots. (Plain black.

Not even a jaunty yellow stitch. Not even a few hearts and daisies doodled in fluorescent highlighter. Good Lord.)

"No comment," Eve said, and flicked a glance at Jacob, who stood broodingly in the corner. She wasn't sure what their party line was, since she couldn't exactly tell his aunt he'd licked her out on a sofa and didn't trust himself not to do it again.

Unfortunately for her, Jacob didn't appear to be listening to the conversation. He continued to brood broodily in silence.

"I suppose it can't be that bad," Lucy said. "He'd be making a hell of a lot more noise if you'd annoyed him."

"Or perhaps I've annoyed him *so* much that he's utterly run out of fury."

Lucy's gaze flicked sharply to Eve's, those frosty eyes narrowed. They studied Eve for one palm-sweating second, as if searching her expression for some sort of mockery or judgment. But she must not have found any, because after a moment, the coldness drained right out of her, replaced by an amused smirk. "Maybe. How are you finding it, then? The job?"

"Jacob thinks he's working me too hard."

Lucy rolled her eyes. "He has grand ideas about labor and human rights."

In the corner, Jacob blinked. "Are you talking about me?"

"Darling," Eve said, "would we ever? Go on, get back to brooding."

He grunted and recommenced staring at the wall. Apparently, he'd decided to actually follow Eve's directive. Amazing. Well, one mustn't look a gift horse in the mouth.

"I've been enjoying it," she said to Lucy. "I like cooking for people." Eve had always known that, of course—but it had never occurred to her that some things could be even more rewarding on a professional basis. Now, she actually looked forward to work every morning; looked forward to taking care of people not just because she had nothing better to do, but because it was her job. She'd spent days waiting for that feeling to fade.

It was only getting stronger.

"I think," she said out loud, "that making people happy sort of—fuels me. I like working hard to give them things. I like seeing them enjoy those things. It's kindness and performance and creation all at once."

"Hm," Lucy murmured, looking pleased. "So you're only moving out to get away from Jacob, then."

"Actually," Eve joked back, "he's trying to get away from me."

At which point, Jacob's distant gaze snapped toward Eve. "I'm sorry," he said abruptly. "Excuse me, Aunt Lucy. I just need to . . ." His voice trailed off, possibly because he couldn't figure out how to say, *I just need to grab Eve by the hand and drag her off into this cupboard.* Which is exactly what he did.

Eve, of course, let herself be dragged. Actually, she was thrilled to be dragged—damn her treacherous nervous system. Jacob's hand was big and calloused in hers, and it held her so tightly. He pushed her into the cupboard, shut the door behind them, and there they stood in the dark.

A curse floated softly between them. "Forgot," he said shortly. "The switch is on the outside."

"It doesn't matter," she murmured, which it didn't, because he was still holding her hand.

A taut moment passed. "Look," he said. "I'm sorry to drag you in here, I just—Eve—you don't really think that, do you?"

It took her a moment to realize what he meant. But once she did, the spark of irritation in her chest, the one she'd been ignoring since Sunday, became a teeny, tiny flame. "Well, yes." She frowned. "Of course I think you're trying to get away from me. Because you are."

His grip on her hand tightened, relaxed. "No," he said firmly, as if the word itself could bend reality. "No."

"Oh, come on, Jacob," she whispered, except her whisper sounded alarmingly like a hiss. A very soft and quiet hiss, but still. "We—things went too far, between us. I know that. And then all of a sudden you remembered how desperately you wanted me out of your house. Fine. Your decision. I'm going along with it. But you're not allowed to pretend it's something else."

There was a long pause before he said slowly, "You're angry. You're angry with me."

"No, I'm not," she snapped, rather angrily. Which gave her pause. Made her examine the irritable little flame in her chest. Made her realize that actually, yes, she was angry, despite her decision to get over this whole thing.

Eve wasn't used to being angry, especially not for long. She was always aware that most people didn't want her around badly enough to put up with difficult conversations, with constant complaints. She was used to swallowing her feelings and replacing them with a smile, to playing the role in which she'd been cast.

But *these* feelings were huge and jagged and spiky in her stomach, and she wanted to spit them out.

"Fine," she blurted. "Fine, yes, maybe I am. Maybe I'm angry with you because—because I thought we were equals, even if you are my boss, but as soon as you made me orgasm you decided to become my benevolent overlord." She ignored the alarmed choking sound Jacob made when she said *orgasm*. "I realize this is awkward for you. I get that. And if you want to throw me out to make it less awkward, fine. But don't act like you're doing it for my benefit, and don't act like you didn't strong-arm me into it instead of *asking* what I wanted to do."

Once all those words had rushed out, Eve felt a bit like an empty pond, her usually hidden depths suddenly exposed to the light. Belatedly, her cheeks warmed. She'd made that speech intending to demand honesty, and autonomy, and all those lovely things Dani was always talking about. But she was suddenly worried it had come off as simply demanding *Jacob*. That she'd revealed, somewhere in her little speech, how badly she still wanted him.

But when the seconds ticked by without his reply, Eve steeled her spine and squared her shoulders. So what if he'd heard that sad, horny, far-too-attached part of her? So fucking what? Sometimes, being convenient instead of real was exhausting. So maybe, from now on, she'd stop.

"Nothing to say?" she asked, and surprised herself by sounding as sharp and superior as her eldest sister. Which made Eve feel rather authoritative. If only Jacob weren't still holding her hand—or rather, if only she weren't still holding *his*—her transformation to absolute badass would be complete.

Then Jacob ruined everything by saying quietly, "Eve. I'm sorry."

Very small, very simple words. They shouldn't be able to punch a hole through her outrage like this, but clearly, Eve was soft.

"I'm so sorry," he repeated, his voice as impassioned as a whisper could be. Which was, apparently, rather impassioned indeed. His hand squeezed hers, and then his *other* hand joined the party, cast and all, and suddenly he was clutching her like a Regency gentleman about to make a heartfelt declaration. "I did strong-arm you, because I was panicking, and that was wrong of me, and I—I was a shit, and you're right to be angry with me, but please, please don't ever think I want to get rid of you. That is the last thing I want. I don't think I could *ever* want that. You're lovely, Evie, and you make me smile every day—multiple times a day"—he managed to sound genuinely shocked by that—"and I can't believe you've been holding this in all week instead of smacking me for it."

Eve decided it was for the best that she couldn't see Jacob in here, because hearing his voice was bad enough. The speed of his words, and the way his sentences frayed at the edges, and that thread of desperation through it all as if he really, urgently needed her to understand, was bad enough.

"Say something," he murmured hoarsely. "Please."

"I . . ." She took a breath. She had the vague idea that she should remain angry despite his apology, based on principle alone, but, well. She wasn't angry anymore. He had just popped all her hurt like a balloon and replaced it with several thousand hopeful, happy bubbles, and really, no one should have the power to change her mood so very quickly.

But apparently, Jacob did.

Drat.

"Fine," she whispered. "Fine. I suppose I understand. And you apologize very well." She paused. "If you would like to compliment me some more before we make up, feel free."

To her surprise, he took that joke as a very serious suggestion. "You are extremely sweet and a very good cook and incredibly pretty," he said without hesitation, "and . . . you have a wonderful sense of humor."

"Ha! I knew you thought I was funny. I *knew* it."

"Maybe I'm just sucking up," he said. But he squeezed her hand again, and she felt an answering squeeze of pleasure in her tummy.

"I don't think sucking up is your style, Jacob Wayne," she said softly.

"If anyone could drive me to it," he replied, "you could."

In that moment, Eve decided that getting on with things might be the adult way to live—but blurting out her feelings was officially the Eve Brown way to live. She much preferred it.

"So," Jacob said after a moment. "Since I never did ask—what *do* you want to do? About . . . everything?"

Now, there was a question. Her gut instinct was to reply, *I want to go home and have my way with you again*—but Eve had spent the last week thinking about all the reasons why that was not a sound choice. First and foremost: she had a queasy suspicion that if she spent too much time with her hands on this man, she'd eventually refuse to let go. And she couldn't refuse to let go; not when Skybriar was just a temporary pit stop on her journey to being her better self. She had a party-planning job to complete. She had parents to make proud, once and for all. She had a mature, adult plan, and staying here in this happy little fairy-tale town with a delightful big bad wolf was not conducive to that plan. It couldn't be, because she wanted it so badly.

Anyway, Jacob wasn't asking for a relationship. He was asking how they should go about not-fucking, which was pretty much the opposite, so she'd better rein in all these secret, silly hopes.

If she was smart, she would want what Jacob wanted: distance. Yet the very idea made her come over all gray, like a rainy sky.

"Look," she said slowly. "I am on a journey to self-ac . . . ac . . ."

"Actualization."

"Precisely," she said. "I know sleeping with my emotionally unavailable boss isn't a mature, sensible choice, so I'm not going to do it again." Even if she was struggling more and more to accept the idea that Jacob could be a bad choice.

He wasn't hers to choose, so it didn't really matter.

"But I still want to be *near* you," she continued. "All right? I just want to be near you. So I vote we keep going the way we always have, and we'll completely forget the inappropriate sex part, and everything will be fine." She hoped.

After a long, long silence, he said, "I see." Then, in a sudden flurry of action, he added, "Come on," and opened the door, and towed her outside like a boat.

Lucy was leaning against the opposite wall with her arms folded and one eyebrow raised. But there was a hint of amusement in her voice when she asked, "Meeting concluded?"

"Yes," Jacob said. "Really sorry, Luce, but we don't need the room. Sorry. Just—more convenient at the cottage. Early hours. Free board. I'm not paying Eve enough, you know."

"No," Lucy said dryly. "I imagine not."

"Right, well, we'll be off now."

Lucy cleared her throat.

"Oh." Jacob released Eve's hand and went over to his aunt. "Thanks, really. Sorry to play silly buggers. I'll see you for dinner this weekend. Bye." He bent to kiss her silvery hair.

"Whatever. Love you, kiddo," Lucy said, and slapped him on the shoulder as he passed.

"Erm, good-bye," Eve said brightly, and that was all she managed before Jacob took her hand again and dragged her away.

CHAPTER SIXTEEN

Jacob leaned back in his oversized, leather desk chair, his phone pressed anxiously to his ear. "Mont? Are you all right? You sound like you're hyperventilating."

"I *am* hyperventilating," Mont replied, although now he was speaking again, he sounded more dazed and confused than low on oxygen. "Did you just—Jacob—did you just call me up and tell me, all fucking casual, that you slept with Eve last Sunday night?"

"I suppose that depends on your definition of *slept with*."

"My definition involves orgasms."

"Ah." Restless, Jacob pushed back his chair and stood. "In that case, I suppose so." He sounded dry and detached, like he really was as casual about this situation as Mont claimed. But he fucking wasn't, hence why he'd caved and confessed all to his best friend. It had been an entire week since the Dildo Incident, and he was crumbling like some ancient cliff because God and fuck and shit and *God*, he wanted to touch her again. To hold her, and taste her, and feel like she was his.

He'd been this close to saying as much on Thursday, in the

darkness of Aunt Lucy's cupboard. If Eve had pushed him then—even a little bit—he would've abandoned his common sense and fucked her however, whenever, and wherever she bloody well wanted. But she'd made it clear that she didn't want anything of the sort—thankfully before he'd made a total fool of himself.

I know sleeping with my emotionally unavailable boss isn't a mature, sensible choice . . .

That completely factual statement should not have stung.

"So," Mont said, "does she know you only sleep with people if you—"

"Shut up," Jacob said crisply.

"If you adore them and you want to marry them and hide them away in your lair forever and ever?" Mont finished.

"You exaggerate." Jacob paced his office for the seventy-fifth time today, wishing that was true. But unfortunately, Mont was right: Jacob didn't like people easily, but once he *did* like them, it was always too far and too fast. He had to temper himself, had to be careful.

Not that he'd been remotely careful with Eve. And it showed.

Take this morning at breakfast, for example. If he hadn't been knackered from another sleepless night of overthinking and berating himself, he might have kissed her glossy, orange mouth over the pain au chocolat, and *then* where would they be? Up to their eyeballs in horrified Trip Advisor reviews, and more importantly, on a treacherous path from safe, long-term friendship to difficult, dangerous romance. Which she didn't even want. So there was no use thinking about it.

"I mean, I can't say I didn't see this coming."

Jacob almost tripped over his own feet. "*What?*"

"Come on, man. Surely you saw this coming."

"I say again: *what?*"

Mont laughed down the phone. "Never mind. Never mind. So, you slept with the attractive woman you haven't stopped talking about in weeks. Shocker."

"I—haven't—" Jacob cut off his outraged sputtering, focused on a nice, blank spot on the wall, and took a breath. "Relaying an employee's increasingly excellent job performance is not the same as talking about her for weeks. And stop being flippant about the situation, Montrose. It's horrific."

"Why? You like the girl. I think she likes you back. Ask her out."

"*No,*" Jacob snapped, because he was sensible and logical and would not be led astray by Mont's shockingly casual attitude toward human connection. Mont didn't understand these things. Mont was charming and classically handsome and inherently flexible, and Mont didn't get tied up in knots over the slightest thing, and Mont had almost certainly never had a woman tell him that he was great in bed but a little too intense out of it.

Jacob had heard that several thousand times and did not want to hear it from Eve. In fact, if he ever did hear it from Eve— accompanied by one of those pitying wince-smiles as she disappeared into the mist—he was oddly certain he might burn Castell Cottage to the ground.

"Christ, mate, stop being so bloody awkward and just tell her how you—hang on." Mont broke off midsentence, his voice fading as he spoke to someone else in the background. "Give me a sec, Tess."

"Are you talking to Jacob?" Tessa Montrose's voice floated down the line.

"Yes."

"Is he having a meltdown?"

"Yes."

"Has that woman hit him with her car again?"

Mont laughed. "Oh, something like that. Now piss off."

"But do you know where my—?"

"No, I don't know where your glue gun is, piss off. Sorry, Jake. What was I saying?"

"I don't remember," he lied. "Put Tess on the phone, would you? I want to talk to her." Something about hearing her voice had given him an idea. An idea about how to make Eve smile, which was a goal he found himself more and more eager to achieve, these days. She made *everyone* smile so often, so easily—he could do the same for her, couldn't he?

He certainly fucking hoped so. She deserved it.

"You want to talk to *Tess*? Charming," Mont said. "Why? You need something fixed?"

"Just put your sister on the phone and stop asking questions."

"Why would I do that when I could keep asking questions and get on your nerves?"

Jacob muttered an insult and drifted toward the window behind his desk. Eve was in the garden, clearing up the empty wrought-iron tables, looking like one of the meadow flowers with her lavender braids and rose-pink T-shirt. She'd started serving afternoon tea outside when the weather was nice. Her idea. And, God, why did it make him oddly hot and . . . *fluffy*, inside, when she behaved as if this job, as if this B&B, was her passion, too?

She walked out from under the shade of an oak and it was like watching the sun rise.

Her mouth was moving, but Jacob couldn't hear her—so he balanced the phone between his ear and his shoulder and opened the window. Eve's voice flooded the room like a glass of ice water on a sweltering day. She was singing "Special Affair," and the sound of it thrust him back in time to last Sunday. To sweet, silvery darkness and her body beneath him.

"Tess," Mont was saying, "I think Jake wants to talk to you. God only knows why."

The words barely registered; Jacob was too busy controlling his cock and his thoughts. Reminding himself that there was no way the world would let him keep a woman like Eve. She'd leave in the end. Everyone and everything left, in the end, didn't they?

The thought wasn't entirely accurate, he knew that, but it *felt* accurate. It felt inescapable.

"Never mind," he said out loud. "Never mind. I'll call Tessa later. Mont, I have to go."

"What? Don't. You're freaking out about something, aren't you?"

"No. Good-bye," Jacob said, and then he hung up. Down in the garden, Eve looked up as if she'd heard his voice. Her eyes met his as if drawn by some magnetic force. She smiled, and waved, and Jacob—

Jacob was hit with such soul-deep affection, he actually lost his breath.

Somehow, he managed to wave awkwardly back. Then he turned away and slumped into the hidden safety of his desk chair. He sat there for God only knew how long, frozen and confused, his chest heaving and his thoughts flying. The sun sank low, and still, he sat. The breeze through the open window turned cool, almost cold, and still, he sat.

But no matter how long he waited, the feeling didn't go away.

Bloody shitting hell. He was in love with her.

How goddamn inconvenient.

♫

As far as Eve could tell, things between she and Jacob went back to normal after that moment at Lucy's. Their version of normal, anyway.

The awkwardness that had muffled their friendship was burned away by the time they'd walked home. They still bickered over breakfast in the mornings, still teased each other over bed making in the afternoons. Jacob started bringing his laptop down to the kitchen, typing away with unnerving focus while she prepared tea and cake for the guests.

It was only on nights like tonight—a quiet Wednesday evening when she'd gone to her room early, sitting on the creaky sofa bed where she almost *never* wanked over Jacob—that Eve noticed a slight tension between them. A barely banked heat. Because as soon as they went up to the B&B's private quarters, he turned rigidly silent.

He nodded stiffly at her when they crossed paths in the corridor. He responded to her calls of *Good night* with vague grunts. Eve wanted to decipher those grunts, but she was worried that understanding his whole tight-jawed restraint thing might push her into accidentally seducing him. Mature, adult women did not accidentally seduce their bosses, nor did they obsess over said boss's grunts like teenagers with a whale-sized crush.

Mature, adult women focused on introspection and personal growth. And Eve really must be maturing, because tonight, instead of reliving the best head of her life for the thousandth time, she was busy with some personal research.

Jacob had asked her, last week, *Have you ever heard of stimming?* and after his explanation, she'd wanted to ask something back. She'd wanted to ask, *Is that what I do? Am I stimming right now?*

But she'd also wanted to figure things out for herself.

So she picked up her tablet, settled back against the cushions, and typed a few words into the search bar. *Autism in adults* brought up countless hits. She was mildly overwhelmed for a moment, but then she closed her eyes and thought, *What would Chloe do?*

Chloe would isolate key, reliable sources. Rather like Jacob. Rather like Dani. The three of them shared a lot of similarities in that regard, but Eve and Jacob shared *other* similarities—silly ones that probably didn't mean anything. Yet, those similarities kept nibbling at her brain like insistent little mice with big, sharp teeth.

Eve clicked on two links: one by the National Health Service, and one by the National Autistic Society. The NHS had an abrupt list of "symptoms": signs of autism that made her smile because they brought Jacob to mind. The same well-known signs she'd seen in TV characters, the kind that didn't apply to her in the slightest. She was never taken as blunt or rude. She didn't find it remotely difficult to express how she felt, and routine had never been her strong suit.

Then she read the words, *Noticing small details, such as patterns or sounds, that others do not.*

Well. That didn't mean much. Not even if it made her heart jump with nervous recognition. Not even if the thought of having a reason for that slight difference—the difference that had led to her obsession with music—made Eve feel strangely . . . known.

She ran her tongue over the inside of her teeth and kept reading.

You may get very anxious about social situations. You may struggle to understand social "rules" or to communicate clearly. You may find it difficult to make friends.

It can be harder to tell you're autistic if you're a woman.

She could feel her pulse thumping against her throat, which was ridiculous. It wasn't as if this bothered her—she was smiling, for God's sake, though she couldn't explain why. A dawning surprise swept over her, and all she wanted to do was catch it in her hands like a warm, bright star and hold it quietly until she'd absorbed it a bit. Reading this stuff felt like climbing, inch by inch, up to the top of a roller coaster; it stirred a thrill of anticipation in her stomach, along with a hint of fear at the unknown. The giddy, uncertain kind of fear that made a sudden drop all the sweeter.

Eve switched websites and found a much more personal, detailed approach from the National Autistic Society, one that discussed the benefits of diagnosis and what it all meant. There was a section called *Coming to Terms with Your Autism*, which Eve found she couldn't relate to. She'd had to *come to terms* with the fact that hormonal breakouts weren't limited to one's teenage years (horribly unfair, if you asked her), but she didn't need to come to terms with the signs of autism listed on these websites. She knew very well who she was and who she wasn't, and she'd already spent a long, difficult time learning to like herself despite those differences. Having a possible reason for them didn't change much.

But then, she also couldn't see herself following the steps on this page that described how to secure a diagnosis. Whereas plenty of other people might want to. So perhaps this was different for everyone.

No, it almost certainly was.

Satisfied, Eve locked the tablet and tucked this latest development safely against her heart. She was still ruminating over what she'd found—and painting her toenails, of course, which was the best way to ruminate—when someone knocked on the door an hour later. Jacob. Would she tell him?

No. Not yet. These thoughts were just hers, for now, until she'd explored them fully.

That decided, she heaved herself off the sofa, her toes spread for maximum safety and minimum smudges, and waddled over to answer the door.

It swung open to reveal a disgracefully tall and alarmingly attractive woman with hair like a thunderstorm, or a '50s lounge singer, or a '50s lounge singer who was also a thunderstorm. *Not*

Jacob, then. The woman flipped her dark, riotous waves over one broad shoulder and said in a low, throaty voice, "Hi."

Eve blinked. Gosh. She'd very nearly blurted out, *You're pretty,* like some sort of overwhelmed toddler.

"We've come," the thunderstorm '50s singer went on decisively, "to take you out." By the set of her sharp jaw and the flint in her doe eyes, that was not a request.

"For God's sake, Tess, you sound like a hitwoman," came an irritable voice from the hallway. "Maybe start with the fact that we're Mont's sisters." The goddess was thrust aside by an equally tall, brown woman with razored short hair and narrowed eyes. While the first woman—Tess?—wore a tight gold dress with enough sequins to confuse air traffic (Eve approved), the second wore jeans and a crisp, white shirt that made her look rather dapper. "Hi. I'm Alex Montrose and this is Tessa. You're Eve, yeah?" She held out a long-fingered hand, and it took Eve a heartbeat to reconnect her brain to her . . . other brain and realize she was supposed to shake.

"Erm," she said. "Yes." She squeezed Alex's hand limply, murmured, "Enchanté," then wondered why the bloody hell she'd said such a thing. Oh, well. She was alarmed, she was taken aback, and her toes were still slightly wet. Under such circumstances, she could not be blamed for a little ridiculousness.

Alex arched her eyebrows, one of which was sharply bisected by a pale scar, before continuing. "We are here to bully you out of the house."

"Well," piped up Tessa, "the B&B."

"Which is a house, Tess."

"And if I called a camper van a—a *car*, you'd be horrified."

"I wouldn't give a flying fuck," Alex said calmly, and somehow sauntered past Eve into the room.

"Liar," Tessa said, and flipped her hair some more, and followed. She turned to Eve, who was still standing, slightly dazed, by the door. "Do you like my hair? Roller set. Twenty-four hours and seven different YouTube tutorials! I had to sleep on the rollers. What a nightmare. Anyway, get dressed."

"You're doing this all wrong," Alex told her. Eve noticed that Alex had made herself comfortable on Jacob's weight bench, of all things, lying back and propping up one knee, staring at the ceiling with her hands over her stomach. She had a thick, dark scar wrapped all around her wrist like a bracelet.

"*I'm* doing it wrong? You're lying on the furniture," Tessa said, but by now Eve had noticed their bickering held zero heat. As if they were simply annoying each other for the fun of it. "Now, Eve, I know this is all very sudden, but Jacob told us you urgently needed to socialize, and we are his only friends aside from Mont—"

"*Friends?*" Alex snorted.

Eve found herself suddenly scowling. "Jacob's only next door, you know. He can probably hear you."

"Good," Alex grinned, raising her voice, at which point Eve realized this was a gentle in-joke, as opposed to actual Jacob-hating, and felt rather silly.

"Well," Tessa said thoughtfully, "we're probably not his *only* friends. He gets on very well with that older lady who runs the cheese counter at the supermarket and also the man who washes out the wheelie bins, but you know what I mean. He wanted to show you a good time, and he decided we were the best option.

Obviously." She swished the hair again, leaving a trail of hibiscus and coconut in the air, and flashed a rather beguiling smile. "So. Are you in?"

Was Eve in? At this point, she wasn't even certain she was conscious. "Erm. I must admit, I'm slightly confused on several counts. *Jacob* wanted to show me a good time?" Jacob had already shown her a good time. Very effectively. And *most* enthusiastically, she remembered, her cheeks flushing. More to the point, he wasn't here to show her a good time now, so what the bloody hell was going on?

"Well, he's not a big fan of going out dancing," Tessa said.

"Shocker," Alex interjected.

"But he thought you might be, and also that you might want to talk to someone other than him, for once, so he told us all about you and we decided you sounded excellent and that we should definitely hang out."

Eve's heart started vibrating, which was alarming, but entirely understandable, all things considered. "He told you all about me? What . . . what did that entail?" She tried to stamp out the tentative pleasure in her voice, but judging by Alex's smirk, she wasn't entirely successful.

"He said," Alex grinned, "that you were funny, and sweet, and then he had an embolism from being too complimentary and refused to say anything else except, *Just be* nice *to her, Alexandra, or I'll murder you in your sleep.*"

Eve bit her lip on a smile. First he gave her the mother of all orgasms. Then he brooded himself into a tizzy about it. Now he was trying to make her happy in a predictably cloak-and-dagger fashion. It was all so fucking *Jacob* she might just pass out.

For God's sake, how the hell was she supposed to resist him? She adored him. It was undoubtedly true that mature, sensible women didn't sleep with their bosses—but it seemed painfully clear, in that moment, that mature, sensible Eves weren't supposed to let men like Jacob Wayne pass them by.

So she wouldn't. She simply *wouldn't*. Maybe she'd made bad choices in the past, but she was changing now. Eve was going to follow everything she felt for this man, and if it all ended in tears, she'd simply face the consequences like the grown woman she was.

Just making that decision lifted a weight from her shoulders. A slow smile spread across her face. She felt the urge to go and throw herself at Jacob right this instant, but first . . .

Well, first, she was kind of missing her sisters, and the two women in front of her were chaotic enough to fill at least a quarter of that gap.

"All right," she said finally. "I'll go out with you."

"Yay!" Tessa clapped her hands, while Alex produced a surprisingly sweet smile. In that moment, with matching dimples in their right cheeks and warm, whiskey eyes, Eve finally cottoned on.

"Oh! You're twins!"

Alex arched an amused eyebrow. "Uh . . . we're identical. Don't tell me you only just noticed."

"Don't be annoying, Alex, who cares if she just noticed? Eve, come on, get dressed. I love your hair. We're going to the pub."

"We *might* go to the pub," Alex corrected. "We don't even know if she drinks."

"If she doesn't, she can have lemonade and peanuts. There's nowhere else interesting to go."

"We can grab some Thai food and eat in the park like respectable reprobates."

"You think I'm putting vintage Cavalli on grass?" Tessa demanded.

"Hold on," Eve said, "there's Thai food here?"

"See?" Alex grinned, triumphant.

"Eve, no, don't, don't be seduced by Thai food." Tessa came over and put her hands on Eve's shoulders, at which point Eve finally realized the woman seemed so tall because she was wearing killer heels. But, judging by Alex's height in shiny, flat brogues, they were also simply very tall regardless. "Listen to me," Tessa said, low and urgent, as if imparting state secrets of international importance. "We can get Thai food whenever we want. Tonight is our first night of meeting and we're supposed to become best friends—"

Alex snorted loudly in the background.

"Which means either we have to get drunk together, or we have to make terrible decisions together. I am entirely open to either, but the point is we need to go out and make absolute tits of ourselves in order to forge a lasting best friend bond because—"

"What the hell do you need a lasting best friend bond for?" Alex demanded. "You have a *twin*."

"Because," Tessa forged on firmly, "all friendships are better in threes, like the three musketeers or *Totally Spies*, so Alex and I need you, and also because you're driving Jacob sideways up the wall and off his trolley—I salute you by the way—and also because I saw you at the supermarket three days ago wearing a T-shirt that said UNFUCK YOU, OR WHATEVER and I desperately need to know where it was from."

"Well," Eve said, faintly stunned. "*My*. Goodness."

"I never," Alex said dryly, "should've let you open the rosé."

"I, er . . . I don't receive many instant offers of best friendship," Eve admitted.

"Then you really must take this one," Tessa said reasonably.

Eve found herself smiling. "Yes, I suppose I must."

CHAPTER SEVENTEEN

Mont's pub, the Rose and Crown, was a cozy mixture of dark wood and green velvet that seemed infinitely suited to the Lake District, and to Montrose himself. Eve spotted him as soon as she entered arm in arm with the twins; he was pouring a glass of gin with a practiced air while chatting to a grizzled customer who looked alarmingly like some sort of biker.

"Mont's cute, don't you think?" Tessa said over the speakers' frantic cascade of "From the Ritz to the Rubble."

Eve blinked, caught unawares. "Erm . . . weren't we just talking about macramé?"

Alex rolled her eyes. "Tess thinks that if you ask people unexpected questions they'll get confused and tell the truth."

"Oh. Well. Yes, your brother is cute."

"Perfect," Tess beamed. "Want to date him?"

"No, she doesn't want to date him, genius," Alex interjected. "Anyway, we're supposed to be bonding. No man-talk. It's boring."

Tessa gave a mournful sigh. "Fine. Fine! Come on. Eve, lemon or lime?"

Eve wrinkled her nose as they approached the bar. "You need to be more specific. In general? In drinks? Appearance-wise? As the base flavor for a citrus drizzle cake?"

"Oh my God, all of those."

"Okay, well, lemon is better in drinks—sharper. Limes look more interesting. But lemon goes better in cake, *unless* it's cheese-cake."

"Best color for a Suzuki GSX?" Alex asked.

"I have no idea what a Suzuki is, but I'm going to say lime."

"Amazing," Alex said. "You don't even know what you're saying and you're saying everything right."

Eve laughed, feeling strangely . . . light. She'd never been in this situation, the kind where you met new people with the aim of making friends, yet didn't experience the crushing weight of self-consciousness. With everyone except her sisters, she felt a slight pressure to perform, to hide away the most annoying parts of herself in order to be liked.

But she hadn't bothered to do that with Jacob, because she hadn't wanted him to like her, at first. So maybe now she was out of the habit, and she was forgetting to do it with the twins. Or maybe she simply wasn't as worried about being annoying anymore, because she hadn't annoyed herself in quite a while.

Here in Skybriar, there was no pandering to friends who found her more useful than lovable. No whining about mistakes she hadn't bothered to fix in her journal. No avoiding her parents' disappointed stares, pretending she couldn't see them or didn't deserve it. No wriggling out of the first difficulty she encountered. These days, Eve felt like someone who kept going, and she liked that someone, so she didn't care quite as much if everyone else liked her, too.

Interesting.

"Eve," Mont said, appearing in front of the barstools they'd commandeered and snapping her out of her thoughts. "The bloody hell are you doing with these two?"

"We're best friends now," Eve said, "like in *Totally Spies*."

Mont rolled his eyes. "Has Alex told you she refuses to be Alex? Apparently, she's Sam."

"Has *Eric* told you he refuses to be Clover?" Tessa piped up.

"Uh, because I'm not a little white girl."

"Don't be so basic, brother-mine. Anyway, you're uninvited from the trio. Eve is Clover now. Isn't she perfect?"

Mont snorted. "Sure. What are you drinking?"

"Lemonade," Eve said firmly. "Just lemonade, for me. Belvoir, if you have it." She'd decided on the walk here that she couldn't get drunk. Not even tipsy.

Because she had plans when she got home, and if Jacob decided to negate those plans, it wouldn't be down to possible issues of consent.

"Yes, ma'am." Mont winked, and walked off toward the fridge.

"Ah, hello?" Alex waved. "What about us? Service, barkeep. Service."

"You can wait," he said. "It's good for you."

Alex kissed her teeth and turned away from him, focusing on Eve. To the right, Tessa was doing pretty much the same thing. Eve suddenly realized she'd never met identical twins before. This close up, despite the differences in hair and makeup, it was kind of trippy.

"So," Tessa said. "You're a chef. I should tell you, I can't cook."

"She doesn't need to cook," Alex added. "She's the provider. She just needs a happy little homemaker husband."

"I thought you said no man-talk?"

"They're like ants. They get into everything."

Eve could see this escalating, so she interjected, "What do you provide?"

Tessa winked and kissed her admittedly impressive biceps. "Everything, baby."

Alex rolled her eyes and pulled out her phone. "Look, this is Tess." She opened up a YouTube channel called DIYTessa. The header was a picture of Tessa wearing red lipstick and waving a hot pink drill. "She makes shit. Like, builds furniture and paints walls and whatever else."

"I create aesthetic spaces," Tessa said smoothly. "From social media projects to local interior design contracts." Suddenly she sounded like exactly the kind of person who could make money talking into a camera: confident, put together, with the polished charisma of a radio DJ or a TV newscaster. Then she grinned and turned to holler at her brother, "Hurry it up, big head," and the moment passed.

Eve took Alex's phone and scrolled through the videos. *Upscaling IKEA Furniture*, *Creating a Feature Wall*, *DIY Macramé Planter*—no wonder Tessa had been extolling the virtues on their way here.

"Wow," Eve murmured. So many videos, so many views, so many followers. The woman beside her had built a DIY empire in more ways than one, and instead of feeling envious or lesser, Eve felt inspired. One day, she wanted to have something like this—well, not *like this*, not YouTube, but something to show for herself. Evidence of a passion committed to.

She would. She was on her way.

Except she realized abruptly that the passion she was imagining was Castell Cottage. Not years of party planning for old school friends who still made her uncomfortable, but years of high tea and recipes. Which was rather a problem, since she planned to leave by the end of the month.

Just the thought was making her queasy. Shit, shit, shit.

She bit her lip and handed back the phone. "That's amazing, Tess. I'll subscribe."

"Oh, thanks. You're a doll."

"What do you do?" Eve asked Alex, not just because she needed to change the subject before she overthought—well, everything, but because she really wanted to know.

Alex ran a hand over her buzz cut and offered a sheepish grin. "Oh, I'm a mechanic."

"She runs the only local autoshop," Tessa corrected sternly. "And she rebuilds classic cars."

"That part's just a hobby."

"It could be a business, if she was more confident," Tessa sing-songed. It had the cadence of an oft-repeated argument.

Alex waved at Montrose. "Seriously, get me some vodka."

Eve giggled—and tried not to feel too at home with these wonderful people, in this wonderful place. Tried not to feel more and more threads twining between her soul and Skybriar. Tried, and spectacularly failed.

But she was still scheduled to leave in less than two weeks.

"Anyway," Alex said, turning back to the group. "Eve. What's your thing?"

"I take care of people," Eve replied. Nothing had ever sounded so right.

♫

Jacob found himself staring sightlessly at the clock for what must be the thousandth time and dragged his eyes back to his computer. Technically, he supposed, he didn't need to update the accounts at 1:15 A.M. on a Thursday. Technically, it wasn't even the end of the month yet, so he shouldn't be doing this at all. But he needed to do *something* while Eve was out—something other than lying in bed, thinking about her, wondering if she was having fun. Something other than calling Mont to report on her movements, which Mont would almost certainly refuse to do, and which would make Jacob an actual, official creep.

It wasn't that he wanted to *monitor* her, exactly. It was just— every five minutes, he found himself wondering if he'd done the right thing, if this evening was making her happy, and the desire to know for sure was kind of eating him alive.

But. No creepy phone calls. Watching people too closely could stifle them. He'd learned that after his first girlfriend had found his spreadsheet tracking the details of their relationship and dumped him outside the local library.

So these accounts would have to do as a distraction. He turned back to his spreadsheet—this one thoroughly legitimate—and typed in a few more numbers before he heard it: the click of a key in the lock. That was the spare key to his private area, the one he'd given Eve shortly after discovering she'd, y'know, moved in.

She was back.

He wouldn't go out to see her. That would be weird. That would be like handing someone an unexpected and unasked-for gift, then hovering as they opened it and demanding to know if they liked it. He also couldn't go out there because he'd made a private vow to himself: no being alone with Eve at night. He could not be trusted. Jacob was certain of that.

So he typed nonsense into his spreadsheet, completely fucking up his equations, as the creak of her footsteps sounded down the hall. *Ignore. Ignore. Ig—*

A knock came at his office door.

Well, shit.

"Jacob?" she called softly. "The light's on."

She'd hated it. She'd hated the entire night and was horrified by his presumption. She'd felt corralled into an evening of socializing, like a child, which was frankly Jacob's worst nightmare, so—

"Can I come in?"

To hit him with a brick, probably. Ah, well. Better face the consequences of his actions like a man. "Yes," he said, his voice rough with—tiredness. Probably.

The door opened, and Eve didn't *look* like she was going to hit him with a brick. For one thing, she didn't even have a brick. Just a pair of white Converse with neon, rainbow laces, hanging from one hand—Converse that had presumably been on her feet, once, because now her feet were bare. And she probably didn't intend to hit him with the shoes, because she was smiling. She was smiling so big that her cheeks plumped and her eyes crinkled at the corners and his heart began to thump a frantic dance beat against his ribs.

"Hi," she said, leaning against the doorway. God, he wished she hadn't done that. She was wearing this tiny white dress, a silky, strapless thing with random flecks of color, that clung to every last one of her curves. And there were many. Her hips strained the fabric, pulling it so tight she might as well be fucking naked. She leaned forward slightly, her movements lazy and loose, and her cleavage basically spilled over the neckline. That dress was precarious, to say the least. It was clearly his duty, as the nearest authority figure, to watch her breasts as closely as possible. The minute they bounced free, he would spring into action and . . . put them back in? No, that didn't seem right.

"I know what you did," she murmured, and he immediately thought back to this morning—to the way he'd fucked his hand underneath the spray of the shower while she sang "Good Morning Baltimore," of all things, on the other side of the wall.

But obviously, she wasn't talking about that.

"Jacob Wayne," she said as she finally stepped into the room, "you are the sweetest man alive."

He flinched. "No."

She sprawled in the chair opposite his desk. "Yes." She raised her legs and put her feet on said desk. Her toes were painted glittery pink. Her lip gloss was glittery pink, too. Bright and brilliant and obnoxious as fuck. He wanted to see it all over his dick.

"Did you organize tonight because you were sick of me and wanted me out of your hair?"

"No," he repeated, louder and faster than before.

Eve flashed him a smug smile. "Thought not."

Shit. It was slowly dawning on Jacob that Eve knew him well enough to possibly guess at his motives for tonight. His motives being that he was pathetically in love with her and he would refracture his own wrist, or in this case, ask Theresa and Alexandra Montrose for a favor, to make her happy. "I just wanted you to make some more friends so you could stop talking my ear off."

"You love when I talk your ear off."

"You're a very social being. I was worried you might die in captivity."

"Now, that, I believe," she said, and he experienced a moment of relief before she went on. "You were looking after me, weren't you? You do that rather a lot."

Shit, shit, shit. "No," he said flatly. "You don't need looking after. You're a grown woman."

"You do that a lot, too." Her glossy lips tipped up into a smile. "The whole 'respecting me' bit."

"It's not a . . . bit."

"I know. That's what makes it a panty-dropper." And then she spread her legs.

Dear fucking Christ.

He saw it all happen in slow motion. Her feet on his desk,

slowly parting. His direct view up the length of her legs, and the way those lush thighs separated until he could see straight up her fucking skirt. She wasn't wearing any underwear. Her pussy was bare and beautifully exposed, as pouting and glossy as her wicked mouth, and at the sight his cock became a fucking crowbar.

He wrapped his good hand around the arm of his desk chair, felt the leather creak and stretch under his white-knuckled grip. "*Eve.*"

She batted her eyelashes. "Yes, Jacob?"

"You're drunk."

"I most certainly am not," she replied with a sweet smile. "You see, I have been trying really super hard not to jump your bones for a while now, and I have been succeeding. Barely. Even though you're so sweet and so—" She made this tiny little growl that shot right through him, that brought heat to his throat and yet more blood to his thick cock, and Jacob thought he might die. "You're so *you*," she said. "You're so firm and funny and ridiculous and precise. You are so fucking you, and I love it."

His heart almost jumped out of his throat. If he hadn't slammed his mouth shut, it might have flown out and landed in her lap.

"I've been trying," she repeated. "But tonight, as soon as I realized that you'd taken it upon yourself to organize friends and fun for me, it became clear that I couldn't hold out anymore. I don't just want to fuck you, Jacob. I want—I want you to be mine." She stumbled over the words, but she didn't stop. She kept going, fast and determined and *perfect*, so fucking perfect. "I didn't drink a drop of alcohol all night, and you may call Montrose if you don't believe me. I drank nothing but lemonade because I knew I was coming right back here to sit on your dick. So. What do you think about that?"

He thought he was on fucking fire, that's what. He thought he'd been hit by lightning, and the electricity was destroying him even as it lit him up, and he would beg for it again and again if given half the chance. He thought the idea of Eve, out all night with *him* on her mind, making choices with the intention of ending up here, might actually rip him in two. That's what he thought.

But what he said, through the steel vise of his jaw, was, "You told me you didn't want to do this."

"I changed my mind. It's a lady's prerogative. I was hoping you might change yours, too, but that's up to you."

"You don't think—I'm—" *God, Jacob, don't ask this question.* But he had no bloody control when it came to her. "You don't think I'm bad for your, er, personal growth, and so on?"

She licked her lips, shifted slightly, and his gaze was dragged back to the treasure between her thighs before he pulled himself away. *Eyes up.* If he was going to make good choices here, the kind of choices that didn't ruin everything, he had to concentrate.

Unfortunately, Eve chose that moment to say, "I don't think you could be bad for me if you tried."

It was quite difficult, after that, not to throw common sense out the window and lunge at her over the table. Thankfully, Jacob had a lifetime of control to fall back on during this, his hour of greatest need. "Let me make it clear that I don't—" He swallowed for a moment before pushing past his discomfort, laying the raw truth between them. "I don't just want to sleep with you. I want everything. I need this to be real. So we can't start something if

it's going to end with you getting bored and disappearing on me."
Don't. Please don't ever disappear.

"Good," she said softly. "Stop expecting me to vanish, Jacob. I'm not going anywhere."

He couldn't take her words literally—people said things like that all the time and didn't mean it as an unbreakable vow. But he understood what she was trying to say, understood that she was serious about this. And the knowledge pulsed through his body like something more vital than blood.

She leaned forward and continued, "You asked me, a while ago, what I wanted out of life. I've been thinking about that a lot, and the answers are getting clearer. I want to be happy. I want to feel like myself. Well, Jacob, you make me happy, and I'm always myself around you, and that—that means a lot. That means more than you know. So I'm asking you to touch me tonight, and if you do, it won't be a mistake. It'll be a choice. And it will mean that things are different from now on. That we're different together."

Fuck, he loved her. He loved her, he loved her, he loved her.

And if she was brave enough to choose him, he would bloody well choose her back.

♫

Tonight had been perfect, but through it all, a quiet, steady urgency had hummed just behind Eve's breastbone. She'd caught herself, a few times, rubbing the place where her heart was because it physically ached. Now she was with Jacob, and the ache was replaced by a melting warmth that flooded the air between them.

She was making the right decision, for once. Of this, she was absolutely sure. Eve was meant to be here with him, and her confidence in that fact was a liberation all its own.

Then he stood and walked around the desk toward her, and conscious thoughts faded away in favor of more basic impulses. Little electric flashes spread from low in her belly, and they felt like want, hunger, need.

She exhaled, hard, and watched him come.

"Is it terrible," he asked conversationally, "that I'm going to fuck you on this desk?"

Her thighs tensed, her nipples tightened, her teeth sank into her lip. But her voice remained light as she replied, "Not in my opinion."

"You know the traffic light system, don't you?"

"As in red means stop?"

"Yes."

"I know it." She reached beneath the neckline of her dress, and snagged the condom nestled between her breasts. Waving it in the air, she said, "Green."

Jacob faltered less than a foot away, looming over her like some sort of horny god. Behind his glasses, his eyes were dark and stormy, and his razor-sharp cheekbones were softened by that raspberry flush. "Where," he asked tightly, "did you get that?"

"There's a dispenser in the ladies' at Mont's pub."

"And you—" Jacob dragged a hand through his hair, his expression almost pained. "You really spent this whole night planning to come home and sleep with me, didn't you?"

It was all Eve could do not to purr at the dizzy satisfaction in his voice. "I thought you'd like that."

"I like *you*," he said roughly, taking that last step toward her. "I—Eve—"

"Mmm?" He sounded as if he was gearing up to say something, but Eve found her attention ensnared by his rather prominent erection. She'd taken her legs off the desk, so he was standing between her spread thighs, his waist at eye level. She only had to look down a *tiny* little bit, and her field of vision was dominated by the thickness in his jeans.

And gosh. *Gosh.* What, was he smuggling a butternut squash down there? The thing was obscene. Eve was absolutely thrilled.

"Eve . . ." he said. "Are you staring at my dick?"

"Of course I'm staring at your dick, darling. What did you think I was proposing we do, here?"

"I was hoping for more than staring, actually. I just—I think I forgot about the way you look at me."

She tilted her head back, meeting his eyes, seeing a world of dark desires within that familiar frost. "And how do I look at you?" she whispered.

He wrapped a hand around her upper arm and pulled her gently to her feet. Then he said, "Like this," and kissed her.

It felt like being consumed.

Jacob surrounded her—the clean, fresh scent of him, the heat and strength of him, the weight of his cast against the small of her back and the delicacy of his left hand on her cheek. He cradled her face and tipped her head back and nibbled at her lower lip, and when she gasped he kissed firmer, harder, more desperate, and sucked at the tip of her tongue. Eve had never had anyone suck her tongue before, but she decided from now on it would be a requirement.

And since she could no longer imagine kissing anyone who wasn't Jacob, that struck her as just fine.

He pressed their bodies together tightly, so tightly, as if he wanted to push his way inside her. Then she felt the fat curve of his dick against her belly and remembered he *did* want to be inside her. They should make that happen soon. Very soon. But right now, she was a bit hazy and melty and all the other lovely, legless sensations that came with being so thoroughly kissed. He felt as if he adored her. As if everything between them was some kind of worship. As if she was more than good enough; she was the best he could ever have.

"Fuck me," she breathed against his lips, and pushed him back against the desk.

"Foreplay," he countered, but his own breaths were quick and harsh. He sat on the desk and ran his shaking hand from her cheek down to her throat. "The first time I saw you, I wanted to touch you right here."

"Before I opened my mouth, you mean."

"Yes. And now you've opened your mouth many, many times, and I want to touch you even more." Gently, he wrapped his hand around her throat and pulled her closer. Then he bent his head and grazed his teeth over the bare, tender curve where her neck met her shoulder. A shiver zipped between Eve's breasts and spiraled through the softening heat of her cunt. She moaned, and he kissed the place he'd barely bitten, hot and wet and decadent.

"I want to learn every single sound you make," he said softly. "I want to be the one who brings you pleasure. Every time. Can I?" His hand went from her throat to her breast. He traced a finger over the edge of her dress for a second before pushing the bodice down in one decisive move.

Eve's breath caught, coalescing into a gasp that remained trapped in her chest. All she could hear was the thud of her own pulse, all she could feel was cool air and Jacob's hot gaze on her nipples, as tangible as a touch.

"Say yes," he murmured, and cupped her in that squeezing, shameless way he had, as if he could spend a lifetime doing nothing but this.

"Yes," she managed, the word shuddering out of her as she arched into his hand.

"Tell me I'm yours now," he ordered, quiet but immovable. He licked his thumb, then touched her other breast. Circled her nipple with that firm, slick pressure while his words infected her blood.

Tell me I'm yours now. It felt as if he'd given her all his secret tenderness, just handed it to her and asked her to take care of it. And she would. She couldn't do anything but. Only—the moment seemed so solemn, she felt a little guilty for finding it mind-blowingly hot as well.

But that couldn't be helped. Because here was Jacob, studying her with steely intensity, touching her like he owned her, asking her to own him. So, really, was it any wonder she wanted to rip his clothes off?

"You're mine," she agreed, unbuttoning his shirt, "and you're impossibly hot, Jacob Wayne. Did you know that?"

He smiled a little, that cautious curve of the lips that made her heart flutter. "I try. Since I know you like it, and all."

"Oh—so you *know* what a mess you make of me." She couldn't stop her own smile, even as fire pulsed through her veins and his bare chest became visible, inch by inch.

"Yes, I know," he said, reaching behind her to wrestle with the dress's zipper. "You are beautifully obvious. Sometimes you look at me and I can *see* you thinking about screwing my brains out. You—" The zipper gave with a metallic whisper and he grinned that wolfish grin, sharp and anticipatory. "Oh, good. Now you can be naked." He pushed the dress down, and when she stood before him completely bare, all the humor left his expression. Nothing remained but stark, explicit longing as he bit his lip and groaned. When he shoved a hand against his erection, Eve felt her clit ache for the want of him. She pressed her thighs together, shifted her hips, but it didn't help.

She was wet and swollen and desperate for one thing only.

So she stopped taking her time and went for his belt.

CHAPTER EIGHTEEN

Restraint forced Jacob to grab Eve's wrist. Heart-pounding need begged him to relax and let her get the fuck on with it.

But if he let go now—when his body shook with the force of his lust, when his mind was teetering at a cliff's edge—he couldn't make this good for her. And he needed it to be good for her, as opposed to good for *him*, which would equal ten minutes of pounding her over the desk until he came so hard his brain fell out.

So he held her wrist, and met her eyes, and said, "Slow down, Sunshine."

She cocked her head, curious. "Any particular reason?"

"Yes. I'm this close to bending you over, and your apparent enthusiasm isn't helping." Because she was just so—into him. So clearly, impossibly into him. Pupils blown like she was high, lips slick and swollen from kissing him, rubbing her body against his like a cat every chance she got. And fuck, what a body—taking her dress off had been a miscalculation, but in Jacob's defense, he'd only ever seen her naked in the shadows. He'd had no idea that the sight of her fully illuminated—all softness and abundance and brown, velvet skin—would steal his higher cognitive function.

She flashed him a brilliant smile and said, "Maybe you *should* bend me over. Right now."

Biting back a moan, Jacob pressed her hand crudely against his erection. "I'm not just shoving this inside you, Eve. No, don't whine. Bad. That would be bad. *Foreplay,*" he repeated. He'd meant to let go of her once he'd made his point, but instead, he was still holding her hand against his cock. Pressing her down, really, and jerking his hips up, seduced by that sweet pressure. Shit. *Stop it.*

"At least let me take these off," she murmured, tugging at the belt loop of his jeans. Looking up at him with those beautiful eyes and that wicked smile and oh, fuck—

"Fine," he said, "fine, fine, fine," and then they were both fumbling with his belt and his fly, Jacob one-handed but twice as desperate, and before he knew it, he was sat there bollock naked on his desk.

He remembered the day he'd bought this desk and kind of wanted to smirk, because if someone had told him, *Hi, I'm from the future, and one day you're going to let a brilliant, ridiculous woman reduce you to a shaking puddle of lust on this thing*, he would've rolled his eyes and moved away from the hidden cameras.

Eve raised a hand to cradle his face, her thumb tracing the curve of his lower lip. "What are you smiling about?"

"You," he replied honestly, and turned his head to kiss her palm.

She smiled back. And for a moment, despite the electric rope of lust crackling from the head of his cock down to his aching balls, the air between them felt innocent and unbelievably sweet.

"Can you keep your glasses on this time?" she asked softly.

"Is this the part where you confess your spectacle fetish?"

Eve laughed and pushed the length of her hair over one shoulder. Jacob's gaze followed the fall of lavender automatically. He watched fine braids glide over her nipple, cascade past her ribs, caress the deep bronze stretch marks at her hips. "Actually," she said, "I just want to make sure you see everything."

"Understandable," Jacob rasped, his tongue heavy in his mouth. "There's a lot to see. Cracking view. Wouldn't want to miss it."

"Mmm," she murmured, her own gaze dipping to his lap. "I agree."

Jacob looked down, too, and flushed at the sight of himself. He knew how hard he was—he could feel it in his fucking skull, at this point—but seeing the evidence was altogether different. Or at least, it was when Eve ran a delicate finger from the fat, glossy head to the thick root, tracing his veins like they were a map. "Can I have this now," she asked, "or do I have to seduce you some more?"

His chest heaved with each sharp, Eve-scented breath. "Sit down," he managed, "and let me lick you again."

"After," she said. "Fuck me hard and kiss it better."

His head fell back, his abs contracted, his dick jumped under her touch. "*Eve.*"

"I know you like being convinced." She slid her hands over his shoulders, then clambered up onto the desk, straddling his lap. Jacob wasn't entirely sure how he kept breathing. He watched her pretty mouth move, but for a moment he couldn't hear a damn thing over the rush of blood in his ears.

Between them, her hot, wet pussy was spread by the length of his shaft. Her thick thighs cradled his hips, and all he could do was lean back against the desk with one hand and take it. Take her. Or rather, let her take him. She rolled her hips and his eyes rolled back in his head. Scalding, silky torture, gliding over his hypersensitive skin. Fuck. "*Fuck.*"

"Happily," she said, and picked up the condom she'd placed on the edge of the desk.

He knew then that he'd be balls-deep in her within ten minutes—but he decided to keep arguing anyway. This was what they did, after all: they argued, and it was good. "There is such a thing," he gritted out, "as dicks that are too big." Which was true. He'd researched extensively during his teens and concluded that if he wanted any form of penetrative sex, which he most certainly did, he'd have to be very careful about it. So, yes, there was definitely such a thing as dicks that were too big—too big to be convenient, anyway.

Eve apparently agreed, because she nodded eagerly. "I know," she said. "I like them."

And now he was remembering that night—the night he'd fucked her senseless with a twelve-inch purple cock and she'd begged him for more. Memory Eve and actual Eve pressed in on him from all directions. He sucked in a breath, looked down, and swallowed hard at the sight of them together: of Eve's plump folds spread open around his rigid prick; of her sweet little clit, glossy and fat; of her rounded belly and bare skin screaming louder than anything else: *intimacy*.

He had her. He had her, and honestly, he'd do whatever the fuck she wanted because she had him, too.

Jacob was about to snatch up the condom when she grabbed a fistful of his hair, hard—hard enough that silvery pleasure sang down his spine and straight to his balls. Then she pressed her mouth to his, and he was no longer capable of thoughts or reason or making decisions. He was just . . . a body. She made him one big, horny, blissed-out body, she grounded him with her weight and her touch, she turned everything Technicolor, and he'd never felt like this in his entire fucking life.

"Eve," he breathed, but the sound was lost in the slow sweep of her tongue. "Eve," he groaned, and she moved to kiss his throat, to rake her nails down his chest and rock her clit against his cock. "Eve," he said, over and over, but what he meant—what he couldn't say just yet, but what he *meant*—was, *I love you. I love you, Eve Brown.*

She ripped open the condom and wrapped him up so fast it left him dizzy. There was the pressure of her hand as she rolled down the latex, so good that his hips punched up as if trying to fuck her fist, and then she was gone. Jacob felt a growl rumbling in the back of his throat and swallowed it, but he couldn't swallow the urge to get inside her soft body. That need was too great.

So he gave in to it. He shifted his weight, braced one foot against the floor and one against the desk chair at Eve's back. Wrapped his right arm around her body, despite the awkwardness of his cast, and gripped her chin with his left hand so she was forced to hold his gaze. Sometimes, eye contact made him uncomfortable. Right now, it felt like stripping her open and learning everything she kept inside, and that was exactly what he fucking wanted.

"Come on, then," he said softly. "Since you want it so bad. Come and sit on my dick."

A long breath rushed out of her and her lashes fluttered. Every little sign that he affected her flew straight to Jacob's cock, and this time was no different. He was moaning well before her pussy kissed his tip. Then she made contact, and—

"Shit," he hissed, pleasure forcing his eyes shut for a moment. He simply couldn't keep them open; sensation swelled over him in a drugging wave, taking away his control. He fought it back enough to open his eyes again, holding her gaze as she worked herself slowly onto his length.

This. *This* was perfection. Jacob had been chasing it his whole life, but fuck, he'd never expected to find it quite like this.

He watched Eve's pupils dilate as he felt her cunt tighten. Watched her lips part as she sank inch by slow, careful inch. And *felt* her surrounding him, easing him into that hot, wet clasp until it was a struggle to breathe. His thighs flexed with the effort of controlling himself; his hips demanded to move, to thrust, to fuck. But not yet. He'd let her soften around him first, until her body wasn't strangling his cock so much as gripping it tight.

And then, when she was desperate and begging for it, he'd fuck her like an animal.

Eve's breath hitched, and he wound a fistful of her braids

around his hand and pulled her even closer. Until every word between them was practically a kiss. "Okay?"

"Okay," she nodded, rolling her hips. Taking him deeper. He released her hair, ran a hand down her body, thumbed her tender clit. Her answering moan was low and decadent, so he did it again, pressing in firm, slow circles, and felt her tight little cunt bloom for him, just a little.

"See?" he asked softly. "Foreplay."

"Better when you're already in me," she rasped, her head falling forward to bump gently against his.

"Yeah. Yeah, it is." His fingers glided through her folds until he found the place where they were joined. He traced her soft, needy flesh and she whimpered, then sank down until his heavy balls were flush against the twin curves of her arse.

Their moans twined together like fragments of the same thread. He kissed her hungrily, clumsily, and she was the same. "Fuck me," she breathed between the hot, rushed meetings of their lips. "Oh my God, Jacob, fuck me. You should've bent me over. Wait, why aren't we in a *bed*?"

His laugh was tight and shaky. "Later. We'll ruin the bed later." Then he gripped her hip for leverage, holding her down as he began to thrust. It wasn't exactly easy. Actually, it wasn't remotely easy. He was glad, though; concentrating on the logistics made it easier to keep from coming. If he had been fucking her in a bed, if he'd been lying over all this brilliance just dicking her into the mattress, it'd probably be over by now.

As it was, he could already feel that rising tide of relief coming for him, an electrical storm of pleasure coalescing at the base of his spine. He gritted his teeth and fucked harder, reveling in the feel of her skin, her softness, the sounds of her sharp little screams. "Eve," he groaned, burying his face against her throat. Somewhere in the back of his mind it occurred to him that his glasses—his spare glasses, at that—were going to be fucked, but frankly, he didn't give a damn. "God, Eve."

"Tell me," she panted, rocking desperately against him, her nails digging into his back. "Tell me."

"So fucking good," he choked out. There was this thing called grammar, Jacob recalled, but he'd forgotten how to use it and it seemed unnecessary. "Fuck, Eve, so good. Do you want more, love? Tell me what you need."

"Yes," she whimpered. "More. Harder."

He wasn't entirely sure how he managed it—sex-induced super strength, or something like—but Jacob lifted her to the side without breaking their connection, rolling them both until Eve was splayed back on the desk and he was leaning over her. The desk creaked. Several files fell dramatically to the ground, as did his keyboard. The desk lamp fell, too, with a loud thud, and suddenly all the light in the room was behind them. But he could still make out the tortured bliss on her face, so he didn't give a fuck.

Jacob grasped the edge of the desk behind Eve's head, held on tight, and thrust hard.

She made a noise that could be described as incoherent, or perfect, or both, and then she held on to him and sobbed, *"Jacob."* Her body arched in invitation, her legs spread wider, and he felt the first tight, tense flutterings of her impending orgasm. If he'd thought this couldn't get any better, that he couldn't burn any harder, he'd clearly been wrong; now everything about him was aflame.

"Do you like that?" he asked, just for the satisfaction of hearing her gasp—

"*Yes.*"

He thrust harder, deeper, and she met him every time, until they were writhing together in a mess of grunts and moans and sweat and sighs, until her breathy sounds became sharp, building screams and her soft, pliant body turned rigid beneath him. There was barely a second of stillness before she shattered, as beautifully as before, her hands twisting in his hair and her body shuddering around him. He watched her with an ache in his chest so intense it made him shudder, too, and then suddenly the ache was everywhere and he was moaning as he came hard, hard, hard.

Dizzy. He was dizzy. But he could feel Eve panting beneath him, could hear her breathless laugh, could see—when he opened his eyes, and when had he closed them?—her smile, like the North Star he used to stare at on the road.

God, he loved her.

But all he said out loud was, "Fuck, that felt good."

Eve had surprised herself countless times, during these last weeks. She'd surprised herself by interviewing for this position, for example. She'd surprised herself by hitting someone with her car— because, regardless of what Jacob liked to imply, that had never happened before. It was usually just cones and fences.

Then she'd surprised herself in increasingly better ways—by

keeping her word and looking after Castell Cottage, and not fucking it up. By getting into this whole chef lark and taking pride in
her job. By making friends and settling down and starting to see
Skybriar, already, as something like home.

But Eve had never shocked herself quite so thoroughly as
she did in the moments following her and Jacob's rather mind-
blowing desk-sex. The moment in which he kissed her, then gave
her a sheepish grin and said, "I'm going to deal with the condom."

"By *deal with*," she asked, stretching languidly, "do you mean
shower your whole entire body?"

He released a laughing breath, then admitted, "Well, yes. But
I'll be quick."

She opened her mouth to reply, and the words, *I love you*, almost fell out.

Thoroughly astonished, Eve snapped her mouth shut. Luckily,
Jacob didn't notice; he was too busy staring at her tits over his
shoulder as he left the room. Bless his one-track mind.

And bless his arse, a bitable curve that flexed with every step.

But when he finally disappeared out of the doorway, the evil
spell of his backside was broken and Eve mentally returned to the
I love you moment. Hm. Interesting. She probably ought to investigate that. Her first instinct was to go to her room and put on
some nice, fluffy pajamas—you know, to settle her mind and thus
facilitate the feelings investigation—but she found she couldn't
leave the office without setting Jacob's desk to rights. Or at least
attempting to. They'd rather decimated it.

It occurred to Eve, as she was gathering papers in a vague attempt at order and fixing his upended lamp, that this sort of be-

havior rather matched the words she'd wanted to say. After all, love seemed the only reasonable motivator for tidying someone else's desk when you yourself could not give a flying fuck about the entire thing.

Of course, it was possible that her love for Castell Cottage had inspired this fit of conscientiousness, and that she'd only felt a momentary swell of love in her heart for Jacob because he'd just given her such impeccable dick.

On the other hand, that momentary swell of love wasn't actually momentary, because as soon as she thought about him, she felt it again: a flood of tenderness and affection, gentle, yet powerful enough to swallow entire cities whole. Familiar, but magnified. Known, but intense. The sort of love you read about in books.

After two weeks. No way. No fucking way.

And yet, by the time Eve finished in the office, carried herself back to her bedroom, and put on the aforementioned fluffy pajamas, that soft-but-strong emotion hadn't gone away.

It wasn't that the idea of loving Jacob *bothered* her. Actually, when she thought about it, she caught herself grinning so hard her cheeks ached and her eyes squinted and her ears sort of popped, and she felt a bit loopy, like she could fall back against the bed with a film-worthy sigh and do nothing but moon over his very excellent qualities for the next nine hundred hours.

But there was also a part of her, small but loud and rather fierce, that insisted she be reasonable. Rational. Adult. She couldn't possibly be in love with Jacob already. It was silly. It was reckless. It was the very definition of immature, absolute evidence that she was making bad choices yet again—only, when she tried to think of Jacob as a mistake, she came up against an impenetrable wall in her mind that cut off such a sacrilegious path completely.

In the end, she decided to do as Gigi had advised. Because when attempting to adult, there was no harm in requesting a little assistance.

Eve strained to listen for the sound of the shower running down the hall, and then—satisfied Jacob was still occupied—she adjusted the silk scarf holding back her braids, picked up her phone, and opened the sisterly group chat. After misspelling her request three times in a row, she decided her mind was frazzled enough without bringing typing into the equation, and hit Record on a voice note instead.

"Hello. I have a question that requires only answers; no nosy questions in return, thank you. How does one know when one is really in love? For example, in *Beauty and the Beast*, how did Belle know she was in love with the Beast and not just Stockholm syndromed? Or, Chloe, how did you know you were in love with Red and not just his excellent hair? Oh, or Dani, how did *you* know you were in love with Zaf and not just *his* excellent hair? Yes. That question. That's my question. Danika, please respond." Satisfied, she sent the message.

It took a moment for blue ticks and jumping dots to appear, but once they did, responses were fired in quick succession.

DANI: I didn't know I was in love with Zaf, remember? You told me.

CHLOE: I find this question infinitely suspicious.

CHLOE: Who is Stockholm syndroming you?

Eve rolled her eyes and sent back, "No one. It was a theoretical comparison."

DANI: Okay, but who are you in love with?

Eve hit Record, opened her mouth, then stopped when she realized she'd been about to say it. She'd been about to say, out loud, *I'm in love with Jacob*, and she would've meant it, too.

Which didn't entirely obliterate Eve's doubts—not when those doubts revolved around herself, around who she was and who she wanted to become, and how wide the gulf was between each state. But it certainly helped.

She found herself smiling again. *I'm in love with Jacob*. It sounded so good, so pure, so precious in her head. So she'd keep it in there for a little while longer, until she was confident enough to say it out loud.

"Were you talking to someone?" As if conjured by her thoughts, Jacob's voice floated through the door a moment before he stepped inside.

Dripping wet.

In a towel.

"Good God in heaven," Eve said, "you have to stop doing this."

"Doing what?" he asked coolly. But there was a slight tilt to the corner of his mouth, a purposeful languor in his movements as he sauntered into the bedroom, raking a hand through his damp hair. He knew exactly what, so she didn't bother spelling it out.

He was clearly terrible at drying himself off, because she could see tiny droplets of water glistening over his pale skin. It made him look like a delicious can of Coke on a sweltering day, sweating enticingly. The downy trail of blond hair arrowing toward his—well, frankly, toward his dick, had Eve's heart pumping like a perky aerobics teacher's biceps, and her clit aching like her head after a tequila hangover. Her mouth went dry. Possibly because all the moisture in her body had moved rapidly down to her pussy.

"Who were you talking to?" he asked softly.

"Hmm?" Eve attempted to scrape her sentiency up off the floor where she'd dropped it. "Oh. Erm, my sisters."

He came closer, his eyes an electric storm. "That's nice. Now put the phone down."

Eve realized belatedly that she was still holding the Record button. "Yes, sir." She let go, locked the phone, and stood up.

"You should come to my room," he said.

She blinked. "Sex in a bed? You spoil me."

"No, not sex in a bed. I mean—" His nostrils flared, even as his mouth curled into a self-deprecating smile. "Well, yes, actually. Sex in a bed. But I meant that you should sleep with me." He caught her hand. "If you want. That's what I meant."

"Oh," Eve said softly, and there was the love again, gliding through her veins, glowing and golden, turning everything in its path to mush. "Okay. Yes. Lovely. That's what I want."

Jacob grinned and tugged at her hand, dragging her swiftly out of this room and into his. She barely had time to process the change of location before he tumbled her onto the bed and climbed over her. Then her entire body was a vibrating nerve again, alive and exposed. He pressed close, his strong thigh sliding between hers with a sureness that made her gasp. Pressure, so much pressure, so insistent and demanding was her Jacob.

"Talk to me, Evie," he murmured, and she realized she'd been holding her breath, and also—

And also, that the idea of talking right now didn't worry her, the way it had with other men. She wasn't nervous about saying the wrong thing, about getting on his nerves with her random trains of thought. She wasn't focused on pretending to be perfectly fun instead of imperfectly strange. Because behind his scowls and his terrifyingly high standards, Jacob was steely enough to take everything she was and say, *Actually, I think I'd like some more.*

But she must have spent too long thinking, because after a moment, his expression faltered, and he made as if to lift his weight off her. "Sorry. Am I—? I know I can be a bit much, in these situations."

She grabbed his shoulder and pulled him back on top of her, her response fierce and instinctive. "No. You are divine. You are impossible to get enough of. Perhaps some people would disagree, but those people don't especially matter, because you're mine." As soon as the words were out, she was mildly shocked by her own venom. But she didn't regret it.

Especially not when he smiled, small and slow and unmistakably shy. "Ah. Well. That's me told." Then he kissed her, with a slight, soft groan that said he couldn't not. As much as she'd grown to appreciate Jacob's control, she liked even better to feel him lose every ounce of it, pouring it into her like an offering. His mouth moved feverishly over hers as if he was afraid she might disappear. His tongue tasted the seam of her lower lip, the corner of her mouth, the vulnerable tip of her own tongue, and his cock pressed against her aching clit in a way she was 100 percent okay with. Ecstatic with, in fact. This was like a direct dick-to-pussy massage and he wasn't even hard. Eve would be leaving 5-star feedback when they were done.

"We can't have sex yet," he told her between kisses. "I'm serious. It's been all of ten minutes and I'm absolutely fucked. I have no idea why I'm doing this."

"We could have sex," she corrected, "if your tongue isn't too tired."

"Eve," he said sternly, which got her hot as hell. "You do realize, don't you, that we should be talking right now? Discussing what just happened and continuing our ongoing and vocal negotiation of consent, et cetera?"

"Shut up, Jacob," she said cheerfully, and kissed him again. Their mouths met softly, their tongues touched lazily, she hiked her leg over his hip and rode his thigh a little. And in the end, it turned out his tongue wasn't too tired. Neither was his dick, after a while.

♫

They did settle down eventually.

Jacob lay back against the cushions, cocooned by warm blankets and Eve's soft, lemon-and-vanilla scent. To his right, he'd propped his cast up on a cushion as usual. To his left, he felt the presence of the woman he'd spent the last couple of hours doing terrible things to—and yet, he was abominably nervous at the prospect of touching her now. Probably because he didn't want to touch her for sex; he wanted to hold on to her like she was something precious, and to never let go.

Despite their roller coaster of a night, Jacob still wasn't confident an action like that wouldn't blow up in his face.

But he might do it anyway.

In the end, he didn't get a chance, because Eve was bold enough for the both of them. And warm enough to keep their fire going when Jacob's pessimism threatened to cool him down. She rolled over and slung an arm across his bare chest, snuggling her cheek against his shoulder. "Can you sleep like this?" she asked. "I thought you might like it."

Eve: always taking care of him. He let his eyes slide shut and sank into the moment like it was a feather bed. "I do," he said, his voice rough. "I mean, I can—I do—stay." That was the point, really. He wanted her to stay, and he needed her to know it. Because he suspected people had let Eve go far too easily, in the past. That she was uncertain sometimes, just like him.

"You know I'm a sure thing, right?" he blurted out.

"*Are* you?" She raised her head with a wicked smile. "And here I thought you were tired."

He rolled his eyes. "Stop that. Depraved woman. What I meant is—I was serious, earlier. You're mine now."

"Very caveman of you," she murmured.

Jacob made the executive decision to ignore that. "You're mine, which means you don't need to worry about me wandering off or—or rejecting you, or—I'm a sure thing," he repeated, because they were veering too deeply into emotional language and he strongly doubted his ability to get it right. "I'm certain. For you. Of you. And things."

She raised her head again, but this time, there was no teasing smile. This time, her gaze met his, midnight pupils enveloping chocolate brown, and she blinked rapidly. "Oh," she said, her voice quiet. And with that single syllable, Jacob's suspicions were confirmed. Eve wasn't used to being held on to.

He could relate.

"Will you tell me something?" he asked.

She lay down again, her head a comforting weight on his chest. "Anything."

His heart squeezed at the word. "Why did you come here?"

She hesitated. He'd expected that. The day they'd met, Jacob had written this woman off as an irresponsible tornado sweeping the countryside, searching for interviews to ruin. Which was, obviously, ridiculous. But in his defense, he'd been under a lot of pressure, and he hadn't really known her then.

He knew her now. He knew that she adored her sisters—so much she never shut up about them—and that her friends back home didn't deserve her, but she talked about their ludicrous rich-girl antics with fondness, anyway, and that she was perfectly capable of working hard and succeeding as long as she was given the space to do so.

All of which begged the question—why *had* she left her life behind and taken the first job she could find out here? Once upon a time, Jacob hadn't cared to know, and then he hadn't deserved to ask, but now? Well. Now, he was the man Eve Brown would tell *anything.* Which felt like one of the top five most powerful positions in the world.

So he waited, and after a moment, she started talking. "This story isn't especially flattering. Toward me, I mean."

"You should know by now," he said, somehow pulling her even closer, "that I'm not going to judge you."

"Jacob Wayne, you dirty liar."

"That I'm only going to judge you a little bit," he corrected, "and that I'll still—" He stopped talking, the words *I'll still love you* yanked offstage by a hook around the neck. Not yet. Seriously, not yet. "I'll still like you," he finished roughly. Nice one. He was about as smooth as crunchy fucking peanut butter.

"Gracious of you, darling," she snorted.

"That is my defining character trait, yes."

"What if I'd killed somebody?"

"I wouldn't be surprised, and I would visit you in prison if necessary."

She gasped, all feigned outrage. "You wouldn't offer to help me hide the body?"

Jacob's lips quirked without permission. "You've been here quite a while, Sunshine, and there's no police sniffing around. So I imagine you hid it just fine yourself."

"Well. Yes. Quite right." She preened at the idea of being a capable murderer, because she was a ridiculous ball of fluff. Jacob kissed her forehead because there was really no other option, not when she was being so obnoxiously cute.

"Now," he said, "stop stalling. Tell me this story."

She sighed. "My parents were angry with me."

He waited for a moment before nudging. "Did you hit them with your car?"

"Spiritually speaking, I think I've hit my mother with my car many times." Her tone was dry, but her fingers were tapping a rapid rhythm against his rib cage. "My mum wants so badly for me to be successful. At anything. And for a while, I gave up even trying. I think failure was one thing, but giving up, for her—that was a bridge too far. They were disappointed with me and I couldn't bear it, so I . . . I left, determined to find something to do. You know, to prove myself. And so, here I am! Trying not to fuck up again."

It wasn't a totally unexpected explanation—and the way Eve spoke about herself was hardly unfamiliar. She said that sort of thing all the time—that she was a failure, a disappointment, that she was trying but had no faith in her ability to succeed. Jacob couldn't pinpoint exactly when those words had started to set his teeth on edge, but the feeling got worse every time. And here? Now? It was the worst it had ever been, like scratching bone.

Apparently, he couldn't bear to hear Eve Brown criticized. Not even by herself. "Thank you for telling me," he said, because manners were useful things, and he'd read somewhere that it was good to start positive before telling someone off. "But Eve, I think it's time we had a serious conversation—"

"Boo," she interrupted. "You know I hate serious conversations."

"No," he said sharply, turning to look at her. "No, you don't. Stop acting like you do. Even the brightest, lightest things still have substance."

She was quiet for a moment, clearly surprised. "I—well—"

"And this is exactly what I wanted to talk about. Eve . . ." He wrapped an arm around her and squeezed, corralling his feelings into actual, useful words. Sometimes her presence made that kind of thing easy, but sometimes, when he was drowning in all the emotions he felt for her, it was incredibly hard. "Eve," he repeated, "I know you think you need to improve yourself, or grow up, or whatever else. But there is nothing wrong with you. You're just . . . a bit different, that's all. You're just sensitive enough for the world to seem too fast and too loud. And you're—you're hurt, I think. You're used to flinching in case you get hurt again. I'm the same, for different reasons, but still. The fact is, you're smart, you're creative, you're dedicated, and you *care* about people. You'd do anything for anyone, even if you were terrified, as long as it was right. And what matters more than that? Tell me one thing, honestly, that matters more than that." Expressing this stuff felt a bit like digging for gold; Jacob labored for what felt like hours (but was actually thirty seconds), and in the end he was mildly exhausted and utterly elated because—

There. There was his gold: Eve's smile.

"You're very complimentary, this evening," she murmured. "I wonder why?"

He rolled his eyes.

And she, just like he'd known she would, sobered up after a moment. "Thank you, Jacob," she said softly. "If you'd said something like that to me last month, I might not have believed you. But I'm starting to see sides of myself I didn't even know were there. So maybe I'll believe you after all." She was teasing, but behind her smile he saw it: a burgeoning trust. Not in him, but in herself. "I . . . I suppose I never really thought of doing nice things for people as a skill. At least, not until I came here, and you offered to pay me for it."

"Well, I'm glad you're changing your mind," he said, "because it absolutely is a skill. I should know. I have to work on it a lot."

She laughed, and it was like little bubbles of sunlight popping against his skin.

"Your abilities," he said slowly, "lie in the places people usually overlook. So you've been convinced you don't have any at all. But you're smart, and you're capable, and if people struggle to see that, it's their problem, not yours." He really hadn't meant to bring this next topic up, but the words spilled from his mouth without permission. "You know, Eve, you're—we're—different. And . . ." He cleared his throat, started again. "Do *you* feel like things are different when you're with me? The way we communicate?"

"Well, yes," she said pertly. "I imagine that's how we ended up in bed."

She had him there. "I wasn't talking about that difference. I meant—you like the fact that I'm straightforward. You say it all the time. Do other people feel . . . less straightforward to you?"

Jacob expected her to reply with confusion, with more questions, with—something ordinary. But she wasn't ordinary. She was Eve. Which is why she shocked the shit out of him by replying calmly, "Oh, I see. Yes, it feels different—rather like talking to my sisters. Easier and familiar, probably because we're both on the autistic spectrum."

His surprise dissolved almost instantly into of-fucking-course laughter. "You already knew."

"Well, no," she corrected, "not before I met you. You've made me notice my own behavior more. So I did some research and drew the obvious conclusion: it's likely that I, like you, am autistic. I assume most of my family is, actually, which would explain why almost everyone finds us incredibly strange. It's an interesting development, but also . . ." She smiled a little, her gaze on the ceiling as she spoke. "I already know who I am and how I am. In fact, I'm learning more about that every day. Having a name for some of those things is satisfying. That's all."

Jacob absorbed that for a moment, biting back a smile of his own. "You're so . . ."

"What?" she asked, rising on one elbow to look at him. The lavender fall of her hair spilled across his chest, and her eyes were like starlit night. "I'm so what?"

"Perfect," he finished. "Eve Brown, you are absolutely perfect to me."

She beamed, so obviously happy it made his heart squeeze. Then she kissed him, and that was perfect, too. They were always perfect together, these days, and most of Jacob believed they always would be.

But a tiny little part of him—the young, cold, worthless part—still wasn't quite convinced. That part had a long memory, and it was filled with loss.

He'd work on that part, Jacob decided. He'd work on it for her.

CHAPTER NINETEEN

Eve was singing.

She'd been singing ever since last night, in fact, and having a jolly good time of it. Today, instead of humming her usual absent-minded refrains, she let every ounce of her joy shine through her voice, creating her own backing track. Luckily, Jacob didn't seem to mind.

She looked up from the blueberry-and-lemon sponge cake she was icing to gaze at him like a moony, devoted cow. Fortunately, he was studying the Gingerbread Festival event map he'd brought down to the kitchen, and therefore completely missed her heart eyes. She took advantage of the moment to explore his now-familiar face: the golden gleam of his severely parted hair, the deep furrow of his lovely scowl, the sunshine-colored lashes hiding his stormy gray gaze. Beautiful, beautiful man. She was of half a mind to drag him upstairs to the store cupboard and have her wicked way with him before high tea.

Again.

Just as Eve began to seriously consider the idea, the kitchen door swung open, shattering her thoughts. She jumped, dropped her icing bag directly on top of the almost finished cake, and released a deep sigh. "Oh, fudge."

Jacob saw the mess she'd made of her cake and leapt to his feet with a determined expression. Apparently, he thought he could rescue her from ruined icing like a knight in shining armor. She was tempted to let him try, just to see what happened.

Then Mont, who was leaning in the open doorway with a smirk on his face, finally spoke. "Hm. Well, now. Whatcha doing down here, Jake?" There was more than a little triumph in his voice.

Jacob scowled at his friend. "Stop the Jake shit." His tone softened as he approached Eve. "How's the cake?"

"Oh, you know," she replied, deeply annoyed with herself as she picked the bag out of the icing. "Splotchy. Slightly dented. Ever so appetizing." She bit her lower lip, her gaze flicking to the clock as she considered her options. "Maybe I can cover up the, er . . . indent with something."

"Something like this?" Jacob asked, and then he reached over her shoulder to snag the glass of fresh-cut lavender she'd placed on the table that morning.

She stared at the flowers for a moment before a slow smile spread over her face. "Yes. Something exactly like that. Thanks, darling, you're a peach." She popped up on her toes and kissed him—just a quick, sweet press of their mouths, already familiar after a single day. Then she remembered Mont, froze, and pulled back sharply—or tried to. But Jacob caught her by the hip, surprise and pleasure merging in his gaze.

Eve blushed. She wasn't embarrassed, or anything; she just got rather warm when he looked at her like that.

He held her close a moment longer, ducking his head to murmur in her ear. "You kissed me."

"I know," she whispered back. "I've kissed you many times since last night, in case you'd forgotten."

His voice dropped an octave. "I hadn't forgotten."

"Right here, guys," Mont said from the doorway. "Literally standing right here."

"Shut up," Jacob advised, before turning his attention back to Eve. "You kissed me in *public*."

"Does Mont count as public?"

"Interesting question," Mont drawled.

Jacob, who had apparently decided to ignore his best friend, continued. "I like you kissing me in public. We should do that more. Whenever we want. Like a couple. Do you agree that we're a couple?"

Eve laughed softly, letting her head fall forward against his shoulder. She'd sort of thought last night made them a couple—not the sex, but rather, all the lovely mushy things she'd managed to make him say. Of course, Jacob was more black and white than that. He needed actual, clear-cut words, and she was happy to give them to him.

But for Eve, even the air between them was everything. It was so absolutely everything that she'd decided, once and for all, to stay in Skybriar. She was going to tell Florence to fuck off—albeit more professionally, since Eve was now associated with Castell

Cottage and had certain standards of behavior to uphold. She was going to forget about little Freddy's cursed bloody birthday party . . .

And then she was going to make a trip home and tell her parents in person that she was sorry, and that she was changing, and that she believed in her own power now. That the things she did—feeding people, helping people, making them feel good—were just as important as counting money or writing contracts. That she respected her own skills enough to use them, fear of failure be damned.

She'd inform her parents, honestly, that she'd found something she loved. (And someone, too, but she'd likely keep that part to herself for now.)

Maybe they wouldn't believe her—*she* could barely believe it, sometimes—but she knew it was the truth. Because when she thought about leaving Castell Cottage, about making it a temporary blip in her past, something inside her said calmly but firmly, *No*.

And when she thought about leaving Jacob, the voice became a hundred times louder.

So, "Yes," she whispered in his ear. "We are absolutely a couple."

He grinned at her as if she'd just single-handedly disinfected and restocked every bathroom in the building, and then he grabbed her about the waist as if they'd spent the last six years apart, dragged her against his body, and kissed her breathless.

"Jesus Christ," Mont muttered, but he actually sounded quite pleased.

He sounded less pleased a moment later when he cleared his throat and said, "Er, not to interrupt, you two, but it looks like there's a goose outside."

♩

Eve had learned many things since arriving at Castell Cottage, but it seemed her education was far from complete. Case in point: she had no idea of the grave threat posed by certain waterfowl until Jacob dragged her outside and told her sternly, "Ducks are little shits. Geese are worse. Swans are worst."

"Ah," she said, "right." She was still faintly dizzy from all the semipublic kissing—and of course, Jacob's *We're a couple* moment, which she had found adorable.

Being this happy should be illegal. Even the goose couldn't dampen her mood.

But it was certainly dampening the mood of Castell Cottage, if the scene on the gravel driveway was anything to go by. A big, gray goose waddled toward Mr. Packard, who'd checked into the Daisy Room with his wife just that morning. At the time, Mr. Packard had been a calm but friendly man in a nice check shirt. At present, he was a pink and nervous man climbing on top of his own car.

"Get it!" he shouted. Then he pointed at the goose, as if anyone could mistake his meaning.

"Are geese dangerous?" Eve asked no one in particular. It wasn't a question she'd thought much on before, but Mr. Packard looked liable to lose control of his bladder, so she was forced to wonder.

"Sometimes," Mont smiled, just as Jacob said grimly, "They are a great danger to the peace and dignity of my establishment, yes."

"A goose can break an arm if it really gets going," Mont went on, "but Jacob's arm is already broken, so he'll be fine."

Eve was horrified. "He has another arm to break!"

"Yeah, but that'd be *really* bad luck."

"Stop winding her up," Jacob scowled. "It's not going to break my arm. It's just a goose. This isn't its territory. It has no reason to resort to arm-breaking, and I'm sure even geese can be reasonable." That said, he stormed off toward said goose with steel in his spine.

"If you're sure," Eve called after him. "Good luck, darling. Godspeed, et cetera."

He waved.

"So," Mont said as they watched Jacob approach the creature. "You and Jacob, huh?"

She felt herself flush. "I suppose so."

"I'm pleased, to be honest with you."

"I knew I liked you."

"Go on," Jacob was shouting, waving his cast around like a battering ram. "Be off with you!"

"Just go steady with him," Mont said quietly.

Eve dragged her gaze away from the sight of a goose all but fleeing Jacob's broken arm. "Hm?"

"He's not as tough as he seems." Mont's voice was quiet, his own eyes on the goose, his focus clearly elsewhere. "That's all. He's not as tough as he seems."

The goose exited the gate and waddled right. Eve opened her mouth to tell Mont that she knew, that she'd be awfully careful, that Jacob's fragile brilliance was quite safe in her hands.

Then she heard a familiar voice floating through the air. Familiar, but impossible, of course.

"Is this it?" the voice asked. And then, "Dear Lord, Martin, was that a goose?"

Eve stiffened, then forced herself to relax. Her mother couldn't possibly be here. That voice clearly belonged to some other lady. A lady accompanied by a man with the same name as Eve's father.

That's what she told herself, right up until the moment her mother stepped through Castell Cottage's front gate, pushed her Dolce & Gabbana sunglasses up onto her forehead, pressed a hand to her chest, and cried, "Eve!"

Then *the rest of the family, oh my goodness*, crowded behind her—Dad, of course, and Gigi, and Shivani, and even Chloe and Danika, hovering at the back. It was a veritable ambush of relatives, which, in Eve's experience, did not bode well.

It didn't bode well at all.

"Oh, fudge," she said.

Beside her, Mont squinted at Gigi. "Is that Garnet Brown?!"

♫

Jacob wasn't sure what he'd expected from Eve's family, but this . . . Well, actually, he thought, as he looked around his packed dining room, this wasn't a surprise at all.

Eve's relatives all had an untouchable air of glamour and certainty, that healthy gloss of attractiveness that surrounded people who had access to the best of everything—food, clothes, whatever. He'd seen people like this many times before, but the part that threw him off was: they all seemed to *like* each other. It was hard to put his finger on how he knew that. Something about the way they'd walked as a group, making space for one another, steps almost in synch, like a pack rather than a simple group of relatives. Or the way they'd bickered through awkward hellos and made odd little comments to each other as Jacob had herded them inside like sheep.

Whatever the case, he could see the love between them like heat shimmering in the air. It made sense, of course, that Eve had been raised at the heart of a family like this. She'd learned her softness from somewhere, after all.

Jacob studied them now, since he'd run out of conversation shortly after *Hello*, and since Eve wasn't here to ease the way for him. There was the mother, sitting stiffly by the window in a pristine suit, her sharp, hazel eyes examining every inch of the room. Probably looking for faults, which shouldn't worry Jacob; his establishment had no faults, the occasional trespass of waterfowl aside. But he still felt a twinge of nervous worry in his gut, because, well . . . this was Eve's mother, and she had the same sharpness about her that Aunt Lucy had, which suggested—among other things—very high standards.

And there was Eve's father, a man who radiated warmth and appeared never to leave his wife's side. He didn't look much like Eve, what with the bald head and mustache and all, but he had the . . . the feel of Eve. He'd nodded and smiled, earlier, as Jacob had led them all in here to wait. And right now, he had a hand on the mother's shoulder, like he could share calm through his touch the way Eve spread happiness through her smiles.

To Jacob's right sat the sisters; pretty, different, close. They were whispering together in the corner, shooting him suspicious looks. The one with the blue glasses looked particularly murderous. The one with the purple hair seemed dispassionately curious, like a scientist who would dissect him if she thought it worth her while.

And then there was the grandmother, and the other older lady who seemed to be her partner. They were the only ones who weren't pointedly ignoring him. Jacob rather wished they would.

"So," the grandmother said. She was wearing enormous sunglasses and, unlike the mother, hadn't bothered to remove them indoors. "You own this place, do you, darling?"

"I do, madam."

"Oh, *darling*. How sweet. Did you hear that, Shivani? But no, no, you must call me Gigi. And this is my darling Shivani, and over there is Joy, having an embolism, and that is Martin, having a quieter embolism, and huddled in the corner like a pair of witches are Chloe and Danika. There, now, we're all introduced and terribly intimate." Gigi smiled beautifully, all white teeth and fine-boned beauty, before producing a cigarette from . . . somewhere. Jacob must have missed the source. "Can I smoke, darling?"

"I'd rather you—"

She held it to her lips, and then the other woman—Shivani—produced a box of matches, and the cigarette was chivalrously lit, and it was all very Hollywood.

"Times of great stress require it," Gigi told him conspiratorially. "But really, I quit in '79. Now, then. What was your name?"

"Erm," he said, "Jacob."

"Fabulous, fabulous." She took a deep drag. "Jacob, sweetheart, are you in any way mistreating my little *dumpling* of a granddaughter?"

In the corner, Joy stiffened. "*Gigi.*"

Meanwhile, Shivani—a middle-aged woman with a waterfall of black-and-silver hair—rolled her eyes. "Oh, Garnet. You ham-handed battering ram."

"You say the sweetest things, dear."

At which point, Jacob managed to gather the wits that question had knocked out of him. "Am I *what*?"

"Well," Gigi said after another dragonlike exhalation, "*I* was dragged up here on the belief that my dear little muffin had gotten herself into some sort of trouble, or at the very least fallen in thrall to an unsuitable sort. Yet here we are, and you seem a perfectly reasonable man, and Eve—well, I could be confused, but I do believe Eve has dumped us all here to wait for her while she serves *cake* to *strangers*. Which suggests to me, darling, correct me if I'm wrong, that she simply works here, as opposed to anything more sinister."

"It's—it's—it's high tea," Jacob managed. *Sinister?* Why in God's name would anyone suspect something sinister? He was about to ask as much when Eve appeared in the doorway and beat him to it.

"What on earth are you talking about, Gigi?" she asked, and he practically fainted with relief at the sight of her. Because Jacob knew exactly how he would behave if any other group of posh, smoking arseholes appeared at his B&B and started looking around like he had something to hide, asking rude questions and generally making nuisances of themselves; he would shout a bit and curse a bit and throw them out on their arses.

But this was Eve's family, and she cared about her family, and it seemed painfully clear that they cared about her. She'd ended up here because she was ashamed of disappointing them. They mattered. And he loved her. Which meant that Jacob was caught between his general—and growing—irritation, and the desire to be, well . . . not hated. Which wasn't a place he'd often found himself, since entering adulthood.

He didn't fucking like it.

But he'd stay here awhile longer, for her.

"And what are you all doing here?" Eve demanded, coming in and closing the door behind her. "Better yet, *how* are you here? I didn't tell anyone where I was."

Her entrance seemed to spark energy into the room. Everyone rose to their feet, with the exception of Gigi, who was busy lounging around and smoking, and her *darling* Shivani, who was busy sighing and rolling her eyes. And also seemed to have secured a steaming flask of tea from somewhere. At least one of Eve's relatives was sensible.

"Well," said one of the sisters—Chloe, if he'd followed Gigi's vague points correctly. "Do you remember, Evie-Bean, when you and I drove to the ballet in Birmingham, but we got lost and Danika came to get us? You turned your location on, so she could find us. And, well, none of us ever thought to turn it off."

Eve opened and closed her mouth like a fish before blurting, "You *stalked* me?"

"She had to." That was Eve's mother, Joy, who was looking vaguely tortured and wringing her hands. "Your father and I know we were harsh, before. But you vanished into thin air and refused to tell anyone where you were."

"So you decided to turn up here and—and heresy me?" Eve demanded.

"I think you mean harass, darling," interjected the other sister, Danika. "And no, that isn't why we're here. Not entirely. We were going to leave you to it, but then Chloe and I got slightly . . . worried."

"Worried? Why?"

There was a pause, and a few more wary looks in his direction, before Chloe spoke. "At first, every time we called or texted you'd tell us about this awful new job and how horrible your boss was."

Jacob tried not to wince. She'd said *at first*, after all, and he supposed he deserved that.

"Then, all of a sudden, you were never free to talk because you and your boss were terribly busy," Chloe went on awkwardly. "With all sorts of . . . after-hours meetings, and *then* last night you sent us a, erm, voice note."

"What voice note?" Eve asked, her face a picture of confusion. But he saw the moment she realized what they were talking about. Jacob remembered it, too.

Eve had been sitting in her room, talking to her phone, and he'd come in demanding to know what she was doing. And then he'd dragged her off to *his* room.

Ah, shit.

"We thought you might be in some sort of sex cult," Danika said baldly. "Those happen, you know."

"A sex cult?" Eve squeaked. "At a bed-and-breakfast?"

"Well," Gigi piped up, "clearly their worries were unfounded, because it looks as though there's only you and Jacob, and sex cults typically require multiple members. Unless that strapping young man from outside is also involved, in which case, bravo."

"Mother," sighed Eve's dad in weary tones.

"What, Martin? I'm not taking this lightly, you understand. I'm simply examining the facts."

Joy spoke sharply over everyone. "The point is, we had no idea what was going on, so we're here to check on your well-being. That's all. We had intended to give you space, wait for you to come home next week—"

"Next week?" Jacob interjected. He hadn't meant to speak aloud, but—well, that was wrong. Pretty much everything said in the last ten minutes had been wrong, but also understandable. This statement, however, stuck out like a sore thumb. Eve couldn't have been planning to visit home next week, because next weekend was the Gingerbread Festival.

"Or was it the week after?" Joy waved her hand. "I don't know. Whenever you were coming back to begin the event-planning job. But you know you have a tendency to pick up, erm, less than suitable men, darling, so we thought we'd better nip up here just to check nothing was getting out of hand."

Event-planning job. Jacob supposed he should be focusing more on the fact that Eve's mother had just called him less than suitable—or had she simply insulted Eve's general life choices?

One of those. And usually, he'd be incredibly pissed by either option. But his brain was a little stuck on the phrase *event-planning job*, trying and failing to absorb it, to move past it, to make it make sense.

He looked at Eve, waiting for her to clear things up. Instead, she avoided his gaze and told her mother, "Jacob isn't *unsuitable*, Mum. He's exceedingly—good. And very—accomplished. And far cleverer than—" She spluttered awkwardly. "Oh, never mind. The event planning begins *after* next weekend."

"The *what*?" Jacob asked, his voice harder than he intended. Couldn't help it. He felt suddenly twisted and prickly, and— awkward and foolish and caught unawares. All the things he most hated to be.

Because apparently, Eve was leaving, and he was the only person in this room who didn't know about it.

Eve's dad, Martin, glared at Jacob with surprising force. "Do you know, son, I'm not sure how this conversation is any of your business."

Jacob stood up straighter, feeling himself ice over. "I'm Eve's employer. Her whereabouts during our busiest season are certainly my business."

"Well," Martin shot back, "our Eve has a lucrative opportunity in event planning beginning in September, so perhaps you won't be her employer for much longer."

Those words plunged Jacob into ice water. He ground his teeth practically to dust, trying to hold on to the leftovers of the day's happiness—but he couldn't. He couldn't. Because all of a sudden, he was uncertain, he was an outsider in his own safe haven, and the woman who should be with him—the woman who should *always* be with him—was planning to leave. Had been planning to leave all along, he realized. When he turned to look at her, the guilt was written all over her face. Her brows were drawn tight together, her eyes huge and shimmering, her teeth sinking into her lip. He wanted to go over there and put his arms around her, to comfort her.

He wanted her arms around *him*. He was so cold. She was so warm. She'd fix it.

Except right now, she was the problem. She was the one who'd made him a fucking fool.

"Jacob," she said cautiously, "after I interviewed here, I agreed to plan a party for an old friend."

"Plan a party?" Joy repeated. "Don't downplay your achievement, darling. Your father and I were beyond impressed when Mrs. Lennox let us know you'd be planning Freddy's twenty-first. She had me on the phone for half an hour yesterday morning alone. You've done very well."

"I wasn't due to start," Eve said, still looking at him, "until *after* the festival."

And there it was. The final confirmation. Jacob's throat felt tight, his stomach roiled, his skin stretched thin and painful over his bones. Of course she'd been planning to leave. What had he thought—that this perfect hurricane of a woman would blow into his life and actually stick around? Fall in love with him? Instead of blowing right the fuck out again?

He shouldn't be surprised she was disappearing so soon. Jacob was easy to leave behind; he'd learned that very early on. What hurt—no, what made him *furious*, so furious his eyes prickled with it and his blood burned him from the inside—was the fact that she'd almost convinced him she might stay. Why had she done that? *Why had she done that?* And why had he wanted her so bad after all of five fucking seconds? He should know by now that other people didn't work like him, weren't intense like him, but she was so right and so familiar, he'd just—

"Fuck," he muttered, and suddenly he couldn't bear to stand in that room in front of all those people, all those strangers. He stormed past Eve and slammed out into the hall, drawing alarmed looks from two guests heading up the stairs.

Heart pounding, breaths coming a bit too fast, Jacob pulled himself together and offered them a smile that felt more like baring fangs. Their alarm didn't fade. Actually, they seemed to head up the stairs a bit faster.

"*Fuck,*" he repeated, and then the door behind him opened and Eve was there.

Her fingers fluttered up to his shoulder. "Jacob—"

"Don't touch me." Her hand felt like a boulder. He jerked away and whirled around to face her, forcing himself to ignore the expression on her face.

The expression that said she was crumbling.

Clearly, his interpretations couldn't be trusted when it came to this woman. Clearly, he always got her entirely, overwhelmingly wrong.

"Why?" he demanded. "Why would you—" He didn't even know what to say.

"You didn't give me the job." Her words were rushed, fumbled,

as she fiddled frantically with the ends of her braids. "At first. I—
you didn't—before I hit you, you didn't give me the job. So then
Florence called me, and she did give me a job. But I had to stay
because I hit you, and you needed help. So I thought I'd just stay
here until the festival was over. The job—"

"I don't give a fuck about the job," he roared, and in that second, it was absolutely true. "You—" *You said you wanted me. You
were supposed to be with me, not make plans behind my back and
stay here out of obligation. Were you still going to leave, after last
night?*

He couldn't ask. He couldn't ask, because experience dictated
that the answer would be yes.

But only children whined when they were left, and only children waited, night after night, for the ones they loved to change
their minds. Jacob was not a child anymore. Nor was he some
pathetic thing to be abandoned and beg for an explanation. He
wasn't pathetic at all.

Even if he *had* been foolishly, hopelessly in love with this
woman, dreaming of a future, while she'd stumbled into his bed
and been ready to stumble right back out.

He took a deep, deep breath, and felt like himself again. Felt
like he was in control.

"Jacob," she said softly. "Don't. You're . . . don't."

He knew exactly what she meant, but he ignored her. It was far
better to be like this, to be distant and safe, than to be—whatever
she'd made him. Far better indeed. "I appreciate your commitment to your work here," he said coldly, "and I understand why
you felt responsible, after what happened. But I don't need you."

She rocked back a step, her inhalation sharp. "I'm saying this all wrong, aren't I? I know I am. Jacob, I wasn't going to leave. I'd changed my mind. Okay? I wanted to stay. Here. At the cottage."

Jacob's shriveling heart leapt at those words, tried to run right for her—but it slammed into a wall of experience. He screwed his eyes shut because he couldn't process all this and look at her, too. She was so beautiful and so precious and so obviously placating him, saying whatever it took because she could see him shattering and her soft heart couldn't take it. Saying exactly what he wanted to hear. Just like she had all along.

It had been a lie all along.

Opening his eyes, he echoed flatly, "You'd changed your mind."

"Yes." The word came out in a rush, more air than substance.

"Did you tell anyone?"

She stared. "I—what?"

"Did you tell anyone?" he repeated, his spine like steel, his stomach roiling. "Like your sisters, or, I don't know—whoever hired you to plan this party? Did you really make the decision? Or did you start to feel bad, and *think* about staying, and now this is happening and you need to fix it so you're just speaking those thoughts out loud?"

"I . . ." She stuttered, blinking rapidly, looking so crestfallen it actually broke his heart. Or maybe something else was breaking his heart right now. It was hard to tell.

"You need everything to be sunshine and rainbows," he said. "You don't want me to be pissed. You don't want me to end this." Because he could see that. He'd be a fool not to see that. Eve looked ready to cry, which was really fucking with his resolve. There was something young and raw in his chest snarling and clawing at him, demanding he let this whole mess go and just have her any way he could get her. That he hold the fuck on to this.

But Jacob knew how holding on ended. It ended with the other party letting go and pushing him firmly—embarrassingly—away. He was thirty years old and he knew what he needed. He needed honesty, he needed simplicity, he needed not to be ambushed by situations like this because his relationship was a moment of pity that had spun out of control. And most of all, he needed someone who would stay. Someone just like him.

So he made himself cold, cold, cold. What a shame this frost didn't bring numbness. "You don't need to worry about me. I don't need you," he repeated. "I have never needed you, Eve." *I have never needed anyone.* "And honestly, I'm pleased you have another option. Perhaps you'll be better suited to your . . . party planning than you are to what you do here."

Her jaw hardened, those beautiful eyes narrowing. "I'm good at what I do here, Jacob."

He couldn't bring himself to lie on that score, not knowing how she worried about failure. Even though he shouldn't care, at this point. "Yes, you're good. But that doesn't make you irreplaceable." He felt a bit sick, saying that, but he couldn't not. Eve's life here was replaceable to her, after all.

Although she wasn't reacting that way. Not quite. She jerked back at his words as if he'd slapped her, and then she took a step forward with her hands curled into fists and said, "Really? So if I just—left. You'd be fine. That's what you're saying?"

She must know the answer was *absolutely not*, but he wouldn't humiliate himself by saying it out loud. He looked her up and down, as detached as he could manage. Her T-shirt today said BEE SWEET, the words surrounded by embroidered little bees. But he'd tried sweet, and he'd ended up stung.

This whole time—this whole fucking time, she'd been here out of obligation. And whatever had changed between them, it hadn't changed enough, not in the ways that mattered. Not in the ways that said out loud and without doubt, *This person is mine.*

He would've screamed that in the street for her, and he knew it was irrational, but it was also him. And he couldn't change that.

"I was fine without you before," he said, "and I'll be fine again."

The words should've felt like satisfaction. But as she flinched away from him, as she turned on her heel and stormed back to her family, as they gathered her belongings and bundled her into a car and drove her far, far away . . .

Jacob couldn't shake the nagging feeling he'd just thoroughly fucked himself.

CHAPTER TWENTY

It was funny how much could change in twenty-four hours.

According to the clock in Jacob's office, it was a little past 1 A.M., and he was absolutely certain that this time yesterday he'd been dizzily blissful with Eve. Or maybe just sleeping next to Eve, which was basically the same thing. Either way, he'd been happy, totally unaware that he and Castell Cottage both were a temporary obligation. That he was making a fool of himself. That the feelings he incited in others would never reach the senseless heights of his own emotions.

But today there was no bliss, and no delusion, either. He'd spent all fucking day storming through Castell Cottage to remove signs of Public Enemy Number One, scrubbing the kitchen from top to bottom and putting things back on the high shelves instead of the ridiculously low ones her adorable—her *annoying*—shortness had required, washing his sheets and also any sheets Eve herself had washed because they all retained a faint scent of vanilla (he'd checked), and so on and so forth.

After all that, he should be sleeping like the dead, but he couldn't so much as nod off—not with a certain weight missing from the left side of his mattress. He was determined not to miss Eve, but his body hadn't quite caught up. Fucking typical. Fucking *infuriating*. So here he was, sitting in his office, staring at spreadsheets until his eyes bled. Funnily enough, it wasn't improving his mood.

With a muttered curse, Jacob jerked open his desk drawer searching for a distraction and found—

An AirPod. Right there, in the midst of his carefully organized sudoku magazines, resting on a heart-shaped sticky note that could only have come from one person. His stomach tensed, and he slammed the drawer shut again. Exhaled, hard. Stared at the wall, and swallowed every forbidden feeling that tried to creep up from his chest . . . until one slipped past his defenses and whispered in his ear.

She didn't actually leave, you know. You sent her away.

Well, yeah. That had been the fucking point: sending her away before she *could* leave. He'd learned very early in life that obligation wasn't enough to make anyone keep him. Eve wouldn't have kept him, either, in the end, whether she realized it or not. So he should just—he should just fucking forget her.

Instead, he opened the drawer again with a shaking hand. Then he lifted out the AirPod and the sticky note, put them both on the desk, and read the flowing lines of Eve's handwriting.

Jacob,

This is synched to my phone. If you keep one, we can listen to the same music while we do the housekeeping!

XOXO
Sunshine

It was the *Sunshine* that did it. Jacob stared at the note for long minutes, memories flickering through his mind like old film. He saw Eve's eyes flash as she fired sarcasm and insults right back at him. Eve's irrepressible smile as she laughed in the face of his irritation. Eve's voice practically singing his name, as if she'd never met a word she liked better.

The feelings he didn't want came thicker and faster, until there were far too many for Jacob to bat away. They crawled over him in a wave of uncomfortable warmth and impossible longing, whispering wild hopes he could never in a thousand years believe. But he wanted to. His heart twisted, almost pulling itself in two, because he wanted to believe those hopes so bad. They washed across his scorched earth like a gentle, cleansing wave, and suddenly, he saw everything a little differently.

Jacob, I wasn't going to leave. I'd changed my mind. Okay? I wanted to stay.

She'd said that to him. She'd said that, out loud, and he'd dismissed it as not enough because . . .

Because he hadn't believed her. He hadn't been *able* to believe her. She hadn't meant it, was just trying not to hurt him. Any other interpretation had felt impossible—still felt impossible now. His heart slammed up against old fears, fears that swore he should tread carefully or end up broken.

But instead of focusing on that—on the threat of his own pain—now Jacob focused on hers. Eve's. She'd looked so fucking sad. And then so hurt. Because—what had he said to her?

Did you tell anyone?

As if he didn't trust her. Well, he *hadn't* trusted her. Only now did he realize what a fucking insult that must be. Only now did he realize that thinking so lowly of his own worth required him to think badly of Eve in turn. And he refused to do that. He'd promised her he wouldn't do that. God, he'd told her he wouldn't let go, and then, at the first sign of trouble, he'd pushed.

A scale tipped back and forth inside him like a seesaw, making him nauseous. On the one side was his own self-doubt, the weight of the idea that no one could stick around. But on the other side was Eve herself. The woman he knew her to be. Sweet, and sparkly, and a little chaotic—and smart, and caring, and *real*.

Eve could do anything. He definitely believed that. Which meant if she wanted to, she could choose Jacob.

But only if he let go of scales and doubts and all the little things that had made him shove her away. Only if he believed in himself, too.

He stood, swallowed, then picked up the note and the AirPod, shoving both in his pocket. Checking the clock, he strode out of his office and down the hall. He managed to restrain himself until he stepped out of Castell Cottage completely and into the cool night. Then he ran all the way to the Rose and Crown.

♪

"Jesus, man, are you okay?"

Jacob stood in the doorway of the Rose and Crown, one hand on his thigh as he bent double, breathing hard. He hadn't been for a run since fracturing his wrist, and according to his doctor's advice, he probably shouldn't have taken that one. But this was an urgent situation, so . . .

Catching his breath, he looked up at Mont, who was all wide-eyed astonishment and obvious alarm. He had a mop and bucket in his hands, and behind him, Katy, the barmaid, was drying glasses at the bar—or rather, she'd frozen in the act of drying glasses, and was also staring at Jacob.

He briefly considered dragging Mont off somewhere private for this little chat, then decided there was no time. If he didn't get answers soon, he might die. Of uncertainty. Or love. Or regret. At least one of those had to be deadly, and possibly all three.

So he straightened up and just blurted it out. "I love Eve and I didn't tell her. Do you think I should've told her?"

Mont blinked rapidly. At the bar, Katy made a strangled noise before putting down a glass and grabbing her phone in what she probably thought was a very subtle move. Fucking teenagers.

"I—I don't know, mate," Mont said finally. "Maybe. Probably. Are we going to talk, now, about why she left?" Because Mont had been bugging him since yesterday about it. So had Aunt Lucy. So, for God's sake, had Liam, the man who never called or texted, managing to get on Jacob's arse all the way from the United bloody States.

"She left because I told her to go," Jacob said. "She'd been planning to—eventually—so I told her to go. Because I thought she'd always leave anyway. I just, I really fucking believed it, Mont, and it seemed so reasonable at the time, I swear it did, but now I'm starting to wonder if it wasn't, and I don't know which half of my brain is the smart half and which half is all emotional and shit."

Mont sighed and ran a hand over his stubbled jaw. "Jacob. Mate. Maybe the smart half *is* all emotional and shit."

Jacob collapsed at the nearest table. "Yes, I've been afraid of that." And afraid of facing just how badly he'd fucked up, hurting Eve with all his insecurities. Shit. *Shit.*

He had to fix it. He had to. Even if she wanted nothing to do with him after the crap he'd pulled, she had to know exactly how vital, how powerful, how perfect she was. He had to *make* her know, even if she despised him. Even if he'd ruined the fledgling magic between them.

"I don't think you need me to tell you all this, Jake," Mont said. "I think you just want me to confirm you're not completely deluded before you run off and do something wild."

Yes. Yes, that was true.

"So ask," Mont continued. "Just ask me."

His voice hoarse, Jacob managed the hardest question of all. "Do you think Eve could love me? If I told her I was sorry, and I—I trusted her, and she—gave me a chance?"

"Yeah, genius. I do. Aside from anything else, you're pretty fucking lovable."

Something in Jacob wanted to ignore those words, to brush them aside as unlikely or impossible. But that something didn't have permission to lead—not anymore. It was old and battered and bruised. It was toxic and it told him such utterly believable lies. It belonged to a far younger version of himself, and it also belonged to his parents. Worst of all, that thing had hurt Eve.

He decided to squash it.

It would definitely pop back up again, but in order to maintain the level-headed analysis he so prized, Jacob would happily—and ruthlessly—continue to squash.

"Okay," he said. "Okay. Thanks. Going now." He turned to leave.

"Hey." A viselike hand clamped onto his shoulder. "Reminder: it's almost two o'clock in the morning."

Jacob deflated a little. "Oh. Right. Yes." No fetching Eve just yet, then. Fetching Eve later. Never mind. He had a feeling he'd be able to sleep, now, so that was something. "Thanks, Mont. Bye."

♫

No matter how hard she tried, Eve couldn't make her old bedroom feel like home. All the things she used to do here—lying in until noon watching porn, ordering new T-shirts because she was bored with the many, many slogans in her walk-in wardrobe, bitching about her "friends" in her journal—felt silly and pointless and wrong. Which, in turn, made the room itself feel silly and pointless and wrong, because it offered no other diversions. She couldn't even focus on her favorite romance novels, since the idea of reading about love suddenly made her feel sick to her stomach.

This was most unfortunate, since she also couldn't get up and leave her room. If she did, she might bump into one of the relatives lingering worriedly about the house, and she hadn't yet decided what she wanted to say to them. She knew she was pissed off about their behavior yesterday, but she couldn't quite articulate *why*.

She was too busy thinking about Jacob.

As in, Mariah Carey's "Through the Rain" blaring from her speakers, the aforementioned journal in her hands, one sad, used tissue on the bedside table—*thinking about Jacob*. She was trying to write something horrible and scathing about him, but she couldn't quite manage it. Every time she put pen to paper she'd remember something terrible, like the way he forced himself to say soft, gentle things when she really needed it, or the way he threw himself around to rescue her from minor disasters in clumsiness, and then she'd cry a little tiny bit. Again.

Although, at this point, she was getting sick of crying. Because yes, Jacob was lovely and blah, blah, blah, but he'd also been monumentally shitty yesterday, and actually, she was rather fucking pissed about that, too. The more she thought about it, the more she suspected she was furious.

She remembered his iron expression as he'd asked, *Did you tell anyone?* and wanted to shout, *This isn't fucking chess. Stop trying to checkmate me.*

She knew she'd done wrong. She'd lied, and she'd lost his trust, and she'd pressed down on a barely healed scar without ever meaning to. But he'd done the same right back, acting as if all she cared about was having her cake and eating it, too. Acting as if she was some sort of spoiled brat, after everything.

So, yes: Eve was pissed.

Satisfied, now that she'd identified the burning in her diaphragm, she put down her pen and flicked back through her journal—back through all the other times she'd been pissed off. Because that was the theme, she realized, as she combed through random dates. Something happened, she didn't like it, so she ranted about it in silence.

Hello darling,

Olivia was absolutely frightful today, so I put corian-der in her lemon drizzle cake and then I blocked her phone number.

Hello darling,

The festival coordinator called me an imbecile for putting up the map boards incorrectly—can you believe that? Well, good luck to him with putting them up right, because I've come home and that poxy little fes-tival can carry on with one less volunteer. I didn't really want to meet the Dixie Chicks anyway.

Good morning, darling,

It's been eight days since Cecelia's wedding. I'm sorry I didn't write sooner, but you are an inanimate object, so it doesn't really matter.

She remembered writing that last entry, just like she remembered the wedding itself. The rush of success that had soured so easily, and the familiar lick of fear when everything started to go wrong. It had seemed easier to give up completely than to face yet another fucking failure. Had been such a relief to come home and vent in her journal and then forget it had ever happened.

But Eve didn't feel that relief anymore. Now, she read over that last entry and wanted to call Cecelia, apologize for the dress, then demand the slander against Eve Antonia Weddings be removed from the internet because those doves had needed rescuing, and all that aside, Eve had done a bloody good job.

Her mind stumbled over the words a little, the first time. But the more Eve repeated them to herself, the smoother they came. *She'd done a bloody good job.* She knew she had. She'd tried her hardest, she'd been organized and capable, she'd bent over backward to make someone else's dreams come true. She'd been *good*.

Just like she'd been good at Castell Cottage, no matter what Jacob said.

Yes, you're good. But that doesn't make you irreplaceable.

The old Eve might accept that statement. The new one wanted to throw a chair.

How dare he think the worst of her, after treating her like she was the best? How dare he push her away after making her feel needed? How dare he act as if she was the same scared, thoughtless woman he'd first met when he must know by now that she was so much more? If he'd given her a chance to explain, she could've told him that she was passionate about Castell Cottage, that her commitment *meant* something.

Although . . . it suddenly occurred to Eve that, despite Jacob's devotion to the B&B, maybe it wasn't her commitment to Castell Cottage he'd wanted to hear about.

Hm.

Hmmm.

It was too soon to tell him about the little seed of love sprouting in her chest, putting down deep, delicate roots. It *had* to be too soon. That's what Eve had thought, anyway.

But what if she'd been wrong?

A knock at the door startled her out of her tangled thoughts. "It's only me, darling," Gigi called, just like she had yesterday evening.

"Come in," Eve said, but her mind was still churning, replaying that last edgy, uncertain conversation with Jacob. Everything had come crashing together without warning, two sides of her life that she'd been learning to handle separately, and she hadn't known what to do for the best.

"Shivani made you breakfast," Gigi said, shutting the door behind her. "A cheese and sun-dried tomato omelet, you lucky thing. She's always shoving spinach at *me*."

"Tell her thank you," Eve murmured absently, but the words were just a reflex. She'd thought—she'd wanted to make it clear to Jacob that she wasn't messing him around, work-wise, and then he'd told her to fuck right off and quite frankly broken her heart. (At least, Eve assumed the throbbing ache in her chest was heartbreak. If it wasn't, it must be the start of some other cardiac event.) When he'd gotten rid of her so easily, she'd felt as if her bones were too fragile to carry her. She'd had to leave. She'd had to run. Except now she was wondering if getting rid of her had been easy for Jacob at all.

She'd been so hurt by his sudden coldness, she'd forgotten what that coldness meant. Forgotten that his barbed wire was just a desperate form of protection.

"Thank Shivani yourself, darling," Gigi was saying. "Come to our midmorning practice in the sunroom. She misses you terribly, as do I."

Eve finally looked up at her grandmother, who was perched on the edge of her bed in a skintight, baby-blue jersey catsuit. "Um . . . I . . . I don't think I can make midmorning practice, actually."

"Gosh," Gigi said. "You look a little dazed, sweetheart. Perhaps we should go and see Doctor Bobby. He was telling me all about these lovely vitamin drips they've had in from America, they'll pep you *right* up."

"No thank you," Eve murmured, disentangling herself from the silky canopy of her princess bed. "I have plans today."

"*Do* you, indeed? How thrilling, do share." Gigi picked up the omelet she'd just placed on the bedside table and helped herself to a bite.

"I'm going to have stern words with the family," Eve called as she strode into the en suite, "and then I'm going back to Skybriar where I will inform Jacob that he can't sack me without due cause, or I shall take him to tribunal, and also that I love him, and if he wants to get rid of me he'll have to say something definitive about that."

There was a short pause from the bedroom before Gigi replied, "Oh, Eve. *Yes.* Absolutely yes. You take a shower, my little moppet, and I will choose your T-shirt."

♫

"I have something to say!" Eve announced as she swept into the kitchen. Then she stopped in her tracks, snapped her mouth shut, and blinked at the crowded island. "Oh. Erm. Hello, everyone."

She'd expected her parents to be pacing about the place, since they both took Fridays off, but she hadn't been prepared to find her sisters and their boyfriends lurking, as well. Still, she would not be deterred. Eve lifted her chin and nodded at the men. "Hello, Redford, Zafir. Since you did not force yourselves into my haven of self-actualization, you are exempt from the coming storm."

Red grinned and leaned back against the kitchen wall, his long, fiery hair standing out against the cream tile. "Nice one."

Chloe rolled her eyes.

Zaf, meanwhile, was busy stroking one massive hand over Danika's back with grave intensity—but he spared a second to turn his dark eyes on Eve and grunt. It was one of his neutral grunts, which she took to mean, *Very well, carry on.* So she did.

"First of all." Eve turned to glare at Gigi, who had followed her in, and then at Shivani, who sat at the breakfast bar. "You two are supposed to be the voices of reason in this house." She ignored the sharp sound of her mother's outraged breath. "What on earth were you doing in Skybriar?"

"I decided we had better go along," Shivani said, her attention on her own omelet, "in case your mother lost her temper and threatened someone with a lawsuit."

Eve faltered. "Ah. Hm. Well, I suppose that's fair enough."

"Eve!" Mum said, her outrage intensifying.

Eve, however, was in no mood. *She* was the outraged one, thank you very much, and over the last twenty minutes of preparation—during which Janelle Monáe's "Make Me Feel" tongue-clicked encouragingly in her ear—she'd decided she had every right to be. So she said firmly, "Clearly, Shivani's caution was warranted, because you behaved horribly."

"Now, sweetheart," Dad began.

"As did you. You're just as bad as each other!"

Dad shut his mouth with an astonished click.

"I appreciate that I've handled some things poorly, recently," Eve said, swallowing as she considered her next words. "Up to and including running off to another county because I was upset about being told off. You were absolutely right to take me to task, because I've been letting childish fear limit me for far too long, and it wasn't fair to myself or to you."

Eve's parents looked equal parts bewildered and relieved, as if these were the words they'd longed to hear but had never expected to. That, more than anything, spurred her on. Clearly, Eve had spent more than enough of her twenties avoiding responsibility—but that ended now. It ended today. Which meant expressing herself fully, being open and honest, being the best person she could hope to be for herself and for the people she loved. The people who loved *her*.

"The thing is," she continued, "there was no need for what happened at Castell Cottage. It's not as if I completely disappeared. I remained in contact with my sisters, and I'm an adult woman with a brown belt in karate."

From the corner of the kitchen, she heard Zaf murmur, "Er . . . she's a what?"

Eve plowed on. "Your worries for me were valid, but instead of *expressing* them, you skipped straight to—to DEFCON Five."

"Actually," Chloe interjected, "DEFCON One is the—"

"Shut up, Chloe! This applies to you, too, by the way. And you, Dan. I appreciate you all being worried for my welfare. But couldn't you have *asked* me about the situation before you all showed up and created a scene at my place of employment? Couldn't one of you have said, *Hey, Eve, we have some questions and concerns about X, Y, and Z, so we'd like to come visit?* Or did none of you believe I'd respond in a reasonable, adult manner? That I'd understand, and give you the information you needed to feel comfortable?" Eve waited for a moment, her jaw tight.

No one spoke, though Mum had the grace to look ashamed. Dad shuffled uncomfortably, too—as well he might, since Mum never did anything they hadn't both agreed upon, and for all his quietness, Dad enjoyed and strongly endorsed his wife's frequent bouts of bonkersness.

Focusing on her parents, she said, "If you want me to behave like an adult, you need to give me the space to do so. Instead, you treated me like a child. I got a job," Eve went on, "for myself. A job I was committed to, and that I—that I loved—" Oh dear, her voice was wobbling. *Stop thinking about Jacob. Stop it!* She cleared her throat and continued. "I did exactly as you asked. But *you* interfered in a manner that damaged my—my chosen career."

Dad, looking oddly pleased, interjected. "Career, is it?"

Eve desperately wanted to say yes, which gave her a flash of habitual anxiety. Sometimes (all right, fine: often) she felt as if wanting things too badly meant dooming herself to fail. But she wanted *Jacob* more than anything, and they couldn't be doomed. So she refused to accept that feeling any longer. Refused to even consider it.

She'd lived in fear of failure for far too long.

"Yes," she said after a moment. "Yes. My career." Cooking to start people's mornings off right, taking care of the little touches that made a house feel like a home, chatting with different guests every day and feeling as if charm could be meaningful rather than a glittering waste of time. That was her career, or it would be soon. Eve knew what she wanted, and she wasn't afraid of it.

"I will always be grateful for the things you've done for me," she told her parents quietly. "For the privileges and safety nets you've afforded me, for the ways you've supported me when I didn't know who I was, even for pushing me to get a grip and make a change. I'm trying my best to make you proud, and I always will. But I'm never going to be like everyone else. I'm not even going to be like the rest of this family, as much as I love you all. I'm a different person and I need different things and I work in a different way, and that's okay."

It occurred to Eve that this would be a convenient time to mention her recent discovery vis-à-vis autism, et cetera, but she didn't want that conversation to be a family argument in the kitchen. She wanted it to be something easy and familiar that she mentioned one day, all casually, and everyone else responded relatively casually, and everything was fine and no one looked at her for too long, and maybe Jacob was there and he held her hand.

So, not yet. Not today. Because this was her knowledge, to do with what she wanted.

Instead of blurting it out, then, she simply finished her outburst with a different truth. "I'm changing. I'm figuring myself out. You need to respect that, and let it continue, because I *am* an adult and

I have been for quite some time. Even if I haven't always acted like it. All right?"

There was a heavy pause during which Eve became distinctly nervous that she might have to put her foot down harder than intended. She found herself wondering WWJD: What Would Jacob (King of Boundaries, First of His Name) Do?

Then Mum swallowed hard and nodded, her neat bob brushing her cheekbones as she stepped forward. "You're right, of course, my darling. I apologize."

Dad came next, catching Eve's hands and giving them a quick squeeze. "We're sorry, Evie. Really. We were just worried about you. But you're correct."

"We're very proud of you," Mum said, pursing her lips in a way that meant she was hiding a smile.

Eve didn't bother to hide hers. "Well, wonderful. Glad to hear it. Very emotional reunion, et cetera, but now I'm afraid I've got to dash so I can win Jacob back, and so on and so forth, so . . . bye!" She kissed her parents' cheeks, then turned on her heel and whipped out of the kitchen.

"Evie, wait!" She'd barely made it down the hall before Dani's voice followed her. Pausing by the front door, Eve grabbed her shoes and turned to face her sister—no, sisters, Dani striding toward her and Chloe hurrying behind.

"What's up? I'm on a tight schedule." Actually, Eve was on no schedule beyond the one that went:

1. Find Jacob.
2. Insist she would never leave Jacob.

3. Proceed to never leave Jacob, regardless of how much he
   may protest.

But she was slightly—only slightly—distracted from that particular plan when she noticed the uncharacteristically nervous
looks on her sisters' faces. Chloe, in particular, might possibly be
sweating. Chloe! Sweating!

"Are you all right, darling?" Eve asked. "Do you need me to
open a window? Are you having a wobble? Is—"

"I'm fine." Chloe flapped a hand, then sighed heavily. "Except
for the part where I'm drowning in guilt."

Eve blinked. "Oh. Erm. I see."

"We're sorry, is what she's trying to say," Dani interjected. "We
were interfering cows and you're absolutely right—we should've
asked a few more questions before jumping to the sex cult conclusion."

"Now your job is all . . . fudged," Chloe said, "and it's all our
fault."

"Not entirely," Dani added. "It was also Zaf's fault."

"Safety first," came a grim, rumbling voice from down the hall.
Eve looked up to discover her sisters' boyfriends were also hovering at the edge of the Group of Guilt.

"Oh, how wonderful," Eve said brightly. "Now everyone is in
my business. It's a venerable party."

"Did you mean veritable, darling?"

"I meant what I meant!" Eve snapped, her temper ratcheting
up by the second. Jacob never asked what she meant. Jacob just
paid attention and focused on what actually mattered and got the

bloody hell on with it, and didn't make her feel silly or frivolous or childish—which was understandable, since she wasn't any of those things. Or rather, she wasn't just those things. She was herself, and she'd demanded he respect that—*all* of it—and now she was going to demand everyone else did, too.

"Right," Chloe winced. "Sorry, darling. I just thought I should admit that—well. That I might possibly have been the one who started the entire visit. Not Mum and Dad."

Well, now. *That* was unexpected.

"Basically," Red piped up from down the hall, "Chloe heard that voice note and decided you were in grave danger."

"And *I* said," Dani interjected, "in danger of what? Having her brains bonked out?"

"But then Zaf said," Chloe went on, "that intimate relationships with superiors were dangerous ground, ripe for potential coercion, and that we didn't even know the man, and should therefore intercede."

Zaf crossed his massive arms over his massive chest and glowered. "Actually, I said it all seemed a bit dodgy and we should give her a ring."

"But then I accidentally asked Gigi for her opinion," Dani said, "and she told Aunty Mary, who told Mother, and it was all over."

All over indeed.

Eve sighed and squeezed the bridge of her nose. "You know what? It really doesn't matter who started it. This entire family is a lost cause and I love you all very much, but we'll pick this up later. I need to get back to Skybriar."

Dani grinned. "Are you wildly in love with your boss? Zaf says you might be."

Eve narrowed her eyes and pointed at Zafir. "Stop that."

He flashed a shockingly pretty smile. "Which means yes."

"Oh, bugger off, the lot of you. I have to go." She snagged her car keys and opened the door.

"Er, hang on a second," Zaf said, his eyebrows shooting up in alarm. "Didn't you run someone over the last time you got behind a wheel?"

Eve glared. "The second to last time, actually."

"Still, though. And aren't you in a rush?"

"Yes, which is why I'd appreciate it if you'd—"

"All right," Red interjected, pushing off the wall—did the man do anything other than lean?—and strolling past her out of the door. "This is easily sorted," he said as he approached the gleaming blue Triumph parked innocuously on her parents' gravel driveway. "All things considered, Eve, how's about I give you a lift?"

CHAPTER TWENTY-ONE

You've got to be *fucking* kidding me," Jacob growled.

Tessa shot him a look from the driver's seat. "Don't you curse at me, Jacob Wayne. I'm a lady."

"I think he's cursing the traffic, actually," Alex piped up from the back seat.

"Yes," Jacob gritted out. He'd assumed that was obvious. It had been over an hour since he'd left the B&B in Mont's hands, yet they were barely eighty miles closer to the address Eve had left on file, an address belonging to one Chloe Brown.

Jacob's original plan had been to get up bright and early this morning, jump in his car, drive or possibly fly to Chloe's house, get Eve's whereabouts from her—or, ideally, find Eve in the guest bedroom—and then . . . er . . . fix things. He was still a little hazy on that part, but he had the necessary passion and determination, and he was also going to grab some flowers on the way so he could get down on his knees and apologize as profusely as she deserved. Seriously. He was going to apologize so goddamn hard, and then some more, and then some more, just to really empha-size the point.

Well—that had been the plan, anyway. But things had gone horribly wrong from the moment Mont had pointed out Jacob shouldn't drive himself with a fractured wrist, and it had all gone downhill from there.

"Then again," Alex continued thoughtfully. "Maybe he *is* curs-ing at you. You never can tell, with Jacob."

Jacob turned to glare at her. "Why are you here again? I'm quite sure it takes *one* Montrose to drive a car."

Alex grinned, looking unnervingly like her brother. "I'm here in case you break down, Jake."

"Bullshit. You're here for the drama."

"Who, me?" She pressed a hand to her chest and pasted on an expression of shock. "God, man. Have a bit of faith."

Tessa giggled.

Jacob let his head fall back against the seat. "I'm going to die of frustration before I ever see her again."

"Was that a sex joke?" Tessa asked.

Alex snorted. "Save those for Eve, my guy."

"Maybe he's practicing."

"Ha! Maybe he's—"

"I appreciate you driving me, Tess, I really do," Jacob said, "but would you two please shut the fuck up?"

"Woo. Touchy." Tessa smirked, hit the brake for the thou-sandth time in the last ten minutes, then pulled up the handbrake. In front of them, what looked like a mile of cars sat bumper to bumper in the late morning sunlight. It was, Jacob thought dully, a beautiful day. Pity he wouldn't be able to enjoy it after his head inevitably exploded.

"You're thinking about Eve again, aren't you?" Alex prodded. "You ever consider, I don't know—calling her?"

Well, there was a diamond fucking idea. Except . . . "I'm trying to be romantic. You know, like in books. She's into that stuff," he mumbled. "Anyway, you know I'm better in person."

"Oh, yeah. Good point," Alex allowed.

"I think it's sweet," Tess said. "I think she'll be thrilled."

Jacob's heart leapt. "Yeah?"

"Oh, yeah. Unless she hates your guts for sending her away, in which case she might laugh in your face and tell you to jog on."

Jacob's heart sank. "Oh."

Tess winced. "Oh my God, Jake, no, that was a joke! I'm sorry. I was joking."

Unfortunately, the situation she'd laid out seemed all too likely. But Jacob couldn't see a world in which he didn't try his fucking hardest for Eve Brown, and if that meant setting himself up for the most brutal rejection of his life, well. He supposed he'd just have to deal with it.

"Leave him alone, Tess," Alex ordered, leaning between their seats. "Hey, do you hear that? Wicked purr." She squinted at the road. "Is that a Triumph?"

"Alexandra," Jacob said, "I truly could not give a fuck." But he saw the Triumph—couldn't miss it, a flash of blue on the other side of the road, steered by a lanky bloke in leather, winding through the traffic with enviable speed. Still, when the temporary traffic lights on that side turned red, the bike had to stop just like everyone else.

Jacob sighed and screwed his eyes shut. Maybe he *should* call Eve. Because with every second he spent not fixing things, all he could think about was the look on her face when he'd pushed her away. And if he thought about that too much, his heart might break as surely as his goddamn wrist.

♫

Red's motorbike turned out to be an excellent idea, because on the way to the Lake District they hit unbelievable traffic. Eve squeezed her eyes shut, took shallow breaths to minimize smog inhalation, and tried not to die of nerves.

Grand gestures were supposed to be executed immediately, otherwise one got all tangled with violent emotion. Like the growing fear that words might not be enough, and the urge to see Jacob now, now, now, anyway.

Then, out of nowhere, she *did* see him. Jacob, that is. She looked up through the visor of her helmet as they reached a temporary traffic light, and on the other side of the cones sat Jacob's car, with Tessa at the wheel and Jacob himself in the passenger seat.

"Oh. My. God." The wind whipped her words away. Which is why, instead of screaming for Red to pull over properly, she pinched him in the ribs. *Then* she screamed. "Pull over pull over pull over pull over pull—"

The lights turned to green, but instead of racing away, Red guided them steadily to the edge of the road and kicked off the engine. "What?" he demanded as he yanked off his helmet. "You dying or something?"

Eve barely heard. Her braids spilled over her shoulders as she removed her own helmet and shoved it at Red before getting off the bike. The other lights would change soon and then Jacob would be gone. He couldn't be gone. She pinned her gaze to the sharp lines of his profile, the glint of his glasses and the sheen of his perfectly neat and tidy hair, and ran—

Except no she didn't, because Red grabbed her wrist in an iron grip and yanked her back. "*Eve!* Would you watch the road? If I let you get hit by a car, your sister will fucking garrote me."

She spun around to scowl at him. "I was watching! Sort of." She really hadn't been.

"Where the hell are you going? I thought we had to find this guy in—"

A flat, impenetrable voice rose over the rumble of traffic. "Let. Go. Of. Her."

Eve turned to find Jacob standing beside her like a column of frost and fury. Judging by the look on his face, if Red didn't respond in an appropriate manner, Jacob might commit roadside murder in her honor. Which was very romantic. She nearly swooned, in fact, but then she decided that losing consciousness would not be conducive to getting him back.

Red's coppery eyebrows flew up as he stared at Jacob. Then his surprise faded into a slight smile, and he released her hand. "You good, Evie?"

"Mmm hmm. Yep. So good. Super good. Thank you for the lift okay bye now!" She grabbed Jacob's arm and dragged him away.

This road was long and narrow, bracketed by the copse-heavy edges of two country fields. Sections of daisy-dotted grass and massive, ancient trees lined the tarmac, and it was into their sunlight-dappled shadow that Eve towed Jacob like an unusually agreeable boat. His out-of-character docility could bode well or ill; she hadn't decided which. Then again, she was struggling to think straight enough to decide anything. All she could do was stare at the man in front of her, from the starched collar of his perfectly ironed shirt to the familiar name tag on his chest that read HELLO, MY NAME IS: JACOB with more cheer than he'd ever managed to offer a stranger. She swallowed hard, her throat drier than a desperation desert. Now seemed like the perfect time to speak, to say the countless things she'd rehearsed on the way here—except her heart was melting like chocolate on a summer's day, dripping down through her rib cage to pool in her stomach, and the sensation was rather distracting.

Jacob's jaw bunched and he shifted his weight ever so slightly from one foot to the other. His hand rose toward his glasses, faltered, fell. Rose again, smoothed over his already smooth hair, and fell. He opened his mouth, closed it, and Eve wondered vaguely if he was having trouble telling her that he still didn't want to see her ever again and, since he'd established she wasn't being kidnapped by a giant tattooed biker, she should go away now.

Everything about her drooped.

Then he bit his lip and said, "Eve, I—I was going to get you flowers."

Her jaw dropped enough to let in flies and let out her garbled sound of confusion. "You were? But . . ." Then slow realization dawned, and she found herself grinning uncontrollably. "That's funny. I was rushing off to tell you that you were an insufferable prick yesterday"—Jacob seemed to wilt before her very eyes—"but also, that it would take far more than that to get rid of me. Because I've chosen you, Jacob, and I trust that choice. So you need to trust it, too. If you can't—"

She took a deep breath, tapping her fingers against her thighs, wishing she had music in her ear to sweep her through this moment. Hoping she hadn't read this situation all wrong.

"If you can't," she continued, "then this isn't going to work. Because I am a grown woman and I need the people around me to respect my decisions. Instead," she added pointedly, "of pushing me away. The thing is, Jacob, I trust *you*. I believe in you. I think this can work, and I really, really want to try. So." She pressed her lips together nervously. "What do you think about that?"

After a frozen moment of obvious shock, Jacob gave her a slow but brilliant smile. "I think I'll do anything you want and everything you need as long as it means I get to try with someone as lovely as you. I think—"

His words were drowned out by a sudden torrent of beeps. They both turned to find Jacob's car being gently steered by Tessa onto a grassy verge, while the cars behind kicked off as the light turned green.

"Just bear with," Alex yelled out of the back window. "My mate's trying to get this girl—it's a whole thing—and we can't exactly drive off and leave them here because they're both traffic disasters, so . . ."

Eve whipped around to look at Jacob. "Um—"

"Ignore her," Jacob said firmly. "She was dropped as a child. Often, I assume."

Eve laughed, but the sound came out a little . . . damp. She wasn't sure why until Jacob gave her a tortured look and cupped her face with both hands. He pulled her close and murmured, "Oh, don't cry, Sunshine," and kissed her forehead, and she was so relieved she almost fell over.

"I *knew* you were bullshitting," she half sobbed, "you awful bastard, telling me to fuck off like that—"

"I'm sorry," he said. "I'm so, *so* sorry, Eve. You're right. I thought everything between us had been . . . something different, and I was the only one who hadn't understood. I thought I was the fool always wanting too much, too hard, and I freaked the fuck out. I shouldn't have done it. I need to . . . to deal with my shit, clearly, and I'm going to. Because we could be something special. We *are* something special, and I won't let myself stand in the way of it."

Eve's half sobs were veering dangerously toward full ones. He just—he was so earnest and she loved him so much and no matter what he thought, it wasn't *all* his fault. "I said everything wrong, I know I did. I was just trying to—reassure you," she babbled, "because I knew you'd be upset, of course you were, but I thought you'd care more about my intentions toward the B&B than my intentions toward you, so I started there—"

"And I should've let you fucking talk instead of rushing to think the worst, because I'm done thinking the worst of you," he said. "I swear, I am. All it ever does is bite me in the arse, and more importantly, you don't deserve it. You're incredible and you're more than worth my trust, and . . . You're the one thing I know I can rely on, Eve. It's fast, and it's ridiculous, but it's true. It's you."

Oh dear. She hadn't been prepared for that. Nor had she been prepared for the absolute tsunami of love and mush and rainbows that dragged her under when she looked at him. God, she'd missed him, and now he was here, and she almost couldn't cope.

Then he made everything a thousand times worse by saying, "My only excuse is that I—I love you. I love you so much and I was kind of terrified, because when you love someone, everything hurts a thousand times more. And I have all this shit in my head, shit that pops up at the worst time and makes me think the sky is falling. I—sometimes I find it difficult to believe that anyone could want me as much as I want them. Never mind someone as amazing as you. And I let that get the better of me. But I'm working on that, because it hurt you, and the one fucking thing I *refuse* to do is hurt you." The words came fast and obviously nervous, Jacob's sharp cheekbones stained a soft pink.

He didn't stop, though.

"I suppose I'm going to have to examine my feelings and all that shit," he said with obvious distaste. "To make sure I don't hurt you again. And it'll be worth it, because I love you. Even if you just stand there staring at me forever instead of saying something." He offered a smile that was more like a wince, his hand cradling her face, the warmth of his body pressed close to hers. He was perfect. He was just overwhelmingly perfect and she couldn't even choke out the words to tell him so.

But she was going to try.

♫

When Eve finally opened her mouth, Jacob's hope swelled. But the only sound she produced was another astonished sob, so he went back to slowly dying.

On the plus side, she was letting him touch her—and she'd mentioned coming back to Skybriar for him, which was good. That was fucking excellent. On the negative side, he'd accidentally admitted the whole *love* thing, which might be a bit soon, so she could be changing her mind about coming back and considering filing a restraining order instead.

Regardless, hiding his feelings hadn't worked too well for him last time, so this time, he'd keep going with the truth. "My heart seems to be throwing some kind of fit, and seeing you cry isn't helping the matter, so if you could at least tell me how to make you stop . . ."

She didn't tell him jack, but she did dry her eyes with her hands and smile. If anything, that made his heart situation worse.

Then she blurted out, "You are so brave and you are absolutely beautiful and I'm so happy you're here, and anyone who doesn't want you as much as you want them is a fucking *donut*, Jacob, because you are just the most wantable man on planet Earth."

He blinked slowly, his pulse thudding in his ears. His eyes were stinging a little bit. Shit. God. He swallowed hard.

Then the opening notes of Corinne Bailey Rae's "Breathless" sparkled in the background, and they both turned to look at

Jacob's car. Tessa gave them a thumbs-up from the driver's seat before pointing at the stereo.

"What an excellent song choice," Eve said.

Though Jacob privately agreed, he muttered, "That woman is a menace."

Eve smiled. "You're very sexy when you're grumpy."

Just like that, the last of his nerves dissolved. "Eve," he laughed shakily, letting his head fall forward until their noses bumped together. "Please. I'm trying to keep things romantic here."

"That *was* romantic," she argued. "Pointing out your hotness counts as romantic if I also love you while I do it."

She said it so casually, sprinkled it into her stream of smiling words. Almost as if she knew that saying it outright might short all his circuits.

"You . . . do?" he asked haltingly, his mind approaching the concept with care, taking a cautious examination. Even if what he really wanted was to jump on her words without hesitation, old habits died hard. "Love me, I mean. You . . ."

She reached up and slid a hand into his hair, and he didn't even mind the fact that she was definitely messing it up. Pushing his head up gently until he met her eyes, Eve murmured, "Yes, Jacob. I love you. I'm sorry I didn't tell you about all my plans, but honestly, they became more and more irrelevant as time went on. As I started to trust myself, and learned what I really value. The truth is, Castell Cottage is my passion, and I love my job, and I want to stay. But also, I love *you*. And I didn't want to leave you. I still don't."

Jacob felt a bit dizzy. "But—you *can* leave me. If you want to. If you need to. I just need to know that when you stay, when you're with me—you mean it. I know you do. I might forget it, sometimes, but I know it, because I know you. Eve—"

"Hey!" A car horn beeped, jolting him out of his giddiness. Well, not entirely. That would be impossible. "Get a room!" someone bellowed.

"Go fuck yourself," Jacob shouted around the heart wedged in his throat. Funny what a man and his various, malfunctioning organs could accomplish when the most wonderful human being on the planet was involved.

Then the ginger bloke Eve had arrived with got off the bike he'd been perched on a few meters away and wandered over to the queue of cars stuck behind Alex and Tessa. Jacob heard the strange man say in a ludicrously friendly tone, "Listen, mate, I know you've got places to be and this traffic's a nightmare, but . . ." His voice faded out of hearing as he walked away. Jacob waited for more shouting and beeping to ensue, but, to his astonishment, it did not. Instead, the ginger leaned against a stranger's car, laughing with the occupants through the window.

"Hm," Jacob said. "He's quite useful, isn't he?"

"You're going soft."

"Do you mind?"

Eve gave him that gorgeous, sunshine smile. "Certainly not."

"Good." Because with her around, he envisioned the softness getting worse. "Now, then—in light of recent declarations—if you could just give me one second to . . ."

She waved a hand. "Oh, yes, whatever you need."

"Cracking, thanks." He let go of her and turned away long

enough to snag a handful of daisies from the ground. He'd intended all this to be much more put together and professional but—well. He was improvising. Going with the flow. Eve frequently managed to make such behavior look magnificent, so he hoped to achieve something half as great.

A few seconds later, armed with his admittedly sparse roadside bouquet, he went back and thrust the flowers in her direction.

"Oh." She blinked, as if that was the last thing she'd expected. "Oh. Jacob." She sniffed and blinked some more.

"Eve, we've talked about this. No crying."

"Shut up and take it, you big baby."

"I could say the same to you." He waved the flowers at her, and she finally took them. Flower transference dealt with, he caught her free hand and met her eyes. "Good. So, to recap: I love you. You love me. We're going home now. Home for both of us. And everything's going to be fine," he said steadily, holding her gaze, "because I'm going to trust you, and believe in you, and give you whatever you need."

"And I'm going to stay," she replied quietly. "I'm going to stay, and I'm going to love you, and I'm going to try. You taught me how much that matters."

Those words burned in Jacob like a forest fire, but they left the opposite of destruction in their wake. Because Eve's love didn't hurt. If his current feelings were anything to go by, it healed.

"Just to be clear," he said gruffly, after taking a moment to collect himself, "by accepting these flowers, you have formally agreed to coupledom and commitment, et cetera—"

"Oh, is that what the flowers mean?" she laughed.

"Absolutely." He hesitated, then pushed through, because she loved him. "Do you have any complaints?"

"Nope."

Jacob grinned.

Then Eve dropped the daisies, grabbed his arse, and kissed him so hard she almost knocked his glasses off. Tessa turned up the music to obnoxious heights. A few more cars beeped, possibly in outrage, but Jacob liked to interpret the noise as support. Either way, he wasn't about to stop kissing this woman for anything. He wrapped an arm around the softness of her waist, hauled her closer, and sank into the familiar sweetness of her lips.

He was still grinning when they came up for air.

EPILOGUE

One Year Later

I can't believe you got Mother in a hairnet."

Eve raised a hand to shield her eyes from the late-afternoon sun, squinting in Joy's direction. "Hardly." The net sat on top of Joy's immaculate bob at a jaunty angle, more like a beret than a food safety aid.

"You'd better do something about that," Danika said dryly, "before Jacob spots her and has stern words."

"I think Dad's got it under control, actually," Chloe murmured. The three sisters watched as their father abandoned his place beside Montrose and Aunt Lucy at the grill to come up behind his wife, saying something that made her laugh as he gently tugged the hairnet into place.

Joy rolled her eyes at him, but she didn't protest. Instead, she turned a flawless smile onto the next Gingerbread Festival attendee in the queue and set about taking their order. Above her hung a burgundy-and-gold banner that read BREAKFAST FOR DIN-NER WITH CASTELL COTTAGE.

It was Jacob's second year securing a place at the festival—and this time, they had a bigger stall, since they'd been such a success last year. Eve had looked into hiring temporary help, but Mum and Dad had—rather shockingly—volunteered their assistance instead.

And Jacob—equally shockingly—had accepted that assistance, despite what he privately termed their *grave lack of appropriate qualifications or experience*. And despite the fact they'd once accused him of running a sex cult, et cetera.

"What are you smiling about, Evie-Bean?" Chloe demanded.

"Probably something Jacob related," Dani supplied dryly.

Eve didn't bother to defend herself. She was too busy rolling her shoulders after hours of serving scrambled eggs, tipping back her head to feel the sunshine on her cheeks, and generally enjoying this moment. Her sisters were beside her, her parents were properly supervised, and Jacob was somewhere in the vicinity hunting down strawberry lemonade. Breakfast for dinner was going fabulously well, with a queue that had barely shrunk all day. And half an hour ago she'd watched a toddler take one bite of her black forest gâteau, grin, then put his face—his whole *face*—into the cake. Which she certainly deemed a success.

In short, everything was right in Eve's world. Everything was absolutely perfect.

Although—she cracked open one eyelid to check the glittery pink face of her favorite watch, a birthday present from Tessa—

this break was scheduled to end in five minutes. Where on earth had Jacob gotten to?

"Why, just *look* at you three," Gigi cooed, popping up out of nowhere in a cloud of Chanel No. 5 and individual Russian lashes. "Sunning yourselves while your parents slave away. I thoroughly approve." She opened her mouth as if to say more, but then Shivani appeared, holding a gigantic ice cream cone and commanding her attention.

"Look, Garnet, it's as big as my head. Take a picture."

"Oh, very good, my love." Gigi whipped out a baby pink Polaroid camera and snapped. The diamond ring on her left hand reflected a blinding shaft of sunlight. "You'll never finish it."

"Watch me," Shivani snickered.

Gigi snorted and slipped an arm around her waist.

"*I* want one of those ice creams," Chloe murmured as the pair wandered off.

As if on cue, Red strolled over with both hands full. "Good thing I got you one, then."

Eve blinked at his sudden appearance, then stared after Gigi and Shivs. "Is it just me, or has our entire family returned in the space of thirty seconds?"

"Charming," Zaf said, as he, too, appeared from thin air. "What about me?"

She rolled her eyes. "Honestly, I had anticipated your arrival. You would never let Danika go without snacks under circumstances such as these."

Zaf's mouth tilted into one of his tiny, subtle smiles. "Hm. You got me there." He held two giant cones, just like Red, and he gave one to Dani. "Come on, sweetheart. Let's go."

Eve frowned. "Sorry? Go *where*?"

"Away," Dani said mysteriously, waggling her purple eyebrows. Since it was summer break, she'd experimented with matching them to her hair. "Cheer up, Evie-Bean. I'm sure you'll get an ice cream, too, eventually."

"Oh yes," Chloe agreed as Redford helped her up. "But probably not until after—"

"All right, Button, let's be having you," Red said, and dragged her bodily away.

Suspicious. Very suspicious.

"Erm," Eve began.

"See you later!" Dani waved over her shoulder as she and Zaf followed suit.

"*Erm*," Eve repeated.

"Remember your angles, my clever little communion wafer," Gigi called across the grass, waving her camera.

"*Pardon?*"

"Smize," Shivani advised, and then she and Gigi turned resolutely away.

Eve sat at her suddenly abandoned table for a good few minutes, feeling slightly dazed. Around her, the Gingerbread Festival continued: there were floats designed by the local schoolchildren traveling slowly down the cordoned-off road to her left, all themed around local history. To her right were the other stalls that made up the festival: ice cream stands, various restaurant stalls, and, of course, the actual gingerbread area.

And behind Eve . . .

Behind Eve stood the man she always *felt* before she saw. A familiar, golden thread wrapped tight around her stomach as she caught the clean, lemon and eucalyptus scent of him.

"Jacob," she said softly, tipping her head back.

He smiled down at her, both hands filled by a pair of ice cream cones. "Hello, Sunshine."

"I *knew* you'd get me one," she beamed.

"Raspberry ripple." He pressed a cone into her hand. "You're welcome."

"And you're in my good books. Come sit with me," she ordered, "and gaze upon all this gingery splendor."

"You want me to gaze upon . . . your brother-in-law?" he asked as he sat down.

Eve snorted. "That was rather good."

"Thank you. I try." They sat practically on top of each other, their bodies pressed together from shoulder to hip to thigh. Jacob's arm found its now-familiar place around her waist, his other hand wrapped around his own ice cream cone. But unlike Eve, who'd already fallen upon her raspberry ripple with animal enthusiasm, he wasn't eating.

He was simply watching her.

His eyes were melting frost behind the frames of his glasses. His lower lip gave under the pressure of his teeth. "Eve," he said. "I have something to ask you."

She swallowed a mouthful of ice cream and looked over at Castell Cottage's stall, where her parents stood watching, Gigi hovering in the background with her camera at the ready.

"Erm," Eve said. "You're not going to propose, are you? Because

I'm still wearing my hairnet, and also, I might get excited and throw my ice cream at you."

Jacob stared blankly at her for a moment, and she felt the first nervous flush of embarrassment. Whoops. She probably shouldn't *ask* people if they were going to propose. But then again, this was Jacob, and if the last year had taught her anything, it was that she could ask Jacob whatever she wanted. Tell him whatever popped into her head. Do whatever took her fancy. So long as she loved him all the while, he would forever love her back—and his love was, above all, comfort.

So she flicked the embarrassment away.

Finally, he blinked back to life and released a surprised little laugh. "No," he said. "No, I wasn't going to propose. But, er, just for the sake of research—if I *did*, and you weren't wearing a hairnet, and there wasn't any ice cream to throw . . ." A lovely blush spread across his cheeks. "Would you say yes, Evie?"

Giddy pleasure sloshed about in her stomach, rather like champagne on a Jet Ski. "Erm," she squeaked. "At the risk of seeming overeager, I do believe I would."

"Good." Jacob sounded deeply satisfied. "Hang on a second." He pulled his phone out of his back pocket, opened up the notes app, and started typing. She peeked over his shoulder and saw the words: *NO ICE CREAM.*

Then he tutted at her and closed the app. "Oi. Nosy."

"Jacob, are you writing a proposal plan?"

"*Nosy*," he repeated, but he was grinning. "Now, as I was saying before you disrupted proceedings—"

"*Jacob.*" Eve was smiling so wide her face hurt, and it was entirely this man's fault.

"Eve," he shot back, arching one severe eyebrow. "Listen."

"Fine, fine!" She schooled her features and cleared her throat. "Yes, Mr. Wayne? How may I help you?"

"You already help me, Ms. Brown. Which is why I got you this." Setting aside his phone, Jacob fiddled in his pocket again and produced . . . a name tag? It was burgundy and gold, rather like the one Eve already wore. He dropped it into her outstretched palm, and she examined it more closely.

Yes; this name tag was exactly like the one Eve had worn all year, except for a minor difference. Written beneath the familiar phrase HELLO, MY NAME IS: EVE was one teeny, tiny word:

MANAGER

Speechless, she looked up at Jacob. "This is . . ."

He offered her the smallest, sweetest smile in the world. "We already do the job together. I was wondering if you'd be interested in making things official."

Old doubts—in her abilities, in herself, in whether she deserved *this* when it was something she wanted so much—tried their best to rise from the dead. But with the ease born of a year's practice, Eve kicked them back into their graves and let the brilliance of this moment wash over her, uninterrupted.

"You want me to be a manager," she said.

"I do," Jacob replied.

"Like you," she said.

"*With* me," Jacob replied. "Always with me."

"Because you love me?"

"Because you're good at it," he corrected calmly, firmly, "and because I need you. Your ideas, your energy, your care—all of it. You're not just my sunshine; you're the sun. You make my business better. You make it ours."

At which point, Eve dropped her ice cream and kissed Jacob so hard, they almost fell off the bench.

"Fabulous, darling!" Gigi cried, and somewhere in the distance, Eve heard the camera whirr.

ABOUT THE AUTHOR

USA Today and *Wall Street Journal* bestseller **TALIA HIBBERT** is a Black British author who lives in a bedroom full of books. Supposedly, there is a world beyond that room, but she has yet to drum up enough interest to investigate. She writes sexy, diverse romance because she believes that people of marginalized identities need honest and positive representation. Her interests include beauty, junk food, and unnecessary sarcasm.

MORE ROM COMS FROM
TALIA HIBBERT

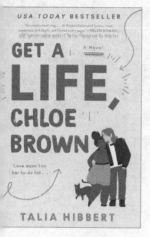

GET A LIFE, CHLOE BROWN

"Absolutely charming...
a flawless balance of humor, heat,
sweetness, and depth, and I loved every page."
— Helen Hoang, *USA Today* bestselling author of
The Bride Test

"This is an extraordinary book, full of love,
generosity, kindness and sharp humor."

— *The New York Times Book Review*

TAKE A HINT, DANI BROWN

As seen in *OprahMag*, *Bustle*, Parade, *PopSugar*, *New York Post*, *Essence*, *Travel & Leisure*, *Ms. Magazine*, *TheSkimm*, *Betches*, *Shondaland*, and *Buzzfeed*! Named one of the Best Books of the Year by Apple and Amazon.

USA Today bestselling author Talia Hibbert returns with another charming romantic comedy about a young woman who agrees to fake date her friend after a video of him "rescuing" her from their office building goes viral...